HALLDÓR LAXNESS

Wayward Heroes

Translated from the Icelandic
by Philip Roughton

archipelago books

First Archipelago Books Edition, 2016

Library of Congress Cataloging-in-Publication Data
Halldâor Laxness, 1902-1998. author. | Roughton, Philip, translator.
Wayward heroes / Halldor Laxness ; translated by Phillip Roughton.
Other titles: Gerpla. English
Brooklyn, New York : Archipelago, 2016.
Originally published in Icelandic as Gerpla
(Reykjavâik : Vaka-Helgafell, 1988. 4. âutg.).
LCCN 2016027339 (print) | LCCN 2016037170 (ebook)
ISBN 9780914671091 (paperback) | ISBN 9780914671107 (e-book)
LC record available at https://lccn.loc.gov/2016027339

Archipelago Books
232 3rd Street #A111
Brooklyn, NY 11215
www.archipelagobooks.org

Distributed by Penguin Random House
www.penguinrandomhouse.com

Cover art: Alberto Giacometti

This publication was made possible with support from
The American-Scandinavian Foundation,
the Icelandic Literature Center (Bókmenntasjóður), the National Endowment of the Arts,
the Lannan Foundation, the New York State Council on the Arts, a state agency,
and the New York City Department of Cultural Affairs.

PRINTED IN THE UNITED STATES OF AMERICA

Wayward Heroes

I

TWO ARE THE heroes from the Vestfirðir that have gained the greatest renown: Þorgeir Hávarsson and Þormóður Bessason, sworn brothers, of whom, as we might expect, much is told in Ísafjarðardjúp, where they grew up, as well as in the Jökulfirðir and Hornstrandir. In all of these places they accomplished great feats. Not much time has passed since learned men there in the west, and women of good memory, could recount of these comrades tales that have never seen light in books – and many an excellent book has been written concerning these two Vestfirðir men. Most of the stories of these warriors we find so remarkable that recalling them once more is certainly worth our time and attention, and thus we have spent long hours compiling into one narrative their achievements as related in numerous books. Foremost among these, we would be remiss not to name, is the *Great Saga of the Sworn Brothers*. Then there are the edifying accounts recorded on Icelandic parchments and stashed for centuries in collections abroad, besides the scores of old foreign tomes containing various well-informed, detailed reports, especially concerning later developments in our tale. Moreover, many an anecdote has been shared with us by trustworthy people who dwelt in Hornstrandir before the district was abandoned, as well as in the Jökulfirðir to the west, which is emptying even as we speak – the harsh immensity of the landscape in those parts being too overwhelming for the feeble folk born today. Finally, we have drawn from numerous obscure sources information that seems to us no less credible than the tales that people know better from books, it being our goal, in the volume that you hold now in your hands, to highlight the heroism of these two men. We bid welcome to anyone, man or woman, who surpasses us in learning and memory and wishes to amend what we have put in letters on these pages, thereby bringing it nearer the truth.

When recounting histories, scholars have generally begun by naming the men in authority where events take place. Here we follow their example, to ensure a better understanding of the unfolding of events as described in this book.

In the days of this story, the southern part of the Vestfirðir, bordering on Breiðafjörður, was in the hands of Þorgils Arason. His estate was at Reykhólar. As a youth, Þorgils had traveled and traded, producing great yield from the little that he initially had. He considered peace more profitable than war, and had purchased both his estate and his authority with silver. As is common among those who have traveled far and wide and encountered numerous gods, he was not much given to heathendom. When Christianity came to this country, he took out two treasures from his trunks: a fine cross bearing the crowned Christ, the friend of merchants, and a likeness of Christ's mother, the great guiding star of seafarers.

In the northern part of the Vestfirðir, in Ísafjarðardjúp, the Jökulfirðir, and Strandir, Vermundur Þorgrímsson held sway. He dwelt in Vatnsfjörður. He was old-fashioned, a heathen, and claimed descent from Norwegian chieftains. He took his revenue in kind from his tenants, and kept his larder well stocked. He was an industrious farmer and had a large number of workers – an intelligent man, if somewhat formidable. He had taken many a woman into his bed, some under the pretense of nuptials. A number of them came in their spare time at holidays just to visit him, several of them quite good catches, yet best was the woman for whom he had paid the bride price, Þorbjörg the Stout, of whom far more can be read in other books than this.

As it happened, these two Vestfirðir chieftains came to power at the start of Jarl Haakon Sigurdarson's reign in Norway, and Þorgeir and Þormóður were but young lads in the Vestfirðir when the Danish king Sweyn took possession of Norway after the fall of Olaf Tryggvason.

Concerning Hávar Kleppsson, the father of the champion Þorgeir, folk know mainly the following: he maintained a little croft at Jöklakelda in Mjóifjörður in Ísafjarðardjúp, a short distance from the chieftain in Vatnsfjörður, and upon his land. The early days of the reign of King Olaf the Stout saw a new wave of

Norse Viking raids on the British Isles, after several generations of relative calm. For most men of the time, however, taking part in such pirating yielded little, and it was rumored that Hávar had returned penniless to Iceland from his Viking ventures. He and several dirt-poor companions of his had gone to see Vermundur to ask for his support, and Vermundur had opened his arms to the men, making one or two of them his farmhands and the others his tenants. Concerning Hávar's feats of prowess as a Viking, we have no report but his own, though the story goes that he felt farm work to be practically worthless compared to deeds of valor and courage, and that far more honor was to be gained by slaying men than by hauling in fish – yet he himself returned from his raids with no other weapon than a single cudgel. Hávar's wife was named Þórelfur, a close relation of Þorgils Arason at Reykjahólar. She was a shrewd and energetic woman, and so well-learned that she knew most of what is told of the North's old heroes, and of the kings that took countries by force.

Farmer Hávar's unruliness soon became known to his neighbors: striking down dead their stray livestock, hacking the heads off their hens and geese when he could, and brandishing his club when they raised a fuss. Most would then flee to save their own lives, but many took their complaints to Vermundur. When Farmer Hávar was out working, his son Þorgeir sat at home listening to his mother's lays. Under her tutelage, his eyes were opened to the only world that could matter to a champion: where helmet-crowned heroes lord it over folk, serve noble kings, slay evildoers and sorcerers, and fight duels with their peers in courage and valor, their reputations remaining intact whether they stand or fall. In the evenings after the farmer came home, he would tell his son how he once fought twelve berserkers single-handedly in Denmark, either slaying three before the others scattered or leveling them all with his sword – the tale varied from night to night. He also described how he killed the berserker Sóti in single combat to the east of Øsel, spinning out the tale as much as he could. What is more, Farmer Hávar had taken part in eighteen major battles in the British Isles with the army of King Adils of Uppsala – that too, was a grand chronicle. It was not long before Þorgeir placed his father on a pedestal with the greatest heroes in his mother's lore.

Of Hávar Kleppsson's wrangles with the men of Djúp no more will be told in this book, except to say that Chieftain Vermundur finally feels he can no longer turn a deaf ear to the complaints of his charges.* He summons Þorgils Arason and says that his liegemen can no longer raise their hens in peace due to this kinsman of his, and recommends that he be provided an abode elsewhere. "It is a hapless situation," he says, "when men return weaponless from war, settle in peaceful districts and start slaughtering people's hens, to make up for feats they could not accomplish in other lands."

Þorgils Arason agrees with Vermundur, saying that he has heard more than his fair share about Hávar Kleppsson. "It is indeed the greatest misfortune," says he, "that such a clear-headed woman as my kinswoman Þórelfur should have been so badly wed."

Þorgils felt far from secure having his brother-in-law within his demesne by Breiðafjörður, so at the next Alþingi he purchased a little piece of land from some Borgarfjörður folk, built a croft there for Hávar, and supplied it with livestock. That same summer Hávar Kleppsson moved to Borgarfjörður, to the place that Þorgils had purchased, which was later called Hávarsstaðir, south of Hafnarfjall Mountain.

It soon became clear that the men of Borgarfjörður were none too thrilled by the arrival of Hávar Kleppsson. Borgarfjörður is a great, flourishing district, and was inhabited at the time by many a wealthy man. Folk there began discussing how they could stave off the calamity of having their fine farmlands saddled with disreputable riff-raff from other parts of the country.

Now we must mention that to the north of Hafnarfjall, at Skeljabrekka, there dwelt a man named Jöður. He was the son of Klængur. Of Jöður it is said that he was never far from any action in the district. He was overbearing and unfair to most people, was quick to the kill and slow to offer compensation, instead flaunting the backing that he had from chieftains. His croft was small and mean – others could only guess whence he got his daily bread – but he owned a remarkable stallion.

Hávar Kleppsson had few farmhands and little livestock.

He did, however, have a red packhorse that he had brought along from the west. This horse felt more at home on the fields and grassy slopes surrounding the farmhouse than on mountainsides.

One fine day in the autumn, Farmer Jöður from Skeljabrekka set out for Akranes with his grown-up son and a servant to purchase grain. As they were taking their rest near Hávarsstaðir, Hávar, who was in the farmyard, shook a rattle, making a terrible clatter. Before Jöður and the others could prevent it, the stallion broke loose and bolted up the mountain slope.

Red, Farmer Hávar's hack, idled disgruntledly by the home-field wall, its lower lip dangling. Jöður said: "Take this gelding and tie it to the end of the pack train. I shall have my grain from Akranes."

His son and servant did as he ordered.

That evening they transported their grain back to Skeljabrekka, past Hávarsstaðir. Farmer Hávar was standing outside. He immediately recognized his horse beneath the Skeljabrekka men's load of grain, took the cudgel that he had returned with from his warmongering days, and walked down the field toward the pack train. He said: "You shall now give me back my horse. What outrageous upstarts you are to take a farmer's things right out from under him, without leave or discussion! Never did I witness such shenanigans back in the Vestfirðir."

Jöður replied: "Yet we have heard much about how you were

driven out of the west for your wrongdoing and hen-thievery, and it is simply staggering that a newcomer to Borgarfjörður such as you should be so brash toward the men of these parts."

At that, Farmer Hávar laid his knife to his horse's rein and cut it free from the pack train, then led it with its load back to his croft. Jöður bade his companions follow him, telling them that he was going to see if he could curb this outsider's insolence, making as if he would steal their grain. They wasted no time, dropped the packhorses' leads, and as a man rode down Hávar. Jöður raised his ax and landed a blow on the back of the farmer's head, staggering him, just as Jöður's son Grímur thrust his spear into his side. There Farmer Hávar fell, leading his horse. Jöður Klængsson dismounted, and, like a true Norseman, hewed frantically at the man with his ax where he lay fallen, spattering blood and brains everywhere. Hávar Kleppsson was at death's doorstep long before Jöður Klængsson stopped hacking at him.

When Farmer Jöður had had enough hacking, he ordered his farmhand to take Hávar's horse and rope it again to the end of the pack train – a stouthearted man could hardly call it a killing if it came with no loot. "But I and my son," he said, "will go and announce our deed."

Þorgeir Hávarsson sat on the homefield wall and watched as his father was killed. The work completed, Jöður Klængsson rode up to the boy and said: "Go home, young lad, and tell your mother that your father won't be shaking any more rattles at the horses of us men of Borgarfjörður."

Then Jöður Klængsson rode away. It was near sunset. When Jöður was gone, the boy jumped down, walked over to where his father was lying across the path, and took a closer look at his body. The blow had disfigured his face, and blood and brains oozed like porridge from the crack in his head. One of his arms jerked at the shoulder before the man went limp and died – that twitch was his last. Þorgeir Hávarsson was astonished at how easily his father died, despite his having fought berserkers in Denmark and brought fire and slaughter to Ireland. He had always believed his father to be one of the greatest champions in the North. The boy stood outside for a long time before going to tell his mother. Finally, he went in. He was seven years old at the time.

2

CHIEFTAIN VERMUNDUR had a kinsman named Bessi, the son of Halldór. He lived at Laugaból, a short distance from Vatnsfjörður. Bessi was highly versed in poetry and law and was popular with everyone, but not very well-to-do. He and Vermundur were not only related but also good friends – Bessi often accompanied Vermundur when he had business to attend to, either at the Alþingi or elsewhere. Bessi's wife had passed away before this story begins, but he had a young son named Þormóður. The lad soon proved to be quick-witted, if somewhat sharp-tongued. From his father he learned poetry and other arts, and even at an early age could relate much lore of the Northern kings and jarls most intrepid in war and other noble pursuits, as well as of the Æsir, the Völsungar, the Ylfingar, and the renowned heroes who wrestled with ogresses. In addition, the lad had excellent knowledge of the great passions men shared with women in the world's first days, when Brynhildur slept on the mountain, and he knew stories of the swans that flew from the south and alighted on the headlands, cast off their dresses, and spun men's fates.* What is more, he was fluent in the uncanny lore predicting the end of the peopled world and the twilight of the Gods.

Þormóður Bessason found life at home with his father dreary. Early on, he made a habit of visiting places where things were more lively: feasts, weddings, wakes, Yule gatherings, or else he went to join the men at the fishing huts or other places where people gathered for work. At such times, it fell to him to cheer up folk with his lays, since winters in the Vestfirðir are long and tediously dark. Soon, when pressed for fresh verses, Þormóður began composing his own. Even as a youth he had such a gift for verse that his poems were on a par with those of other skalds.

At Vatnsfjörður, Chieftain Vermundur had numerous domestics and a good store of slaves. Both poor men and criminals made their way there, in addition to invited guests and visitors from all over the Vestfirðir who would come to speak to Vermundur and ask his advice. It was not long before Þormóður became a frequent visitor to Vatnsfjörður, finding it much more entertaining there than at home in Laugaból. Many in Vermundur's household welcomed his visits warmly, though the householders themselves were not quite so open-armed. Folk there had no end of amusement listening to the lad's tales in the hall at the close of day.

A woman from the Jökulfirðir, Kolbrún by name, was visiting Vatnsfjörður with her young daughter, Geirríður. Kolbrún was from Norway. She had sailed for Iceland along with her husband, the ship's skipper, and taken winter lodging with Vermundur. That same winter, her husband, the Easterling, died suddenly, and it was rumored that Kolbrún had devised his death.* Then for a time she and Vermundur carried on quite a torrid affair, but when another young woman caught the aged chieftain's attention, he broke off their relationship and sent her to dwell in Hrafnsfjörður, one of the most desolate areas in all the Jökulfirðir. Vermundur sent a Norwegian slave, named Loðinn, with Kolbrún to serve her. Loðinn was a hawkish man who kept mainly to himself; he was very hairy, bearded, and bushy-browed – hence his name.* He kept his eyes lowered most of the time, though those who claimed to have seen him look up said his eyes gleamed like a snake's. During haymaking, mother and daughter would pay visits to old acquaintances in Djúp, the slave Loðinn leading their horses. The housewife had a good short sword that she entrusted to Loðinn's keeping, though she would take it from him during boisterous, drunken gatherings. Kolbrún was so robust that few could match her in tests of strength. She was quite portly, yet had a good-looking face, and the best eyes of any woman, dark beneath her brow. She was known to be rather pettish if displeased and harsh to people whom she did not like – or, folk said, even more so to her lovers. For this reason, more men preferred to jest with her than try for her hand – and besides, she had very little to show for herself.

Once at day's end when folk were gathered in the hall at Vatnsfjörður, Þormóður sat for a long time singing verses, regaling the company with lays on noble kings, famous battles, and many a valiant slaying. As is wont when evenings draw on, calls came for tales of the love that men won from shieldmaidens of yore.

One man said: "What a rotten scandal, to be forced to listen over and over to the story of when Lady Sigrún trod the road to Hel to kiss the dead Helgi, or of when Freyja clamped her thighs around Loki, or yet again of when Sigurður came upon the armor-clad maiden asleep on the mountain, slit her byrnie down to her crotch, and ravaged her before she woke up, while nobody ever sings love-verses on the noblest women in the Vestfirðir in our day and age. What would suit us all better is a lay about what is on everyone's lips: how the housewife in Hrafnsfjörður beds her slave Loðinn twice a year; first when only nine nights of winter remain and the ravens have laid their eggs, and later when summer begins to fade and the hay has been gathered from the homefields."

Many others joined in, pointing out the need for verses composed in honor of such a noble lady as Kolbrún of Hrafnsfjörður. At that time, however, poetry about women was held in very low esteem, and it was considered such an affront to address verses to a woman that her relatives had the right to avenge it with murder.

"I am not much good at making love songs," said Skald Þormóður, "and besides, I see little use in slandering a woman who has done no wrong."

The gathered company said that it was unnecessary to put

the woman's name into any verses he composed – whoever was meant would be plain.

Mistress Kolbrún of Hrafnsfjörður scoffed at this conversation and declared that men who composed love songs were incapable of enjoying women in other ways.

Þormóður said: "My father Bessi Halldórsson told me that it ill beseems a real man to make up lays about women's loves – such poems are for pansies alone, and paltry fellows who lie about in inglenooks sucking curd-teats."

The conversation in the hall at Vatnsfjörður now died down for the night, and folk went off to bed.

But the next evening after supper, Þormóður stepped forth and asked for silence, announcing that he had composed a poem about Mistress Kolbrún of Hrafnsfjörður, as requested by the assembly the previous night.

Many of them had forgotten last evening's gibes, and were not keen on continuing. They had gone to bed late, and that, plus work and all the curds they had just downed, made them quite drowsy. Yet some of them stayed up to hear the poem, giving Þormóður the nickname Kolbrúnarskáld: the Skald of Coal-Brow. Some of the women, however, said that the name he deserved better was Kolrössuskáld, the Skald of Coal-Rump, and they always used that name for him whenever he came up in conversation later. No one remembers clearly how the poem the young Þormóður composed for this woman went – it has been removed from most books or scratched out. Some folk of old must have thought it unseemly, yet it more likely smacked of youthful frivolity than the earnest effort of a full-grown man who makes verses on loves denied him. Most written accounts agree, however, that Kolbrún from Hrafnsfjörður neither cursed the poem nor praised it – and as the lad went off to bed in an outlying shed where his kinsman Vermundur put beggars, rascals, and dogs, he ran his hand along the bedframe of the mother and daughter from Hrafnsfjörður. The mistress lay nearest the frame, and the girl against the wall behind her. The woman bade the lad stop. "How old a man are you, Skald Þormóður?" she asked.

He told her his age, which some say was fourteen at the time, and others twelve.

She reached for the skald and sat him down beside her on the bed. Reliable sources say that the lad had never before known that so great a woman could exist in the world.

"It astonishes me," said she, "that such a young man should foist verses on us women, against which we have little recourse. And it is unexampled in all the world for a little boy to make a woman his laughingstock – we women find it dishonorable enough to hear poems about us composed by men with more to them than you. But in this case, the precept shall prevail that words rule over works, and from this moment on, you shall never be able to escape me. This is my reward for your poem. I also declare that when you have become a man, Þormóður, you shall ever and always be drawn to me, wherever you go, yet shall never be nearer than when you set your course farthest."

Having spoken these words, the woman let the skald go for the time being.

3

ÞÓRELFUR, ÞORGEIR Hávarsson's mother, came from Hordaland in Norway, a region harsh and forlorn, where it had long been the custom for men's sons who had little chance to thrive to travel abroad and acquire wealth through plunder. Some went to Russia, others to the British Isles. In Hordaland, those who never undertook a Viking raid were deemed worthless. Yet none knew more valiant tales of the trials of the Vikings, their battles and sea-voyages, than those who never ventured from home. Among these, it was the nursemaids who had the best stocks of lore. In fair verses, they extolled the Vikings' feats: the prowess, valor, and gallantry that true men display in distant lands, yet do so more rarely the closer they are to women. For the young sons of Hordaland crofters, such lore was the only provision and dowry that they received from their mothers before leaving home – and likewise, Þórelfur had little else to lavish on her son than tales of the prowess of champions of yore and paeans to kings who win the devotion of ambitious crofters' sons with their bounteousness, rewarding stout hearts with weighty rings.

Never once did Mistress Þórelfur mention when Hávar Kleppsson, the Viking from Hordaland, fell by his homefield wall without raising a hand in his own defense. As a rule, she spoke of Hávar as an intrepid hero who had ravaged distant lands with fire and fought at the forefront in the battles of noble kings. The only tales that Þorgeir heard of his father placed him firmly beneath the banner, making it quite clear to the boy that the kings owed everything to Hávar, even treating him as their confidant at fateful moments. For the boy, Farmer Hávar was the living embodiment of a "battle rouser," a name given by skalds to men of swords and slaughter. Housewife Þórelfur taught her son that glibness is best left to the waifs, geezers, and crones who begged from door to door. Words, she declared, are entirely worthless but for the praise befitting kings, swords, and battle. A hero, she stated, says little about most things, neither commending nor disparaging, uttering not a word beyond what he is prepared to back with arms. She insisted that the only persuasions capable of solving a dispute are the truths spoken by swords. A man's doughtiness in conflict, his valor and cunning, prove his worth. Whether his life is long or short, whether he stands or falls in battle, makes no difference, if his deeds are resplendent with glory. His value lies in his stoutheartedness, whether fighting against overwhelming odds or taking his enemy unawares and striking him dead. Nobleness means enduring no man's taunts, avenging injury, making open foes of traitors, and striking first.

Þorgeir's mother said that a valiant man should pledge truest faith to the most freehanded king, for good fortune attends such a king. If, on the other hand, the king grows tightfisted, then it is best to break that pledge. Never must a courageous man see his name disgraced for choosing peace when it is time for a fight. His mother said too that a good Viking never spares a woman or a child in war. The fame of any man who followed this sound advice would resound throughout the world as long as the Midgard Serpent was bound.

In her poverty, Þórelfur nurtured the lad as best she could, doting on him as though he were a guest of high esteem, long anticipated and a hundred times welcome, and upon whom the family's honor and prosperity depended. The few blessings that their rather barren patch of earth could provide were always her son's first. If she found a berry on the slope, she brought it home for him. She never burdened him with chores, instead teaching him that farm work was for beggarly folk and fishing was for slaves. She did, however, encourage him to sail, and to learn to steer a ship, so that someday he could set his own course across the world.

Mistress Þórelfur's greatest grief was that she had no weapon to give her son, apart from Farmer Hávar's club. When Þorgeir asked why his father had no assortment of fine weapons, as great a warrior as he had been, the housewife replied that he had lost his sword in a shipwreck.

Although French swords have hardly ever held a higher place than in Icelandic poetry, it is commonly believed that the Icelanders' poverty at the time the sworn brothers grew up was such as to prevent almost everyone in the land from owning a decent weapon – apart from the wealthy, who purchased them abroad for vanity's sake or received them as gifts from great lords.

When Þorgeir Hávarsson was twelve winters old, his mother sent him west to her kinsman Þorgils at Reykjahólar, to give the lad a chance to learn the manners and customs of chieftains. There was little joy at Reykjahólar when southern horse-traders delivered the lad there. Þorgils Arason owned and oversaw a great many farms and trading ships, leaving him little time to tend to this kinsman of his who had shown up at his door, and he sent word to the maids to lodge the newcomer with the farmhands.

Next morning, the foreman announces that Þorgeir is to go with the other boys to feed the pigs. To this, Þorgeir says little, and sits tighter in his seat.

That day and those following, Þorgeir continues to mope, obstinately ignoring any chores assigned to him. When Þorgils is informed of his kinsman's reluctance to work, he sends for him and tells him that his workmen are finding it quite hard to budge him. "Would you prefer, kinsman," says Þorgils, "that I assign you a task?"

Þorgeir replies: "My mother never said that I was to feed pigs."

"What job would she have you do?" asks Þorgils.

"Slay with a sword," replies Þorgeir Hávarsson.

"And where shall you begin?" asks Þorgils.

"No need for you to ask," answers Þorgeir.

"Yet your mother is fully aware that the men of Borgar-fjörður compensated your father's slaying, to the satisfaction of all, long ago," says Þorgils. "Nor do we have much heart for killing. The days are long past when men earned their keep through conflict."

"You certainly do not sound like much of a chieftain to me," says Þorgeir Hávarsson. "It is time for me to go home to Borgarfjörður."

"No sense in that," says Þorgils. "If the pigs are not to your liking, go and watch the men butcher seals or flense whales, smelt bog iron or make charcoal. Or go to the forge to see our good smiths at their craft. We are also busy erecting a timber church to Christ, the lord who is peer to the emperors in the lands where we trade. We would have both his friendship and his mother's, who steadfastly supports all merchants, and is a sight better than your mother, our kinswoman Þórelfur. Pay a visit to the housewrights shaping boards for our church, and learn to use a saw or a plane. Or will you join a ship's crew, and haul cargo for the merchants? Here many a man, both old and young, labors at useful industry. Sword-rattling profits us little."

Things then went as they had seemed likely to from the start, with little love lost between the two kinsmen. Yet Þorgils cautioned his foremen not to express their annoyance with the boy or raise his hackles. Þorgeir did not change his ways. He was disinclined toward almost all work, and paid little heed to others' opinion of him. When the smiths forged hot iron, however, they would occasionally allow the boy to handle the hammer or pump the bellows – for which he turned out to have quite a knack. Þorgeir grew so fond of iron that if he found rusty scraps lying around, he would bring them home to his bed and sleep on them. It was customary then to ration out stockfish and butter to the workers by the week. Þorgeir traded the farmhands his share of butter for iron, saying that he thought it beggarly to eat butter – "Iron is more to my taste." He took a great liking to those who wielded weapons, and always turned up for games, soon proving his mettle in them. Otherwise, he never showed whether he liked things or not, and nothing enjoyed by other youngsters seemed to make him happy.

One day in early summer, between the weaning of the lambs and the start of haymaking, a group of men came riding from the north, over the heaths. It was Vermundur Þórgrímsson, the chieftain of Vatnsfjörður, on his way to the Alþingi. Vermundur stayed the night with Þorgils at Reykjahólar. These two chieftains were on good terms, each holding his own share of the Vestfirðir. As usual, Bessi Halldórsson of Laugaból accompanied his kinsman Vermundur, sticking close by his side. Þormóður Bessason had joined them as their groom. Early the next morning at Reykjahólar, Þormóður was woken to tend to the horses. The sun was still in the north and there was dew on the hayfields, the sea glistened, and white vapor hung lazily over the hot spring in the still of morning.

As Þormóður, bleary-eyed, looked out the door, he noticed a young man standing in the yard, with a shark knife hanging from his belt, a heavy meat cleaver perched on his shoulder, and a kettle lid in his hand, as a shield. This fellow was as shoddily dressed as he was armed. Þormóður held nothing but a poor whip and a bridle. His drowsiness drained from him the second he caught sight of this youth, who seemed of similar age, all accoutred for battle on such a mild morning. He walked over to him, standing there with his weapons, and looked him up and down. The weapon-bearer gave no indication that he wished to converse with him, or that he noticed him at all.

Þormóður greets him and asks: "Why are you wide awake at night, fellow, when most folk are enjoying the great blessing of sleep?"

"I cannot sleep," answers the warrior, "because I am constantly pondering where I might find men worthy of dying by my weapons."

Þormóður asks: "Are you he who shall avenge his woes?"

Þorgeir replies: "Of that I am not certain, at least not as certain as I am that you are the Þormóður who climbed into the old crow's bed. Folk are puzzled as to why you made verses about an ogress instead of praising the women from southerly lands who soar high in the sky in the likeness of swans and spin the fates of men."

Þormóður says: "That lay will not prevent me from lauding your valiant deeds once word of them spreads. Due to my youth, the only indulgence I could grant a woman was poetry."

Þorgeir replies: "When word comes to you of deeds of mine that you deem fit for praise in verse, I will be your friend."

"Will you permit me to handle your weapons, fellow?" asks Þormóður.

"My weapons could stand improvement," says Þorgeir. "I myself banged out this old cleaver, but the day will come when I serve a king who shall present me with a Frankish sword."

"Have you chosen a king, by any chance?" asks Þormóður.

"I will back the king who spares neither savagery nor stout-heartedness in carving out a kingdom for himself in the North," replies Þorgeir.

"It seems to me," says Þormóður, "that in you, Þorgeir Hávarsson, a great warrior has been born into this world. Therefore, I vow and declare that when you have done your very first deed of renown, worthy of the gift of Óðinn, I shall journey wherever you may be and deliver you a lay. Thenceforth we shall never part company, but together seek out the ring-breaker we know to be noblest, and pledge ourselves to him."

Of their conversation at that time, no more has been recorded.

4

AT ÖGUR IN Djúp lived a widow named Katla, whose husband had perished at sea. She was a wealthy woman. When this
story begins, she had a young daughter, named Þórdís, called
Þórdís Kötludóttir after her mother. Among Mistress Katla's
household was an Easterling by the name of Skati, who had
missed his ship one day and hired on as one of her laborers. He
was an enterprising man and quickly took over management of
Katla's farmstead. Skati was considered a demanding taskmas-
ter, and was unpopular with the household and slaves. Many
people said that the only thing Skati was after in reward for his
service to Katla was the satisfaction of seeing her farm's wealth
grow.

Skati was a great one for talking. He had many tales to tell
of warfare and plundering, and often regaled folk with stories
of his exploits on Viking expeditions, when he threw in his lot
with sea-kings. They had come away victors in numerous battles,
in the Baltic as well as in Ireland.

Þórdís Kötludóttir loved listening to Skati's tales. He often
had the girl on his lap, his hands clasped around her ankles, as he
sat in his mistress's bower at evening. Skati told of the Vikings'

raids on foreign lands, how they burned people's houses to cinders and cut down any man who could fight and posed them a threat, as well as old folk, infants, and anyone else who proved a hindrance. There was no better plunder to be had, however, than living women, who could be traded for silver in England and Denmark. Skati also told of perilous battles he had fought as a Viking, when, of his entire band, only he and the king were left standing in the end, and were seized and led to a dungeon in chains. Their only hope then was in the intercession of a *dís*, or one of those good women known as princesses in foreign lands. The girl, sitting there on the Viking's lap, often dozed off before Skati and the king were rescued from prison. She liked falling asleep listening to the tales told by this man, whom she did not doubt was the greatest warrior in the North.

At Ögur there was a young slave named Kolbakur, who was Irish. Katla's husband had purchased him on one of his voyages abroad, when Kolbakur was a boy of ten. Seven years had passed since then. Kolbakur was a red-haired, squint-eyed man, rather short-statured, but exceptionally fair of form: he had broad shoulders and a slender waist, lissome limbs, and small hands. He was not particularly strong, but did most of his chores better than hardier men. He was the deftest of fishermen, and the nimblest at rounding up livestock in the mountains. Kolbakur was never first to make conversation or jest, but if addressed, he would respond lightheartedly and spiritedly. When he was alone, a shadow fell across his face, as if he were mulling over things hidden to others.

It annoyed some of the freedmen to see this slave, hardly more than a child, do most of the farm work quicker and better than themselves. They loathed fishing next to him, watching him catch fish after fish while they got barely a bite, or seeing him run up steep slopes that made them quail. He was often harassed out of sheer envy. Foreman Skati, in particular, was quite hostile toward this Irish lad, brooding, as he often did, over the way high-minded Norse chieftains had been driven from Ireland to end up behind cows' rumps in Iceland. Their kingdoms had been sundered, after they had won them with gallantry and valor and subjected the Irish to the rule of law, while those excellent men who had not been killed or driven out had been forced to stretch their necks beneath Irish heels. Skati thought it fair and fitting that Slave Kolbakur taste the humiliation that the Irish had inflicted on the Norsemen when they drove them away.

When Þórdís Kötludóttir was a small child, she found it funny to see Kolbakur abused and laughed merrily, as children do at others' misfortune. The Norseman Skati was no less contented to please the girl, and was constantly finding fault with Kolbakur's work. If Kolbakur so much as broke a tooth of his rake during haymaking, Skati would grab him and shove him to the ground, while hurling gibes at him. It certainly did not befit a Norseman to stand up for a beaten slave, and most folk acted as if they saw nothing. Yet none but the children laughed out loud.

As time went by and the girl grew, she became less jocose. She no longer found it as amusing to watch slaves being thrashed, and, as might be expected, turned her mind to more interesting means of passing the time.

Word went round Djúp that a fair flower had sprung up in Laugadalur: to be more precise, the skald Þormóður Bessason, who entertained folk with his lays, and was a friend of chieftains and favorite of women.

Report also came that the son of Hávar Kleppsson of Ísafjörður, whom the men of Borgarfjörður killed, was now in Reykjahólar. This lad's name was Þorgeir, and he was such a warrior, even at his young age, that he went round armed day and night and never spoke a word to anyone. People said that the doughtiest of men would find him a handful in a contest, and that the *dísir* had most likely preordained great glory for this lad.

One day in early summer, some men came to Ögur from Hornstrandir to buy stallions, and Kolbakur was sent to the mountains to drive the herd down. As the men were standing at the corral, watching the horses descend, the colt thought to be the finest in the entire herd broke from the others and galloped back toward the mountains, whinnying shrilly in a rutting frenzy. Kolbakur rode after it for some distance before turning back – the path the young stallion had taken being impossible for a rider.

Besides those from Hornstrandir, quite a crowd of men, women, and children had gathered at the corral for amusement. The sun shone in the dry air and gleamed on the steeds, which had newly shed their winter coats and were plump as seals. The girl Þórdís Kötludóttir had also come, along with other women.

Slave Kolbakur had been unable to round up the stallion, and was now on his way back without it. As he rode toward the corral, Foreman Skati ran into his path, grabbed his horse's reins, yanked the boy off the horse, slapped him across the face and shoved him to the ground, then pulled the slave's shirt over his head, tore the whip from his hand, and lashed the boy's naked back several times before finally hurling it at him as he lay there groveling.

Skati The Easterling was the most courteous of men, comely of appearance and most stately in stature, with a bright countenance and the fairest eyes of all.

When Slave Kolbakur was fairly certain that Skati had had his fill of beating him, he got to his feet and hastily pulled up his trousers, his cheeks slightly red with youthful modesty, and then smiled apologetically at those who had witnessed this incident.

The horse-traders carried on with their bargaining.

Late in the day, Þórdís went home. She and the other young girls had passed the time during the horse-trading in fun and games, and they soon forgot the incident just described. Kolbakur and an aged manservant had rowed to a sheltered spot to fish, and they came ashore just as Maid Þórdís was walking across the homefield. Kolbakur was dangling his catch on a string. The girl stopped and addressed him at once:

"Why do you chase after horses and slaughter fish, Kolbakur?" she said. "It would beseem you better to become a hero and skald."

"I am a slave," said he.

"How can a man as comely as you," she asked, "be a slave, for others to beat at will?"

"Heroes and skalds came to my home in Ireland," said he.

"Why do you not cry when you are beaten?" asked the girl.

"I do not cry, young woman," said he, having laid his fish on the grass as he spoke. "I do not cry because heroes and skalds burned down my house; because they slew my father in his field and thrust a spear through my grandfather, just a frail old man. My grandmother was on her knees praising her beloved friend, the blessed Columbkille, when a man bashed in her skull with a blow from his ax. That is why I do not cry. Then they took my infant brother, unwound his swaddling clothes, and tossed him naked between them on their spear points. My mother and my young sister they dragged away wailing to their ship. And that is why, young woman, I do not cry."

The girl stared at Kolbakur for several moments, without another word, and then walked away.

5

ON THE NEXT day, Skati the Easterling went to visit his mistress in her bower and presented her with good silver. "I have gotten you this in trade for horses."

"You are a gem," said the woman. "Sit down. I shall prepare you some dainties."

She beat eggs and mixed in wine and honey.

Her daughter was there as well, standing by the window opening, whose frame and membrane she had drawn aside.* The girl stared out, listening to the chirping of the birds. She did not turn to look when the Easterling walked in. He said:

"Why does Mardöll not laugh as usual for her Viking Skati?* Does she not wish to sit on the warrior's lap tonight? We had not finished the story of how I fought with the Wends and they clapped me in irons."

The girl made no reply. Mistress Katla said: "Keep your custom, child, and sit on your foster-father Skati's lap. Away with peevishness and timidity – such dispositions do not suit little girls."

The girl answered: "I shall do as you wish, mother – but it is you who have most at stake, for I am no longer inclined toward nursery rhymes."

Skati laughed, lifted the girl to his lap, and warbled her part of a lullaby. Then he took up the story of how the Wends captured and enchained him. The centerpiece of his tale was a place of cruel dreams, a dark and foul dungeon whose floor and walls were crawling with lizards, toads, and other poisonous creatures, some of them bristling or shaggy with hair. When a warrior, however, tells of the worst of all places he has visited, he must never admit to having felt fear – that is out of the question. Skati went only so far as to say that it had been a rather dull dwelling. One time, he recounted, he heard a peculiar noise in the dark, and, still in his shackles, edged nearer to the wall to try to make it out. From there he heard what he thought was a fiddle being bowed deep in the earth, and a woman singing along in spellbindingly beautiful tones.

On most days, it made the girl drowsy to sit like this on the Easterling's lap, leaning up against him and feeling his grip around her ankles as he rambled on with his stories, but now the girl sprang with a shriek from his grasp, shook her fists furiously at him, and showered him with the most scornful of names.

Her mother asked her the cause of this tantrum.

She replied: "He laid hold of my knee."

Mistress Katla stopped her beating and looked at her foreman.

He said: "I never knew the girl to have a woman's touchiness. Until now, she has never made a fuss about where I lay my hand."

"Keep your paws where they belong," said Þórdís. "And hereafter, you shall never touch me. I am going now to see Kolbakur, who is far nobler than you."

When the girl had left the bower, Mistress Katla said to her Easterling: "It is quite clear," she says, "that my daughter has come of age, and your lullabies have been far from my liking for some time. She has now sensed the situation more clearly than I had seen it: your fondness for her is growing, and will grow overmuch if you cling to this place for too long – you faithless man."

This said, the mistress raised the whisk she had been using to beat the eggs and honey, and with it whacked the Viking's upper lip.

The slave sat with his dogs on the homefield wall. One of his tasks was to scare off sheep from the homefield during the night. The girl walked up and sat down on the wall beside him, drooped her head, and plucked blades of grass. He asked what was on her mind. She raised her head slowly, looked him in the eyes and said: "I want to ask a trifle of you."

He inquired what it might be.

She said: "I want you to kill the Easterling."

"I was not aware that you loved him so much," answered Slave Kolbakur.

She asked why he said such a monstrous thing.

He replied: "My kinsmen have told me that when a Norse woman loves a man beyond all else, she will seduce an assassin into murdering her beloved, and then marry the murderer."

She laughed and replied: "It may be true that we women choose, if given a choice between two men, to marry the one we love less. And indeed, we may also condemn our lovers to death if their affection should turn to other women than us. But I do not know whether I am fond enough of Skati to give myself in marriage to the man who slays him. In short, I weary of hearing how he put Wends and Kurs to the sword, while my mother sits by with her cheeks flushing red, waiting for me to fall asleep to his tales. I find myself shunning him more the more tales that he tells, and I am now determined that if any man is to lay his hand on my knee, it shall be you."

"I shall risk neither," said Slave Kolbakur. "Neither laying hold of your knee nor slaying your Easterling – for which bootless acts I would forfeit my life."

"Would you just be beaten, then," said the girl, "and never lift your neck?"

"My being beaten matters little," said he. "'Ever may a living man come by a cow.'"*

"Your wisdom is hardly heroic," said the girl. "Where did you learn it?"

"When old Grímnir and I go out fishing, he teaches me lore

of his that is not austere to the point of spooking fish. 'Halt may ride horses, handless may herd.'"*

She replied: "I wish to learn this lore from you, and any other that you know. Nor are you required to kill the Easterling – just as you prefer."

"Why should I hazard to teach you this lore?" said he.

She said: "Would you have me return to the Easterling and tell him that it suits champions to slay men with swords, not beat them with whips?"

"Your words are your own choice, young woman," he said. "But for you I will perform no other task than what befits a man taken captive in war."

She said: "My mother has built me a loft, with the window facing the mountain. But the frame is fastened so tightly that it cannot be moved. In my abode, I would have a window that I may open and shut at will, as my mother has in her bower. Now I would ask you to loosen the frame and fix it with bolts, that I might unbolt it to hear the birds chirp in the evenings."

He said: "Carrion birds might fly in."

"What flies through my window," said she, "is of no matter to you. Let me just say that I prefer not to use the main door when night falls."

"I would never have guessed a woman fair as you to be a night hag," said he.

"Is your whole intent to belittle my friendship and vex me?"

asked the girl, the corners of her mouth twitching as she fought back tears. Then she looked up, glared at him, and said sharply: "I would have such a window in my loft," said she, "that I might fly out with my spinning to a certain headland where I know two young warriors dwell – one of whom beats iron into a sword, while the other embosses a shield with ancient tales. On that headland I will lay aside my swan's dress and spin their fates."

He replied: "I will loosen your window frame for you, that you might fly out and fix their fates."

6

ONE DAY ÞORGEIR Hávarsson came to speak with his kinsman Þorgils in his sitting room at Reykjahólar. At Þorgeir's waist
hung an inferior-looking sword, and he held a spear and a shield
at the ready. He took his stand opposite his kinsman and gave
him a look that might have been called audacious.

"You have no words of greeting for us, your kinsmen?" asked
Þorgils Arason, with a laugh. "Or am I to rise and serve you?"

"Greeting others is an unmanly custom," said Þorgeir
Hávarsson. "Laugh at me as you wish. Due to our kinship – and
your being a man of wealth and might – I am entirely at your
disposal."

Þorgils said that it was in fact a great honor to the family tree
to have sprouted such a sprig as Þorgeir. "But shall we speak to
each other with weapons drawn?" Without rising from his seat,
he reached for a fine, hefty sword lying on a shelf, drew it from
its sheath, and pointed it at Þorgeir. Upon beholding such a noble weapon, Þorgeir nearly dropped his own. "Or," said Þorgils,
"shall we behave like men and keep the peace as we converse?"

Þorgeir laid his weapons on the dais, and Þorgils sheathed
the sword and put it back on the shelf.

Þorgeir said: "I have endured the gibes of you kinsmen of mine in Reykjahólar for quite some time now, and many would say that I am no peevish man to have put up with such treatment for so long. Your place for me was with your dogs, and I have not had any clothes other than my own, apart from what I pressed your slaves into giving me. The time has now come for me to thank you for your hospitality. I intend to go south to Borgarfjörður."

"What business do you have in Borgarfjörður?" asked Þorgils Arason.

"I must pay a debt that my mother and I owe a farmer there," said Þorgeir. "She is not fond of us being indebted to folk outside the family."

"Say no more," said Þorgils Arason. "It is obvious that you are descended from fools on your father's side, if you believe that manslaughter makes you more of a man. When I was in the Orkney Isles, one of the servants of King Christ in Rome told me that his lord would do away with militarism and its accompanying campaigns, and instead grant men wealth and prosperity through trade, benedictions, baptisms, church-building, land acquisition, the keeping of servants, and celebration of the Divine Office. It would be more propitious for you to saw panels and plane altar boards for the church that I intend to dedicate to Christ within the next few years than to trudge southward to slay folk. This winter, I will bring clerics here to sing Masses for us and baptize all those who, out of sheerfoolishness and paltriness, have been depriving themselves of such excellent boons."

Þorgeir replied: "I learned from my mother that many an outstanding man has challenged White Christ to single combat, and he has dared to fight with none.* He must be a milksop, and I would rather serve almost any other king than him. My mother has also told me that the power that waxes in men and gods is called the Earth-force, and is fused from the hardness of stone and the succulence of plants, as well as the ferocity found in a wolf's tooth. I am convinced that Christ has not received this power, while other gods mourned and withered away when they lost it – and so it will go with men."

Nothing further of the two kinsmen's conversation will be told in this book. To continue with Þorgeir Hávarsson: he set off for Borgarfjörður with no possessions but his poor weapons and the tatty clothes on his back. Winter set in, freezing the lakes and rivers. Nothing is told of Þorgeir's travels until he arrived at Skeljabrekka late one evening around bedtime. He knocked at the door. A manservant came, asked who was outside, and invited the visitor to enter, but Þorgeir said that he never told slaves his name or accepted their invitations. "Where is Farmer Jöður?" he asked.

"What do you want with him?" asked the servant.

"I have a debt to settle with him," said Þorgeir.

The servant went in and reported that a stranger was at the door, wishing to pay a debt to Farmer Jöður, but that he apparently never entered people's houses at the invitation of inferiors. Jöður called to his son to come with him, and they both grabbed axes. They went to the door. The brightness of their lamps burning inside blinded the father and son to the world outside. Þorgeir, however, whose eyes were adjusted to the dark, saw the farmer's silhouette in the doorway, and he thrust his spear ferociously into the farmer's belly, driving the man back into his son's arms. Without hesitation, Þorgeir swung his ax at the farmer's son's head and cracked his skull. Having struck down the farmer and his son and leaving both lying there dying in the doorway, Þorgeir continued to thrash them for some time, to ensure that they did not escape death. In those days, Norsemen were greatly in the habit of using their weapons, badly forged from inferior steel, as bludgeons, being too blunt to bite. Having taken his fill of flailing and flogging, Þorgeir went his way that same night, not stopping until he reached his mother's door at Hávarsstaðir in the faint gleam of dawn.

Þórelfur welcomed her son gladly and asked him the news, but he had little to tell.

"Did you stop at Skeljabrekka?" the woman asked.

"The highroad cuts through their hayfields," said he.

"Did you meet anyone there?" the woman asked.

"Less I," said he, "than my spear and my ax."

He then asked her to walk with him into the light, where they could see that his clothes were bloody and his weapons and hands were smeared with gore, and that his face was spotted with the blood that spouted from the bodies of the Skeljabrekka men under his blows. Now he poured out every detail of the slayings to his mother. Hearing his report, Þórelfur embraced Þorgeir tenderly, before ordering a servant to slaughter a lamb, declaring that she would hold a feast for her son.

The law decreed that a killer was compelled to make his slaying public before sundown of the same day, on pain of being deemed a murderer and deprived of the law's aegis. It was his duty to go to the nearest habitation where he felt his life was safe, and to announce the deed to a resident there.

"Here we have neither the manpower nor the wealth to keep you from the clutches of the Borgarfjörður men a single day more," said Þórelfur. "Now eat your fill of the lamb, and I shall bundle up the remains for you for the road. Return as quickly as you can to my kinsman Þorgils – the bonds of kinship ensure that he will take you back in, though little love is lost between you two. Men have come here by boat from the Borgarfjörður dales, on their way westward to Snæfellsjökull to buy stockfish. They have been waiting out the headwinds in an empty hut nearby, but now the wind is shifting, it seems, to a light southerly. I will ask them to give you passage, and you must announce the slaying to the first man that you meet west of Mýrar. Those there will hardly think it news. Then you must find your own way over Breiðafjörður to your kinsman at Reykjanes."

Nothing is told of Þorgeir's journey westward to Reykjahólar, except that Þorgils Arason's brow darkened when he saw his kinsman again. To him, Þorgeir's arrival boded nothing but ill. "What mess have you gotten yourself into?" he asked.

Þorgeir told him freely how he avenged his father.

"That case was settled long ago, and compensation duly paid," said Þorgils Arason. "Am I now to be hounded by lawsuits from distant parts of the country for your nighttime slaying, you fool?"

Þorgeir replied: "It is clear now how weapons become me, kinsman, even when their edges are flawed. My mother always told me that I should be a killer."

"No surprise there," said Þorgils. "In none do the Viking ideals of piracy and pugnacity wax stronger than in old widows in remote valleys. In our day and age, little distinction is to be had in costuming oneself like a long-dead sea-king from Norway – there is far more to be found in following the example of the lord of Rome, who offers good men profit through peace. Yet many might excuse you for the deed you have now described – stupid man that you are."

7

THE STORY SPREAD widely – and was thought most heroic – that in the space of one night, a mere youth had struck down both a champion of the caliber of Jöður Klængsson and his son, the most promising of men, and in doing so fulfilled the ancient, sacred, and legal obligation of avenging one's father. It was not long until news of Þorgeir's redoubtable deed was reported at Laugaból in Djúp. Þormóður the skald was highly impressed by this achievement, and sat down immediately to compose *Þorgeir's Revenge*, a lay of twenty stanzas. He asked his father's leave to go south to Reykjahólar for the Yule festivities, to present the lay to his friend. Bessi said that for now, he was free to travel as he chose, yet he had an inkling that Þormóður's occupation was as little needed elsewhere as at home.

Þormóður was nearly full-grown when he made his trip to Reykjahólar. At that time, most men in Iceland were short and bandy-legged, gaunt and swollen-jointed, knotted and twisted by gout, blue of complexion and shriveled. Their plight was to toil away in that inimical land, in storm, wind, and rain, on mountainsides and at sea. Most had no fatty meat to sustain them. Þormóður Kolbrúnarskáld was supple of limb and slender of build, straight-legged and light of foot, pale-skinned, bushy-browed, and dark-haired. At that time, it was common to overwork children at their chores, scarring them early, but Þormóður bore no signs of such excess. He was genial to all and ready-tongued with women.

After his arrival in Reykjahólar, Þormóður recited *Þorgeir's Revenge* for the gathered household. Few had anything to say about the poem except Þorgeir himself, who stated that it would be on people's lips as long as the North was inhabited. Yet he deeply lamented that his poverty should prevent him from granting its skald a fitting reward, and declared that instead, Þormóður would have his friendship as long as they both lived. These two friends, however, seemed less to enjoy the commoners' respect than their own for each other.

More than once, while sitting outdoors, they bandied visions of ancient kings consecrated to the gods: Jörmunrekur, King of the Goths, Helgi Hundingsbani and Sigurður Fáfnisbani, King Hálfur's champions, and other outstanding men. At times, Norns flew by in swan dress, stretching their necks and singing, and they heeded their songs, feeling as if some were sung precisely to them. Eagles flew by as well.

Their conversation frequently turned to the contemptible state of things in Iceland, when free men were forced to haul fish or chase sheep in place of pursuing wealth through war, heroism, and manslaughter, or doing other deeds worthy to be praised in poetry, such as those their forefathers had accomplished in Norway. Their lives, they felt, would be worse than unlived if they failed to carry out exploits that would be unforgettable to unborn generations. They deemed it a shame and an abomination that the land should be kingless, with not a man fit to raise an army and campaign in longships. They agreed to lead warriors' lives, paying not a whit of regard to the opinions of churls and slaves, making enemies in the manner of true gallants and building their fortunes through stout-heartedness, enduring no taunt and sparing no man, near or far, who considered himself capable of defying them or calling himself their equal.

As so often happens, those who travel their own road find it fraught with obstacles, and it was far from clear to the two how to attain the glory their hearts were set upon. They thought they might try taking passage with merchants, to seek out Vikings or kings whom it would be an honor to serve in the lands of the North, the British Isles, or east of the Baltic. At that time, no monarch of great fame ruled Norway. Since the fall of Olaf Tryggvason, the land had been governed by Danish jarls, along with Norwegian freeholders who were styled petty kings but who lived under the jarls' wings and ate from their hands. To the Icelanders, it seemed there was little glory to be gained in that old fatherland of theirs. In Ireland, the Norse chieftains were tottering. The parents of both comrades had dwelt there for a time before being driven out by the Irish. Many a Norseman felt it a cruel fate to be expelled from the bliss of the Isles, after having courageously founded a kingdom there, and to be borne bereft of joy to a land rising obstinately and imposingly from the outermost sea.

One day the two comrades went to see Þorgils Arason.

He asked what they had on their minds. They said:

"We have had quite enough of idling here fameless in Iceland, eager as we are to do deeds of renown. Will you arrange for us to meet a chieftain abroad who would avail himself of the backing of doughty fighters?"

Þorgils said: "Nothing but harm and misfortune result when killers and skalds come together, and landless liegemen should concern themselves more with honing their skills in hooking flounder and hunting seals than in sword-rattling and palaver."

They told him they found this answer wanting, and of no avail for their needs.

"If you wish to pledge yourself to foreign lords," said he, "then go to the king for whom I am building a house of glory here at Reykjahólar. It is my advice that if you serve a king, it be him. He is so great a sovereign that the very emperor in Constantinople is but his foot-page. I will now give you the chance to quit the company of my dogs, and lodge instead with my priest."

For some time it had been the law in Iceland that all should be Christian in name, and the land's leading men had bound themselves to covenants with foreign lords and merchants requiring the baptism of the commoners. For this task, they engaged itinerant clerics and wandering bishops that merchants had found on the loose in foreign lands. The Pope had decreed that Iceland belonged to the see of Bremen. At that time, however, it was uncustomary for envoys in the North to carry letters, and in any case, the Pope himself had spent little time issuing them. Nor had our countrymen in Iceland learned the Latin alphabet, and few could tell for certain whether the clerics that the merchants brought with them from foreign marketplaces had any backing from the archbishopric or the Lord Pope. It meant little for these men to produce written tokens to corroborate their stories, for at that time, most letters that passed from land to land were forged, and what is more, few could decipher them. In that century, as long before, the preaching of Christianity was carried out more by eccentrics and doltish adventurers than by the true stewards of the Holy Church. For Icelanders, the best choice was to take these traveling prelates at their word, or else remain unbaptized. Frequently these men of God proved to be murderers, thieves, or excommunicates. Some were English or Irish, and others Saxon, while several called themselves Armenian – these were black and ugly and lay with every woman they could get their hands on. Folk say that they were heretics. These clerics often had gangs of ruffians in tow to assist them with baptisms and Masses, as well as the extortion, murders, and other acts of aggression that followed. Things went on in this way until better-placed men in Borgarfjörður established a learned school at Bær and brought in Rudolf of Rouen, a worthy Frenchman, to teach Icelandic clerics the arts of book-learning and music.

At that time, the old religion was very much in decline, as folk began heeding the new. Most, in fact, soon abandoned the old gods. Noble chieftains vied to build churches and baptize as many people as they could, in order to increase the numbers of their liegemen. They promised each and every churl manifold boons in Heaven when he was dead, if he would come to church to hear the paternoster and learn about the champions of White Christ.

Although instruction in the paternoster and other sacred lore was somewhat patchy at first, due to the scarcity of priests, and unintelligible in the mouths of foreign clerics, the chieftains took pains to fasten bells and crosses to their churches, to the people's delight. Some placed statues of the champion John the Baptist in the middle of their churches, in the place that Thunder-Þórr had previously occupied in the temples. The Irish, and those who had lived among them, esteemed Patrick and Columbkille, otherwise known as Columba, above most of the Lord's champions, while others from the British Isles and the lands of the North venerated fair Cecilia and the little maidens Sunniva and Belinda. At the time, Mary was less loved by the Lord Pope than she later came to be. It was also considered obligatory for a comely crucifix to be fastened above the chancel entrance of all churches, or at the door to the nave. It was not yet customary to depict the Crucified One naked, with a forlorn face and pitiful expression, as later became common. Rather, he was decked out in an elegant, knee-length royal mantle and splendid cordovan hose. On his head he wore a tall, imperial crown, and he stood two-footed on a block on the cross, grave in his bearing, like a great landowner, or fierce, like a warrior-king.

It was the opinion of many that Christ could serve them no worse than the gods that they had brought from Norway: Þórr the Thunderer, King Freyr of the Grand Phallus, and Óðinn the Evil of Ásgarður, all of whom had helped them least when the need was greatest. More than one peasant said that it cost him nothing to believe in whatever gods the rulers chose, as long as he was left in peace to worship the crags and rocks, bluffs and peaks, hills and mounds that his forefathers had occupied when they died. What is more, there were those who put faith in their own might and main, and asserted that nothing availed them but their own strength. Some believed in their breeding stock: stallions, bulls, rams, or boars, and some in ravens, claiming that the gods were reborn in these creatures. Those who had spent time voyaging, however, declared it far more profitable to barter with foreigners peacefully than to fight them. Through peaceful trade, their friendship could be purchased as well. Yet this they could not do unbaptized, for Christians were forbidden to engage in commerce with heathens. To a man, they said that overseas, folk were considered mere fools if they did not know that White Christ wears the tallest gold crown of all sovereigns. Even the emperors in Constantinople had laid their necks beneath his heel.

A priest named Jörundur lodged in a storehouse at Reykjahólar. At the far end of it was a platform, and there stood his bunk. This man was scarcely over twenty and had done more shepherding than schooling, but a wandering English bishop had ordained him as priest to Þorgils' church, and taught him a few Latin letters and one antiphon, to whose tune he sang most of the verses that he knew and could not be avoided, such as the paternoster and Credo. Jörundur had a stole, or a brocaded scarf, to lay over his shoulders when he sang, but no other vestments. He also had a tattered copy of the Psalter, which Þorgils had bought for him. Written on several leaves in the back of this book were the holy Pope Gregory's dialogues with Peter the deacon, in which Gregory imparts sacred wisdom by means of wondrous tales. The end was missing, but it was no matter, because Jörundur could not read, though he did spend long hours racking his brain over the book.

Christianity in Iceland was then still poor and feeble, without lands or a bishopric of its own, and lacking any appeal to youth. When the sons of better men showed little interest in joining the clergy, lowly folk were chosen for the job, namely the sons of freedmen, slaves, or crofters, who served lay chieftains who had built churches, singing Masses in them to the best of their ability and receiving their pay in stockfish or seaweed. These clerics could be beaten with impunity, like any other paltry folk, if ever they shirked their tasks.

Jörundur the priest was cheerful, frail, meek, and beardless. He had carved a crucifix for himself from a block of wood, but the man hanging on it was quite unimposing, with only a thin fringe of beard and wearing a wretched, stubby crown. Slack and scrawny, this god hung on the cross, where he ruled Heaven and Earth in an everyday tunic. On the torso of the Lord God there was room enough only for the sword that the Romans thrust into his heart, and Jörundur had carved the wound into the wood and daubed it with red. Most were of the opinion that this image bore less resemblance to the King of Heaven than it did to Jörundur's father, who was a slave.

The sworn brothers had one bunk between them and the cleric another, but these new roommates were suspicious of each other and exchanged few words at first. Þorgeir Hávarsson's habit was to sleep sitting up in bed, rather than lying down. He kept his shield strapped to him as he slept, with one hand on its handle and the other on his sword hilt, and his ax on his knees. It was his belief that heroes slept in this position, and never lay down.

Twice a night, Jörundur had the task of getting up, lighting a lamp, and singing from the Psalter to his friend Christ, son of Mary, as well as commemorating the begetting of the Lord in his mother's womb, and repeating the exhortations that the Archangel Gabriel and Queen Elizabeth, mother of the champion John the Baptist, gave to the maiden when she conceived immaculately.

On the first night that the two comrades slept in the cleric's lodging, they were woken from sleep by loud, piercing singing in Latin. As might be guessed, this rude awakening agitated them to no small degree.

Þorgeir said: "We have heard that Christ is craven in a fight."

The cleric finished his office, bowed his head and carefully made the sign of the cross, and then asked: "Are you men unbaptized?"

They said that they could not be certain what clerics had gabbled at them before they were old enough to talk. "What was White Christ's greatest battle?" they asked.

Jörundur the priest reached into his trunk and pulled out the crucifix, held it up to them, and said: "This was his greatest battle. And this wound, which oozes blood and water, is a sign of his victory."

"There is little glory in dying without killing someone first. What battle did he fight that he could personally boast of?" they asked.

The cleric said: "He rose from the dead, livelier than ever before. Indeed, though he submitted himself to torment and death, no creature could do him harm, since he himself had created everything in the beginning, when he dwelt in the Kingdom of Heaven in his youth. He is so skilled a craftsman that he made the entire world from nothing. Though his kingdom may be good here on Earth, it is but a flimsy bubble compared to his kingdom in the next world, where a light shines fairer than the sun."

Þorgeir asked: "How did he treat his enemies after leaping down from the gallows?"

The cleric said: "Although Christ was fastened to the cross by evildoers and then pierced with a spear, no one could keep him captive in Hell any longer than he himself willed. He has made all men his sons, both good and evil. This is why he does not grow angry with his creation when it treats him ill, but instead takes pity on it."

"How many women has he had?" asks Þormóður.

"The souls of men and women sprang from his head and played at his feet as he sat enthroned in joy in the Kingdom of Heaven before the creation of the world," said the priest.

Þorgeir said: "Our mothers told us that the only truths are those backed by swords, and the only great man is he who either slays his enemy or makes him his slave."

"Greater," said the cleric, "was the victory of Christ the son of the Virgin when he gave all men equal share in his birthright, than that of the kings who burdened men with the yoke of slavery, and a greater deed of prowess it was when he first fashioned men's souls, lavishing the same precious fabric on both king and slave, than it is to make war on folk and send them to their deaths."

Þorgeir said: "Never did Christ or any other sorcerer fashion my mother Þórelfur a soul, yet she bore an unflinching son."

"It is written in holy books," said Jörundur, "that old Loki, whom both learned and lay call Lucifer, he being the loosest – and lousiest – of clerics, used his wiles to entrap souls, beguiling them with falsehoods. And when the souls of men began to entangle themselves in murder, day and night, and wives to double-cross their husbands through adultery, then it was that Christ displayed his full munificence and authority, when, with his overflowing wealth, he ransomed both king and slave at the same price, lifting and straightening the infirm and the bent, teaching them many a bloom-bearing hymn."

Þormóður now said to Þorgeir: "Would it not be better for us to lie with your kinsman Þorgils' bitches and lap up slops than to stay here with this foul rogue and listen to his night-time nonsense?"

"You speak soundest of all men," replied Þorgeir, who had gotten to his feet, fully armed. "And we have been done no small disgrace, to have been lodged with a feeble fool who places the gallantry of good men and the wickedness of slaves on equal footing."

Þormóður said that it would serve Þorgils right to kill his priest.

"That we shall not do," said Þorgeir, "for it would break all my bonds of kinship with Þorgils and put us outside his protection. Someday, before it all ends, we may find ourselves in need of a place of refuge here in the Vestfirðir. But that will not stop us from chastising this cleric."

They now seized Jörundur and pulled off his tunic, but because the man was weak and poor, wearing a hairshirt patched many times over, they did not have the heart to beat him long into the night. Besides, whenever they touched him, their fingertips stung, as if they had grabbed nettles.

Afterward, they went out under the open sky. The Vestfirðir night was still and starry.

8

NOW, AS YULE drew near, the two comrades took to free-loading from others throughout the Vestfirðir, calling partic-ularly – and always uninvited – on better-off farmers holding feasts. Þormóður did the talking, and in general folk did not find his tales and poems unentertaining, though not all were equally glad of the comrades' company. They were not easy to please, and took liberties and rattled their weapons.

Wherever they stayed, it was their habit to challenge men to trials of strength, and in this, Þorgeir took the lead. They invited some to bouts of arm-pulling, yanking them down off their bunks – which was in fact an offense punishable by blood vengeance, though none would have held such a grudge as to pursue it. They challenged others to the game of "rawhide-toss," which some call "hide-in-the-corners." Five men play this game at once: one in the middle of the room and one in each of its four corners – the man in the middle is said to be "out." A wet rawhide is twisted into a ball and tossed from corner to corner of the room, while the man who is out attempts to catch it. It is thus trap-ball and tug-of-war all at once. The game often ends in roughhousing and fisticuffs, or even worse, choking or suffocation, if the wet hide is wrapped around someone's neck or head – but weapons are forbidden in this game. He who wins the hide is the one left standing in the end, having never been driven to the floor. In this game, the two comrades generally had the best of it. Þormóður was so nimble that he could not be knocked off his feet, while Þorgeir was so strong that he could shove nearly every other man down, and such a tough competitor that the others were often left reeling by his thwacks to their snouts, blood pouring from their nostrils and mouths. That Yule, the sworn brothers spent their time in these sorts of games and others.

Farmer Bessi, Þormóður's father, was far from fond of this gallivanting of theirs throughout the district, and sent them word to come take their meals and lodging at Laugaból, instead of imposing themselves upon strangers. The two comrades returned there after Yule. It was a rather unhappy place for warriors to be: the valley lies far from the sea and is rarely visited by others in winter. Its normal occupants are sluggish churls, little given to sports or heroics. The comrades slept until late in the day, and when they woke, they spent most of their time bandying saws, tales, and poems about heroes of yore, or harping on their vows to yield to no foe, to be bested by none, and never to beg mercy of an enemy, but always to fight with every ounce of strength, until the bitter end.

It was customary each winter, as the sun began to climb higher, for young men from the district to meet to play games on the lake at the lower end of Laugadalur, near Laugaból, and this they did now. The weather was mild, chilly at night but sunny by day, and the ice was firm. The young men engaged in various sports: wrestling, horse-fighting, trap-ball, and tug-of-war. Many a grown man was there with his son, seeing to it that the players followed the rules. Young women had also come to watch, sitting on the bank of the lake or the flat ground above it, taking the midday sun. Some wore linen hoods on their heads, and were accompanied by their mothers or nursemaids, or else had bondwomen to look after them. During a break in the game, Skald Þormóður walked over to these girls, greeted them, and began chitchatting and jesting with them. There was one girl with pretty eyes and a fairer hue than most of the other women. She regarded this visitor of theirs with interest, yet remained somewhat guarded, as if she preferred to wait and see how things would unfold before revealing too much. Nor were her eyes and replies entirely free of humor, as though she were amused by this slender, well-spoken sportsman, without trusting him too deeply. Now shouts were heard from the ice, calling for Þormóður and another man to join the game. Just as he was about to take his leave, Þormóður turned back to this young woman and asked whether his eyes were deceiving him. "Is this," said he, "my neighbor from Ögur?"

She laughed and said yes, but then expressed her surprise at how long it had taken him to tell her from the others.

He took her hand, drew her away from the group of women, and, while her back was turned to the assembly, said: "You are the only woman to whom I would wish to address a lay."

She abruptly stopped laughing, fear filled her eyes, and her cheeks turned red.

"You will dare no such impropriety," she answered tersely, in a rather low voice, and with a tear in her eye. "My slave Kolbakur would kill you. He is sitting on the bank over there, watching as we speak. Rumor also has it that you had your platter full composing your lay for Kolbrún."

"I shall make you a longer and better lay," said he.

"I will be shamed throughout the district," said she, her eyes now blazing.

"Then I will come to meet you another time, but alone," said he.

She replied: "How astonishingly bold you are to say this to my face in plain sight of all, giving them cause to raise a hue and cry about us."

"Then next time I will speak with you hidden from others' eyes," said he.

"I have no say in your comings and goings," said she. "But do not endanger yourself any more than me, now that spring is coming and the nights grow brighter. Yet I will be no man's concubine."

"Sudden death alone could keep me from coming to you."

At these words, Þorgeir Hávarsson shouted out for Þormóður to come rejoin the game. When Þormóður Kolbrúnarskáld heard his sworn brother's voice, he left the girl at once.

At that time, many a man skilled in the games lived out west in Djúp. These men were little pleased to be bested by outsiders who turned up for their contests, such as Þorgeir Hávarsson, and they played against this interloper as fiercely as they could. Nor did Þorgeir himself hold back. They jostled on the ice, and Þorgeir knocked some of them senseless. Several farmers' sons urged the others to grab their weapons and face down this man. Respected, well-intentioned men, however, stepped in and managed to stave off further trouble between Þorgeir and the local swellheads.

Chieftain Vermundur of Eyri had been enjoying the games that day, but when he felt that the younger men's roughhousing was getting out of hand, he made ready to leave and called to his kinsman Bessi to ride with him to his boat.

He said: "I think it might be a good idea, kinsman, for your son Þormóður not to seek his cronies in other districts, lest he find in those places no other men than the kind we have driven out of the Vestfirðir for their thuggery, or that have sentences of outlawry for manslaughter hanging over their heads. I would be quite happy if you sent Þorgeir Hávarsson away. He is scarcely less of a troublemaker than his father was, and no good influence on your son Þormóður."

At the conclusion of the games, Þormóður went back over to where the women were sitting to continue his conversation with the girl, but she was gone. He asked where he might find Þórdís Kötludóttir from Ögur.

They said that the slave Kolbakur had led her horse thither, lifted her into the saddle, and taken her home.

Þormóður was idling despondently on the ice opposite the group of women when his comrade Þorgeir Hávarsson walked by.

"Are you looking for someone among these women?" asked Þorgeir.

"There was a girl here a short time ago, but now she is gone," said Þormóður. "And I feel as if this day has lost all its luster."

"We shall not let luster befuddle us," said Þorgeir.

"I wish to compose a lay for this woman," said Þormóður.

Þorgeir said: "The skalds of old would have called it unmanly

to make verses about beggar girls, the daughters of bumpkins, and not about the women who shine in the sky in swan-
likeness."

"It so happens," said Þormóður, "that I am less fond than I
was of women that fly through the air."

"That, you shall regret most," said Þorgeir Hávarsson. "He
who truckles to a woman is lowest laid."

Þormóður Kolbrúnarskáld looked at his friend Þorgeir
Hávarsson and smiled. "No need to augur me calamity," he said,
"for when the end draws near, I shall praise your head as beseems it."

Now folk made ready to head home from the games. Farmer
Bessi Halldórsson led his horse over to where the two comrades
were standing. He said to Þorgeir:

"You played very hard, Þorgeir. Two things are certain: you
are quite a daredevil, and great fame awaits you. Yet we here in
Djúp scrape by on farming and fishing, and are little inclined
toward contests of courage against heroes, simply for the sake
of pride. It would thus please us greatly if you would desist from
displays of prowess while among us, for it is difficult to see what
the result might be should more days come when men's sons
are knocked senseless by outsiders when folk gather for amusement. Now I will offer you this horse and my good cowl, if you
head south tonight over the heaths. I ask you to indulge me in

this for the sake of your friendship with Þormóður, and thereby to spare me any trouble that I might meet with because of you. In the agreement between our kinsman, Chieftain Vermundur, and your father Hávar, it was stipulated that your family should keep to the south of the great fjords – the result of events that I need not go into now."

The two comrades did not think they had the wherewithal to continue swaggering around the Vestfirðir as they had done for some time, especially if it were making the chieftains bristle. Þorgeir accepted the horse and cowl and made ready to ride south. Þormóður said that he would ride with him.

"What shall we do when the weather warms up?" asked Þormóður Kolbrúnarskáld. "Shall we become summer laborers and hire ourselves out for butter and stockfish?"

Þorgeir answered: "If we are now to be denied farmers' hospitality, we would be better off roaming the countryside and demanding whatever we need. But it is likelier that our exploits will be few while we have no ship to sail. It crosses my mind that my father had a fishing boat, which is no doubt rotten and leaky by now. We can repair it, and then assemble a band of vagrant folk and go raiding here in the west. There are numerous narrow fjords in this corner of the country, separated by mountains sheer to the sea, and many a scattered, scantly-manned farm, making it hard to assemble a force against Vikings. We shall procure wares in valiant fashion: claiming stockfish, whale oil, woolen cloaks, homespun, and tusks from farmers, and forcing those of means to buy peace with whatever valuables – gold and silver – they possess. When we have gained ample spoils, we shall kill our men and trade our wares for weapons and shares in a ship, and sail to foreign lands."

That night they set out from Laugadalur, riding in moonlight over Þernuvíkurháls Ridge and leading their horses over Kleif, one of the steepest paths in the Vestfirðir, before traversing the snow and ice of Kollafjarðarheiði Heath to Breiðafjörður. They had grand schemes and plans, and grew ever more resolute in their intentions the more difficult things seemed. On the evening of the next day, they arrived at Reykjahólar and were given food to eat, but few folk there passed the cup to them in welcome. They slept through the night, and next morning called people together as witnesses, for now they meant to swear solemn oaths by the Earth. The ground was frozen too deep and too solid for cutting fresh turf, so they took some icy turfs from the stackyard and crawled under those, opened veins and mingled their blood with the soil, at the same time declaring their sworn brotherhood: that from then on, they would both face the world as one and evenly divide all the spoils that they took through bold warring on other men, and that he who lived longer would spare nothing in avenging the other. Christian folk laughed at the ludicrousness of these two frozen-turfers agreeing to go halves on the lice crawling over them, and said that such losers would likely never have any other loot to share.

Then the sworn brothers part. Þorgeir Hávarsson goes south to his mother in Borgarfjörður to procure a ship, and Þormóður Kolbrúnarskáld travels back westward to Djúp.

9

OF ÞORMÓÐUR'S JOURNEY there is this to tell: he rode
the same route back, over the heath, stopping for the night in
Ísafjörður and sleeping well into the next day before heading
home to Laugadalur. The weather remained calm. That evening
he drew near Laugaból, but instead of going all the way home,
he turned his horse loose and started hiking up the mountainside. The moon was new. Toward the top of the mountain was
a lake, its water frozen. Þormóður was so light of step that he
flew rather than walked over the mountain that night. He ran
down into Ögurdalur alongside the river that flows from the
lake, a path rarely taken.

The main door at Ögur faced Djúp, whose waters are both
a highroad and a field of plenty. Þormóður came down the
ravine behind the farm, took a look around and noticed a medi-
um-sized window facing the slope. The window had eight panes
of membrane, fastened with sinews. He climbed up to the window ledge, spoke the girl's name several times, and fiddled with
the window. The girl started from sleep, terribly frightened, and
asked who was outside.

Þormóður said it was he.

"What is on your mind?" she asked.

"I have composed a lay in your honor," said he. "Pray let me in."

"I am no jarl. Away with you and your piddling lay," she said. "I will never let scrappers and scamps into my house, nor skalds with their silly love songs for women."

"It is the best lay ever made," said he.

She said: "There is no chance that I will do my mother the dishonor of heeding your lay at the time of day that can bring greatest disgrace to us women. And now it is proven, as she has always said, that you are a horrible miscreant."

"Open your window and see for yourself what sort of man I am," said he.

"You will wake Kolbakur with your ruckus, and he will come and kill you," said she.

"I fear your will more than I do your slave," said he. "Or would you rather I deliver your lay outside the window?"

"Waking my mother and our servants with your gibes will not diminish my disgrace," said she.

"Shall I perhaps try my knife on your window-skins?" he asked.

"It was the foulest of days by far when I first set eyes on you," said she. "Why did you not leave with your friend, that nitwit Þorgeir?"

"Because," he said, "I love you more than him."

She said: "What have I done to cause you, Þorgeir's crony and Coal-Rump's delight, to seek me out over mountains by night just to lie to me and make me cry? Away with you forever."

"If you let me in, I shall whisper in your ear," said he, "and wake neither Kolbakur nor your mother nor the household. My lay will lull you to sleep."

The girl replied: "Never shall any man say to another that Þórdís of Ögur leaves her window open for visitors at night – and you are a hideous scoundrel to expect a simple maiden to behave like a strumpet." With these words, she drew back the bolts that Kolbakur had made to fasten her window frame, pulled the frame aside, and let the man into her bower. Images of gods were carved on the bower's pillars and the stiles and rails of her chair, but they were only half-done – Christianity having come to Iceland before the artist completed his work. The new moon shone on the half-carved jaws of the cats that Freyja drove across the sky. After opening her window, the girl stepped out of her shoes, jumped back onto her bed, and curled up in the corner. When Þormóður had come inside, however, he did not launch straight into his lay – it seemed he had a lot to say first. She declared that she would not heed anything but the lay – "and this is all wretched knavery."

He said: "Much seems to us skalds more needful, when we sit near to women, than reciting them verses we made when they were far away. We would rather lay our hands on their knees."

"I am no little girl," said she, "yet I have never heard such an abomination as the one you now speak, that a man should lay his hand upon a woman's knee, and it is more than base of you to propose such a thing – yet I will allow it for now, and you shall deliver your lay as you do so."

Commencing upon his lay, he felt her knee move welcomingly, as if this were not the very first time a man had touched it. "How can this be?" he asked.

The woman remained silent for a long time in the dark, but shed a few tears. When he pressed her for an answer, she replied coldly: "I will never tell a soul."

He sulked and shrunk back from her, saying that no man should trust women. She dried her eyes on her arm and the back of her hand, and sat up straight. "Why not ask me instead what I thought of the lay?" she said.

"Tell me, if you think it is of any worth," he replied.

"It has less to say of the women who shine in the sky in swan-likeness and spin the fates of valiant men than it does of hags who halter men's necks and ride them by night – and I am no such woman."

10

SUMMER ARRIVED AND Þorgeir Hávarsson lingered in
the south, delaying the sworn brothers' plans for Viking maraud-
ing in the west. At the Alþingi, a lawsuit was brought against
Þorgeir for the slaying of the Skeljabrekka men, and his kinsman
Þorgils Arason spoke in his defense. Þorgeir avoided outlawry
– the killings were judged excusable, since the father and his
son had forfeited their rights when they murdered Hávar, yet
full recompense was to be made for them, and Þorgils paid the
penalty.

As summer wore on, Þormóður Bessason began hankering
after his sworn brother, and felt that Laugadalur was a wearisome abode for a stouthearted man who sought fame and glory.
He showed little interest in work and was reproached for it by
all. In those days, nearly everyone was obliged to labor for a living, apart from champions who dwelt on outlying skerries and
ate seabirds for their sustenance, or who lingered in mountain
gullies, tracking the pack trains – not to mention the pampered
and pompous dames who lived with hardly a care.

It was the custom of Mistress Katla of Ögur to supervise the farm work in summer and rake hay with the women on fine-weather days, particularly after banishing her foreman, the Easterling. Her daughter Þórdís stayed indoors, skimming milk or spinning wool. On serene midsummer days, when the cat lay on its back on the slates before the farm door and the workers were out in the hayfields, Þormóður Kolbrúnarskáld came over the mountain to visit the maiden. He sat with her for long periods of time, though no one knew what they discussed.

One day, Þormóður goes to meet Þórdís and tarries with her so long that the workers are returning from the fields for the evening just as he is leaving the farm. At the door he runs into Mistress Katla, who is the stateliest of women. He greets her. Mistress Katla returns his greeting amicably, asks how he is faring, and invites him to join her in her sitting room. He goes in with her. She asks him to sit. Then she says:

"Your visits here, Þormóður, are now of such a nature that I simply cannot sit by any longer and do nothing. Everyone can see that you are seducing Þórdís. You are taking advantage of the fact that my daughter and I have little by way of support from kin, to defend us when we are dishonored, while you have the backing of your kinsman Vermundur when pestering widows and folk of low means."

He replies: "I meant not to vex you and Þórdís, and in all truth, she is dear to me."

Katla says: "In that case, Þormóður, I give you the opportunity to take her as your wife. Here we have land aplenty: wide hayfields, copses and meadows in the valley, fat sheep, horses, and cattle – our own mouse-gray cattle of merman stock.* Eiderdown and eggs in the spring, fish in the lakes, rivers, and sea, banks of flounder in the deep, seal hunts in the fall. Either that, or you desist from your visits and harm the girl no more than you already have done."

Þormóður replies: "I am a man meager in wealth, and most would call it an unequal match if I were to gain such a goodly wife as Þórdís, when I have neither cut another man down nor voyaged by sea. It would suit me better to go and do battle for a king and take others with me into death than to pledge myself now to a wife and farm."

With that, he goes home to Laugaból.

A few days later, just as he was leaving to cross over the mountain, his father Bessi called to him from the farmyard and asked for a word with him. Þormóður turned and walked back to his father in the homefield. Bessi said:

"When I was young, it was hardly thought heroic to be trysting with women by night – and even less so in broad daylight. Such a thing was certain to harm a young man's fame, wasting his manhood in such a way."

"It seems to me, father, that I am old enough to determine my own comings and goings," said Þormóður.

"Never did I hear my parents say that trysting suited the young any more than the old," said Bessi. "Good men take wives – they do not dally with women. My kinsmen and I will support you in your courtship of a wife, if you wish. But you will have neither my support nor others' against Katla's bravoes."

After reprimanding his son, Bessi walked off, leaving Þormóður sitting at the outskirt of the homefield, mulling over his options. It seemed certain that he would be much better off complying with his father in this matter. Þorgeir's tardiness in returning still nagged at him, and this dawdling around for lack of ships in the district got very much on his nerves. Finally, he fell asleep in the field.

How often has it happened that men's plans lose steam as they sleep? So it was with Þormóður. When he woke, neither Bessi nor anyone else was in sight – only the sun in the northwest over Greenland. The cows lowed eleven times in succession, which betokened dry weather. Þormóður picked up his ax from the grass, and then headed for the mountain.

It was dusk by the time Þormóður came to Ögurdalur, and he waited until bedtime before descending the slope. When he felt that the household was asleep, he went to the girl's window. She unbolted the frame and let him in. They spoke together quietly in her loft for a long time. Near dawn, they heard the sound of someone riding from the farmyard, and the cock crowed.

Þormóður jumped up at the clatter of hooves, and asked who would be riding at that time of day.

Þórdís replied: "That would be our slave Kolbakur, taking weft for my mother to Heydalur in Mjóifjörður. The good weavers there have a cloth of hers on their loom."

A short time later, sunlight shone through the girl's window. Þormóður said that it was time he went home. She said: "I want you to take another path home to Laugaból. Go round the inlet at the foot of the slope – not over the mountain." She said that she had dreamed many things.

He said that he would take his customary route. Of two things she could be certain: he neither feared for his life, nor did he put faith in dreams.

"Will you take some hanks of blue yarn for me to Mjóifjörður?" she asked.

"What do you want with homespun?" asked he.

"It may well be," said she, "that I have need of some homespun for patching. Here in the west, women have won verses from skalds for doing as little as stitching gores to the seats of their breeches."

He said that it would be as she chose. She wound the hanks of yarn very carefully about him, underneath his shirt.

Early that same morning, an old gelding stood in a grassy hollow beneath the scree on the mountainside. It had a worn saddle and rope bridle, and plucked listlessly at the dewy grass.

Þormóður saw no sign of the person in charge of this steed. As he started clambering up the scree, rocks both big and small began tumbling down toward him, skipping into the air and clattering as they struck, giving off sparks, smoke, and a burning smell. Þormóður had the feeling that this was no normal landslide, and that he would be reckoned a coward if he turned aside, so he stuck to his course up the slope. On the top stood a large boulder, with a man peeking out from behind. It was Kolbakur. He had stopped toppling rocks and made a breastwork of the boulder – whence he pointed his spear. Þormóður climbed up to the boulder and hewed the ambusher's spear in two. Then he hoisted his ax and swung it down on the slave's shoulder, but the weapon bit no better than a piece of whalebone. Kolbakur struck back with his ax at Þormóður's chest, but he might as well have been thrashing a sack stuffed with wool, for all the harm he did. To their wonder, iron could bite neither of them in this battle. Þormóður flung down his ax and charged his ambusher, and they began grappling hand-to-hand. For some time they wrestled in this way, yet both were lithe and young, and neither could get the better of the other. In the midst of the scuffle the slave's smock was torn, revealing the blue weft underneath. Þormóður laughed and said: "Let us sit down and unravel our webs." They stopped brawling and sat down. Kolbakur cast off his smock and pulled out twenty hanks of yarn. Þormóður took off his tunic and unwound just as many. "The same Norn spun for us both," said he.

Kolbakur did not reply, but plucked a piece of sorrel from the scree and stuck it in his mouth to chew on. Lying close by was his spear, in two pieces, and Þormóður's blunt ax was wedged between two rocks. The yarn was strewn around them like newly felled trees.

Þormóður said: "You are a courageous man to battle against me, as unskilled as you are with weapons. I have no heart to kill you, though it is well within my grasp. You have this yarn lying here to thank. I would like for us to make peace. But first you shall tell me what there is between you and Þórdís."

Kolbakur said: "I am a slave. She is a woman."

"Have you ever spoken such words to her as others may not hear?" asked Þormóður.

Kolbakur replied: "Master Hólmkell bought me in the Hebrides when I was ten years old. She was too young to know the difference between a free man and a slave. We played together as children."

"Have you set foot in her loft since she grew up?" asked Þormóður.

"It was I who fashioned the window through which you slip late at night," said Kolbakur.

Þormóður asked: "Have you ever laid hold of Þórdís's knee?"

"I ask for no mercy from you," said Kolbakur, chewing his sorrel.

"Remember that you are a slave, and that your life is in my hands," said Þormóður.

"I am not dependent on the favors of others," said Kolbakur. "There is but one who will not only free those who are fettered, but also resurrect the dead."

Þormóður asked who this might be.

"Josa mac De is his name,"* replied Kolbakur. "All who are bound shall greet him in joy, for he casts those who oppress others into burning fire."

"Is this fool that you speak of akin to the craven son of the Virgin, who dwells in his hall in Rome and has a gallows for a high-seat?" asked Þormóður.

"I am an Irishman," said the slave. "I have no interest at all in the hall that you mention, or in who is in charge there. What I do know is that Josa mac De has more than enough dukes to do battle for him: Patrick the farmer and Columbkille the priest, Columba the seafarer and Kilian the skald. His beautifully-inscribed stone crosses tower higher than the peaks of my home in Ireland."

"What news this is," said Þormóður Kolbrúnarskáld, and he fell into thought. "Will you then swear an oath, Kolbakur," says he, "by Josa mac De the Stout, that you have never slipped in through the window that you yourself fashioned for the maiden?"

"Cut down her slave right here, if you will," said Kolbakur, "and I will rise once more as her king."

Þormóður Kolbrúnarskáld stared long at the slave, astonished at such speech. Then he got to his feet slowly, weary as he was. He said no more to the slave, but walked off toward home, leaving his ax behind. The slave remained sitting there on a rock, chewing his sorrel. Lying at his feet were their blunt weapons and the blue yarn. Once Þormóður was out of sight, the slave stood up, gathered the yarn from the scree and tossed it over his shoulder.

II

AFTER HIKING a short distance, Þormóður's leg begins to feel peculiar, though more with numbness than pain, and he finds it hard to walk. At the same time, he feels ill. He is also surprised to find that his leg is wet, as if he had stepped into a lukewarm mire. He sits down on the mountainside to see what is wrong, and finds that his shoe is full of blood – it has clotted on his stocking, too, and is oozing from his leg. He has a wound on his calf, by no means a slight one: most of the flesh had been ripped from the bone when one of the tumbling rocks hit him. He tears a strip from his linen tunic and wraps it around his leg, then scrambles down from the mountain, making it home with great difficulty, and great loss of blood.

This injury left Þormóður bedridden for a long time – the gash simply would not heal properly. He was unable to get to his feet before winter, and then could only hobble. He was extremely anxious about Þorgeir Hávarsson's absence. The champion must either have gone overseas, or else was dead, and things were not looking promising at all for his own fame. No sooner, however, was he fit once more to be up and about than his attention turned toward seeking out the comforts of his ladylove at Ögur, and in doing so, to let courtship replace the deeds of fame and glory that looked likely to remain forever unaccomplished. Nine weeks had passed since his last visit to the girl. The fall brought obstinate weather: ceaseless sea winds and snowsqualls. One stormy night he could no longer sit quiet. When the household was asleep, he took his father's best horse and rode to Ögur. He descended the slope behind the farmstead and whistled at the girl's window. She woke, frightened, and asked who went there in such weather.

"Who do you think?" said he.

"It could be so many," said the girl.

"I am cold," said he. "Let me in."

"Why you rather than the wind?" said she, yet she unfastened her window in the storm, and he slipped in. She fastened it again and lit a lamp, but said nothing to him. He asked her why she was so dispirited. Dressed in a long shift, she sat down on her chair, began weeping bitterly, and hid her face in her hands.

"Why must I see you again? How I have scolded my slave for not killing you!" she said.

He asked her why she spoke so coldly to him.

"I have not yet mentioned the greatest disgrace you have done me: that you did not kill my slave, and instead have become the laughingstock of the district – such a champion as you presume to be."

"How can you be astonished," said Þormóður, "that I did not slay your slave, nor he me, after you wrapped us both in the same web? It was not due to cowardice that I did not slay him, but because I chose to share half a living slave with you rather than to allow you to have him whole – but dead."

She said: "Now I know that you do not love me, since you spared him. I will free my slave and make him your equal, and your better."

"Do not weep so miserably," said the skald. "One day, when the sun is shining on land and sea and Mistress Katla is sitting at home with all her household, I will ride through the main gate at Ögur."

The girl dried her tears on the hem of her shift.

"Will you be riding alone, then?" she whispered. "For my mother will set the dogs on you."

"That day, I will ride in fine company," said he. "My father will be with me, as will Chieftain Vermundur of Vatnsfjörður. They will send word to your mother, and she will invite us in and serve us ale. They will make their proposal in proper form, requesting that her daughter be made my wife. On our behalf, Vermundur will offer great amounts of land and chattels."

"It is astonishing how much you can lie," said she. "Yet it is said to be a sign of love when a man lies to a woman – and a woman loves a man when she believes him though she knows he lies. It is good to hear you lying. Lie to me!"

"Our marriage contract will be sealed with sage words and shaking of hands," said he.

By now the girl had almost completely dried her eyes.

"On that fine day," said she, "when you ride through the main gate to us, accompanied by your father, Farmer Bessi, and Chieftain Vermundur, and all the bounties of the land in Ögur are granted me as my dowry – on that day, will you love me, Þormóður?"

"On that day, we will waste no time in vain prattle," said he.

"Will you deliver me a lay, then," asked she, "that I know for certain is meant for me and no other woman?"

"Men take wives to make poetry unnecessary," said he. "From that day on, neither you nor your mother shall ever be disgraced."

The girl was now consoled, and she rose from her seat and embraced him tenderly. She said: "I have heard women say that it is better to be wed to a man than to have a lay from him. It must be true. From that moment on, I will never ask you for another lay."

Squalls hammered mountain and sea with a tumultuous din, and clouds drew over the moon. In the midst of the storm a door opened, letting the wind shriek through the house as if a whistle were being blown. A ruckus was heard from the vestibule. "Visitors! Out the window, quick as you can!" she exclaimed, jumping into bed and pulling the bedclothes up over her head.

He said: "I am not moving. I run from no man."

From below came men's voices and the clanking of weapons, mixed with the howls of the storm. A frightened servant was ordered to tell where the widow's daughter had her bed, and then the ladder was tramped by hard-frozen shoes.

The visitor who stepped into the girl's loft looked more like a sea-monster than a man: he was iced over with snow and sea spray, and the house creaked beneath his hooves. His spear was ice-coated as well, up to its tip. Þormóður stood by the window, his ax raised. But when the visitor lifted his icy hood, and the light fell on his weatherbeaten lips, hairless as a youth's, Skald Þormóður dropped his ax, sprang toward the man, and greeted him warmly.

When the girl realized what this meant, she swept back the curtain surrounding her bed, stuck her long legs out from beneath the bedclothes, and smoothed down her shift as she got to her feet. The girl was bare to the nipples, and her hair flowed about her shoulders. Fire burned in her eyes as she spat these words at the visitor: "Dead man!"

A man who is doomed to hang and waits only to be hoisted on the gallows-tree can no longer envision bloom-bearing life – in his eyes, it is all the vainest abomination. Nor did Þorgeir Hávarsson acknowledge in the least the presence of the woman whose loft he had entered, but said instead to her lover: "Here," said he, "have I come, Þormóður, to call on you – with a ship."

Þormóður replied: "So many bright days this summer did I spend waiting for you, that I find it hard to see why we should sail through foul storms on winter nights. Yet I will not go back on my word and oath to you. Tell me your will, and skald shall follow hero as of old."

Þorgeir said: "Many a dim night have I gotten to my feet while others slept, brandished my weapons and bit my shield-rim in uncontrollable longing for the glory that is won by slaying men and ruling the world, or being slain to great renown. Here at last is a ship. I have repaired it myself for the most part, for lack of funds to pay smiths, and I have hired a crew of vagrants to sail with us to win fame. Now I would have us sail to the Jökulfirðir and along Hornstrandir and kill all who say they are not afraid of us. When that is done, we will be free to do as we please in the north. I have heard tell that in those parts dwells a great warrior named Butraldi Brúsason, who has spread word that he fears no man and will not stop until he has felled every swaggerer and swellhead in the Vestfirðir. I am convinced this warrior poses us no small danger while he is alive, and I advise setting out this very night to find him, arouse his hostility, and fight with him to the bitter end, taking no rest until we have won the victory from him, and showing everyone how mighty we are."

Þórdís butted in: "What great folly to choose to sail by night in precarious weather, only to hunt down outlawed thieves up north in Hornstrandir, wreck your vessel and be eaten by fish, rather than dwell in present bliss."

Þormóður girded his breeches, saying: "Men do not become skalds and heroes by dwelling in their present bliss. The saga of us sworn brothers will never be told if I dally at your side this night."

The girl went up to Þorgeir Hávarsson and walloped the champion's ear. "Trolls take you!" said she. "Your fame will be greatest the day you are ripped apart by dogs and ravens."

Þorgeir gave a little laugh, without looking at the girl.

Finally, Þormóður said to her: "It is for love that I have traversed this mountain to you. Yet as much joy as our trysts have brought me this many a night, I love you the most the night that I leave you."

12

ÞORMÓÐUR ASKED NOTHING further, but walked with his sworn brother Þorgeir to the boat. The snowsquall had passed, but a bank of grim clouds seethed on the horizon. The sea swelled as the moon shone on rime-caked islets and reefs. Awaiting them at their destination was an average-sized fishing boat that rocked back and forth on the breakers, having little ballast. Aboard it stood weathered men with frozen beards and eyebrows, knocking ice off the sail yards and ropes. Þorgeir presented the crew to his comrade: first there was a father and son from down south in Kjalarnes – homeless men who hired themselves to farmers for their keep. Also from the south was a thief, Tjörvi by name, whose life was bereft of the protection of law. Þorgeir's fourth crewman was named Oddi – called Lúsoddi, for his lice – he was a man of little wits, who, for most of his life, had been dependent on his impoverished mother at Akranes, but had started begging door to door by the time Þorgeir hired him.*

Þorgeir addressed these men as follows:

"This man is my sworn brother, Þormóður Bessason. He owns half this ship and everything aboard it. He is a greater skald than any other now living in the Vestfirðir. You are to heed his commands and prohibitions as though they were my own, for we stand as one in everything. Now drink your fill of the whale-oil keg, and then we shall sail west round Rytagnúpur and keep to sea until we come north to Aðalvík. I have heard rumor from there of the blustering of the man who calls himself the greatest warrior in the Vestfirðir, Butraldi Brúsason. We shall attack him and kill him."

The crew thought Þorgeir had spoken most manfully, and they heeded his orders. Þorgeir took the helm as soon as they left the lee of the land, and Þormóður acted as skipper. There was a crosswind, and they spread the sail and tacked hard. The boat bounded over the waves, but heeled drastically and shipped water to leeward, while the crew all bailed as best they could.

They had not sailed very long before a black snowsquall hit them, with fierce gales and churning waves that thrashed the boat and pelted it with spray hard as gravel. Þormóður reefed the sail and let the boat run before the wind. It was dark as pitch around them, and the frenzied storm wrenched all control from their hands. The strakes and ribs cracked, water poured in time and again, and most cargo that was loose flew overboard. Only the bailing pails in the hands of the crew had anything to say, and no one knew which would come first: whether the boat would sink or be smashed.

When they caught a glimpse of the sky once more, and the tiniest whiff of moonlight, they found themselves west of

Snæfjallaströnd, near the peak Geirsfjall. Above them glinted a spray-lashed, ice-coated cliff face.

They worked hard to hold their craft clear of the cliff to avoid wrecking it, before attempting to beat northwest to open sea and push round Rytagnúpur, yet were scarcely free of the final cliffs of Snæfjallaströnd when the sky blackened anew and the winds howled with fresh fury. This blizzard blew far longer than the first – and then their rudder snapped. Throughout the night they were tossed uncontrollably, until finally the waves slackened. When the clouds finally broke, snow-laden mountain ridges towered on both sides. Þorgeir asked Þormóður whether he recognized these peaks.

Þormóður said: "I do not believe things will worsen if we let ourselves be borne for a time on our present course. Yet little did I think that I would glimpse these peaks tonight."

Soon afterward, the late-midmorning sky cleared enough for them to spy Orion's three milkmaids.* They were now some distance up a narrow fjord that had but scant foreshore and mountains towering at its end, their precipitous faces hung with menacing crags, blue and naked, shoals at their base and a river running to the sea. They caught the odor of cowsheds and smoke from a human dwelling. They made land, and hauled their vessel ashore. Naught remained of the few valuables they had but the oil-keg, which was lashed astern, and the weapons that they had strapped to themselves.

Þorgeir asked his sworn brother if he still thought he knew where they might be.

"I would be farther off than I thought," said Þormóður, "if that jutting mountain there is none other than Gýgjarsporshamar Crag, where tracks of ogresses can be read on the rock, and the fjord itself, Hrafnsfjörður, the innermost of the Jökulfirðir fjords. I have often beheld these regions in my dreams."

"Then we have strayed to a foul spot," says Þorgeir, "for our last-resort landing. It is clear that our comrades have little spirit left for sailing, and besides, our mast is broken, our sail gone, and our rudder in pieces."

The voyage had left the entire crew cold, drenched, and spent, and their clothing hard blocks of ice. The lad from Kjalarnes was so exhausted he could barely walk, and his father was frostbitten – both were sorely in need of relief. The sky was tinted with the first flush of dawn, but it was still a long time until sunrise. A little farther down the fjord they found a farmstead, where no one was stirring yet. Þorgeir asked his sworn brother to go to the window and wake those inside. Þormóður replied:

"You are our leader. It is you who shall wake them, and bid them the gods' good fortune. But if in your venture you prove unsuccessful, by all means call on me."

Þorgeir went to one of the windows and shouted that there were visitors outside, and that those inside were to open the door.

A woman asked who went there.

"Champions and warriors," said Þorgeir.

"So you are not men of peace?" asked the woman.

"I hope that we will never commit such a howling offense as to sue for peace with others," said Þorgeir. "We yield to none."

"What do you ask of us?" said the woman.

"We ask nothing of anyone," said Þorgeir. "But we would have food to eat and fire to thaw our clothes and a place to sleep. If you will not give us these, then send out a man or two worthy enough to do battle with us."

The woman replied: "It has hardly been the custom here in the fjords for wet, weary men to fight against farmers for bed and board. What a foolish man you are! What is your name?"

"It is I, Þorgeir Hávarsson," he said, "along with my company. We challenge every man of any mettle here in the fjords to come and fight us."

Þormóður Kolbrúnarskáld then said: "Now it is my turn, brother."

He went to the window and bade them good fortune by gods and men.

"Who goes there?" said the woman.

"None other than I, Þormóður Kolbrúnarskáld," declared the visitor. "And I know for certain that there are women here in the Jökulfirðir that have heard this name."

Upon his speaking these words, the door opened, and there on the threshold stood a woman, with a blue mantle tossed over her shoulders. This woman had large eyes and dark brows, and emanated more warmth than other women. She opened her arms to Skald Þormóður, kissed him tenderly, and bade him and his band welcome to her home, for as long or short a time as they wished. She had awaited this moment so long, she said, that she had nearly lost hope of its coming – but now the men of theirs that were frostbitten or helpless must be borne in, and life restored to those who were at death's door. They had ended up at the dwelling of Mistress Kolbrún in Hrafnsfjörður. Slave Loðinn went out to tend to the livestock, without greeting the visitors.

"Now it makes sense, brother," said Þorgeir, "why you were eager to steer toward the fjords, when we should have sailed deep off the headlands. Farthest from my mind when we left behind Borgarfjörður was calling at women's knees in the west."

"The only way," said Þormóður, "for your saga to last longer, brother, was for me to lie about our course when we were pressed hardest."

Þorgeir said: "While we are here, we shall rule this farm, and ask nothing of women."

"That is good news," said Mistress Kolbrún. "Too long have my daughter and I lived widows' lives here, ridiculed by most. I am glad to have visitors of manly mien, both to delight us and to avenge the provocations that we have had to endure from wicked men."

The sworn brothers now entered the house there in Hrafns-fjörður, dragging their bone-weary comrades with them. Fires were lit in the hall and they were given fresh clothing, while their wet garments were hung to dry. Kettles were brought out, meat was boiled, and porridge was heated, and the exhausted men gradually revived. They began wiping down their weapons, cleansing them of rust and salt. Then the men were shown to their beds.

It was late in the day when Þorgeir woke up. The weather had worsened again, with freezing snowsqualls. Þorgeir woke his men and told them that they had not been hired to sprawl on their bellies deep in the fjords – awaiting them elsewhere was seemlier work. The mistress said that the weather was foul, and that they need not put themselves at risk. They were more than welcome to linger there with her, she said – the longer, the better.

Þorgeir said that the weather was the least of their concerns – they cared little whether others called it foul or fair. "Neither frost nor tempest can hurt us, for we have no wives, children, or beasts to tend."

What with their boat being so battered and barely fit to float, besides being buried in snow in its shed on Skipeyri Point, and with the inner fjord slathered with ice, further sailing was out of the question. Þorgeir said that if the ice and freezing weather hindered their seafaring beyond any reasonable length of time, he and his men would hike over the mountains to Hornstrandir. She asked what he was planning to do there. Þorgeir said:

"There is a man named Butraldi, a great champion. He has spread word that he flinches before no man. He makes his abode in Hornstrandir. I will attack him and kill him. I have vowed to slay any man who thinks himself as valiant as I."

She asked what would come next.

Þorgeir said that when champions and other men of moment in the north were all dead, he and his sworn brother would be free to take whales and other great catches on Hornstrandir.

Mistress Kolbrún laughed and said: "What peculiar men you are, wanting to hunt down wretched outlaws on Hornstrandir and flense whales, when there is more valiant work much nearer."

They asked what work that was.

"It seems to me more valiant," said the mistress, "to kill free strongmen in human habitations – those who oppress widows and other poor folk – than to chase after derelicts or cut apart whales."

They asked whom she meant.

She replied: "Across the fjord at Sviðinsstaðir live a farmer named Ingólfur and his son Þorbrandur. They have made their farm on a shelf of Lónanúpur Peak. These men graze their cows and sheep on my land, though they have their own scrap of moor on the mountain above. And they pull heaps of skate, flounder, and plaice from the water within a line's cast of my homefield."

Þorgeir said: "We do not deem it death-worthy for a man to make his living, as long as he is inferior and likely to fear us."

The mistress says: "I have neglected to say what we women suffer worst from men: something against which, by nature, we have no defense – and now I am speaking to you, Þormóður, who have made me a lay greater than any woman in the Vestfirðir has ever been granted, and which was so well delivered that if a kinsman of mine had been my defender, you would have lost your life for it long before. As it happens, Farmer Ingólfur of Sviðinsstaðir laid me in his bed for a grievous moment last Yule, after he and his son found my daughter and me in tears at our bereavement and lack of ale, when we had not a drop to gladden us. He has kept up with this new habit of his and refuses to desist – and his son Þorbrandur has dishonored my daughter. Both she and I are wearied and worn from putting up for so long with such an abominable affront and abasement."

As Kolbrún concluded, Slave Loðinn laughed in the doorway. She said to the slave: "I will never love you, you poltroon, so much that I put weapons in men's hands to kill you. Be gone from the sight of us free folk!"

Þorgeir turned his gaze to his sworn brother, as if asking what solution he might have for this matter.

Þormóður said: "Clearly, a woman so valiant should never have to endure the tyranny of wicked men for too long. She absolutely does not deserve for us to refuse to deal with these two, or to delay in doing so. It is time this woman saw our mettle in more than just poetry."

"On your feet, lads, and repay the mistress's hospitality," said Þorgeir Hávarsson. They stood up, took their weapons, and went out.

13

THEY REACHED Sviðinsstaðir late that evening, after all there were sleeping. Not far up the mountain, the farm hunkered on a shelf that dropped sheer to the sea. A low wall encircled the buildings. Up beneath the mountain's eaves trickled rivulets now swollen with ice. Þormóður went to a window and wished the household peace and plenty. Someone inside asked who went there and what business they had.

Þorgeir Hávarsson spoke thus: "At your door are the sworn brothers Þorgeir Hávarsson and Þormóður Bessason. We have come here to challenge you to fight with us, for we have heard that you are doughty men. We will kill you, and when you are dead, we will take away your cattle and carry off on your horses what chattels we can find. Defend yourselves stoutly now, while you still have your lives."

The person inside asked if there was any hope of them suing for mercy from the two warriors.

Þorgeir said no. "We have trusty report," said he, "that you lavish amorous attention on certain women in the neighborhood, and graze your livestock on their land without having proposed marriage to them. They will no longer put up with such an affront."

Farmer Ingólfur replied that neither he nor his son would beg for their lives, since life was of little worth when it was granted by wicked men. He declared that they would die here willingly, weapons in hand, if that were verdict of the Norns, and fall at the feet of their two barren cows and the stack of skate they had curing in the muckheap for winter food stores – these being their only possessions. As far as women's love went, he said that it was better to trust a sick calf or a coiled snake, as the old saying went – women are most inclined toward a man on the day that they bring about his downfall and death. The father and his son then put on their clothes, took their spears, and went to the door. They had two servants, one a slave, and the other decrepit with age. These two crawled out through the ash-hole, the old man with a cudgel in hand, ready to rain blows on Þorgeir's men – while the slave ran off up the mountain, unwilling to fight. When the farmer and his son tried to go out, the sworn brothers blocked the doorway and jabbed their weapons through it, until a sudden rage seized them and they thrust and hacked their way in, to feel warm blood splashing onto their faces. Soon father and son were slumped by the wall, a whistling coming from deep wounds to their chests. The sworn brothers swung away with their swords at the men's bodies until neither a groan nor a cough could be gotten from them.

Þormóður and Þorgeir called to their men and told them that Ingólfur and his son Þorbrandur were dead, and that the others there should be given quarter. The old man had been overcome, and the slave was up on the mountain. The moon shone. The sworn brothers dragged out the corpses, which were now just one big clot of blood. They laid the men on the slates before the door and marked them for Óðinn according to ancient custom, treating them carefully and solemnly. They placed the old man a good distance from his master and left him unconsecrated to the gods, but no sooner were the visitors gone than the old man stood up – alive – and grabbed his cudgel. Just as the old man rose, the slave returned from the mountain.

Ingólfur and Þorbrandur had two yearling calves in the cowshed and a lean old draught-horse, while their sheep fended for themselves out in the open, as the land at Sviðinsstaðir was too bleak to yield much hay. The farmer and his son had no other food stores apart from their winter provision of skate in the muckheap. Þorgeir suggested they load the skate on the nag, but Þormóður was reluctant to do so, calling it rather wretched plunder to deliver to so goodly a woman as Kolbrún, and in the end they left behind calves, steed, and skate, and brought back only their renown.

Mistress Kolbrún and her daughter Geirríður were standing at the door when the two heroes returned from Sviðinsstaðir. The women said that they knew the sworn brothers brought good news, kissed the men, and led them to the hall. Þormóður and Þorgeir immediately recounted the outcome of their journey. The hall at Hrafnsfjörður was none too small – there had been fishing sheds and other such dwellings here in this fjord before it was finally settled. Kolbrún and her daughter had decked the hall's walls with hangings, particularly where they were near to collapsing, and stout driftwood logs burned on the floor. Mother and daughter washed blood from the hands and faces of their guests, and cleaned their weapons and clothes. They asked for details of the fight, and what deeds the Sviðinsstaðir men had done before they fell. They laughed to hear how those relentlessly amorous men were denied escape and slaughtered like foxes at the mouth of their den. Many a dainty was brought to the sworn brothers to delight and reward them for their work: singed lambs' heads, blood pudding and broth, cured brisket and rams' testicles, and finally, warm ale. Kolbrún served Þormóður and Geirríður served Þorgeir.

The warriors asked Kolbrún what consequences she and her daughter expected, and who might undertake the prosecution for the slaying. They replied that it was the two dead men who had carried the most weight in the innermost fjords, and that no others dwelling there would be eager to test their strength against the sworn brothers. Mistress Kolbrún said that when she saw fit, she would go to meet her old friend Chieftain Vermundur in Vatnsfjörður and compensate him for the slaying of his liegemen, Ingólfur and Þorbrandur, if he would accept it, since they were kinless men. The sworn brothers asked her where her money might be. She said: "I believe that I still have enough under my belt to compensate Vermundur for arranging the deaths of men of his who abused us. And as long as you are in my house, no one will harass you, thanks to your prowess and my friendship with Vermundur."

Þorgeir Hávarsson sprang from his seat and said: "I did not sail here from down south in Borgarfjörður for us to use a woman's undergarments as our breastplate and shield. Where is Vermundur's kinsman Butraldi at this time, and how is he armed?"

"It would be news to us here in the north if Butraldi Brúsason were keeping men awake at night," said Mistress Kolbrún, laughing. "Fill horns for these warriors, Geirríður."

Þorgeir Hávarsson was short and rather bandy-legged, like most of his countrymen. He had blue eyes, ruddy skin, light-brown hair, straight teeth, and thick, red gums. He frowned at other folk and sat hunched and dour in lively gatherings, smiling only when murder or other great deeds crossed his mind. Even when the girl Geirríður sat at his feet and held him by the knee, and his horn was full, his thoughts were far from the feast, for it nagged him not to know whether somewhere out there was a champion his equal or better.

"Why so aloof, Þorgeir? Am I not a beautiful woman?" asked Geirríður Kolbrúnardóttir. "It is rare for men not to pinch me when I serve them a drink. Do you not see how the skald recites verses to my mother, rhapsodizing most manfully? One would think you might be at least as frolicsome with me – younger woman that I am! Now lay your head in my lap, you, and I shall hunt out your lice, and tell me the while how you slew my gallant Þorbrandur, and whether he screamed as the steel cut him."

Þorgeir said: "No need to hunt lice on me for that. He and his father met their deaths well and bravely."

"Did you not hear Þorbrandur utter any last words to me as your spear pierced his belly?" asked the girl, lifting herself from the dais to Þorgeir's lap and wrapping her arms round his neck.

"Both father and son proved to be stouthearted men, eager to defend their possessions, meager as they were, and unsparing of their last breaths in vilifying the women that had betrayed them," said Þorgeir.

"I have no idea how stout a heart Þorbrandur had, nor do I particularly care," said the girl. "What I do know is that he was better than you at laying his head in a woman's lap, and that you seem more suited to assaulting innocent men by night and murdering them than to satisfying women. You were a poor trade."

Þorgeir rose from his seat, letting the girl slip down between his feet. He stepped over her and said:

"Þorgeir Hávarsson will never have his praise sung in days to come for having been better than other men at groping women. Þormóður and I have been foully duped by this mother and her daughter into killing their lovers only to put us into their shoes – thus proving the old saying that women are always worst to those they love most. My advice is that we cross the mountains to Hornstrandir tonight, and there undertake more needful work."

"You mean to tear us away from so noble a feast," said Þormóður, "without having done our duty to such goodly widows?"

Þorgeir said: "I am not to be blamed for your choosing an amity deadlier than all discord: a woman's favor. And no one but you shall pay the price for it."

Þorgeir put on his jerkin, girt himself tightly, called to Lúsoddi to follow him, and walked out of the hall. Geirríður stood on the dais and watched the door shut at the hero's heels – and at this sight, blood rushed to the girl's head.

"Þormóður," said she, "go after him and kill him, if you are not craven."

He replied: "My attachment to my sworn brother Þorgeir may be night one moment and day the next, but such an exploit as you urge, I would never once consider. For now, though, I mean to enjoy your favor. Let us be merry!"

14

THERE WAS A hard frost and the wind heaped the snow into drifts, but the sky was clear and lit with auroras. Þorgeir Hávarsson hiked up and out of Hrafnsfjörður that night, setting his course beneath Gýgjarsporshamar Crag and over Skorarheiði Heath to Hornstrandir. The going was laborious and Lúsoddi sought bare spots, while Þorgeir called it unmanly to skirt such thin snow – the only thing that suited doughty men was to march directly into what lay ahead, be it a snowdrift or bare ground. When Lúsoddi started to find the path quite steep, Þorgeir asked whether he had never heard of where Hlórriði drove with his he-goats.*

They reached Hornstrandir around the time that folk rise for the day, and came to a farm where several people were at their chores. Þorgeir asked where the champion Butraldi was. They said that he was preparing to depart for Djúp to visit his kinsman Vermundur, as was his custom when winter arrived in the north.

"Why should he go there?" asked Þorgeir.

They said that when winter came to Hornstrandir, thieves

and outlaws had little opportunity to drink milk from cows at pasture or to sleep in cowsheds.

"Where has Butraldi hidden his treasure and other spoils?" asks Þorgeir.

They said that they had never known him to have any treasure apart from Vermundur's leave to roam Hornstrandir all summer, to the vexation of most, and that he slaved away at the fishing stations down south in Arnarfjörður during winter.

Þorgeir said: "I have never heard tell of Butraldi Brúsason wielding fishing gear. You men of Hornstrandir are liars."

They burst out laughing and answered: "Whether better-informed folk dwell in other districts, we are not certain, but it is clear that more powerful men than us here in Hornstrandir will be needed to fell Butraldi Brúsason."

Þorgeir asked what made them laugh so hard. "What weapons does Butraldi have?"

They said that he was known to have one weapon that made people give him whatever he demanded. "But you," they said, "need not fear this weapon, should you two meet."

Þorgeir bade them have food and a bed ready, and then left to seek out Butraldi. He and Lúsoddi traversed steep heaths and passes, or shoals at the feet of massive cliffs, for here the land rises sheerest from the sea of almost all places on Earth. At every habitation they encountered, they inquired of Butraldi.

That evening they came to a small farm at the foot of a mountain. Three wayfarers stood at its door, demanding shelter of the farmer. It was Butraldi Brúsason, and with him two rogues. Butraldi scowled and grimaced at the farmer, and then ordered him to slaughter a fattened calf and hold a feast for him and his comrades, with women to do their bidding, if any were on the farm. The farmer, who was a rather paltry fellow and somewhat advanced in years, said that they certainly did not have the provisions to grant such great men fitting welcome – he had no living calves, and the women were doddering with age.

"Would you rather that I piss in your well, then?" said Butraldi.

At these words, Þorgeir Hávarsson walked up with his follower, Lúsoddi. Þorgeir halted in the farmyard, hoisted his ax to his shoulder in warrior fashion, edge upward, and said:

"It is I, Þorgeir Hávarsson – and it is good, Butraldi, that we finally meet. I have come here to challenge you to a fight and kill you."

Butraldi Brúsason was unimposing in appearance, but very bandy-legged. He was past his youth and had thin, gray down on his jowls, shallow bug-eyes, a broad jaw and a wide mouth. For a weapon he had an old spear, as rusty as if it had been dug from the ground, while his fellow travelers bore only iron-tipped staves. Butraldi was wearing a poor lambskin pelt, and his companions wore frayed homespun jerkins. They had all wrapped their feet in shreds of cloth and scraps of hide. Þorgeir Hávarsson, it is said, expected a gruffer response to his hurled taunt, but not what now happened, and which we here tell.

When Butraldi Brúsason realizes that others have joined them there in the farmyard, and that the newcomers are keen to fight straightaway with earlier arrivals, his heart does not quiver mouselike at their challenge. Instead, he stops making faces at the farmer, and in the failing light thrusts out his chin toward Þorgeir Hávarsson. With his turned-up, big-nostriled snout, he sniffs and snuffles at the newcomer, lips curling like a cloven-hooved grass-grazer scenting ewes in heat, then lets loose with an ear-splitting, salacious, shrill bray, like a studhorse at the peak of arousal, followed by hideous laughter, with such monstrous snorts and facial distortions that none have seen the like.

Þorgeir Hávarsson cannot be said to have been unstartled to hear such grotesque sounds erupting from a human being. Butraldi's vagabond henchmen stood a little way off, leaning on their staves in the snow, but when Lúsoddi heard the noise, he took off round the corner of the farmhouse and hid, keeping himself as far as he could from danger.

The farmer was so overjoyed at Þorgeir Hávarsson's arrival that he dashed up and embraced him, without letting the fighter's sword and shield slow him down. He declared it evident that

Óðinn wished to protect him, having sent him, old and useless, on one and the same evening, not just one but two great men and eminent warriors to gladden him, and he invited them both into his home, if they would deign to put up with his poverty. "But," said he, "I would ask one thing of you, good sires, in return for my hospitality: that you do no heroic deeds in my house, nor perform any other exploits worthy of praise while the world lasts, for I am fainthearted, as are my womenfolk. We cannot bear to see men's blood."

The heroes and their men were shown to seats in the hall and a lamp was lit for them, the day being done. Þorgeir Hávarsson sat at the innermost end of the bench, his ax on his shoulder. It was cold in the house, and Butraldi and his men tried to keep themselves warm by playing at hand-pulling and hank-tugging – and, since no fires had been lit on the floor, he joined them in dolphin-leaping or somersaulting, or hanging in skin-the-cat from a beam. Occasionally he went over to Þorgeir, plucked at his clothing and howled. The old women brought in two plates – the warriors were to eat from one, and all of their followers from the other. Served on the warriors' plate was a piece of cheese, not overly soft in texture, and a short rib from a horse. The farmer stood in the doorway and bade them eat heartily. It was an ancient custom for folk in Iceland to make the sign of Þórr over their food, or else that of the cross if they esteemed Christ higher. Butraldi spent no time on either, and instead seized the rib straightaway with both hands and began devouring it, leaving Þorgeir to deal with the cheese. This is attested in the old books. When they had eaten, Þorgeir wrapped himself in his cloak and settled back down in the corner with his ax. The farmer brought them sheepskins to lie on, before going to extinguish the lamp. Þorgeir insisted that a light be left burning in the hall all night. Butraldi took a skin and made his bed near where Þorgeir was sitting, lying face up across the bench, with his head hanging over its edge – making it very easy to chop off with one stroke. Þorgeir was astonished that Butraldi seemed not to fear him one whit. The warrior fell asleep at once and began snoring up a staggering storm, as though the Midgard Serpent were on the loose. His spear, that most wretched of weapons, lay on the floor. Þorgeir was incredulous, and kept an eye on the man.

Around midnight, Butraldi woke and began squirming and scratching and rubbing his legs with his feet, yawning vigorously at the same time. He said:

"A cow is lowing behind the wall, making me antsy in the dark. It must be evil."

Þorgeir said nothing.

"Shall we not," said Butraldi, "have some fun and games? The nights here on Hornstrandir are long and dull. I suggest we hunt and kill fleas. It would be most merry, I think, to bet on who can kill the most fleas in my sheepskin in between the cow's lowings."

Butraldi laid his sheepskin between them, took a shiny silver coin from his pouch and placed it on the sill above them. "Here I have good English silver – this coin is worth half a mark. What will you wager against it?"

Þorgeir had resolved not to speak a word to this man beyond the truths found in point and edge, and therefore still said nothing. Nonetheless, he could not take his eyes off the coin that the fighter drew forth – it was the first time that Þorgeir Hávarsson had ever seen struck silver. Butraldi began running his paws over the fleece, to his own great amusement, but both because the light in the hall was on the faint side and the creatures were quick to escape, it took him a long time to kill any fleas – yet he did manage to dispatch two or three by the time the cow lowed next.

"How many did you get?" asked Butraldi.

Since Þorgeir had not been playing, Butraldi retrieved his silver coin from the sill, and, sniggering, declared that he had won it in the game. He then drew forth another coin, twice as big as the first, and wagered it in a new bet. Þorgeir Hávarsson's eyes widened at the sight of this coin. Several moments passed before the cow lowed again, and Butraldi snatched up this coin as well, with immense peals of laughter and other monstrous noises. For a third time, Butraldi laid a wager, pulling a gold ring from his pouch and placing it up on the shelf. Yet whether it was because Þorgeir found the man and his game more wearisome the more fleas that he killed, or because the cow had stopped lowing altogether, he became so drowsy that he could no longer fend off sleep – and nothing more of that night shall we tell.

Next morning, Þorgeir Hávarsson wakes and opens his eyes. He is alone in the hall, and his ax is lying between his legs, having slipped from his hands as he slept. His traveling companion Lúsoddi is gone, along with the others. It is milking-time there on Hornstrandir, and Þorgeir calls the farmer out of the cowshed and asks where his night-guests are. The farmer says that they left before the Star was at midmorning.*

Þorgeir says that he is thirsty and would like a drink of milk before he goes after Butraldi and the others. "They have," says he, "taken my servant Lúsoddi with them."

The farmer says: "I fear I must tell you that this morning, Butraldi and his comrades drank my cow dry."

Þorgeir says, "Then bring me a jug of water."

"Worse luck there," says the farmer, "because Butraldi and his mates pissed in my well in payment for their lodging, and now the water is undrinkable. It confounds me that a tramp such as Lúsoddi should stick himself under Butraldi's wing – as if he will have more shelter there. To abandon such a great hero as Þorgeir Hávarsson, for an udder-sucking well-pisser!"

15

IT WAS LATE in the evening when Kolbrún led Skald Þormóður to his bed. He tried laying his hand on her knee. She said:

"I have heard that a maiden in Djúp lies alone in her loft, and that you turned the youthful lay you made for me into a song of praise for her. It hardly beseems a little girl to give ear to a poem made for a mature woman, or for her to presume to appreciate something suited to a self-reliant widow. You can be absolutely certain of this, Þormóður: I will never lift this mantle of mine high enough for you to take hold of my knee, unless you swear an oath to me that you will never lavish your attention on another woman. First, though, you must rework the lay that you composed for me of old – making it mine once more – and then deliver it to me tonight, properly."

Þormóður replied that she truly had a just claim against him in this matter, and that it took little trouble to transform a poem – before launching into the *Lay of Kolbrún* in its original form. The mistress was better contented.

Now the night passed, and the next day, and the skald was indulged there in Hrafnsfjörður. He was free to choose to loll in bed, if he wished, and have his meals brought to him, or to warm himself by the fire in the hall. As day turned to evening and he lay dozing, Mistress Kolbrún donned her mantle and went to the guest room. Silently she opened her guest's bed-closet, then laid her hand on his leg and woke him. She said:

"My daughter demands all my attention – which is why I come so late to attend to my guest in his bed. She is inconsolable over the loss of her fancier, Þorbrandur, and his slayer Þorgeir has fled north to Hornstrandir. Yet now, despite the hour, I shall mend your swathings and brush off your cloak."

After tending to his clothing, she sat for a time at his bed-side, but complained that her knees were cold. He tried laying his hand on her knee to warm her. She bade him abandon his whim, and wept bitter tears.

He asked her what caused her distress.

"I have," said she, "heard such stories of you that my mind cannot be eased at present."

He asked what stories these might be.

"I have heard," said the woman, "that when the little maiden in her loft in Ögur felt my lay sufficiently refashioned in her favor, she requested that you make a lay for her alone, lauding her above all others, particularly for having more knowledge in matters of the bedchamber than other women in the Vestfirðir."

He said: "It is news to me if any verses that I made for that woman – if verses there were – traveled so far afield."

"Her swain, Slave Kolbakur, learned the lay and taught it to his friends," said the mistress, "and it has now become the butt of jokes among fishermen, maidservants, and beggarwomen here in the west, as well as among that slavish rabble most in need of bawdy blather for whiling away the hours when the weather is too poor for fishing."

He said that it was certainly far from courteous, when a man converses privately with a woman, not to recite her a love-poem if she asks, but it was folly and whoredom for a woman to share such a poem with others. "And I never expected of Þórdís," said he, "that she would dally with her slave, to my derision."

The mistress said: "You men imagine that you have free rein when it comes to us women, particularly once you have grown out of our care. Know, too, it is true what they say: a woman's knee is always cold. You shall discover, Þormóður, that the path to me is all but blocked, unless you have something to offer."

He asked her what she expected. She replied:

"You are to turn the lay that you made for the ogress in Ögur to one of praise for me, and recite it in my ear. You may, if you wish, lay your hand on my knee as you do."

Þormóður agreed to her terms, and then took the lay that he had previously made for Þórdís and reworded it in the mistress's honor. Nothing further occurred that night or the next day, and Þormóður and his companions took their ease there in Hrafnsfjörður.

Toward midnight of the third night, when most folk in the Jökulfirðir had gone to bed, Skald Þormóður was suddenly surprised to see Mistress Kolbrún sitting at his bedside, clad in her mantle, for the night was freezing cold. The woman's expression was melancholic. He asked her what it is that made her so mournful, and whether her knees were as cold as last time. She replied:

"I am certain your hand is warm, Þormóður, yet it remains to be proven how suited you are to warming my knees. There is no going back on the fact, however, that on the day you came here, the first thing I asked of you was that you go and kill my suitor, and I sent you to him when he had no web spun around him. On the other hand, I have heard that in Djúp, Þórdís Kötludóttir wrapped her truelove in hanks of yarn before sending you out to kill him."

Þormóður asked whether the mistress had considered any other trials or tests that might allow him to prove his fidelity to her.

She replied: "You still have not made a lay for me alone – one that cannot be refashioned to the glory of another woman."

He said that he could not imagine how a lay might be made for one woman only, so that it was impossible to twist it at will to fit other women.

She said: "I do not ask you to sing the praises of the bright moons beneath my eyelids, nor of the magnificence of my locks or my alluring hue, nor of any of the other things that men find to praise in women with whom they dally. I know full well that my eyes are not bright in the least, and though my hair was raven black of old, the day is drawing near when I will join the other hoary-headed crones. My youthful complexion is gone as well, and instead of having a figure that you skalds liken to aspens and other slender trees, I am certain you would describe me as fleshy. Thus any lay that you make for any other woman, but reword for me, is mockery, not praise. No longer will I hear or put up with such poetry. And you yourself, skald, are absurd."

He said: "It is not in the nature of a skald to endow the world with the countenance it might have when viewed from the beds of decrepit crones – rather, one should be a hero first and a skald second, and let stoutness of heart rule one's lays."

"No woman do I wish less to be," said she, "than one who is praised by a hero."

"What sort of woman would you be?" asked he.

She said: "I have sat here so long at your bedside that such a sharp-eyed man as you could hardly have failed to notice the little strawberry mark here on my skin. I would like you to make a poem about this mark – then, I believe, it will be impossible to twist it into praise for another woman."

He said that he truly desired to compose this poem for her, and asked the mistress not to leave him before it was finished. Reliable sources say that he composed his *Strawberry Ditty* that very night. Upon his reciting it, the woman listened appreciatively, and in reward called him her Pet and her Jewel, declaring that that night, for the first time, he had indeed risen to the name given him in his youth, when he was called Þormóður Kolbrúnarskáld.

At dawn that same morning, however, Þormóður Kolbrúnarskáld has the impression of waking up and drawing aside his bed-curtain. He leans forward on his pillow, looks down the hall, and sees that the servants have all gone to their chores, indoors and out. Then, in an instant, the house is lit with bright light, as when a snowstorm lifts – yet it is not sunshine, and is accompanied by great cold. To his eyes, the hall's walls appear wider and its rafters higher than he had thought they were, and he wonders how such a magnificent homestead came to be in such a remote fjord. The hall's woodwork is carved and decorated beautifully with dragons, birds, men, and other creatures from ancient tales. He cannot comprehend how he failed to notice earlier what sort of house he was dwelling in, which was assuredly as magnificent in every detail as the renowned halls of kings of yore, where events occurred that were of consequence for the entire world. As he gazes at this great hall, he hears a loud noise of wings flapping over the roof. At the same moment, the door through which the mistress had left just a short time ago opens up, and in steps a woman of gigantic size. Her face is pale, and she fixes him with her stare. She is nobler of mien than all other women, yet he feels that she bears a great resemblance to his friend the maiden in Ögur. The woman is accoutered as befits a Valkyrie, in a chain-mail tunic reaching down to mid-thigh. Round her midriff she wears a belt with a great buckle, in the custom of women of old. Her shoes are tall and her knees bare, her hair cut shoulder-length. On her head this woman wears a splendid helmet, and in her hand she holds a gold-inlaid spear. Draped over her arm is her swan-dress. The woman stops at Þormóður's bedside and says:

"You have betrayed me once more, and this time much worse than when you ran off with Þorgeir. What do you intend for me now?"

This vision troubles Skald Þormóður deeply – that a maiden in the blossom of youth, delicate and the slenderest of all women, should have become, in the blink of an eye, a towering earth-goddess, mighty in flight and bearing splendid arms. Her face, which he had left yesterday swollen with sorrow, glowers fearsomely at him today from beneath its helm of terror.

He says: "I am the lover who rides halt and handless,* and the love of you women is the only game in which no man can be a champion apart from him who chooses not to take part. That is what distinguishes Þorgeir and me. How shall we resolve this, Þórdís?"

She replies: "You may writhe here like a worm as long you choose, in the snares of the evil woman who inhabits the abyss.

Yet until you have put my poem back in order, I will shed no tears for your plight."

Saying this, she jabs her spear into his brow between his eyes, startling him so greatly that the vision ends and his eyes dim, while his head throbs with such pain that he feels as if his eyes will burst out – and all his strength abandons him.

16

ON THE SAME morning just described, Mistress Kolbrún of Hrafnsfjörður and her daughter Geirríður set off on a journey to Chieftain Vermundur's, accompanied by Slave Loðinn. The rivers and lakes were all ice-bound. Their journey passed uneventfully, and on the third day they reached Vatnsfjörður.

When Kolbrún and her daughter entered the hall, Vermundur was sitting in his high seat, speaking with visitors. He asked the others to leave the room while he had a word with these women. They went up to the old man and greeted him with kisses. He directed the girl to a seat on a little stool at the edge of the dais, she being his bastard child, but bade the woman sit at his footboard, where she wrapped her arms blithely around the chieftain's legs. He asked her what news was on everyone's lips.

Mistress Kolbrún told him of the frost and harsh storms lashing the Jökulfirðir, yet she declared it far harsher when folk had to endure the aggression of browbeaters who arrived without warning in the district. These men had settled on a mountain crag where they had no land for their livestock and begun fishing on other farmers' shores.

Vermundur declared this bad news.

"Luckily, that leak has now been plugged," said the woman.

"Such news is more to my liking," said Vermundur. "Can you tell me more of what took place?"

"For quite some time, we suffered the wearisome unneighborliness of Ingólfur and his son Þorbrandur, whom you allowed to settle across from us in Hrafnsfjörður, on the mountainside where there is no grass."

Vermundur said that they were, to be sure, kinless seafarers who had shipwrecked there, but had become trusty liegemen of his. He asked how they were getting along.

Kolbrún replied: "In brief, they are dead. I have had them killed. And many would say that my daughter and I had an excuse for it, considering their arrogance."

He asked what wrong they had done. She said:

"They had two bulls that they drove constantly onto the land you gave me. And they grazed their ewes on my land in the summers, driving them and their lambs over other farmers' pastures and stopping only after reaching my own, because they knew that few there would defend a poor widow."

Chieftain Vermundur declared it quite unconscionable to have two such doughty men killed for so little cause. What bravoes did you hire for this deed?"

"Your kinsman Þormóður Bessason and his sworn brother Þorgeir lent me their support in this matter," said she. "It was valiantly done, to mend the lot of a penniless woman."

Vermundur said that such deeds would never be left unredressed under his jurisdiction, no matter who did them. Any upright man would say that one's bull gnawing another's grass is no cause for neighbors to murder each other – if such a thing were law, most of those inhabiting the Vestfirðir would be forfeit of their lives. "Yet it puts me in a particularly tight spot if those who claim my protection take the lead in such deeds."

Kolbrún said: "I have not yet mentioned the far-worse crime committed by this father and his son – wishing to spare you that story for the sake of my long-held love for you. As far as Farmer Ingólfur goes, he visited my house so frequently that had you been there, you would have dealt him a fate not much different than the one he has suffered now. He wanted me to yield my farm to him and become his concubine, but not his lawful wife. Many a woman would have been excused for having let herself be stained by such a man as Ingólfur, for he was an accomplished, courtly man, having dined at the table of the jarl in Orkney."

Vermundur said: "When I was younger and abler than now, I had what I wanted from women without killing men, and I would prefer that you keep all of your gallants rather than have them kill each other."

Kolbrún said: "Again, I have yet to tell you the greatest disgrace inflicted on us by the father and his son, when they asked for the hand of your daughter Geirríður on behalf of Þorbrandur Ingólfsson. No sooner had he held the betrothal feast for the girl than he ravished her in my house, and then put off fulfilling the marriage promise."

"Geirríður," said Vermundur, "are you so loathsome that you make your fiancé a fugitive?"

"I was born a bondwoman and belong with the by-blows," said the girl, "and for it I have paid my dues. Yet luckily, Þorbrandur is now dead, for I loved him beyond all other men – so much, in fact, that I have not lived a happy day since he shunned me."

Vermundur said: "My head will hang in shame if you two persuade me into granting your errand boys, Þormóður and Þorgeir, their lives, though some might say that their deed owes more to your heinousness than to their own stupidity, and it is a shame that the law no longer allows for women to be burned."

"I can hear that you are angry with me, Vermundur," said the woman. "Will you not accept redress for the men of Sviðinsstaðir from the purse you gave me long ago, which still hangs at my belt?"

He said: "I will accept no redress from you – and that purse dangling from your belt, you may open to other men. But now I give you two choices. The first is that I have Þormóður killed, so that in my jurisdiction innocent men do not lie unavenged in sight of all – and Þorgeir's head shall go into the bargain, despite the risk of retribution by powerful men. The other choice is that you leave Iceland, and never return hither as long as I live."

"I can scarcely believe," said she, "that you would be such a scoundrel, Vermundur, as to have your kinsman Þormóður slain, or to stir up conflict in the Vestfirðir by provoking that money-bags at Reykjahólar for the likes of Þorgeir. As for Þormóður, he was but a motherless boy when he first landed here at your door, and delivered me a little lay, for which he was named Kol-brúnarskáld – my skald – and in return I promised him that if he ever needed refuge, he would find it with me. He is now a member of my household. It is my design that when he grows a little older, and I am but a decrepit crone, he shall wed our daughter Geirríður."

"My daughter will never entangle herself in that snare," said Vermundur. "As always, the designs of you women can be truly outrageous. I do not want Geirríður to go home with you now to Hrafnsfjörður, but instead, to remain here and learn better manners than those she has been accustomed to lately. And if I do not have Þormóður killed this winter, then I will do something with him far worse in your eyes: I will wed him to Þórdís of Ögur."

17

NOW THE STORMS abated and Þorgeir Hávarsson's men grew weary of dawdling in Hrafnsfjörður, devoid of spoils or a leader. They found themselves increasingly less welcome the longer they stayed, until finally Mistress Kolbrún served them no other fare than tough whale-flesh, prompting them to make ready to leave. Since they had little pluck for sailing leaderless, weathering Horn in winter, they left their vessel in the boat-shed at Skipeyri, where it had been stored for some time, and set off on foot in search of their leader, taking the shortest route northward over the mountains. Nothing is to tell of their journey until they came across Þorgeir by an inlet in the northern part of Hornstrandir, where he had settled into the little hovel of a crofter, whom he made his slave, along with the three crones in the man's household. Þorgeir welcomed his companions gladly and ordered his slaves to serve them what food and drink they had, and asked the news of his sworn brother Þormóður Kolbrúnarskald. The men said that Þormóður was bedridden down south in the Jökulfirðir, infirm and nearly blind from raging headaches, so bad that he could not bear the slightest glimmer of daylight.

Þorgeir was weary of farm life on Hornstrandir and day-dreamed of exploits yet to be accomplished, and now that his men had joined him again, he decided to get on the move. He determined to visit the farmers in the region to discover what items of profit they had for stalwarts and Vikings. As they roamed from farm to farm, they discovered that the farmers gave them all they demanded, in terms of food, drink, and shelter. Yet whether it was because of people's destitution in these northern abodes, or else because the farmers hid from them any commodities they had, Þorgeir's gains from these places proved far less than he had hoped – disappointing, as well, were the inhabitants' submissiveness and their unwillingness to hold their own against powerful men. Brave and valiant men, bent on spoils gained through stoutness of heart, had little business in those parts. Every time that the men of Hornstrandir were given the opportunity to defend their possessions by passage of arms, they gave the same reply: they had nothing to defend from such great and dauntless champions but the vermin crawling over them and the wind in their guts – nor did they have any arms to speak of but knives for flitching fish and saws for sawing driftwood. The deadly axes that they had inherited from their fathers were now little more than rusted junk.

Now the story moves eastward to Víðidalur, to the farm called Lækjamót, where there dwelt a farmer that most books name Gils, the son of Már. Farmer Gils was a great fisherman and hunter. In his youth he had sailed far and wide to trade. He was respected by his fellow merchants as bold and enterprising, and his voyages brought him substantial wealth. He was one of the finest men in his district, of those who were not chieftains or persons of rank. He was much in the habit of fishing and hunting in outlying places and on the commons, taking seabirds, big fish, and seals.

Report now spreads of a whale stranded to the east of Horn, on the Eastern Commons at the foot of the cliffs. Gils Másson and four of his slaves happen to be on a boat near where the whale washed ashore, and they are the first to begin flensing the carcass. Þorgeir Hávarsson hears of the stranding as well. He immediately loads a small boat with the tools and other things necessary for carving up whales, intending to acquire a supply of oil – a great commodity. Gils and his men have been butchering the whale for two days before Þorgeir lands his boat at the site. They greet each other and exchange a few words. Þorgeir then says:

"You have made great headway with the butchering, and now it is time that you rest and head home, and let others have their turn."

Gils Másson replies that he is little inclined to leave the whale, but that they will not stop others from joining them. The whale had stranded on the Commons, meaning that every man is entitled to take from it what he can cut.

Þorgeir says that the whale will be shared between them, both what is cut and uncut.

Gils Másson replies: "We will not yield to you what we have already cut. Who are you, for that matter?"

Þorgeir states his name and says that they are no cowards – neither he nor his men will tolerate intimidation or taunts. "You have chosen the worst course," he says. "We will now give you the option to fight – and then we will see how long you can keep the whale from us."

Gils says: "It does not surprise us that a hero such as you should wish to perform exploits more praiseworthy than chasing that cow-sucker and well-pisser who is the most despicable of all vagabonds ever to roam the Vestfirðir – particularly when you cannot even catch him. Right now, folk all over Iceland are laughing at how the hero let a measly wretch make a fool of him. That man, they say, must be downright stupid."

Þorgeir says that as far as his stupidity is concerned – as with anything else – weapons alone would be the true judge.

"That is fine by me," says Farmer Gils.

Now both sides arm themselves and make ready to fight. Þorgeir chooses to fight against Gils, who has a reputation as a formidable combatant. "And I am eager," he says, "to show you my mettle." He warns the others not to involve themselves in their fight, and sends his men off to the stony ground north of the whale's mouth to fight with Gils' men.

It was an old Norse custom, much practiced in Iceland by men engaged in combat, to be sure to strike the first blow. The man who managed to impale his enemy or slice off his head before he had his guard up was considered most doughty. At that time, people never slew each other for sport, but rather, for their own profit, and they judged a conflict by its outcome. Long afterwards, it became fashionable for French minstrels in their chansons to reserve highest praise for killings that were carried out with artistry and courtesy. That was in the age of chivalry – when Icelanders were pummeling each other with rocks.

In war, a man is hardly ever fortunate enough to catch another unawares or murder him in his bed. It may also happen that troops are unable to avoid each other on open ground in broad daylight, leaving them no choice but to fight. In Iceland, battles were conducted according to an old Norse practice: men would pair off and hammer away at each other as long as their strength lasted, using shoddy, blunt little axes, for the Norsemen were poor smiths, forced to use poor-quality metal. Nor did they have any skill in wielding swords, though rich men in Iceland bore such arms for the sake of pride. Yet if men wielded their axes doggedly in battle, and especially if they went into a rage, these weapons constantly proved more effective than excellent swords forged in the Southern Empire,* or in France or the British Isles.

In combat, it was crucial to come at one's opponent from the side, or better yet from behind, and strike him a blow where he was vulnerable. The exchange of blows was continued until one of the adversaries fell exhausted or fled. The man with more stamina to endure the pounding generally had the better of it – the first one winded was knocked senseless or had his head cracked open where he sat, lay, or crouched. Although some books state that the Norsemen had axes so sharp that they could cleave men from head to toe, the way wooden rafters are split, or cut men's heads off and slice their limbs off their bodies without needing a chopping-block, or halve a fleeing enemy with one blow, making him fall to the ground in two parts, we believe all this to have been dreamed up by people who actually wielded blunt weapons.

Farmer Gils Másson was past the prime of his life, and he wearied quicker than Þorgeir Hávarsson – nor was he endowed with the same Þórr-like strength as Þorgeir, by dint of his youth. The farmer chanced to lose his footing on the gravel, and Þorgeir hoisted his ax and cracked the man's skull, causing blood and brains to well from the wound. It was an old Norse custom that if a man wounded his enemy so badly that his spirit ebbed out of him and it seemed unlikely that he would get up again, he was to cease all hostilities, and instead, comfort the man as he took his dying breaths and treat his body respectfully. This was deemed valiant. Þorgeir now did the same. He sat down next to the man and cradled his head on his knees, until death overcame him.

When Farmer Gils was dead, Þorgeir looked around for his fellows, whom he had sent to fight Gils' men in the scree north of the whale's mouth. He found the men all safe and sound, having done little battle. They all sat there by the whale, sharing the provisions brought by the men of Húnavatn, cutting big slices of smoked lamb flank and munching cured shark. Þorgeir declared that there was not one single example in the old stories of such miserable slaves attending doughty men. The lives of such recreants should be forfeit – filling their bellies while their masters fought! From the very beginning, it had been the pride of serving folk to lay their lives on the line for their leaders.

Belching loudly, they asked how it had gone. They had been so hungry that they could not be bothered to follow the contest between their betters. Þorgeir said that Farmer Gils Másson was dead. This news took the wind out of the sails of the slaves from Húnavatn, and they got up, cheeks stuffed, and went and laid at Þorgeir's feet the axes and short swords and other cutting tools that they had used to butcher the whale. Þorgeir said:

"As it happens, I am not in the mood to kill such no-accounts as you, though it would be right. Take your boat this minute and row back to Húnafjörður, and take the corpse of your master Gil with you, but leave all the whale meat here."

They replied that they were obliged to do as he bade them.

Þorgeir and his men now turned to the whale and claimed all of it for themselves, cut and uncut. None who dwelt in Hornstrandir dared come near – nor did they get any of it. Þorgeir and his men procured kettles and rendered blubber in them over driftwood fires, and traded what was left of the whale carcass to farmers in exchange for homespun.

18

AT THE CLOSE of winter, Þorgeir and his men set off from Hornstrandir, hiking over the mountains to the Jökulfirðir to retrieve his ship and pay a visit to Þormóður Kolbrúnarskáld. Þormóður could not yet bear the light, feeling as if even the faintest glimmer would completely undo him. Nor could he bear the voices of living things – they were like to drive him mad. He could only eat food intended for small children – a little piece of halibut or baked starry ray – and he drank only lukewarm milk. Mistress Kolbrún concocted for him every sort of elixir known in the Jökulfirðir and Djúp. Throughout the winter he confined himself to his bed-closet, with the curtain drawn, the smoke-hole shut, and the door tightly closed. The mistress never left his bed, night or day. During the day she sat in the darkness at his bedside, working her spindle as quietly as she could. Most of the time, he could hardly bear his own state, except when she wrapped her arms around him, like a distressed child.

Þorgeir and his men fit out their craft and launched it. As they worked, a huge seal cow lay there on the sandbank, watching them with its man's eyes, which lacked even the slightest glint of friendliness. They then rowed their craft over to the homefield, by the foot of the hill named after the ogress Fljóð. The seal cow now lay on a rock on the beach and did not take its eyes off them. They were convinced that this seal was evil.

They came across Slave Loðinn and stopped to question him. Þorgeir asked where Þormóður Bessason was. The slave replied:

"How am I to know what curs might be hiding in the corners of the mistress's pantry? Go find out for yourselves, instead of pestering other people."

When Þorgeir pushed open the door, letting in sunlight, they found the skald wrapped tightly in Mistress Kolbrún's embrace. Over the winter, Þormóður had lost the robustness and color of youth, and was now shriveled, weak, and pale, while the mistress was plumper – she was an even fleshier woman than before, with a rosier complexion. At the visitors' arrival, she stepped from the bed, covered the skald with the blanket, and took up her spindle.

"How low you lie, brother," said Þorgeir Hávarsson.

Þormóður said: "Greater men than I have lain as low."

"I shall lie so when I am dead," said Þorgeir Hávarsson, "but never for a woman." At these words, he tore both yarn and spindle from the mistress's hands and flung them to the floor.

The mistress rose rather slowly from her chair and said: "I expect that you, Þorgeir Hávarsson, shall be laid lowest by men so utterly contemptible that no vengeance shall ever be wrought upon them. Yet to you, Þormóður, my friend and skald, I wish to say that even if you let this hero drag you from my arms today, and you chance to become a lucky man or skald to a king, we agreed this winter that you will never again find refuge anywhere but in the arms that I have wrapped around you."

Saying this, the mistress gathered her things from the floor and left the sleeping room.

"We would do well to kill this witch, who has been sucking your blood for far too long, Þormóður," said Þorgeir. "Open up the doors, lads, and cut the turf from the smoke-hole, and go and harpoon the seal that was lying there below the homefield and bring it here to the bedside, alive."

After his men harpooned the seal and dragged it inside, Þorgeir ordered them to puncture one of its veins and let the blood run into a bailing pail. Then they gave Þormóður the seal's blood to drink, and as the skald felt the warm blood running down his throat, the haze cleared from his eyes and strength returned to his legs, and he dressed and grabbed his weapons. Þorgeir Hávarsson led him to the boat. The moment that the skald drank the seal's blood, he forgot all about women, and his thoughts returned to weightier tasks. They boarded the boat, hoisted the sail, and sailed out of the Jökulfirðir, doubled Rytagnúpur and set course for Horn. The story goes that no sooner had they hoisted sail than Þormóður Kolbrúnarskáld's head cleared so completely that his mind re-opened to poetry, whereas throughout the winter, he had found himself tongue-tied every time he tried to compose a verse. Reliable sources say, however, that on this voyage, he restored the lay that he had composed for Þórdís of Ögur to its original form, dedicating it to Kolbrún, his nurse, in payment for the bed and care she provided.

Some learned men have named the period that the sworn brothers now entered their "golden days." It is said that during this time, their guardian spirits were more favorable to them than ever before or after.

One day, Þormóður was walking beneath some cliffs, searching for birthing stones.* The sun shone brightly, making his head grow heavy, and he sat down on a rock on the beach. He noticed that the cliff face stood open, and sitting there in a cave were two women, so preoccupied with something that they heeded naught else. These women were most imposing: one was dark of brow, the other bright of visage. It looked to him as if one was an ogress, and the other a Valkyrie. These women were busying themselves tossing a little egg back and forth, without stopping, and reciting this verse as they did so:

> *Freely we fling*
> *from damsel to damsel*
> *dear to the skald,*
> *Þormóður's life,*
> *each with her half:*
> *two to his one.*

"What will you portion him?" asked the dark woman, who inhabited the abyss.

The other, who bore the hue of the sun, replied: "I shall portion him a homestead: the most splendid place in Djúp, farmhands and beasts, houses and servants, all the best bounties in Iceland. I shall bear him two daughters: one shall be fair as the moon, the other as a star – whereas I myself shall be the sun to him. What will you portion him?"

The ogress said: "I will portion him the greatest poverty one can suffer at the outskirts of the world, and by him engender daughters most akin to death, whose names are Night, Silence, and Desolation. Yet at my knee he will know such a wonder as neither heaven nor earth can match or augment or surpass, until the world ends and the gods are dead."

At these words, this woman stood up and walked into the cliff face, taking with her Þormóður Kolbrúnarskald's life-egg.

19

THE SWORN BROTHERS had their men fish, hunt, and forage, and they berthed their boat in little inlets in the evening. They never strayed far from the boat. They took great pleasure in the sport of searching cliffs for seabirds and their eggs, lowering themselves on ropes from the brinks of the cliffs and ransacking the ledges and crevices for spoils. The cliffs that men descend for seabirds can often be a hundred fathoms or more, and those who forage them feel safer after they have abandoned their footholds entirely and dangle freely in the air than they do inching themselves over their edges. This task is one of the most enjoyable of any done on Hornstrandir.

The men kindled fires beneath overhangs and sometimes under the open sky, for plentiful firewood was found there on the beaches, and they slept in tents on the land when the weather was fine. When the weather took a turn for the worse, they went to farms and offered to fight for lodging, though the farmers would give up their beds to them without a word. Young men stared at the heroes, captivated, and in their presence, other men seemed of little moment. Young women stared as well; some offered to wash the heroes' clothing, and others to rub their heads with soap. As for slaughter and plunder, they achieved little, for the farmers had a natural defense in their poverty and paltriness.

The sworn brothers often sat on bright evenings in calm weather on the grass-grown clifftop of Horn, which looks northwest over the sea toward the end of the inhabited world. They watched for the wakes of great fish on the surface of the sea, and the columns of spray from the spouting of whales. Dolphins leapt and seals frolicked, and a pod of porpoises headed due north to the heart of the ocean. More than once, they discussed how any man with the strength to capture these creatures, and to take their blubber and tusks, would have the means to trade for a longship and make war on more people than those who inhabit Hornstrandir. Swans would also fly in from the sea, stretching their necks and sounding in flight. Then the heroes would sit silently, for they knew that these were the *dísir* of the Lord of Hosts, women superior to any other, who select champions for Valhöll and turn their backs on cowards. The sworn brothers declared it the highest wisdom in the world to be able to understand the din of such birds and to interpret their flight.

One day as they sat at the edge of the clifftop, watching their men fishing at the base of the cliff, their conversation went as follows. Þormóður asked:

"Are there any two men in all the Vestfirðir who live as contentedly and cheerfully as we?"

"That I do not know," said Þorgeir. "It seems more remarkable to me that no one has ever heard of two equally doughty men sharing such fraternity, either in the Vestfirðir or elsewhere – and may the hour never come when either of us begs for life or mercy from any man."

Þormóður Kolbrúnarskáld said: "Can a better place exist than the one we inhabit now? None dare oppose us, and all as one give us whatever we demand, without a word, while women ask us our leave to hunt out our lice."

Þorgeir said: "I think that any place where we might make enemies worthy of death at our hands, or of cutting us down with their weapons, would be better than here."

"Yet it is hard to forget that Egill Skallagrímsson, the greatest hero ever to have lived in Iceland and its best skald, died in his kitchen in the company of crones," said Þormóður.

"No man is a hero who is well married and has beautiful daughters, as Egill did," said Þorgeir. "A hero is one who fears neither man nor god nor beast, neither sorcerer nor ogre, neither himself nor his fate, and challenges one and all to fight until he is laid out in the grass by his enemy's weapons. And only he is a skald who swells such a man's praise."

Þormóður said: "Are there two men living anywhere whose friendship is so strong that nothing could ever diminish their concord and sworn brotherhood?"

Þorgeir replied: "Truth to tell, there is no firmer friendship than when two men are such great champions that neither need look to the other in anything, until one of them is slain – at which point the other shall do all he can to avenge him."

Growing on the cliffs that rise from this sea – the outermost of all seas – high up on their faces, on narrow, hard-to-reach ledges, is a certain herb, whose like in fragrance, nutriment, and healing potency is not found in hayfields or gardens. This herb has a hollow stalk nearly as tall as a man, and its upper part is pliant and sweet and a cure for most ailments. Due to this herb's enticing sweetness, heathens have named it "cravewort," whereas Christians have given it the Latin name *angelica*, after the angels and archangels seated nearest the throne of Christ in Heaven.

In late spring, the sworn brothers often climbed down to cliff ledges to gather cravewort. One fair-weather day as they were enjoying themselves in this task, Þorgeir was cutting stalks so enthusiastically, yet heedlessly, that the edge of the narrow cleft where his feet were wedged crumbled beneath him, and he lost his balance. The cleft's surface was so loose that all it took was the weight of one man to break it. Since the hero had not yet been claimed by Hel, however, he was able, as he fell, to grab hold of a cravewort stalk growing out from a tuft of grass in a crevice in the cliff face, and hang onto it. Below him was a drop of a hundred fathoms, whereas above, only a few fathoms separated him from a narrow path leading to the cliff's brow.

On the cliff face where Þorgeir now hung, there was neither a shelf nor a spur nor any other toehold, nor any chink or handhold by which he could heave himself up. His only life-thread now was one pitiful stalk of cravewort.

As for Þormóður, he had clambered down onto another ledge to gather this herb, and lingered there doing so for quite some time. He and Þorgeir could not see each other. Upon cutting his fill, Þormóður tied what he had gathered into a bundle, placed it on his back, and hoisted himself to the top of the cliff. The weather was calm and the sea still, and the sun shone in a clear sky.

Þormóður lay down on the overhang to wait for his sworn brother, but the cries of the seabirds lulled him to sleep. In fact, the sworn brothers were not that far away from each other – if Þorgeir had called out even a little loudly, Þorgeir could easily have heard him. Yet on this, the old books all tell the same story: nothing could have been further from Þorgeir's mind at that moment, hanging as he was from the cliff, than to call his sworn brother's name only to beg him for help.

Þormóður, the books say, now sleeps soundly on Hornbjarg, eventually waking late in the day. He wonders about his sworn brother, and starts calling to him from over the brink. Þorgeir does not answer. Þormóður climbs down to a ledge, whence he shouts loudly, startling birds into flight all over the cliff. Finally, from down below him, Þorgeir replies: "Stop scaring the birds with your shouting!"

Þormóður asks what is taking him so long.

Þorgeir replies, saying: "It matters little what is taking me so long."

Þormóður asks if he is finished gathering cravewort.

Þorgeir Hávarsson then gives the reply that has long been remembered in the Vestfirðir: "I think that I will be finished when the one in my hand comes out."

Þormóður begins to suspect that not all is as should be with his sworn brother's cutting of cravewort, and he clambers hastily down to the cleft from which Þorgeir has fallen. He peers over its edge and spies his sworn brother hanging from the cliff. The cravewort stalk is quite frayed, and on the verge of breaking. Þormóður tosses a rope to Þorgeir and manages to pull him up to the cleft. They then climb the narrow path to the top of the cliff.

Þorgeir Hávarsson did not thank his sworn brother for saving him, nor did he express gratitude for it in any other way – in fact, it seemed as if he harbored some sort of grudge against Þormóður for the incident, and things grew colder between the sworn brothers from that point on.

20

ONE EVENING, some farmhands from the district rowed a little boat up under the cliff. With them were three men from other parts. Þorgeir recognized them as belonging to the household of his kinsman Þorgils Arason of Reykjahólar, and leading them was one of Þorgils' work foremen. The newcomers greeted the sworn brothers amicably. Þorgeir Hávarsson offered his apologies for the lack of seats more comfortable than sea-beaten rocks, yet invited them to sit down all the same, and ordered one of his men to cut them pieces of seal blubber and another to look after their boat.

These men said that they had ridden from Reykjahólar over heaths and glaciers, and had left their horses nearby. They had been sent here to the north by Farmer Þorgils of Reykjahólar, to deliver the message that Þorgeir Hávarsson had been sentenced to outlawry by the Öxaráþing for the slaying of Gils Másson, and was thus under obligation to leave the country that summer. They said that reparation had been paid for the sworn brothers' other killings. The chieftains in the Vestfirðir had helped bring about the settlement, and the penalty had been paid by Bessi Halldórsson for his son's part in Þorgeir's deeds. The messengers also brought word from Þorgils that a trading vessel down south in Rif lay at the ready to sail to the Orkney Isles. Þorgils Arason owned a share in the ship, and it was his will that the sworn brothers make their way immediately to it and leave the country.

"Is it not obvious that we should do as your kinsman Þorgils says?" asked Þormóður. "According to the law, any person in the land has the right to kill us."

"We will do as no man says," said Þorgeir Hávarsson. "We would be wise, however, to seize the opportunity to go and search in foreign lands for kings or other worthy chieftains who might desire the service of heroes and skalds. I am tired of listening to the grumbling of churls in a kingless land."

They had stored their wares under small piles of rocks or in boxes made of driftwood: seal blubber, whale blubber, and whale oil, as well as some homespun that they had extorted from farmers. Fish and seal meat they had dried on rocks or hung on racks.

"We have good wares here – we cannot leave without these spoils," said Þormóður.

The messengers said that they did not have the horses to carry their goods over steep heaths and arduous mountain paths. "How did you procure these things?"

Þorgeir said that the wares they had gathered here had been procured by better means than most others, having been fought for most manfully and valiantly, and having cost several doughty men their lives – though some of it had been caught by their slaves or taken by force from cowards. However, since the sworn brothers' minds were now on more momentous things than stockfish and whale oil, he said that it was of no consequence to him if this booty were left here for seagulls. Yet when it came time for them all to board the boat, their men sat themselves down on rocks and said that they would not move – they wished to remain here instead. These men were clad mainly in tatters, and their shoes were all worn thin.

Þorgeir Hávarsson said: "I can see that you, being the slaves that you are, look more to your bellies than to the honor you have in following heroes – and no valiant lad lets himself be tied down by cattle he may have slaughtered or oil that he has drained from other people's whales. It is a greater haul than any other to know that somewhere, you have gotten the better of most others. Now let us be off, knowing that we never once needed to beg mercy of or make peace with any man, or to agree to any terms apart from those that we set for others."

They replied: "Now you shirk your promises to us, intending to leave to the birds the wealth that we toiled and scraped to gain for you, and to drag us, unarmed, down unknown paths. Yet we have risked our lives for you, and what little honor we have.

These rags wrapped around us are more tattered now than when we joined your company, and they were shoddy then. There are also some in your company whose frostbite from the winter has not fully healed – and is in fact festering. Are we now to pay for not being as smart as Lúsoddi, who chose to flee with the man here on Hornstrandir who was cleverer than you, Þorgeir, and who could have been your slayer if he had felt like beheading you when you slept beneath his ax?"

Þorgeir Hávarsson said: "It looks to me as if we should cut down these miscreants here by this cliff."

Þorgils Arason's men wanted nothing more than to get to their horses as quickly as possible and ride south straightaway, rather than be caught up in slaughter. They bade the sworn brothers not rattle their weapons at these vagrants and needlessly waste their own time – the tide was rising beneath the cliffs, and the oarsmen would have more than enough work holding the boat steady. In the end, the sworn brothers stepped aboard, and their ragamuffin men, escaping death for the time being, dug into the provisions that the heroes left behind.

They now rowed to an inlet where the messengers had left their horses, made them ready and rode off, taking routes over mountain passes, high glaciers, and heaths that their horses could handle. They spent the nights in the fjords. In the countryside there, it was thought a grand event when these heroes, Þorgeir Hávarsson and Þormóður Kolbrúnarskáld, rode by.

Young people thronged them to have a look, while women peeked out from thresholds.

It is said that the riders were much in need of food when they came down from Drangajökull Glacier. They found lodging for the night in Skjaldfannardalur Valley. They were brought cods' heads, incredibly hard, as the residents stood in the doorways and timidly observed the visitors. The cods' heads were hardly filling, and Þormóður took to reciting bawdy verses as he tore pieces from his, while Þorgeir flung the head-bones and gills violently to the floor, rattling the walls and rafters. The sworn brothers were pointed to a dark passageway leading to the sleeping room, but they said that they would sleep where they were, and neither removed his clothing nor rose from his seat; instead, they propped their shields on their knees and leaned their axes on their shoulders before dozing off. Near midnight, however, Þormóður was woken by his ax falling from his grip onto the bench, and he got up to go see what women he could find.

As for Þorgeir, he wakes to a little ray of light shining down on his nose through the window in the roof, and he sneezes loudly at the pungent smell of the hall's earthen walls, common in the summer. He looks around, but does not see his sworn brother Þormóður, so he takes his weapons and goes outside.

The air is cold and there is dew upon the grass, and the sun is rising over the glacier. The household is still asleep, apart from the farmer's son, who has come down to let the ewes out of their night-time enclosure and herd them away from the homefield – where he spies the visitors' horses standing. He calls to his dogs and sets them on the horses, but the horses are hungry from their long journey and will not stop grazing. Some face down the dogs. When the farmer's son sees this, he loses his temper and drives his spear into one of the horses. This happens just as Þorgeir Hávarsson steps out of the house. He raises his spear straightaway and goes down to the foot of the homefield to have a word with the farmer's son. "Now," he says, "you must wield your spear against a man, rather than a four-footed beast."

The spear that the farmer's son brandishes is hardly useful for anything but prodding stubborn bulls – and some books say that it was only an alpenstock. Nor does the lad have a shield with which to defend himself, so he decides to retreat into the lamb shed located at the foot of the homefield.

Þorgeir pursues him. Behind the lamb shed is an enclosure for hay, empty now at the start of the summer, and the farmer's son retreats there. The doorway from the lamb shed into the enclosure is too narrow and low for so big a man as Þorgeir, and he is disinclined to bend down. Instead, he adopts the plan that always seems to work in the old stories: to tear his way in through the roof – which, in this case, is patches of turf laid over posts, to shield the hay ricks in winter.

Þorgeir Hávarsson stands on the wall and the farmer's son crouches in the enclosure, and both jab their spears at each other through the turf. They keep this up until the shaft of the farmer's son's spear breaks, at which point Þorgeir jumps into the enclosure through a gap in the turf, hoists his ax over the lad, and starts hacking at him so furiously that it looks as if seven axes are whirling in the air. The lad slumps against the earthen wall, bleeding from innumerable wounds – before giving up the ghost.

At around the same time, Þormóður Kolbrúnarskáld crawls out from one of the farm's windows, and is standing in the farm-yard when Þorgeir returns from this deed. They rouse their fellows, declaring that they have had enough of sleeping in the dens of churls, and say that they are ready to be on their way. Upon mounting his horse, Þorgeir walks it to the farm door and declares himself the slayer of the farmer's son, adding that the fetches of champions, the raven and the eagle, have been given their tidbits, and vengeance has been taken for last night's disgrace, when heroes and skalds had been made to eat cods' heads. Then the others mount, and they ride off together.

The day was bright with sunshine and a breeze blew off the glacier, and the sworn brothers were in a festive mood. Yet as they drew near to the middle of this district, their path split into numerous other ones, making it difficult for them to know which was best. The sworn brothers rode ahead of their companions, and they came to some paths by the banks of a river. As they discussed which to take, they noticed a man walking against the wind, with a bundle of brushwood on his back. The wind pushed hard against the man's burden, causing him to stagger. Þorgeir Hávarsson called to this man across the river and asked his name and where the paths led. The wind and the noise of the water, however, prevented the man from hearing the travelers' words, and he made no reply. Þorgeir called out several more times, but the man bearing the brushwood continued on his way without answering.

Þorgeir said: "That man is more than a middling fool to refuse even to look at Þorgeir Hávarsson and his sworn brother."

"I suspect that this man is not very sharp-sighted," said Þormóður, "and he looks to me to be unsteady of step, as blind men are wont."

"Then why does he not answer when those who are the greatest heroes in the Vestfirðir call out to him? I will certainly put up with no taunt from him," said Þorgeir.

"Perhaps he is deaf?" said Þormóður.

Þorgeir said: "Where does it say in the old tales that a man saved himself by pretending to be blind and deaf when men of might rode by? I feel certain that the man both heard us and saw us, and will now think us weak if we do not catch him."

He drove his horse into the river, rode over to the man, and thrust his spear into his chest, and the man, sorely wounded, fell beneath his burden. He clutched at his chest and groaned. Þorgeir leapt from his horse and started hacking at the man's neck to take his head off, though the task went incredibly slowly due to the dullness of his weapon, despite the champion's firm intent. Finally, however, the head came off its trunk, and the man lay there dead on the ground in two pieces, his bundle of brushwood next to him. Following this, Þorgeir rode back over the river to Þormóður. At that moment, their fellow travelers from Reykjahólar arrived. They declared this a great deed, done by a true hero. On a hill a short distance away stood a little farm. A woman was raking the homefield, and children played by a creek. The group rode to the farm and announced the slaying, saying that the hero with the stoutest heart in the Vestfirðir had come. As everywhere else, the folk there marveled at how dauntless a man Þorgeir Hávarsson was.

Later that evening, after following the shoreline for some time, the travelers came to a shoal beneath the coastal cliffs. At ebb tide, it was possible to walk with dry feet there beneath the cliffs, but at flood tide it was impassable by men or horses. The company had one of two choices: either wait until ebb tide, or follow barely negotiable paths over the mountains. When they approached the shoal, the tide was coming in. The men from Reykjahólar rode in front, while the sworn brothers lagged far behind, conversing about the things that were always foremost in their minds: Þormóður proclaimed the happiest man to be the one who took delight in women's charms by night, while Þorgeir insisted that he was the one who charged boldly into combat by light of day. As before, Þorgeir declared the man felled by the weapons of his enemy to be better off than one who truckled to a woman.

As they were bandying these ideas, they came to the shoal. They dismounted their horses, tightened their girths, and let them graze, before Þorgeir said, quietly: "Although you are a man who loves women, Þormóður, you are clearly the most skilled with weapons of any man that I know. In not one single contest have I seen a man knock you off your feet, and at times I find myself pondering which of us sworn brothers would be the victor if we tried our strength against each other."

Þormóður then said: "I have often lain awake by your side as you slept, Þorgeir, and watched your chest move to the beating of the heart that I know to be braver than all others, and gazed at your neck, knowing that no stronger pillar has ever borne a man's head."

Þorgeir said: "Why did you not behead me then?"

"You have no need to ask, friend," said Þormóður. "You might well remember when you came upon me conversing by night with the woman I esteem higher than many others: it took but one word from your lips to make me leave her and board ship with you, despite the winds being as cold as they were. When I watch you sleeping, I find most laughable the augury sent me by the Spear-Lord, Mímir's friend, that one day I should hold your bloody head in my living hands. Grant that then, these slender, weak arms of mine carry out the vengeance that we swore in our oath to the earth. And you shall ride first across the shoal."

Þorgeir looked and saw that the tide was much higher, and that their companions were riding speedily ahead. He did not wait, but drove his horse into the flood tide between the cliff and a breaker roaring in. Þormóður paused to see how it would go for his sworn brother – and soon the water was higher than his horse's loins, forcing it to swim. Finally the man made it, just as the wave crashed against the cliff. Þorgeir dismounted on the opposite side of the shoal and beckoned Þormóður to cross. Yet when Þormóður went to mount his horse, it ran off up the mountain – and the sea between the sworn brothers was now impassable. Þormóður cupped his hands round his mouth and called out:

"I do not know which of us would win in single combat with the other, but the words that you have spoken now will divide our company and fellowship, and I sense clearly that you have not yet come to terms with me saving your life this summer."

"I did not mean all that I said!" shouted Þorgeir Hávarsson.

"You said what you were thinking," replied Þormóður, "and what you no doubt have thought oft times before. And now we shall part for the time being. Fare you well."

At that, Þormóður turned back, walked to a nearby farm, and asked for conveyance home to his father in Laugaból.

21

AS FOR ÞORGEIR Hávarsson, he rode south to Rif and boarded the waiting ship, in which Þorgils Arason owned a share. The merchants were of the sort that did business with others if the occasion presented itself, but otherwise, in fine Norse style, plundered in places where no one seemed likely to defend their possessions. The first few days of their voyage they had clement weather, before the wind picked up enough to make them think they would soon reach Shetland, where they intended to trade their wares for silver. Just as they assumed they were nearing land, however, the wind died, leaving them in a damp, dreary, stubborn sea fog. In those days, seafarers did not know of the lodestone, their troubles thus being multiplied when the Star was hidden. They lost course and drifted aimlessly for days, before their journey ended with them wrecking on some rocks, and their ship filling and sinking along with its sailyards and rigging. Many men perished there, including the shipmasters, who all drowned. Accounts say that seven men survived this shipwreck, after washing onto a barren skerry in the night, exhausted and destitute. Þorgeir Hávarsson was among the survivors. He was wearing a tunic and was girded with the short, single-edged sword that he always had with him. That night, a man asked him how he was faring. Þorgeir Hávarsson replied:

"I am faring well, and I have more than enough to suffice me as long as I have my sword to kill the men that I do not care for."

At dawn the fog lifted and the castaways found themselves on a stony outcrop in a cluster of skerries off a rocky shoreline, yet not very far from land. Among them was an old seafarer who claimed to recognize the place, saying that it was Ireland. They did not hold out much hope of making it to shore, spent as they were. Nor could they light a fire on the skerry, and they lacked both food and water. They took turns standing and waving a cloth on the outcrop's highest point, whence they could clearly see thin lines of smoke ascending from people's dwellings on land, the buildings reflecting in the air as the sun warmed it. They beheld what they thought were fair castles, topped by towers with shimmering crosses. Yet it seemed very much as if the land's inhabitants had more pressing things to do than attend to castaways. When it was Þorgeir Hávarsson's turn to wave the distress flag, the others called on him to do so, but he replied:

"It will never be reported of Þorgeir Hávarsson that he flapped a kerchief to plead for help. I would rather be left to die on a skerry than live as a starveling. It was never foretold to me that I would suffer the misfortune of having to live off another man's mercy. Therefore I will die here, rather than endure abasement."

Three days and three nights passed, and the castaways had neither food to eat nor water to drink. Sitting there, they watched as the corpses of their comrades drifted up onto the skerries around them, and soon their own numbers began to dwindle. Numbness overcame them as they sat through the nights on the rocks – and then death followed.

When the sun rose on the fourth day, three men remained alive on the skerry: Þorgeir Hávarsson and two merchants. On that same day, however, a boat was launched from shore. Three men rowed out to the skerry, led by the eldest of them. They were all covered in carbuncles, and their faces were disfigured with sores and boils. The eldest was the most hideous of them all, his face and skin looking like a lion's scalp turned inside-out. These men gazed ceaselessly toward heaven and exchanged antiphons as they rowed. They now brought their boat up alongside the sea-battered rocks. Clutching his cross, the old man stepped unsteadily onto the skerry and bade the castaways welcome, but they had been numb for so long that they were barely able to return his greeting. The old man addressed them in various tongues, lastly in Norse, asking who they might be. They said that they were merchants whose ship had wrecked – some of their fellows had drowned, while some sat there on the skerry, frozen and lifeless. Two had given up the ghost that night. The elder begged their pardon that better haste had not been made to come to them on the skerry and see to their needs. "For the past three days and nights," he said, "we have been enormously occupied, holding observances in honor of the tooth of St. Belinda, our patroness, hardly ever desisting from prostrating ourselves in tearful adoration and praise of this blessed, most glorious tooth. We celebrate such commemorations for three consecutive days and nights four times a year. Yet now that these days of thanksgiving are over, we have made it our priority to come to you and invite you who are still alive to become our masters, and we will become your servants for the sake of Christ, son of Mary, the god whom we Irish name Josa mac De. As for your departed, we shall sing offices as needed."

The merchants said that there was little need to sing over men who were dead, but much more to tend those who still bore signs of life. Þorgeir Hávarsson said:

"For certain, I will not abandon these comrades of mine who still have life. I must inform you that I am a Norseman, from Iceland, and we cannot be bought with beneficence. You shall have little thanks from us for saving our lives if we are not as free as before to do as we please. And if you wish to have peace from us, I advise you to kill us at once."

As Þorgeir Hávarsson spoke, the elder raised his rood ever higher, and responded by singing an antiphon from Holy

Scripture, beginning "Love thine enemies." He then kissed the warrior tenderly and bade him welcome from the land where, trustworthy books had told him, night was so bright with sunshine that folk saw clearly enough to pick lice from their kirtles. The castaways had nothing more to say for now, and they boarded the boat as the monks sang them welcome with a lordly hymn of praise from the Psalter, before taking hold of their oars.

As they drew near land, the dwellings turned out to be much less stately than in their hazy reflections. They saw the ruins of many old houses, while the only ones still standing were ramshackle at best: mainly miserable, dome-shaped hovels of piled rocks that seemed far better suited for storing stockfish. The only building there of any note was a low church, with a conical spire topped by a wooden cross. The clerics dwelt in hovels scattered over the surrounding hills. There were no cattle, but goats grazed on the scrub and bleated. The castaways were led into a cold, dim, drafty hall, where they were served goat's milk in wooden bowls and coarse bread of unmilled grain – and that was all the fare they received. Upon finishing their meal, the monks said that Christ required their song and that they could do no better for the castaways at present, though they were welcome to rest against the hall's south wall and pick out their lice.

Now that their lives had been saved, the merchants began to complain: they had given all they owned to purchase the cargo that was now sunk, and each bewailed his loss louder than the next. The one had a wife in Shetland, the other children in the Orkney Isles – and they were so far away from their friends. Þorgeir Hávarsson said that he bemoaned only one thing in his heart: that he had not yet found a king who was so grim and mighty that he never spared the life of a woman or a child and sank merchants in bottomless bogs. He said that they would be far better off ridding themselves of sorrow by focusing on the disgrace of the monks watching their shipmates languish on the skerry for three days, before kneading bran and chaff for the living and inviting them to loll beneath a wall. It would be manlier, he told them, to demolish the monks' temple and kill them than to lament what was lost.

Although the merchants were more naturally inclined toward peace and quiet than Þorgeir Hávarsson, they grew weary of their long idling by the house wall, seeing no other living thing but goats and hearing only the chirping of the birds. They got up to see whether anything of value was to be found in this place, or whether any weapons were hidden anywhere, but they found nothing of any use. Each hovel had a rood made of two rough pieces of wood, set cross-wise and wound with bast at the intersection, and one wooden bowl. For beds, the hovels had only low earthen mounds covered with slabs of rock, and stones for pillows. As they peeked through the temple doorway, they saw the monks sitting in the sanctuary, chanting. The comrades found the chant rather dull, and had little idea what it meant. The monks chanted for a large part of the day, as the visitors stood at the door and pondered what to do next.

Finally the monks had chanted their fill and started trickling out of the temple. They were cheerful of countenance, though thin and bony, swollen with putrid sores, and soiled with filth and pus. Each of them vanished into his own hovel, like bugs crawling beneath rocks.

Last from their church came their master, the elder who had come to retrieve the merchants from the skerry that morning. He greeted the visitors kindly and invited them to his hovel to share his evening meal, and they accepted his invitation gratefully. His hovel was extremely forlorn – the wind slipped in through its walls, and its only furnishings were rocks. A ragged monk served them. The master asked how they felt now at day's end. Þorgeir answered for them, saying that their lice were drowned. The meal was served in two bowls: one containing dulse, and the other, water. As the monk served them, he chanted and genuflected. The master received his share with an antiphon in gratitude to Christ, a blessing, and other laudations. He then took a handful of dulse and set it aside for the poor, and invited his guests to eat.

The merchants ate what was served them rather than go hungry, spitting out scuds and worms, yet Þorgeir Hávarsson sat apart, moodily, and declared that he was no dulse-eater. The master gulped down his meal with the greatest relish, like an epicure popping delicacies into his mouth from a rich man's banquet table. He gobbled the dulse fronds with all the bugs and vermin clinging to them, lecturing to his guests non-stop about Holy Scripture as he did so, pointing out in particular how Christ filled the bellies of five thousand people with three loaves of bread and two fishes, and had twelve baskets left over. The merchants listened courteously to his chatter, until Þorgeir Hávarsson said:

"I am not here to listen to old stories, but instead, to take your life and possessions or fall dead by your hand. All that others own, I count as mine unless they defeat me. Now, if you have a life-egg or rune-stick or other such talisman, I order you to hand it over, and I will destroy it – but any treasure that you are hiding from us, you are to reveal."

The elder asks: "What do you want from us, brethren?"

Þorgeir said: "Silver and gold and ivory."

The elder said: "We have treasure enough in our souls, which Josa mac De ransomed from the Enemy and remitted to the mercy of God, but we have nothing resembling ivory, apart from the tooth that was taken from the mouth of the virgin Belinda, which we venerated and glorified of late. Today we concluded our homage and laid it in its shrine, where it will remain until Christ's Mass."

"What weapons do you have?" asked Þorgeir Hávarsson.

"Only one," said the monk. "Yet it is a weapon to which each and every conqueror must bow – namely, poverty in Christ."

Þorgeir asked what proof he had of this.

The monk said: "Before the Romans, who ruled the greatest empire in the world, hung Christ on the gallows, they first ripped apart his kirtle and shared it among themselves. Yet at the moment that Christ was hung naked on the cross, he became not only the vanquisher of the Roman Empire, but also the Lord of all creation."

"I never heard my sworn brother Þormóður say anything about this," said Þorgeir Hávarsson, "despite his being a skald and knowing many a fine tale. And I find it hard to see how you could defeat anyone in battle."

The elder said: "There was a time when we had the richest church and most splendid monastery in Ireland, until the sons of Lochlann arrived here under bark-colored sails: Norsemen whom we called monsters and brutes. They wrecked our monastery and murdered all of the brethren, and in a single hour burned all of the books that we had collected over five hundred years. They broke or smashed every holy relic in the brethren's possession, and ran off with anything of monetary worth. The sons of Lochlann wreaked the same havoc eighteen separate times. Finally, the brethren and I grew weary of rebuilding our church, and we had even begun to doubt whether Christ was the true King of Heaven and Earth, when he did not raise a finger despite his friends suffering such persecution, until he sent down from the Kingdom of Heaven the angel who has been named Michael, to strengthen our hearts. Michael told us this:

'Let it be known to you that the sons of Lochlann, who sail in black ships, have as little control over you as the color of the hairs on their heads. Rather, Christ made them the hammer that he used to wreck this temple eighteen times, when its brothers were sluggish in honoring his love. He has proclaimed that if any of his friends on Earth seek to exalt themselves above the poor, they shall be called his enemies, and their houses, however gloriously they are constructed, shall be the gates of Hell, and Christ will tear them down. And their books, however wisely they are composed, from great erudition, shall be burnt. And though you vaunt the bones of the saints that have been the staunchest of the Lord's stewards to kings and dukes, and gloated over your purchase of splinters of the Holy Cross, you shall be granted no relief as long as you pride yourselves on your name and rank above those who have nothing. Disperse your holy relics to heathen lands – the best that you own – that they may beget works of the Almighty and miracles among evildoers and heretics, and take every bell and image, every book and cross, chalice, and coffer and bury them deep in the earth. Take your cows and slaughter them for those in need. Yet you shall purchase naught for yourselves but the tooth of the virgin whose name is least known of all God's holy maidens. When she was defiled at the age of twelve, on the anniversary of the Assumption of the Mother of the Lord, she sunk this tooth into the nose of her defiler. This tooth is revered in the Kingdom of Heaven above all other teeth, it being three inches long and four wide. The maiden's name is Belinda.'"

The merchants were greatly in awe of this story, and said that it must be an extraordinarily well-made tooth, and asked how much silver the brethren would demand for it.

The elder said: "The excellence of this tooth can easily be told. A year after we brethren had abandoned our possessions and bought the tooth, Norsemen came calling once more, and when they found nothing here of any worth – nothing at all, in fact, apart from barefoot men – they beheaded the adults among us, tossed our bodies over the cliffs to feed sharks, and sailed away with our heads, because they believed that without our heads, we would never meet Christ, our savior. As for those of us who were still in our youth, they shackled us, transported us to other lands, and traded us for merchandise. After the sons of Lochlann departed that time, there was nothing left of this place, where we stand now, but for our blood on the rocks – and the tooth of Belinda, the holy maiden."

When the merchants heard that the tooth was not enough to guarantee victory, they began to harbor doubts. "How did you manage to return here, then, you monks," they ask, "when they had sailed away with your heads?"

The master replied: "The archangel Michael appeared to us once more, after we had been beheaded. He delivered to us a lengthy discourse, interspersed with antiphons and hymns, saying: 'No holy relic is mighty enough to shield a man who trusts in himself, his vigor and prowess, beauty or health, wisdom or learning – he who puts most faith in these things will be first to fall. For there is only one who is truly beautiful and hale, wise and learned, stouthearted and vigorous, and his name is Josa mac De. You brethren have either been made shorter by a head and thrown to sharks, or men have bartered you in foreign lands – some of you have been traded for honey, and others for tar. That is how it goes for those who put their trust in what is of least value to mortal men. Yet, since Christ looks amicably upon you, he has sent me to pledge to you, on his behalf, the grace that alone will open to you the gates of Heaven."'

The merchants asked what this grace was, and whether, with its help, one might establish a profitable market.

The elder said: "I will now answer your previous question, concerning how we returned here, despite having been either beheaded or bartered. In brief: the same men who buy us to-night, we shall sell tomorrow – and the poor men whom you behead at sundown, each and every one shall rise again with two heads at dawn. Those men whom you shackle now shall shortly be borne on wings. Mortal men shall defeat their enemies only by first offering to Christ their wealth and fame, beauty, health, and vigor, wisdom and learning, and courage. When we brethren once again raised a temple over Belinda's tooth, the angel smote us with the sores named leprosy, the most precious of Christ's graces, for by their power, the gates of Paradise were opened to the poor man Lazarus, on the very same day that a rich man burned. No son of Lochlann has ever again ventured upon our shores."

At the conclusion of this story, Þorgeir Hávarsson stood up and walked out. He wandered aimlessly among the hovels for a time, before eventually finding a path leading out to open country. He took it as an evil omen when black goats bleated at him as he headed down the path.

22

ENTERING THIS story now is a man named Thorkell Strutharaldsson, nicknamed "the Tall." Thorkell led a band of Vikings and commanded a fleet of ships. Some historians place him with the Jomsvikings, but English books state that he was a Swede. Thorkell had traveled far and wide with his men and fought many battles, either on his own initiative or in the service of foreign kings and dukes, fighting for them against any enemy whatsoever. Thorkell and his men demanded their pay in advance and a share in the booty when the victory was won. Whenever it looked likely that the king they supported would be worsted, they would ally themselves with their enemies and fight against their former friends as vigorously as they had supported them – and they took pains to be present when the spoils were divided.

Thorkell the Tall was always victorious in battle, and numerous lesser chieftains and other small fry sought to join his force – men who had few ships and little means to harry well-defended places. Thorkell's band often lacked in numbers – his men's lives being briefer than their fame. Many of them died of fatigue and hardship, besides the manifold ailments that beset seafarers. Some were killed during raids or taken prisoner, and many deserted the band. Thorkell constantly had to send men abroad to recruit new forces to fill the gaps. Norse landlopers were their preferred recruits – those who pursued adventure and glory, but had little or nothing to live on. Thus was Þorgeir Hávarsson, coming from Ireland, drawn into Thorkell the Tall's band.

At that time, England was ruled by a king named Æthelred, or Aðalráður in the Norse tongue. He did little to defend England from its enemies, and far more to collect taxes from his subjects. The English were not much convinced of the need for many of the taxes he imposed upon them, obliging him, like numerous other kings, to collect some through coercion and tyranny. When foreign belligerents threatened the country, Æthelred habitually bought them off, thus assuring bands of brigands from abroad – including armies – of booty in England. Æthelred loved his queen Emma above all others, and every moment that he did not spend collecting taxes, he spent sitting in his castle musing upon this woman, while carving birds from bone.

We lack the space between the covers of this book to recount all of the exchanges between Thorkell the Tall and Æthelred, which, for the longest time, hardly ever varied in nature. Thorkell never grew weary of showing up with his forces and challenging Æthelred to a fight. Each time they landed on England's shores, they did so where its defenses were flimsiest. They would then take hostages and send Æthelred word that he had a choice:

either ransom the hostages and pay tribute, or fight. If a foreign army presented terms to Æthelred, he would fall ill, seized with great fits of vomiting and terrible gripes, and not a word could be gotten from him but this: that he would willingly pay the tribute that his enemies demanded. Englishmen name this type of tribute Danegeld, or *gafol*.

By the time of this story, Æthelred had paid boundless sums in Danegeld. The English peasants, on their part, had had enough of counting out their money to Æthelred, and took it upon themselves both to defend their possessions against him and to muster forces to defend the lands and towns of England from the plunderers who tried to yoke their king with tributes. To King Æthelred, however, such acts constituted nothing less than breaches of the peace and high treason. He considered hostile foreign armies less of a threat than his own subjects, fearing that the peasants would overmaster him, take charge of his army, and deprive him of his throne and kingdom.

Now once again, Thorkell and his men demand an exorbitant sum in silver from Æthelred, landing an army on the banks of the Thames to show they mean business. As usual, Æthelred pledges to pay the tribute claimed, yet finds it difficult to fulfill his pledge. The Vikings, growing impatient for payment, accuse Æthelred of swindling them and lead their army to Canterbury, where both the king and the archbishop have their seats. Thorkell has gathered a great host from Ireland, the isles of Orkney and Shetland, and the lands of the North, and, as always, every man in the army expects great gain from this war with Æthelred. When Æthelred hears report of this army, and that it intends to take Canterbury, his old ailment rears its head: first, he vomits terribly, and then has trumpets blown to summon his troops to war. Yet he does not go to face his foes, Thorkell the Tall and the Norse Vikings, but rather, commences a campaign against his own subjects, the peasants in the territory of Wales, in an attempt to extort enough money from them to hand over to Thorkell as tribute. He personally commands this campaign – declaring, as was true, that the men of Wales are not staunch Christians, for which reason he will now appropriate their wealth – their pure silver, struck and unstruck, wrought and unwrought, and other valuables – and kill every one of them if they refuse to relinquish it.

As for Thorkell the Tall, he and his men grow weary of waiting idly for Æthelred's tribute, and determine to pillage the neighboring shires and seize anything of monetary value they can lay their hands on, in addition to cattle and butter. Yet the yield of their plunder turns out to be less than they had hoped – the peasants have been fleeced many times over, leaving little but the bones in their necks. The longer they wait for Æthelred's return with the tribute, the wearier the Vikings grow of plundering the poor, and they determine to besiege Canterbury. Having a rather scanty population, particularly for mounting a defense against a Viking fleet of two hundred and forty ships, the town is taken without a fight. The Vikings seize everything of value within it and burn the town's churches and monasteries, as well as the king's castle, to cinders. They take hostage great numbers of the town's leading clerics, wellsprings of true doctrine and models of purity in England, both monks and nuns, and lay hold of Bishop Godwine, Abbess Leofrun, and numerous other noble men and women, as well as the king's steward in the city, Earl Ælfweard, and many other aldermen. Finally, they take captive his lordship the archbishop, Ælfheah, one of the greatest aldermen and friends of Christ that has ever lived in England. He is eighty years old at this time.

English books record that the Norsemen then burnt every house in the town to cinders, and cut down any person unable to escape. Droves of dead bodies floated down the Stour River, says one book, and the town's soil and water both ran red with blood. Women and youths they loaded onto ships, calling them their cargo. When Æthelred eventually returned from his campaign, bringing the money that he had squeezed from the Welsh while his castle burned and his monasteries were ransacked and destroyed, Thorkell and his men doubled the sum of the tribute that they had imposed upon him, and demanded ransom for each and every one of the hostages. Æthelred, distraught at the prospect of paying such a supplement to the huge amount previously stipulated, pleaded for mercy from Thorkell, but

Thorkell retorted that he sailed for profit, not pleasure, and that his sole obligation to his men was to let them plunder freely wherever they had hope of gain. He proclaimed such to have been the proper purview of valiant adventurers since the beginning – not paying heed to the whines of those who lacked the mettle to hold onto their own. Æthelred, having already fleeced his own people, had no idea where to turn, and took to vomiting mightily. Once again, Thorkell grew weary of the delay in payment, and he called for an assembly outside the castle wall at daybreak on Palm Sunday. The hostages, he stated, were to be dragged thither from their dungeons. The district's commoners were bidden to attend this assembly, and the king to send his stewards. Thorkell now summoned those in his fleet most skilled in the application of awls, tongs, shears, knives, and hatchets. In charge of them was a youth from Vestfold in Norway, pale of visage, short, and tremendously stout, with a broader rump than most men, so plump that he waddled more than walked. His name was Olaf Haraldsson, and the Vikings called him "the Stout." He had very small hands and wore a ring on each finger – two or three on some, in fact – and two silver belts round his waist, one on top of the other, but because of his great girth, the belts had broken asunder, and were held together with bits of twine tied through and around the buckles.

The hostages were led out. A great crowd of men and women had gathered, most of them in clerical garb. Olaf Haraldsson said that the prisoners were to be tortured according to their equivalent worth in silver or butter, and in the order appropriate to their rank and excellence. Those least likely to earn the Vikings much money or butter, such as lay brothers or poor nuns, besides common clerics, were to be maimed first, and most leniently. Next would come the choir-brothers and canons, followed by abbesses, and finally abbots and bishops, as well as earls and aldermen and their wives. These were disfigured in various ways: some had their hands and feet severed, others had their noses or ears chopped off. People mutilated in this way were nicknamed "nubsy" or "stubsy" by the Vikings. No small number had their eyes gouged out. Numerous times that day, requests were sent to King Æthelred to pay the captives' ransoms, yet his constant reply was that all the coffers in England were empty, as were the butter-larders. That day, Ælfweard, the king's steward, and various other English aldermen, as well as Bishop Godwine and Abbess Leofrun, had their hands and noses chopped off or their eyes gouged out, and the same went for numerous others of the spiritual estate and clergy. After the hostages were tortured, they were led away and sent to Æthelred. From that day on, most folk of any mark in England fell under the designation "nubsy" or "stubsy".

Last to be led forth was Ælfheah, Archbishop of Canterbury, who was doddering and blind. A pale young man walked at his right side, enraptured as he chanted shrilly from the Psalter. Thorkell the Tall said:

"We hardly see the need to gouge the eyes out of the head of a blind and grizzled gaffer such as this, and we would hope that Æthelred agrees with us. Go and tell the king that we shall set this man free unmutilated, provided he first hands over eighty hundreds in silver to redeem his head."

The man acting as King Æthelred's spokesman stepped forward, bowed to Thorkell the Tall and said:

"The venerable master standing there in chains is not only the spiritual father and patron of King Æthelred, but also brother and companion of none other than the apostle Peter in Rome, who speaks on behalf of Christ himself – and for this man, we shall pay whatever sum you name. This we declare by the king's authority and that of Holy Church."

The royal spokesman's declaration was received joyfully by the Vikings, and all as one proclaimed Archbishop Ælfheah to be a truly sublime man of God. It seemed as if their shouts and applause would never come to an end. Yet when they finally quieted down, a single, weak voice, cracked and quivering, was heard asking for the crowd's attention. The voice's owner bade the envoys of King Æthelred tarry and listen to what he had to say. Addressing them was Master Ælfheah himself, in fetters:

"Convey this message," he said, "to my son King Æthelred and my brother Pope Sergius: never shall any price be paid for my head apart from what Christ paid on the cross when he ransomed my soul from Hell. If my life is to be bought now for less, I shall never again lift my eyes to behold this world or the next."

Thorkell the Tall's cohorts were a sight less cheerful when they heard this reply from the archbishop's lips, whereas Thorkell himself said that old Ælfheah was a man with a gallant heart. "For now," he said, "naught else shall be done. Bring the old man back to his tower."

At the conclusion of their day's work, the Norsemen were not yet contented, and they ordered an abundant supply of ale-barrels brought and opened and a great quantity of meat boiled, and lit fires and held a grand feast there on the banks of the Thames.* As they feasted, they declared old Ælfheah a true son of the Devil, meaning to deprive valiant warriors of eighty hundreds in silver for the sake of his own arrogance. They pronounced it a damned disgrace for craven monks to cower in the bosom of that gallows-carrion Christ and fleece doughty men of their livelihoods. The more they chewed this over, the more agitated they grew. Finally, most asserted that they would not put up with any more provocation from Christians who caused them to lose their share of ransoms or spoils. After eating and drinking for quite some time, and with the celebration at its height, various noble members of the fleet raised their voices above the crowd and proclaimed it utter madness to spare the old fool who, that day, had defied such champions as themselves. Their leaders ordered that Archbishop Ælfheah be brought out once more, and this was done. The old man was dressed in a red stole and had had his beard groomed respectably. The young man, Grímkell, stood by his side and chanted. They led Ælfheah to the middle of the square and pulled the stole off him. The old man stood there in nothing but his kirtle, woven of coarse tow and heavily knotted, and his wrists and ankles were shackled. The crowd began pelting the bishop with big knucklebones from oxen and other bones leftover from the boiled meat, as well as bulls' horns and anything else handy. A voice in the crowd rang out – it was Olaf Haraldsson the Stout. He declared:

"They say that more sods can be found in a band of Vikings than anywhere else. But where are they now – when you hold your tongues as beef bones are flung at such a maidenly swain as the one standing there singing?"

At these words the men roared with laughter, pulled the boy from the archbishop's side, and sat him down among them. The old man stood there alone on the square, in his shackles. He held himself upright at first, his eyes raised as though he were blind, muttering a few words that the other men could not catch. Yet, say English books, after being repeatedly pelted by ox-bones, the archbishop finally sank to the ground, his body and limbs covered in bruises and his skull broken. Thus did the Norsemen beat to death, on that day, *Alphegum archiepiscopum venerabilem.*

23

SOURCES SAY THAT Olaf Haraldsson had two small ships of his own in Thorkell Strutharaldsson's fleet, having been given them as a tooth-fee at home in Vestfold.* Olaf had been seafaring since he was a child, at first doing the tasks normally assigned to young boys, and later, after growing older, commanding his own men. He had sailed his ships far and wide and done battle from the Baltic to Spain, and many years later found skalds to sing the praises of his exploits in distant lands. The story went that he defeated the Gotlanders in battle when he was twelve years old, and then occupied the island and subjugated its inhabitants. He also claimed to have fought and defeated an army of innumerable knights in Kennemerland. Yet, if truth be told, no one had ever really heard of him until the day he joined Thorkell Strutharaldsson. Small bands of Vikings that sailed with few ships found it ever harder to subdue folk who inhabited the coasts of the Northern lands, lacking, as they did, the manpower to conduct raids where there was hope of plunder – such places were generally well defended. They were forced to settle for harrying where there were no defenses, the catch being that such places had no spoils either, and the youths that dwelt there were so emaciated and the women so spent that they were practically useless for selling or enslaving. Instead, the Vikings had to content themselves with plundering cows if there were any, or else goats, and salting them down in barrels – and it seemed to them a lucky day if they found anything at all to eat. Quite often, numerous men on the ships became incapacitated due to lack of provisions, and many died of scurvy. Few of them had any untattered garments to wear.

When Olaf the Stout and his men joined up with Thorkell the Tall, they were finally able to eat their fill. Within Thorkell's company, the rule was that every Viking had the right to keep the possessions of any man he managed to fell, but when halls or churches were plundered, or town coffers were emptied, the chieftains were in charge of dividing the spoils. If the booty were plentiful, the chieftains first dealt out weapons and clothing to their troops, and afterward money.

Immediately following the capture of Canterbury, most of those in the Viking fleet arrayed themselves in the clothing that they had stripped from the townsfolk: many a hard-boiled Viking wore a monk's cowl, while some sported lavish chasubles embroidered with gold or carried croziers as staves. Killers with tangled locks and unkempt beards donned bishops' miters, or adorned their heads with gold lace and other diadems of abbesses. When the chieftains could fit no more gold rings on their fingers, they threaded them onto ribbons and let them dangle from their belts.

One day, Olaf the Stout walked among his men to get a sense of their well-being, and had a good look at their clothing and weapons. Among the troops was one man who seemed less disheveled and bedraggled than most of the vagabonds and landlopers gathered there. This man had the look of a warrior and a fierce bearing, though he wore a plain tunic and carried inferior-looking weapons.

Olaf said: "Your clothing is poor, fellow, and your weapons are not what I would call formidable. Choose from my attire what you will."

The man in the tunic replied: "I am no beggar. I did not come here to receive alms, but to win glory."

"Then why did you not get yourself better clothes in Canterbury?" asked Olaf Haraldsson.

"Because," said the man in the tunic, "the only men I encountered in that town worth taking a moment to swing a sword at – the ones we call monks – were more akin to women in their defenselessness. There were also a great many women, most of them with child, whereas the men that were capable of fighting were at work or away at war. It hardly beseems me to strip the clothing from monks and nuns, or pregnant women, and don it myself. I would rather wear my tunic, which I took from Farmer Gils Másson when I killed him on Hornstrandir – it was what I was wearing when I brought myself safely to Ireland."

Olaf the Stout asked who this man was that spoke so boldly. It was clear he was no milksop.

"Þorgeir is my name, son of Hávar, and I am an Icelander," he said. "Since you offer me finer attire, I must tell you what my mother and sworn brother Þormóður Kolbrúnarskáld said: that the only gifts befitting a valiant warrior are those that a king grants him according to his worth at the conclusion of a battle. I will fight in this poor tunic of mine until I and my weapons win a cloak more suited to a doughty fighter, but if I am struck down by another man's arms, then it is right that when it happens, I be wearing this simple tunic – nothing better. I hope that the next time we do battle, I encounter the sort of champions that my mother told me can be found waging war. It will then be revealed what sort of man I am, despite these poor clothes of mine."

Olaf the Stout then said: "Strange men you are, you Icelanders, who submit to no king and trust only in yourselves. In this world, such a thing is rare indeed. Yet if you had the choice, what king would you submit to?"

Þorgeir Hávarsson said: "I pledge such troth to you that I will do only as you command."

"This," says Olaf, "is spoken valiantly – and no one has ever made such a pledge to me before. You will surely make a splendid king's man. I bid you accept this gold ring from me, for I expect greater things of you than of other men."

Now that the Norsemen had accomplished the great exploit of laying waste to Canterbury, their opinion of their own excellence grew to no small extent and they reckoned that all of England would be theirs for the taking. They held important councils on the banks of the Thames, and their leaders agreed that the time had come for them to pay better attention to London than they had until then. It was the richest and most populous place in England, and the only English town that had never been taken by a foreign army. The Vikings had heard that more wealth was amassed in that town than any other. Many a distinguished English alderman and lord dwelt there, as well as rich merchants who outfitted ships for long trading voyages. There were also numerous wrights and craftsman who produced manifold wares: weavers, tanners, goldsmiths, and other skilled artisans. The Norsemen looked on it as a desirable occupation to rob the locals of their valuables, weapons, and money, as well as their household belongings and other useful things. Thorkell ordered his army to whet and polish its weapons, to prepare its ships for battle and sail them up the river, declaring that he intended to attack London, and he promised each man ownership of all the spoils he couldc lay his hands on, yet no more than he could carry away himself. Everything that had to be borne on horseback, as well as carted off in wagons, would remain the undivided property of the army, under the control of King Thorkell. That was Viking law.

The fleet sailed upriver, the troops aboard making a belligerent clamor, blowing horns and bellowing and shaking rattles.

King Æthelred's army marched from inland to meet them and halt their progress, but the troops lacked both ferocity and steadfastness, as well as faith in their leaders to oppose the Vikings – besides the fact that at that time, not a single naval fleet in Europe was capable of fighting against Norse sea-kings. English books state as well that there was discontented murmuring and dissension in the English ranks, and King Æthelred's commanders were preoccupied with undermining each other. Some of them wished to be friends of the king, and others to renounce their oaths to him – and English clerics assert that many a good man in the king's army took bribes from the Norsemen. Some of them betrayed their lord free of charge and entirely on their own initiative, in the hope of personal gain, and the army fell into great disarray.

As for King Æthelred himself, when he received news that the Viking army was on its way to London, he began vomiting more terribly than anyone has ever been known to, and lay bedridden in an out-of-the-way dwelling. Æthelred's men were either killed or taken captive, apart from those who retreated inland and managed to hide themselves in forests or farms. The Vikings held course for London, arriving in the evening and mooring their ships tightly together on the river below London Bridge; they prepared to storm the town walls at daybreak. There was no army in the town, and none to defend it but the townsfolk themselves. When the Londoners came to realize that an overwhelming force was marching on their town, every one of them made preparations to defend his home and his possessions, each with the weapon, implement, or tool that he had at hand – there being a general shortage of arms normally considered suitable for war, and fighting men to wield them. Most of those who had any skill in arms were at work in the fields of their masters or served in Æthelred's army, or had hired themselves out to other kings or sailed away on trading voyages. The men left in town were mainly old or children or youths, besides numerous women and cripples. There were also large numbers of lepers and beggars, as well as noseless fornicators and handless thieves. When the horns signaled the attack, and the Vikings, shouting and screaming, rushed onto the piers, rattled their weapons, and erected ladders against the city walls, they encountered these folk, each jabbing with his own lance. Some of the townsfolk fought with brooms, others with pokers, some with shovels or pitchforks, and many with clubs and sledgehammers. Graybeards and paupers, as well as maimed thieves, fought with their crutches, and children with their toys. The townsfolk showered rocks on the Vikings, while respectable dames and poor women joined in the attack, some pregnant, others carrying babies in swaddling clothes on their backs. Unspoiled maidens and foul whores stood side-by-side and poured boiling urine over the attackers, while others hurled simmering pitch or pumped water on them from the river. Flaming brands were cast at the fleet – fires broke out widely and leapt from ship to ship. It was not long before the fleet was one massive blaze, and great numbers of the Vikings' ships sunk. The townsfolk also managed to wreck all the ramps and ladders that the Vikings had thought would gain them access to the city. Every Viking that did manage to make it over the wall was surrounded and thronged by the crowd and pummeled with all sorts of base bludgeons, or stabbed with carving knives and table knives, files and awls, pins and knitting-needles and shears, or bitten to death by the inhabitants and ripped to living shreds and thrown to the dogs.

English books say that at this point, when King Æthelred hears this news, he is so terrified that the spew sticks fast in his throat, like an avalanche obstructed by a narrow gully – for the fear that a land's rulers have of foreign conquerors is slight compared to their fear of their own subjects. When Æthelred hears how the townspeople of London are relentlessly burning and sinking the Norsemen's ships, and boiling the Vikings in piss and carving them up with table knives, he feels utterly betrayed – to learn that now, in the space of one morning, the wisdom handed down by sage English kings of old, that the Norsemen are invincible, is to be proven false by a crazy rabble, weaponless and ignorant of warfare, after England's army has fled to the woods or hidden itself in manger stalls. Æthelred rises from his bed, hale once more, and sends men in haste to Thorkell Strutharaldsson the Tall to deliver the message that he wishes to parley with him and sue for peace with the Vikings. The Vikings respond quickly by retreating from the town and rowing their ships down the river – those that were not burned or sunk. They summon King Æthelred to meet them at the mouth of the river. There they make a pact that is often cited in English books, with King Æthelred promising to pay the Vikings a tribute of four-hundred-and-eighty hundreds in silver. Æthelred, being penniless, offers to open every door in London to the Vikings, and to designate them protectors of the city, and he pledges to command that they be honored above all others by the people of the land and loved most fervently of all their leaders, and to place at their disposal, beyond all other authorities in England, all the city's property and revenue. Thorkell and most of his men, being landless from birth, had never imagined claiming lands or kingdoms for themselves, but only of pillaging for kind or cash. In return for King Æthelred's offer, they pledge their true willingness to defend him from those subjects of his who stubbornly pit themselves against illustrious warlords and eminent conquerors using table knives and ladles, brooms and crutches, or who pour piss on the heads of men of renown.

24

AS MENTIONED earlier, King Æthelred had a wife named Emma – the most becoming of queens. Emma was a native of Normandy, and a sister of a great lord of whom we now tell: Richard, Duke of Normandy. Both she and her brother were descended from Rollo on their father's side. By the time of this story, Duke Richard had landed in many a scrape, though few of these incidents shall be recounted in this book – most learned men, however, agree that he was among the more sensible of rulers.

Stipulated in the covenant between the dukes of Normandy and the kings of France, their overlords, was that the former were obliged to maintain large, well-outfitted armies at all times, yet not to defend their capital of Rouen, but rather, to support the French monarch when he made war on other kings. The duke of Normandy's army was paid its wages in silver – a significant source of revenue. Richard thus kept only a small garrison in the town, resulting in a lack of sufficient manpower to ensure that taxes need not be collected through a show of force – and the same went for the other demands that he made on the populace. For this reason, the peasants conspired against Richard, and, unbeknownst to the duke, met in assembly with representatives of many different districts to discuss ways to better their conditions. The territories – counties and duchies – neighboring Richard's own were governed by men whom he could hardly call friends. These took every opportunity they could to provoke him unjustly, each encroaching on the duke's authority as best as he could, and thereby enriching himself at the expense of the others. One such encroacher enters our story now, a count by the name of Odo – called Oddur in Iceland – who ruled over Chartres.

Duke Richard lodged a complaint against this count, for the following reasons: Odo had married Duke Richard's sister, Maud by name, who brought him in dowry a rich, spacious county, called Dreux in the French tongue. In the Icelandic tongue, it is called Draugsborg. After living for a time with Maud, Odo grew tired of his wife and fonder of most other women, and he sent Queen Maud to a convent, where he had one of the holy maidens serve her a poisoned drink. Despite having rid himself of his wife and taken other women, however, Count Odo would yield neither the castle of Dreux nor its surrounding lands to his brother-in-law Duke Richard. Richard now reclaimed the land from Odo, and they wrangled over it to the point of exhaustion. The ill will between the two increased, and each sent an army against the other: Richard ordered his forces to burn the county of Chartres, and Odo dispatched troops to ravage Normandy. The two armies, however, never truly fought it out, especially since most of the men on each side married into each others' families during these wars – that is, those who were not closely related or intermarried already. Folk from opposing camps settled down next to each other as if they all belonged to one and the same territory, rather than the two wrangled over by the count and the duke. While these sovereigns, swollen with wrath, fomented war between territories and preached thrashings, slaughter, and revenge for the love of Christ, causing their champions to chomp on the edges of their shields, their subjects invited one another to feasts, nuptials, and baptisms. All of these things combined to make it no easy task for Duke Richard to press his suit against Odo of Chartres, his brother-in-law by chance, rather than choice.

Now the story shifts to King Thorkell the Tall and the Vikings. They made themselves at home in London as the honored guests of King Æthelred, receiving from everyone whatever they demanded, emptying the coffers of London and loading their ships with everything of value they could find in the town. Yet, after drinking dry most of London's ale stocks and eating up everyone's meat, and slaying most of the townsfolk they disliked, and lying free of charge with every woman they fancied, and having no chance for further exploits in the town for now, their grand adventure coming to an end, they grew dreadfully bored and demanded that Æthelred direct them someplace where deeds could be done. Sitting in London drinking ale was not the life for them, they said – they were bent on glory, and desired gold and jewels, or to go where the goods and treasures and other spoils they had acquired in London could be traded for coin.

King Æthelred replied: "Great is your courage and your thirst for achievement, Vikings, and I will surely regret it deeply if I lose such defenders as you. If truth be told, I have never, since I lay in my mother's womb, been as hale as I am now, ever since your arrival in London. Yet it seems to me that God has not intended for me to benefit any longer from your fellowship or support, and I shall therefore tell you what bargain I would make with you upon parting. I have been sent word by my brother-in-law Duke Richard in Rouen, that, like many a good king, he finds himself sorely pressed by his enemies, both from within and beyond his realm. In short, my brother-in-law Odo of Chartres sent his wife Maud to an abbey and had her murdered there, but now refuses to relinquish her dowry of Dreux to Richard. Since Richard has hired out his army to fight for King Robert in France, he lacks the manpower to wreak vengeance for his griefs closer to home. He is therefore offering excellent sums of money, along with other emoluments, to any company that will lend him support in marching against Odo and killing him and his rabble, and pillaging his territory and burning down Chartres."

When the Vikings heard this declaration, they took counsel and debated whether to throw their lot into this sovereign chess-match at the bidding and supplication of Duke Richard. To the wiser men in the company it appeared that the exploit here proposed would bring them great fortune. They sent a hasty reply to Duke Richard in Rouen, stating that King Thorkell the Tall was fully prepared to offer his forces in support. The Vikings outfitted their ships and rowed down the Thames, and upon entering the English Channel, they encountered a good wind. They hoisted their sails, headed for the mouth of the River Seine, and sailed upriver until they reached Rouen Castle, where they dropped anchor and sent envoys to inform the duke that King Thorkell Strutharaldsson had arrived, along with his vassals and personal guard, at the request of King Richard.

Those in the castle were in no great rush to welcome the army – but at the end of the day, the duke's legates finally came to meet Thorkell, bringing word that the marauders were to bathe themselves, comb the lice from their heads, and rub soap into their hair and rinse it, before presenting themselves to Duke Richard.

Many a red-blooded man in the fleet considered this an outrageous injunction. For ages, sea-kings had deemed it far more regal to don lace-trimmed mantles and loads of weighty rings and jewels than to scrub and bathe themselves with soap and water, like women or pansies. Yet the Vikings dared not disdain this order, knowing as well that many a highbred baron, from both France and farther south, graced Duke Richard's court. Only the highest standards of courtesy were adhered to in Richard's castle, and those most lacking in fine manners were the greatest objects of scorn.

When Thorkell and his men arrived at the castle, they were led to the royal assembly hall, where Duke Richard presided over his counselors and bishops and other men of rank. King Thorkell and his men were not exactly polished in appearance, nor were they practiced at pacing stone floors. Their raiments, though wrinkled, were embellished with splendid swords in sparkling hilts and various other decorations, and the shields they bore were gold-rimmed. Duke Richard did not let the Vikings come very far into his hall, but instead, he rose from his high-seat to go and meet them, accompanied by his marshals and bishops. Richard was short in stature, slender in build, and dainty of step – as he approached them, he held the haft of his sword in one hand and made the sign of the cross with the other. It was as if he were faced with tearing his way through a multilayered spider's web. Duke Richard did not bow to his visitors, nor they to him, but he bade them welcome in the French tongue, and, summoning his interpreter, addressed them in these words as they stood there near the door:

"My lord Thorkell and other distinguished commanders, I wish to inform you that with Christ's guidance, we are engaged in manifold conflicts with men inside and outside the borders of this land who have made apparent their malevolence toward myself and God and Holy Church, and who are now besetting us. In these affairs I would ask your support, and offer you both advance payment when you begin, and a share in the spoils afterward. We deem it our most pressing task to take the fight to Count Odo, who styles himself Sovereign of Chartres. Odo of Chartres is an unrighteous ruler, who has flaunted the laws of Holy Church by beguiling women whom Christ, the son of Mary, did not intend for him, and murdering others whom Christ did not intend for him. Such a sovereign deserves nothing better than to lose his head. I ask that you join forces with me in killing this lecher and laying waste to his land, for the sake of our love of Christ and the righteousness that the blessed John the Baptist and the high priest Melchizedek wish to see rule the world – as do God's beloved kinswomen, Sunniva and Belinda, patronesses of chastity. Yet we will not disavow that for this noble task, we desire no man in our company that has not received baptism and the Holy Spirit in water and word. I hereby give you the opportunity to be baptized forthwith, and cleansed of the evil spirit. Those who refuse to be baptized, however, are the enemies of Christ and ourselves and our Lord Pope and all holy men and women, as well as the counts and kings and archangels and thrones that righteously rule in Heaven and on Earth. Our bishops, who stand here with me, have therefore vowed to grant absolution in the cleansing flames of Purgatory to every Christian man who is eager, through divine inspiration, to bring down such an obdurate, unrepentant, and malicious rogue as Odo of Chartres."

After King Thorkell Strutharaldsson and his men returned to their ships, he summoned the chieftains in charge of his fleet and addressed them, telling them that a tasty morsel was theirs for the taking: chests full of gold – besides the immeasurable plunder they were promised upon subduing a mean-spirited, piddling count who ruled a territory nearby. Yet there was one catch, said Thorkell – with which some of them would be none too pleased. The Duke, he said, has given us a choice: either to be baptized, or never to fight beneath his banner.

The chieftains spoke up and voiced various opinions on these tidings. Many in the fleet had in fact been baptized earlier, or prime-signed,* for the sake of engaging in commerce with Christians, though few gave any thought to the religious tenor of the act. Far greater numbers among the fleet were heathens to the bone, and there were a few who considered any open practice of Christian beliefs to be more than sufficient cause for killing. Several exclaimed that Norse Vikings would never bend their necks to Christian men, or obey their commands – instead, they would set Rouen ablaze and murder the Duke and his bishops.

Again King Thorkell addressed his troops. He asked them to bear in mind that the men of Rouen were more than capable of exacting retribution – this would be different than slaughtering livestock and defenseless rabble in little coastal villages in Friesland or Jutland or Semigalia, or up north in Karelia. Richard, he stated, had both a well-armed company of chosen men to defend his castle and the backing of powerful kings in southerly regions. He reckoned it would be wiser to avoid risk by earning their keep through a paltry count such as Odo of Chartres than to wage war against rich sovereigns over which god lied least to people. It had often been proven in England and elsewhere that the friends of Christ were scarcely less doughty than those of Þórr. "Nor is it any secret in the army," says Thorkell, "that my serving lad of late has been an English youth whom we call Grímkell, formerly valet to Ælfheah, the leading man among the Christians in England, whom you pelted with bones on the banks of the Thames. This lad is both skilled in interpreting dreams and a seer, and because of his gift of second-sight, he knows many a hidden thing in and upon the Earth, as well as what occurs above Hliðskjálf, the very seat of Óðinn, and he can tell all the news from Niflheim. This lad is a friend of Emperor Christ himself. I have it on good authority that Christ has sworn a solemn oath to wreak vengeance on us for the wrongs that we have done to his friends and kindred, and vowed that his vengeance shall be more portentous than the world has ever known, unless we yield to him in the matters that are of importance to him. Or," says Thorkell, "is there a stench coming from

White Christ that causes you to reject good money – and earn his hostility – rather than make him our friend?"

King Thorkell's sensible persuasions hushed the chieftains' grumblings, and when the assembly came to an end, fewer were of a mind to reject the rewards offered, despite the conditions imposed. Each chieftain now returned to the company under his command, to explain to the men what profit they could derive from baptism and the Holy Spirit.

25

IT IS SAID that among those assembled aboard Thorkell the Tall's ship to debate the fleet's acceptance of Christianity was the lad Olaf the Stout of Vestfold, who commanded two of the fleet's ships, his tooth-fee. He was eighteen years old at the time. He moored his vessels alongside the other ships on the Seine River at Rouen Castle. After returning to his ship in the evening, Olaf roused his crewmen from sleep and assembled them. He spoke as eloquently as an experienced commander who habitually exhorts his troops, and many a man remarked that when Olaf focused on a cause, his lack of experience in swordplay and other noble pursuits was made up for by his silver-tongued persuasiveness.

He commenced his address by stating that now, at that very hour, Norse Vikings were being offered a greater haul than any man had heard of since the days of Harald Fairhair, when the Norsemen's fortunes soared so high, and their excellence in equal proportion, that foreign kings vied to yield them their lands and give them their daughters to wed, as when King Charles in France handed Normandy to Rollo, and his daughter Poppa to boot. "And now," he continued, "Rollo's descendant in Rouen, Duke Richard, has heard of the great glory you won in England by your stoutness of heart and your valor, and the invincibility that causes all the world to tremble. Now, out of fear, he proposes to relinquish his lands to you, to give you leave to make war on French sovereigns and crush them at will, and to take of the land's bounty whatever you desire, as well as princesses and queens and other distinguished dames, all for free and according to your needs. In order for you to indulge blamelessly in the entertainments to be had from a victorious campaign of manslaughter, arson, plunder, and rape, Richard demands nothing of you in return, apart from the trifle of receiving baptism and the Holy Spirit and becoming Christians." Olaf now informed them what he had heard at the assembly of the fleet's commanders. "There," he said, "those distinguished fellows who boast more ships than me spoke their minds, and all seemed to be in agreement, both the eminences among them and those in charge of but a few small ships."

Olaf the Stout continued his address to his troops, as follows:

"In brief, I consider myself to be better versed in Christianity than other men here in the fleet, as a result of my experience in slicing off the noses and ears, cutting out the tongues, and gouging out the eyes of more learned men and nuns than most other Norsemen, a task entrusted to me because I am thought to have excellent surgeon's hands. I have not yet seen sign of a Christian losing heart despite being maimed – far more of them, in fact, laugh as they are mutilated. I suspect that the world will perish at Ragnarök before such men can be conquered. I also wish now to disclose to you all that not one single day has passed when I do not recall the manhood of Ælfheah, the English archbishop, when we pelted him for our amusement with bones and horns. I have long felt, ever since we stoned that cleric, that our weapons and ships are not as effective as they once were, though our axes are broader than in other lands, and our warships swifter sailing than those of any other king in all the world. I am surely not as wise as our leader, King Thorkell Strutharaldsson, yet I know, no less than he, that the understanding of hidden things, the benefit of books, the art of song, chivalric manners, and skill in noble swordplay, and therewith the respect of worthies in the south, is all had from Christ, not Óðinn, though the latter is said to know the language of birds, and has conversed with Mímir's head. I also feel that the time has come to put an end to a widely believed lie: that Christ the son of Mary is no match for Þórr in his fierceness and severity, or for Óðinn in his guile. Why would Þórr not have smashed the world beneath his hammer if the gallows tree of the son of Mary were not a tougher cudgel – one which my kinsman Olaf Tryggvason let flash in the air over Norway?* I have a suspicion that no Norse king shall ever again be victorious without the support of these fellows, and I am told that my namesake sits at the high-seat with Christ in the royal castle called Munvegar,* which is found in the Kingdom of Heaven. I hope that we never make the heinous mistake of eschewing conflict when gold and silver are to be had, even if we take up arms for holy, spiritual teachings of the sort that we hardly imagined to exist when, uneducated and ignorant, we first left home and which even now we do not fully understand – such as what woman Christ intended for Odo in Chartres to take to his bed. It seems to me a better course to exact Christ's revenge on Odo for his inconstancy to his lawful spouse, and thereby ransom ourselves from the snake pit that Christ intends for his enemies, rather than to slay men and salt down cattle on the desolate coasts of the North, where divine teachings and courtesy and pious morality are lacking."

In the annals of Rouen, the baptism of the Viking fleet is counted among the greatest of events ever to have taken place in that town, not least on account of its manifold consequences, of which only a tiny portion will be recounted in this little book.

When news of the Vikings' imminent conversion spread throughout the castle and town, and then the surrounding region, the entire duchy of Normandy praised the Lord. On the day appointed for this great ceremony, a huge throng of people flocked to the town from all sides, singing and praying, in order to witness that horde of evildoers, known to be among the most abominable of men on earth, humble themselves and submit to Christ. Early that morning, the cathedral filled with people, so many that those who arrived late could not gain entrance. Due to the size of the crowd, the clerics commanded that none should be brought into the church for baptism except the chieftains and other leaders of the Viking fleet – the rest were to be baptized on the cathedral square under the open sky. Water was now brought in buckets, and blessings were chanted over them. This benediction transformed the water, bestowing on it the power and quality of the waters of the Jordan, the river where, Holy Scripture tells us, White Christ himself was baptized. Ropes were used to mark the bounds of the ceremony on the square – within them the Viking host was to be granted the sacrament of baptism, while the populace stood outside the sacred space to behold this work of the Almighty.

That day, the clerics in Rouen certainly had their hands full. All the bells were now rung and every horn or flute in the city was blown, creating a tremendous din that touched and softened hearts that had been untouchable until then. Then the monks began exultantly singing Lauds. As soon as they concluded this office, they went straight on to the *Te deum*, and the bishops, in their finest array, moved in procession from the castle, leaning on their crosiers and preceded by a stout, imposing cross. In the path of this procession, firewood was burned – wood that the kings of the East had brought to the White Christ as a tooth-fee

when he lay newborn in a manger, alongside an ass and oxen –
while deacons and acolytes walked behind the bishops and bore
their trains. Also taking part in the procession, in the name of
God, were Duke Richard and his barons and other high-rank-
ing men, some wearing gold and gemstones, others polished
byrnies and gilded helms. Their exceedingly splendid gold-inlaid
swords flashed and sparkled, as did their wondrously embossed
shields. Finally, bedecked in white christening robes, came the
chieftains from the Viking fleet, followed by the clerics who
were to act as their godfathers. There, cloaked in white linen,
were gathered numerous scruffy old friends of Þórr, their locks
tangled and beards matted, walking in procession with their
great broad shoulders hunched, heads hanging, chins thrust
out, brows knitted and mouths turned down in frowns, glanc-
ing here and there as if following the advice from the *Sayings
of the High One*: "Before crossing a threshold, take a good look
around you."* Together with these were squat men with pot-
bellies, bandy-legged, bull-necked, pale-haired, ruddy-cheeked
rascals, grinning as they waddled along. The rabble thronged
round, their tongues flapping with praise and eyes glistening
with tears of joy to witness such an appalling gang of thieves
and villains adorned with the cloak of light, ready to be anointed
with holy water and chrism and to receive absolution for their
evil deeds, such as stealing cows and setting fire to Europe for
seven generations.

Inside the church, each chieftain was assigned a divine guardian angel and saint, in addition to a godfather, and each was christened with the name of his own particular patron saint through anointment with holy water and chrism. They were then called one by one into the confessional. In the agreement made with Duke Richard and the bishops, it was stipulated that the Vikings were to confess their sins and crimes against God, although they had no clear understanding of what creature it was that the clerics called sin, or what god they had committed crimes against, or how one can commit crimes against gods. As for the articles of faith, they were certainly less studied and reflected on by the chieftains than professed as a means to gain profit.

As regards the rest of the host, the men were arrayed in ranks on the square, and bidden to lift up their hearts to God. Then the clerics went among the ranks with buckets and sprinkled water from sponges over them, thereby baptizing the entire horde at once. Some of them received but a meager dose of chrism on their heads, while entire rows had to content themselves with just one angel or saint, and large numbers of them had to share the name and patronage of just one heavenly guardian. Most of the names of these guiding spirits were in Latin, making it difficult for the men to remember what they were christened, and many a man retained the name that he had been given in childhood, when he was sprinkled with water as a heathen.

It is said that when the fleet's chieftains urged their men to receive baptism, each and every one of them was at liberty, in a manner, to make his own choice – the pact with Duke Richard was to be submitted to freely. Yet with the following proviso: any man who did not wish to receive baptism would have leave to take to the woods of Normandy and live as an outlaw, and to keep whatever spoils he could get his hands on, without, of course, being permitted to fight beneath the banner of Duke Richard.

No books tell of whether anyone in the fleet chose to take to the woods rather than submit to Christ the King of Heaven and Duke Richard; quite a few, however, said that they had already been baptized elsewhere, even though they had forgotten their name and faith for a time, and others were nowhere to be found on the morning they were due to report to the church. The same happened with Olaf Haraldsson's two little ships: one man was missing when the count was taken, and the chieftains were puzzled as to who it might be, since no crewman admitted to losing a comrade. Such was the excitement over the impending great events that the missing man was quickly forgotten.

As for Þorgeir Hávarsson, when he heard that the Vikings intended to be baptized, hoping by such a contrivance to gain money and fame for themselves, he could not help but shake his head at the folly of it all. He did not care for Christ any better than before, or for the Holy Spirit either. Those men who owned ceremonial garb took it out from their small trunks, happy now to be treading the most profitable path and bidding farewell to the heathen gods that had never done anyone any good. In the midst of the fleet's busy preparations in the night, Þorgeir crept along the gangways and manropes between the ships on the river and boarded a merchantman, unnoticed by the ship's watchmen. Þorgeir looked about for a place to hide, but found none apart from a tar barrel, not entirely empty. He decided that it would serve to avoid Christ, hopped in, and pulled the lid over his head. The stench in the barrel was the worst he had ever smelled, yet he found it far preferable to being baptized.

Time passed, and in his barrel Þorgeir could hear the echo of the pandemonium in town, as pipes and horns were blown, bells rung, and organs poured out resounding song – a merrymaking that he could hardly find more disagreeable. Then, long after everyone had gone into the castle, folk had been baptized, and the bells had ceased to ring, and the clergy were singing Mass, Þorgeir heard a voice, near to where he was hiding in his barrel on the merchantman. It was most unpleasant; a hoarse, cracked and ragged voice reciting some sort of lay and constantly repeating the same verse while changing the wording each time, as if composing on the spot and making it ever more gloomy and solemn.

Þorgeir could make out that the lay was in praise of the greatest of all of King Thorkell the Tall's many outstanding exploits: his victory over the English, when he sacked London and endeared himself to King Æthelred, after first ravaging Canterbury. The lay named that battle as the seventy-first that Thorkell had fought, and the most glorious. It told of how hundreds fell to the blue battle-mattocks of Thorkell's warriors in a single hour of the morning – neither eagle nor she-wolf went hungry that day. The river reddened with wound-sweat when Thorkell wrecked London's wharfs. That game, said the lay, bore no resemblance to the one men play when they lay bright brides on their bolsters or kiss young widows – many a maiden wept in the gloam of that morning. The lay had the following burden:

> Fearsome was the fray,
> fiercely battled Thorkell.

Þorgeir Hávarsson lifted the barrel's lid and emerged, black with tar. Sitting there by the deck cargo was a tall bard, with green tartar on his teeth and his chin showing through his beard. He was wearing a tattered and torn black cloak, and his bare, sinewy forearms sported two bands of gold, both of them heavy and worth a great deal.

Þorgeir said: "I am tired of listening to your twaddle. What a liar you are – and a feeble skald – when you say that we sacked London. Who are you, anyway?"

"My lay, *Glory of London*, was not intended for your ears. Why have you not gone with the others, to be sprinkled with water in place of tar?"

"I am an Icelander," said Þorgeir Hávarsson, "and I have little desire to follow others' customs. There may be good booty for the taking in Rouen, but I am no more desirous of Christ here than I was on Hornstrandir, when my sworn brother Þormóður Kolbrúnarskáld and I cut cravewort from a cliff face."

The graybeard looked up and stared hard at the man, before answering: "You are speaking to the Jomsviking Þórður, the Skald of Strutharaldsson. I will not, however, kiss you in greeting, though we are compatriots – for you are all covered in tar. You strike me as a rather unfortunate man."

"There is no need," said Þorgeir, "for you to speak poorly of me or to augur me ill, when you spout lies about King Thorkell's glorious siege of London. The lays of my sworn brother Þormóður were of a different sort, as were the ones that I learned at my mother's knees. Those lays were all made from true events and the magnificent deeds done when hero faced hero in battle – and they exalted those forefathers of ours who were the noblest men in the world: King Sigurd Fafnisbani and the other Völsungs, as well as the Gjukungs and Helgi Hundingsbani, and then Rognvald, Jarl of Møre, and King Ragnar Lodbrok. You, on the other hand, prate about us having bravely conquered London: yet you know better than anyone that in London, piss and pitch were poured on us, and we were sliced with table knives like cured shark, and those who did these deeds were women and decrepit, helpless old men."

Skald Þórður replied: "It goes ever for kings as for vicious dogs: they lie on their spines when their bellies are scratched. That is the lot of skalds. And chieftains know well that the fame they gain from us skalds lasts them longest. Nothing is dearer to any king's man than verses exalting his sovereign, to feel the praise poured on his king drip onto him. Every warrior loves hearing afterwards of how bravely he comported himself in battle, no matter how frightened he actually was, or how useless his king really was – or, no less, if he had been drenched with piss. What chieftain do you serve here in the fleet?"

"The one whom I believe has more glory in store for him than any other young chieftain, for he has sailed with fighters since the age of twelve and fought many a great battle. He defeated the Frisians and occupied Gotland, and his name is Olaf Haraldsson. I would rather you made verses for him."

Skald Þórður replied: "It has not been my habit to versify about kings who command few ships. Poetry composed for petty kings always proves to be labor in vain. All that I have heard of this Olaf is that farmers in Kennemerland rode to the coast to meet him, bringing him gifts and intending to trade with him, but in a grand display of his arrogance, he had them all killed by way of greeting – despite their being unarmed – and then salted down their horses for provisions. One thing more I know of Olaf Haraldsson: that the Gotlanders thrashed him aboard his own boat when he was twelve and came to plunder them – this he called making the Gotlanders his tributaries and occupying their land. The skalds that come after me will laud him in verse, if they find themselves lucky. As for me, I find my skills in the noble art waning, dear fellow; I am hardly able any longer to exalt those friends of mine who need it most. I long once more for the fish I caught when I was young, in a lake in Iceland lying between pasture and heather, called Apavatn Lake. To the east of it we behold Mount Hekla, and the heads of its fish make men skalds. *Glory of London* will be the last of my poems, if I manage to finish it, for I have asked leave of my friend Thorkell to return to Iceland to die. From here on, others will step in to determine kings' reputations. And you, Þorgeir, are a foolish man not to have gone to the castle to be baptized."

"Why did you not go to the castle yourself?" asked Þorgeir Hávarsson.

"I am doddering, and have no desire to betray Óðinn in my old age. I wish to go home to Iceland, to a lake on a heath where I can catch a few fish. Another skald will occupy the seat that was mine, and by Christ spread the good names of kings whom we extolled by Óðinn and Þórr."

26

THE VIKINGS SAILED inland up the rivers, while Duke Richard rode overland with his barons and bishops, as well as the bodyguard that always accompanied him, in the custom of kings. When the Vikings reached the river Eure, which borders the county of Chartres, they went ashore, leaving men to guard the boats. The region is mainly a vast plain, and from a distance a cathedral can be seen standing prominently on a hill, dominating the landscape. There stands the town of Chartres, girded with walls and towers. In old Icelandic books, the place is called Hill-in-France. Since the recent hostilities between Odo of Chartres and the Duke of Normandy had dwindled to nothing after neither had gained the upper hand, there was no one on guard in the town, and the next thing the townsfolk knew was that a hostile foreign army was standing at their gate, making a rather unpleasant commotion, blowing flutes and beating drums and shaking all sorts of rattles. Next, these raucous newcomers raised a war cry and, without further ado, broke into the town and began pillaging and burning. Whatever they encountered – man, dog, or other living creature – they assaulted.

It is said that in those days, Chartres Cathedral was one of the greatest houses of God north of the Alps, and administered by the wisest of clerics. It was built with a high tower of many storeys, where folk could take shelter when the town was besieged or battles were fought within its walls, every resident taking with him whatever possession or possessions he valued most highly – silver and gold or precious stones. When the church was full, portcullises that not even iron could breach were lowered before its doors. The Vikings now assaulted the cathedral, but the portcullises had been lowered to stop them. Word spread that Odo of Chartres was inside, with his bishops and mistresses and other dignitaries, as well as an abundance of jewels.

At that time, churches were not as exquisite in materials and workmanship as they later became. Folk did not yet know how to construct columns and arches for tall buildings solely from stone, but set beams in the walls to bind the stonework and supported the vault and roof with rafters. For an entire night and day, the Vikings besieged the cathedral, and by evening they began to lose patience. Several voices said that it would be wiser to burn the king and the other folk inside the church, rather than wait for the wickedest of all fiends, the rabble, to rise up and ambush the besiegers in the town. Among the Viking horde were several who had devoted themselves, to some degree, to the Christian faith – these declared it sheer recklessness to reduce such an outstanding temple of God to ashes. In the end, they said, Christ would be ill disposed toward those who carried out such a deed. Yet there were also those, no less Christian, who reckoned it a far worse crime that Count Odo bedded women whom Christ rejected, and neglected those he had been given by holy sacrament. They declared the laws of Christ to be more precious than an earthly house built by mortal men. The Vikings debated this theology for some time without coming to an agreement, whereupon King Thorkell stated that the case should be submitted to the judgment of those who apparently knew Christ's will most clearly – that is, the bishops. Envoys were now sent to the bishops to ask them to decide whether this church should be spared, and with it the miscreant they had come to kill. "Or does Christ wish the church to be burned, along with everything in it?"

It has always been the case that great warlords never sleep more soundly than when a crucial battle is being fought – and now, Duke Richard of Normandy was fast asleep in a castle room near the town gates, as was Archbishop Robert, Richard's brother. They had ordered that they were not to be woken unless Odo was taken alive, for they wished to be present when he was dismembered.

Now Richard and his brother get a rude awakening, when envoys of the Vikings come to ask whether Chartres Cathedral should be burned, with its holy relics, together with the king, the noblemen and their possessions, as well as the town populace, including women and children.

The duke rises and summons the clergy there to council. Having, however, but small store of books by which to seek guidance in Holy Scripture and the Church fathers, Robert, Bishop of Rouen, announces that he has reached a verdict, after fervent invocation of the Holy Spirit and chanting of three paternosters – besides whispering an *Ave Maria* with sighs and tears – and sends word to his Christian brother in Christ, King Thorkell Strutharaldsson the Tall, as follows:

"Assuredly, Christ holds it neither laudable nor just, for any reason whatsoever, to set fire to churches and burn kings inside them, or commoners, women and children, or other wretched folk. Yet it should be kept in mind that although Christ is a great fisherman, he will not be caught in his own net. He is too skilled a lawman to be snared in the laws that he himself has laid down. Thus, he overrides his own laws whenever they become a bulwark for the fiend who dwells in Hell, and who is so clever, cunning, and underhanded that he has frequently wrapped himself in a mantle of light and adorned his own head with the halo granted to saints alone, in order to dispute with learned men over articles of faith and refute their dialectic. It is also the greatest of heresies for people to believe that Christ ever stated, *in carne* or *in spiritu*, or that the Holy Spirit ever decreed *in synodo*, that churches and holy relics, clergymen, women and children or other defenseless folk are to be spared, *de facto*, from destruction by fire, come what may – for example, when the stewards of Satan deprive good jarls of their property or disown virtuous princesses, and in doing so deluge the world with vainglory and arrogance. In such a case, a swift verdict shall be rendered: when Satan rears his head, no decree issued by a king or alderman or lawgiver or warlord shall apply, or by a bishop or magistrate or tax collector or warden, or any other of the king's or God's servants. Neither shall the Ten Commandments, which God inscribed with his finger on tablets of stone for Moses, remain in force, and Christians, for the love of Christ, must in fact burn children and women and other wretches, exterminate beasts and birds and grasses, and set fire to churches and holy relics, if, by this means, they are able to defeat the Enemy. *In nomine patris et filii et spiritus sancti.*"

Having received the bishop's verdict, Thorkell the Tall orders that timber, hay, and tar be piled around Chartres Cathedral and set alight.

When the Norsemen went to war, it was an old custom of theirs to gather together all the infants they found, remove their swaddling bands, and skewer them on their spear points. The Vikings had learned early on that the more horrendously they behaved, and the more terror they employed, the less resistance was put up by the populace, and the more readily lands and towns were surrendered to them. The Norsemen deemed it a paltry campaign if they failed to maim three dozen defenseless individuals for every fighting man they killed, and it has always been thought fitting that this ratio be maintained by bands of valiant warriors – those who have any respect for fame and heroism – when they make war on other lands.

After ravaging the town throughout the day and setting fire to the cathedral, the Vikings treat themselves to a feast that evening, rolling casks of red wine into the square, and boiling meat. An excellent banquet commences as the flames consume the cathedral's timbers. Among the entertainments is the reciting of the lay *Glory of London*, composed by Þórður the Skald of Strutharaldsson in praise of Thorkell the Tall – describing how he wreaked destruction on London and satiated the eagle and wolf.

The Vikings had spent that day in town indulging in all kinds of pleasures, as befitted fine men, and they adorned themselves for the feast in all the finery and jewels that they had looted. Some of them sported several gold rings on each finger, according to old Viking custom, and a few were clad in three scarlet mantles, one on top the other, or were girt with two swords, though not a single man in the Viking host knew how to wield such weapons. Some decked themselves with enameled tankards and other drinking vessels, rosaries, amber and coral, women's shoes embroidered with silver, miniver, or tanned hides, or even rolled-up, artfully woven tapestries. Hanging from the belts of others were the heads of the women that they had raped that day. They felt as if they had the world at their feet, and as if the future shone with beautiful light. As they feasted, they delighted in hearing their praises sung, and boisterously joined in with the refrain and the final stanza. They gave free rein to their tongues at the banquet table as they competed in pledging vows – and many a valiant vow they made. Some vowed never to fight again for any other king than Christ, since he had given them articles of faith, revelations, and sacraments to defend by force of arms instead of spending their time salting down cows on the coasts of the North, for the sole purpose of filling their bellies. As they made their vows, they ardently praised their new god for his almighty works and prowess, and especially for having led them to such a prosperous royal town as Chartres. Several vowed to marry the woman they had loved in childhood, in the valley or on the island or headland where they had grown up, but to trade other women in England for tar, and then become freeholders, petty kings, or holy men in Norway.

The Vikings declared it wholesome for young children to die on spear-tips when their mothers had been taken captive or beheaded, their fathers slain, and their homes burned to cinders. By means of such a death, these children were consecrated to the Spear-Lord, Óðinn. The man who was oldest in the band and best with children was generally assigned to look after them, and was named the Friend of Children. His job, at feasts, was to ensure that the children lived until the warriors were sated. Then, when the men were ready for the entertainment, the Friend of Children would remove their swaddlings and toss them into the air one at a time, naked. Where an infant came down, a Viking would be standing with his spear at the ready to skewer it. Then the child would be tossed aloft three times from the spear-point, before being cast off it, dead. The Norsemen always hollered up a storm at this game. Newcomers to the band were called upon to play first, and then those who were more skilled at this sport. That evening in Chartres, as the cathedral burned, Þorgeir Hávarsson was called upon to raise his spear. The Icelander rose slowly to his feet, still gnawing a knucklebone, and said:

"I thought, when I joined your company, that I would be among men – I did not join to play games. I do not consider myself more cowardly than any of my valiant comrades, though I am less inclined than you toward those arts in which manhood and prowess are lacking; nor do I see what need there is for tossing these infants into the air. Back home in Iceland, my mother taught me that all fun and games are useless, little beseeming red-blooded men. Nor do I recall any of the poems of my sworn brother Þormóður Kolbrúnarskáld praising warriors for jabbing spears into sucklings."

One man said: "Barons as noble as Christ and Óðinn can never be fully repaid for their assistance, and these are but trifling sacrifices compared to those made of old, when doughty men and kings were hung from trees or burned for the people's prosperity. You must be a godless man."

Another man said: "It is my belief that the happiest of children are those hoisted on spears, for they laugh merrily as they fly through the air, until they are dead and in Heaven, where Christ our foster father sits with his friend, King Olaf Tryggvason. You must be a stupid man."

A third man added: "Word has spread in this band that you are unable to satisfy women, Þorgeir Hávarsson, and it is little wonder that such a man quails at games with children. You must be both a sod and a poltroon."

Þorgeir Hávarsson answered these men as follows: "From Earth I received my might and main, and I will never turn my mind to mirth, and neither bow to women nor hoist children, nor sacrifice to the gods, and never hope for assistance from any man, woman, or god, but only from Earth. Nor will I ever lay a weapon to an unspeaking infant or any man that lacks the manhood to defend what is his. Yet if any man among you thinks himself a match for me, I challenge him to fight me in single combat. I will not heed idle prattle, but only the true declarations of weapons."

It was law among the Vikings that peace be maintained between the various bands during war, and that he who wrecked this peace was a *níðingur.** The chieftains decreed that Þorgeir's challenge to single combat offset the men's taunts, and let the matter drop. They were gathered to celebrate the death of Odo of Chartres, and no one had the right to spoil the others' merriment. Nor was any man obliged to toss infants on spear-points unless he wished it.

27

THAT NIGHT, when the flames from the cathedral rose highest over the plain of Chartres and the feast was in full swing, the tramping of hooves and a blare of trumpets sounded in the darkness. A distinguished company of legates came riding up, carrying torches and bearing flapping banners. These men asked where the Duke of Normandy was lodged – and for the second time that night, Duke Richard was woken.

The legates brought tidings from Robert Capet, King of the Franks, that yesterday Count Odo had fled by a secret route from his town of Chartres, along with his bishops, mistresses, and other dignitaries, and taken refuge in a fine monastery where he kept his treasure. From there Odo had sent a complaint to Robert Capet, indicting Richard, Duke of Normandy, for unleashing arson, murder, and rape in his domain – the havoc being wrought by a foul mob of foreigners under Richard's command who were still wearing the gowns in which they had been received emergency baptism in Rouen. King Robert had his envoys drive home to Richard that he alone was supreme monarch of the realm of France, and that he alone, by the grace of God, bore the name and title of King of the Franks. He would have his vassals bear in mind that they lived under his rule and ate from his hand, and were so ignoble that they could never hold titles higher than duke or earl. The king also had his legates stress that hostilities between the men of Rouen and Chartres were to cease. From now on nothing more was to be given to the flames – and there should be no more murders, rapes, or other heroic deeds. In addition, no one was to reach out his hand to filch so much as a shoe patch in Chartres, or to harm even a single hair on any child's head, and the foul mob from Norway calling itself Vikings was to leave his realm. As for his vassals, Duke Richard and Count Odo, they were ordered to appear before the king in Paris after peace was restored in the land and the Vikings were either dead or gone. He would then settle their dispute and assign to each the territory he thought fit for them to hold, while he himself would take over Dreux, the demesne over which they had fought, and which was Richard's sister's dowry when she was married to Odo. With King Robert's message came the warning that he had an invincible army to the west of the river, with a great company of knights, as well as all manner of siege engines, war wagons, catapults, and Greek fire.

After receiving the message from the King of the Franks to the Vikings, delivered via Duke Richard's marshal in the middle of the night, Thorkell Strutharaldsson hastily convened a secret meeting with several men of rank in his company, before going to Duke Richard's marshal and addressing him loudly and angrily:

"It seems we are in dire straits, being forced to defend ourselves, in the heart of enemy country, against the invincible army of the very King of the Franks – Duke Richard of Normandy duped us badly when he proposed we take part in this campaign. Moreover, it was treacherous of Richard to conceal from us that Robert Capet is not his staunchest friend, setting us at odds with one of the richest, most powerful monarchs in the world. Richard has delivered us to Frankish swords and Greek fire, and lured us into fighting, as foot soldiers, far from our ships, against a company of heavily-armed knights manning war wagons. When Richard invited us to sail from England to fight for him, we thought that we would be allying ourselves with a Norman army at the ready, but it appears that the Duke has hired out his army to the King of the Franks, and now we find ourselves in the predicament of having to fight our master's army. Just a short time ago, Duke Richard called us marauders and ordered us to bathe ourselves and kill our lice, when his own retinue consists only of ground lice that call themselves counts and barons and dare not show themselves near clashes of arms. Duke Richard has also made a bargain with us to adopt the Christian faith, and it is extraordinary that we Vikings, who were heathens yesterday, should be the only ones that could be mustered to recover the wealth that Richard's sister pledged to old Odo to bed her. She must have been hideously ugly. This Richard seems to us both a petty king and a craven one – you may tell him that it would be fitting for us to kill a milksop like him and renounce the faith."

Of all the dukes in the line of Rollo who have ruled over Normandy from Rouen, Richard is believed to have possessed one of the sharpest political minds. He summons several of the bishops and counts accompanying him and takes counsel with them. They agree that although Robert Capet has forbidden any further warfare in the county of Chartres, there is still more than enough work left for the Vikings in pacifying Normandy and killing the peasants and other inhabitants who do not recognize Duke Richard's authority.

The duke now rides with his retinue to meet the Vikings and greets them cordially, kissing those of their leaders who appear to hold most sway. This time he speaks to them in the Norse tongue, glibly and fawningly, calling them his kinsmen or brothers at every other word, never addressing Thorkell Strutharaldsson as anything but "sire," and asking no one to kill his lice or wash his head before speaking to him. He says:

"I wish to thank you first with words, Sire Thorkell and our other Norse brothers and doughty Vikings," he says, "and then with gold and silver and other splendid objects, for the support that you have given us in discomfiting, albeit in small measure, Odo of Chartres, one of the greatest lechers in France. Yet for the moment, we shall do no more, since Robertus Capetus, King of the Franks, our friend, and, after Christ and the Pope, our overlord, wishes his vassals not to be slain, for he fears that such a deed would be detrimental to the common folk. Though it was tragic misfortune that Odo escaped with his life, and that Chartres Cathedral burned along with most who sought refuge there, you are not to think that the deeds of renown that I had in store for you are completed, or that your hope of gaining wealth has been reduced to nothing, despite things here having taken a turn for the worse – peerless champions and illustrious warriors as you are. I now have an exploit for you that promises to be far more gallant and profitable than any you have so far accomplished. I have heard that when you pledged to unleash your forces on Odo of Chartres, you thought my army, which I intended to ally with yours, rather paltry. Not to beat around the bush: even those men here in Normandy that have not been recruited by the King of the Franks but are capable of bearing arms, are treacherous churls. They hold White Christ in low regard, and instead have Cabbage-Christ and Onion for gods, choosing to toil away in the dirt like worms or to stroke their wives' bellies rather than accomplish anything to the glory of their king. They care not a whit when men who despise the sacraments pillage our lands and wealth, and they stubbornly resist paying taxes, squandering their labor instead in ditch digging and other earthwork, or erecting fences and building bridges and mending roads, or many other kinds of miserable drudgery, instead of maintaining my barons and their castles. In the rare times that we have managed to muster the peasants to make war on our enemies, they have betrayed me, and taken women to wife in the lands of our enemies, and begun worshiping their Cabbage-Christ and Onion according to their despicable, childhood habit, instead of fighting and dying for their king or returning victorious. Now the peasant leaders have been meeting behind our backs to discuss how best to promote their own advantage at the expense of ours. My request to you, Sire Thorkell my brother, and to you, my kinsmen and successors of my great-grandfather Rollo, is that you cross back over the river into Normandy and wreak vengeance on the traitors and turncoats that have conspired against our kingdom and the royal office invested in us, the dukes of Normandy, at the inspiration of the Holy Spirit, by the Frankish king Carolus Simplex, the Pope, and Christ, Son of Mary, and the archangels, to be held in the sight of Almighty God as long as the world lasts."

Upon Richard's finishing his speech, King Thorkell Strutharaldsson's anger abates. The Vikings are better disposed toward Richard now than they were just a short time ago, and they heartily welcome being entrusted with new deeds of glory to perform. "Has anyone," they ask, "ever heard of a Viking going back on his pledge to an open-handed king?" Moreover, the Vikings declare their willingness to have bishops accompany them, ready to deliver Christ's verdict whenever necessary, such as when they might burn churches, as well as to offer them absolution if they burned them unjustly.

28

THE INHABITANTS of Normandy whom we call the peasants of Rouen had heard the news that their ruler, Duke Richard, had brought a Viking army to Chartres to do away with Count Odo. The peasants had no apprehension of danger until the king turned this army on them and began pacifying the land: beating or maiming the common folk, burning their houses, and hanging those whose loyalty he questioned. At first, the peasants put up little defense, to the elation of the Vikings – it was as if they suddenly found themselves licking ladles full of honey. Each and every object made of silver that they found in people's houses, struck or unstruck, as well as of tusk or bone, they grabbed and carried off. They tortured lowly folk into pointing their fingers at the firebrands conspiring against the duke, and wherever they settled for the night, the first thing they did was erect a gallows and hang the peasants that they had taken captive that day. They were very fond of halting in the vicinity of cathedrals and monasteries and ordering all the bells rung, trumpets blown, and God's word preached. In general, people avoided going anywhere near the executions, apart from the king's barons, who sat clad in plate armor atop their horses, visors shut, their gold-inlaid swords raised, as the bishops and the other prelates, arrayed in their vestments, stood gathered around the gallows, chanting. The lower clergy had their hands full granting absolution to those about to lose their lives. A curious crowd of commoners had assembled to watch the executions, to gaze upon the glory of the barons and high clergy, witness the pomp and ceremony, and hear the chanting and solemn formulae used in the blessings. Gathered there too were various hangers-on, harlots, and vagabonds, and those eyeservants of chieftains that are found everywhere and can always be paid to shout and jeer when folk are strung up, willing and eager to clap their hands for anyone in command of fire and the gallows.

By now, the peasants of Rouen had had more than enough, having for some time witnessed their houses being reduced to ashes. News flew from village to village that their ruler was leading a horde of Norse Vikings against them – Rollo risen anew. The Rouen peasants assembled in groups, moving by night but hiding by day in woods or marshes or haystacks. Their weapons were cudgels, which have always served peasants well – all manner of billets and implements that could be used as clubs, most of wood, but some clad with iron. Books on the art of war state that nothing is more perilous for a valiant warrior wielding a sword or other noble weapon than to find himself pitted against a peasant armed with a post or a tree stump, and indeed, learned men believe that Þórr's hammer Mjölnir was made of wood. The Vikings had known since days of old that even if their weapons were both longer and stronger than swords, it was folly for them to launch an assault against gangs of men fighting with clubs.

One evening, after darkness had fallen and the day's catches had been hoisted properly on the gallows as food for the ravens, accompanied by confessions, extreme unction, paternosters, *Ave Marias*, *Misereres* and other sacred hymns, and the barons had invited men to a feast, the peasants came rushing out of the woods en masse. Some of them brandished implements such as shovels and pitchforks, and others various cudgels – poles and fence posts, bludgeons and rammers. The latter began trouncing the Vikings, while the former started slashing and stabbing them.

The Vikings had had no forewarning of this assemblage, and thought that they were under attack by a countless throng. Many a doughty Norseman was knocked unconscious and pummeled into mush by base weapons of a kind never glorified in poetry. Fishing nets were dragged over some, and after they were entangled and rolled up in the nets, women came and flung their boiling, liquid weapons at them – weapons that have kept many a Viking and glorious hero warm indeed in far-flung lands, but which are never named in books or other lore chronicling major battles. Scores of valiant fighters lost their lives there, ingloriously. Many more, however, took the course of action that has always served Vikings best in a pinch: not to wait for the worst. Each fled as fast as he could from his spoils and his share in the booty, and let darkness and night conceal him. The barons of Rouen spurred their horses and rode off, too, and Duke Richard did the same. In addition, the folk that had gathered for pastime, vagrants and wenches, vanished like dew beneath the sun, while the bishops went off to the church to chant the *completorium*.

As for Þorgeir Hávarsson, there is this to tell: when the chieftains bid each man save himself, and most take to their heels and vanish, he alone stands his ground, calmly, in Icelandic fashion. After standing there for a time, he observes folk approaching him with lighted lanterns. These men holler something in the Frankish tongue at him, which he suspects is a question about who he is and why he has not fled like the others. He hollers back in the Danish tongue, which he had learned at his mother's knee:

"I am an Icelander," says he, "and I do not recall old tales ever mentioning valiant fighters fleeing from battle. It has always been the vow and war cry of us Vikings that, when we enter the fray, we shall fight to the end and never desist as long as any man of our company remains standing. Others may do as they will, but I will never be made to belie what I learned from my mother in my childhood, and from my sworn brother Þormóður Kolbrúnarskáld and other good skalds in the North."

Upon saying these things, Þorgeir Hávarsson raises his ax, meaning to have at these men, but all they do is jab at him with boles and posts and laugh and mock him. The more enraged he becomes, like a berserker, the more they ridicule him. A large crowd gathers, women and children, to enjoy the unfolding scene, making Þorgeir Hávarsson feel as if he has ended up in a bad dream. Since, however, he shows no sign of abandoning his assault, they raise their shields, press upon him, seize him, and strip him of his weapons. They chop the blades off his spear and ax, toss the shafts aside, and keep the iron. His short sword, his most treasured possession and the only thing he saved when he was shipwrecked in Ireland, they take from him. One of the peasants raises it, still in its sheath, and breaks it in two over his knee. These things being done, they let Þorgeir go, ordering him to scram like a stray dog, and snapping and wagging their fingers at him. Then they turn their lanterns away from him and are gone.

Throughout the night he wanders in unknown territory, weaponless and in a miserable plight. He strays onto marshy ground and tumbles into a ditch. He then finds himself entangled in a large, thorny thicket, and struggles for a long time to push through it. Next he comes to a dense forest, where stinging nettles grow from the sward and serpents wriggle in the grass. He has no idea what destiny awaits him, because he cannot hear the din of wings of those women who fly in swan-dress to determine heroes' fates – and now an adder coils round his foot and bites him.

He rambles through the forest for a time, but his foot starts throbbing with pain. A wave of dizziness and nausea hits him, and then regret for how the things that he learned at his mother's knee are in fact turning out. Finally, he loses all his strength, breaks out in a cold sweat, and lies down in a glade. He finds it quite ludicrous to be laid low by an adder's bite rather than a weapon, and that the wolves will have only what the snake leaves behind.

29

THAT NIGHT PASSES like any other, and day dawns over the forest in Rouen. Þorgeir Hávarsson is woken from sleep by a huge flock of sheep trampling him where he lies. A young lad with a long staff is herding the flock. Just then, the boy finds himself staring at a man who looks anything but able-bodied, rising to his feet among the sheep and cursing whomever it was that drove the stupid animals over him. The lad tells him that it is foolish beyond belief to lie down on a sheep track, and bids him who did so to clear off immediately. Since neither of them understands the other, however, nothing happens between them for some time apart from an exchange of exclamations, until they finally have nothing more to say. The lad then drives his flock to pasture. But on his way back home, he sees the champion leaning against a tree trunk, head hanging. The boy thinks he must be ill, and, taking pity on this foreigner in the name of Christ, son of Mary, lays hold of the hem of his tunic to lead him to the nearest house. Þórgeir's foot is very swollen, his entire body aches from the bite, and he is shivering violently. The lad from Rouen has to hold the Viking up. The sun now rises over the forest. After walking a little way down the forest path, they come across a low farmhouse under a tall tree, its leaves waving in the breeze over the roof. Smoke drifts slowly and lazily from the chimney in the morning calm, as dew-drenched cows chew their cuds in their nighttime pasture.

The boy helped the champion to the house and opened the door. The interior consisted of a single room, and lying in one corner was a huge sow, with piglets suckling her as she dozed. In another corner slept a woman in a shift, an infant child in her arms and a cauldron of milk simmering over a low fire next to her. Stout butter pats and hefty cheeses stood on a shelf. From the rafters hung bunches of Cabbage-Christ and Onion, as well as meaty carcasses.

The shepherd boy woke the housewife, showed her the sick man he had found, and entrusted him to her care before going his own way. The woman rubbed the sleep from her eyes, got up straightaway from her bed and greeted the visitor, bidding him come in and sit down. She removed his clothing and bathed him, rubbed a suitable ointment into his swollen foot, and then bandaged it and prepared a bed for him. She brought him cheese and butter and turnips, but he did not eat a single bite. He said:

"Here Norsemen have had little glory."

The woman did not understand what he was saying. She put

on her overclothes and went out to milk her cows, asking Þorgeir Hávarsson to look after her baby in the meantime.

As Þorgeir Hávarsson was lying there that day, seriously ill, visitors showed up at the door: neighbors of the housewife, come to speak to her. Between them they bore a dead body, which they delivered to the woman. The corpse had been brought from the gallows and had a noose round its neck – it was the woman's husband. Þorgeir thought he recognized him as one whom the king's men had accused of taking part in the peasant gatherings, and thus of being disloyal to Duke Richard. The Vikings had hung him yesterday. The Norman woman burst into woeful tears when she saw what they had delivered her. She was overwhelmed with sorrow, and women from neighboring farmsteads came to succor her, lest she be alone in bearing her grief.

Þorgeir suffered so miserably from the adder's bite that he could not move. He was feverish and delirious, forced to lie bedridden in this woman's house, along with a corpse, a suckling infant, and a sow. Around the same time that the farmer was laid in his grave, Þorgeir began to show signs of recovery. A wake was held for the farmer, attended by the wife's in-laws, relatives, and neighbors – cheese and meat, leeks and wine were served at the gathering. During the feast, it struck the sick man that the housewife did not look too kindly on him, and there were altercations between the widow and her kinsmen. Þorgeir sensed that it had to do with him – they were likely discussing the most suitable way to kill him. Some drew gleaming knives, which led to further ruckus, causing the sow to stir and start grunting. Þorgeir was fairly certain that he could expect less mercy from the spear side of this family than from the distaff side. Some of the widow's female kin came to his bed, lifted the bedcover off him and took a close look at his foot, and then at his build, commenting to each other as they did, but no misdeed was done him for the time being. Several of the widow's guests lingered late into the night, but when the last finally left, she shut and bolted the door at their backs, went to her guest's bed, sank to the floor before him, and wept bitterly.

Þorgeir Hávarsson, the warrior, was little practiced in comforting women, and he did nothing. She sensed clearly that her guest did not understand her tears, any more than the words that she attempted to speak to him – instead, he lay immobile as a block of wood, with a stunned expression, like a man who has woken from sleep to discover that a terrifying lion has crawled into his bed as he slept, ready to grip him in its claws and devour him if he blinks. Finally, the woman decided to dry her tears. Then she opened the door and walked out into the night.

The housewife was away for quite some time, while the candle burned faintly in its holder. When she returned, she brought with her a wretched, raggedy old crone. This woman could speak the Norse tongue, and the housewife sat her down at Þorgeir Hávarsson's bedside. The old woman asked first how he was feeling, and then his name and where he was from. He told her all of these things.

"You take great risks, poor devil, journeying such long distances over the churning sea, or forcing your way through briers and vipers' nests in distant lands, only to burn down the houses of poor foreigners you know nothing about, or string up farmers on their own land in southerly regions of the world, along with other distinguished men who have never before come before your eyes or harmed you in any way. What is it you want, Þorgeir?"

He said: "I am a Viking. We were hired by your masters to defend them in Normandy. Yet it is no secret that the battles we have fought have been most unlike those described in the stories and lays of old that I learned from my mother and other noble persons in Iceland."

The crone replied: "The only kind of lore I have no time for are those lays made by skalds when they shirk most what is nearest the truth. But Christ has created all men to be men of peace, even though rulers and heroes constantly want to kill us."

Þorgeir replied: "I do not know what sort of person you are, old woman, and will thus never admit that your Christ is wiser

than my mother Þórelfur or my sworn brother Þormóður Kolbrúnarskáld, and I hope that we sworn brothers will never be
beguiled into making peace with others."

She said: "I am an old woman from Rouen and you a young
lad from the North – but it may be time that I tell you a tale,
you simpleton. You are hardly anything new to us in Normandy.
You Norsemen have been visiting our coasts for ages, to destroy
our lives and plunder our food, and even when the countryfolk
here gathered men to oppose you and sent you packing, you always showed up again after your chieftains assembled another
handful of robbers to harry us. When it seemed hopeless that we
would ever be free of the plague of your raids, our foremothers
took things into their own hands. Instead of letting Norsemen
continue to cut down the common folk here for ages on end,
many a fine woman in this country upped and pulled one of
those foul miscreants into her bed and bore him Frankish sons.
Unspoiled farmers' daughters and noble damsels joined in this
action, along with prostitutes and tramps, as well as widows
of men the Norsemen had killed. Even King Charles' daughter, Poppa, bedded the pirate and outlaw from Norway named
Rollo, who was so stupid and fainthearted that he neither could
nor dared to ride a horse. She turned him into a man, and made
his sons and daughters Frankish."

Þorgeir said: "Why then, if the Rouen peasants are men and
Frankish, and have had enough of Richard their king, do they

not form an army against us in warrior fashion, and meet us in battle with Frankish swords, stoutness of heart, and savagery, and kill him? Such a thing would be more valorous than sneaking up on people by night and threatening them with fence posts or entangling them in fishing nets or scalding them with broth and piss."

"Trolls take your valor and your warrior fashion," said the old woman. "And as for your murderous deeds, they are worthy of praise by none but the fools who sniff along after you, whom you call your skalds. Now, Þorgeir Hávarsson, you have this choice: you may stay here and marry my granddaughter, the mistress of this house, since you Vikings have hanged her husband. She saved your life tonight, when her kinsmen and brothers-in-law were determined to kill you. You owe this woman your life many times over."

Þorgeir Hávarsson thought things over for a little while, before saying: "To little avail have good skalds sung of the glory of kings and immortalized the fame of high-minded warriors, if I am to sit here and grow soft, squandering my manhood in love games. My sworn brother, Þormóður the skald, and I had other things in mind the day we parted at the shoal. Þormóður will hardly find much in me worthy of his verses when he hears that I lived out my life and lay down to die as a peasant in Rouen, among swine and babies, with Cabbage-Christ and Onion – even if my wife was beautiful and worthy. He will find little cause to leave his home and ladylove and set out to avenge me. The world must have grown rather flat if heroes are not to be found anymore but in women's arms."

The ragged old crone said: "You have chosen as I expected you would, and it is just as well. Off with you, then, to perform deeds befitting a warrior: setting fire to people's houses and killing everything that draws breath for your sea-kings or sovereigns – all in order to rule the world."

At these words, Þorgeir, though not fully recovered, rose from his bed, pulled on his shoes and threw on his tunic.

The dauntless hero and the Norman woman exchanged few words in parting. The housewife flung a broom at him as he limped out the door, while the old woman remarked that there went a leper who would assuredly suffer an inglorious death someday, detested by all and succorless.

30

A KING NAMED Sweyn, the son of Harald Bluetooth, ruled over Denmark. In their books, the Danes call him Twobeard, and the Icelanders Forkbeard. In English books he has the nickname Father-Slayer, after having adorned himself with far more glory than any other king by fighting against his father and killing him. In his childhood, Sweyn had been received into Christianity by the German emperor, but had renounced his faith and now desired to kill all Christians, clergymen in particular.

King Sweyn heard report of England as a place where intrepid kings might win great renown, so he assembled an imposing fleet in Denmark and sailed with it to England in order to harrow the land.

The Danes arrived in England's east, and ordered a part of their troops ashore and the rest to remain aboard ship. Sweyn Bluetoothsson was quite a different king from Thorkell Strutharaldsson. The latter was a sea-king whose experience was solely aboard ships, making him more of a marauder than a conqueror. He gave little thought to subjugating countries, even when given the opportunity, which is why he plundered King Æthelred's

England of all its valuables rather than occupy it. Sweyn, for his part, was more bent on conquering countries than plundering them, and his men diligently subdued towns and shires. Wherever they came, they began immediately to reorganize things to their liking, and beheaded or mutilated the leading aldermen and clerics, while sparing people's property. Many Englishmen came to parley with King Sweyn and pledge him their allegiance, stating that they preferred their king to be a foreign, heathen patricide and sworn enemy of Christians than a native, devout Christian king who carved bones in peacetime and vomited in wartime, and never commanded his troops against anyone but his own subjects.

As for King Æthelred, he was as generous as ever to his foreign enemies, and just as King Thorkell had obtained from him all the struck silver that he demanded, along with other treasures, so too did the newly arrived king receive almost everything that he desired. King Æthelred's first reaction was to vomit mightily, as usual, and to remain beneath his bedsheets as Sweyn subdued town after town. When Æthelred was finally able to speak again, he sent to King Sweyn to inquire of his demands, and to inform him that all he asked would be his. Sweyn, however, sent back word that he demanded the kingdom of England.

King Æthelred had yielded all of his wealth to King Thorkell, and now he handed over his realm to King Sweyn, leaving him with nothing but Queen Emma and seven birds carved from bone. Some compassionate fishermen then offered him their boat and transported him and his queen to Rouen, where he met his brother-in-law, Duke Richard, and supplicated for his aid.

The Vikings had stopped their attacks for the time being and, as defenders of Duke Richard's realm, were entertaining themselves in Rouen, some in the castles and others on their ships. As was usual when Vikings hired out their services to kings, the townsfolk met their every demand. They spent many an evening drinking in taverns and recounting to each other tales of their valiant deeds and their exploits in battles throughout the world, as well as the perils they had faced at sea, not to mention the distinctions bestowed on them by kings and high-born maidens. In addition to this, they attended the churches on the numerous holidays and festivals observed by the clergy. Frankish books state that every harlot in the town flocked there to find customers, particularly on high holy days. The commoners also took great pleasure in viewing the gloriously arrayed countesses or bishops' mistresses, as well as praiseworthy abbesses strutting in scarlet cloaks bordered with lace down to their hems, and wearing wimples adorned with gemstones.

Duke Richard now met with the Vikings, to request, on behalf of his brother-in-law Æthelred, that they sail to England and help drive King Sweyn Bluetoothsson out of the country, promising them rich rewards if they managed to subjugate the

English to Æthelred's rule once more. At this entreaty, some of the Vikings' brows sunk down to their noses, and they protested that the brothels in Rouen were far more elegant than those in England, the wine sweeter, the church festivals more frequent and lively, the chanting more admirable. The climate was so good in Rouen that grass grew in midwinter and cows continued to give summer milk. Yet others in the company were all for great ventures, rather than living for womanish entertainments or toiling away at haymaking – they declared that the Vikings had taken a turn for the worse if they denied themselves glory and chose instead to dally over trollops, gape at monks croaking evensong, or admire livestock grazing. All agreed, however, that there was little hope of further glory in playing the henchmen of such a pitiful king as Æthelred. It was to be regretted, they said, that Thorkell the Tall had not seized the opportunity to make himself king of England. They were convinced that Sweyn Forkbeard must be a hard-nosed king if he had not even shirked from killing his father.

Time passed as they pondered whether to sail to England, until news came to Rouen that some welcomed joyfully: King Sweyn Forkbeard was dead, the victim of illness. The Danes had sailed away, and England was now without a king. At this news, the Vikings did not hesitate to pledge their support to King Æthelred, so they rigged their ships and prepared to sail to England.

As previously recounted, on the day that the townsfolk were mutilated in Canterbury and the venerable Ælfheah was pelted to death, a young lad stood at the archbishop's side, his gaze fixed on Heaven, his face fair and his eyes beautiful. The chief torturer, Olaf Haraldsson the Stout, stepped forward and proclaimed this boy too maidenly to die, and asked that his life be spared. Having struck Ælfheah dead, the Vikings went up to behold this youth who had stood beside the holy man and chanted as he was martyred. They all found the boy very comely, and various among them said that they would be happy to have him as a wife. When King Thorkell heard these gibes, he declared that no man was to dare humiliate the lad. "He shall serve me, and I will be his guardian," said Thorkell. King Thorkell kept the lad constantly at his side, and lodged him in his own chamber. The Vikings could not pronounce the boy's Latin name, which he had received in holy baptism, and instead called him Grímkell. Thorkell treated him as a great confidant, and consulted him on a variety of things.

After Thorkell became a Christian, he grew even fonder of his foster son Grímkell, and asked him about many things he had previously thought insignificant, particularly concerning the Christian church – who its rightful rulers were, and what weapons they had. It seemed to the Viking that the bishop of Rome was the one in charge, and then the lesser bishops, and that they used magic and Latin spells and other sorcery, against which Óðinn and the old Norse gods had no defense, including the power to excommunicate their foes and put kings on thrones, and Christ the heavenly smith had shared this power with his bishops when he dwelt in this world, before he was martyred. The Viking made a point of learning about Christ and his stewards, and determining which things said about him were true, and which were untrue. Until the hour that the Vikings became Christians, all they had ever heard was that those deeds were right and those words true that could be backed with weapons or bribes, and that any other justification for words or deeds was quite useless. Yet now there was this new idea derived from the example of the saints, that some deeds were right and others wrong, not by the nature of things, but according to divine wisdom. King Þórkell found it quite troublesome that the bishops should be the only ones capable of interpreting the will of Christ in matters of greatest interest to a warlord, such as how battle was to be conducted against Christian men, what justified burning innocents and other wretches alive, and when Christ deems it right and proper to set fire to churches.

For this reason, King Thorkell declared his intent to appoint a bishop as his right-hand man in weighty matters, to deliver verdicts on Christ's precepts for murder, torture, and the desecration of churches, as well as for the slaughter of the poor and the weak. Archbishop Robert, however, was less than enthusiastic about the need to ordain a bishop for King Thorkell, saying that it was Christ's will that bishops have their seats on land and sing in cathedrals, and not be roving the seas.

In the town were some wandering Armenians, who claimed to be clerics and lawful successors of the apostles, and that they had been driven from their homeland by the Seljuks, a people who followed the prophet Mohammed. Armenians profess neither Byzantine Christianity nor Roman, but Gregorian. The Vikings came across an Armenian bishop in a tavern in the town, and expressed their desire to pay him to ordain the lad Grímkell as bishop – but the itinerant was reluctant. First the Vikings offered him ale and wine, and then silver. It was only after they showed him burnished gold, which the archbishop verified to be well struck, that he sent for his fellows, some other traveling clerics who were in town. For the longest time, these clerics refused the task, calling it a scandalous abomination for Christ to reveal his mysteries to pirates and thieves from the northern end of the world. The more the bishops drank at the Norsemen's expense, hearing the constant jingling of the precious Frankish gold in their ears as they downed their ale, the warmer they grew toward the matter, until finally – being nearly penniless – they gave in.

Every church in town was closed to heretics, and there was a ban on providing them places for any of their sacred rites. Thus, Grímkell was ordained bishop in a common marketplace, in the midst of horses, Cabbage-Christ, and Onion, as well as the slaughtered hogs and other victuals the peasants had brought to market. The blessing was brief and the chanting strained, and the Vikings stood guard over the ceremony, shooing away boys and dogs that the clergy stirred up against them. When their work was done, the wandering clerics left with their gold, but Thorkell sent trustworthy men to testify at the council of clerics, named the *capitulum*, that the ordination had been performed and that Grímkell had received his ring and crosier.

Canon law stipulates that any man who accepts an office or is ordained by a wandering bishop is to be excommunicated, yet that neither God nor men nor the Lord Pope himself can repudiate a man's ordination or sacred ministry if he is a true successor of the apostles – and neither the *capitulum* nor suffragan bishops were able to deprive Grímkell of his bishopric.

31

WHEN THORKELL the Tall and his troops landed in England, they encountered few Danish defenders, and fought only minor skirmishes. Yet Englishmen came from inland to meet Thorkell: clerics and laymen, rich and poor, weeping profusely with joy at King Æthelred's return, and entreating him to remount the throne. No king, they declared, was more beloved to them than he. Nature itself, they cried, had bestowed him on them by the will of Christ – particularly if he would govern them more circumspectly than he had done until then.

As written earlier in this book, Æthelred was such a peaceable king that he made war on none but his own subjects, and then only if he found himself forced to strengthen their Christian devotion or collect unpaid taxes, especially after having surrendered all his own wealth. In truth, it was said, warfare was so abhorrent to him that he began vomiting at the mere mention of other kings, and took to his bed if they were reported to be near. His delight was to remain in his castle – not to hurl rocks down on his enemies, but to watch his spouse Emma promenade through its halls, while he carved birds of bone or created silver filigree for her. He firmly believed that Queen Emma was the fairest woman in all Christendom or beyond. He would give all he owned, his estates and castles, as well as the possessions of every Englishman, their houses and farms, along with the entire kingdom of Britain, only to be able to live in peace with this woman, for whom his heart practically burst with affection. For this reason, King Æthelred has been called one of the most inept kings ever to occupy the throne of England.

Æthelred, however, had not long returned to his peaceful, leisurely life in his castles, leaving the country's defense to Thorkell and his men, before another fleet came sailing from the east, comprising more ships than had ever been seen off England's shores. The troops aboard this flotilla, including numerous great and dauntless champions, made war by sea and land against any force that opposed them. For a very long time, Thorkell and his warriors had followed a policy that was more profitable to them than battle: never to put their lives at risk if they encountered a doughty army. When they asked who was now preparing to attack King Æthelred's forces, they were told that it was King Cnut Sweynsson from Denmark, whom the Danes had chosen to be king of England, to take control of the realm that his father Sweyn Bluetoothsson had seized in that country. Each and every man who did not pledge perfect allegiance to Cnut from the start would lose nothing less than his property and his life.

Although Thorkell the Tall had never occupied another

territory, he was such a mighty naval commander that he could demand as much tribute as any one of his fellow Danish kings wherever he landed. He obeyed no man's command in matters he was convinced were his own to decide. Now it seemed that England was being threatened by someone no less formidable at sea than Thorkell Strutharaldsson. While pointless skirmishes between Vikings and Danes were taking place off England's coast or on its headlands, the leaders of the Vikings held long deliberations as to whether they should make a determined attempt to defend England against King Cnut, and what it might cost them.

While this is going on, and no final decision has yet been made by the chieftains nor any order has been issued by King Thorkell, it happens late one night that one of Thorkell the Tall's subordinates, so low-ranking that his name is not given in the books written about these events by learned Englishmen, orders some of his best men, forecastlemen all, to launch a boat under cover of night and row out to the Danish fleet anchored opposite. As they approach Cnut's fleet, the Danish watchmen hear the clanking of the oars and order them to halt, and the man in charge of the rowers replies:

"We are unarmed."

The watchmen ask who they are.

The other answers: "I am Olaf Haraldsson of Norway, here to entreat peace of King Cnut."

The watchmen aboard the king's ships shine their lanterns on the boat to get a look at the men, and notice that their leader is wearing several gold rings, three cloaks, two silver belts, and tall boots from France, inlaid with gold. When the watchmen see these tokens, and that there are no weapons aboard, they direct the boat's crew to King Cnut's fortification a short distance up on the headland.

At this point in our story, King Cnut Sweynsson was eighteen years old. He and Olaf Haraldsson were much the same age – but were quite different in character.

Olaf the Stout had grown up aboard ships, with the sights and smells of salt and tar, rotten seaweed and vomit, lice and decay, rashes and scabs, scurvy and itching, and the sweaty stink of sailors long unwashed. He had no education, apart from the tall tales and hashed and hackneyed poems that sailors swapped to stave off tedium and steel themselves – all of them about battles and sea perils, deeds of derring-do and feats of renown, as well as obscene anecdotes on the shenanigans of ogresses in the North, or vulgar verses about the gods.

King Cnut Sweynsson was reared in the residences of kings and bishops, in halls or castles. In his youth, he learned the arts fit for men of high estate: skill in arms and knightliness, and how to wear one's weapons or clothing in the manner of noblemen, as gracefully as the barons who served the emperor. From childhood, he had served the bishops sent to the Danes from Bremen, and they never let him out of their pincer-grasp even when his father, Sweyn, turned apostate. Clerics had taught Cnut how to read from Latin books and chant antiphons in the choir. He learned, too, how to pray at the altar with tears and sighs, both *genuflectens* and *prostratus*. Cnut was pale and pop-eyed, as is common among his lineage, and he had thick yellow hair. He was as intemperate in his merrymaking as he was lacrimose at the altar. He wore a light blue kirtle and had laid aside his red mantle. Richly embroidered shoes adorned his feet, and from his belt hung a curved Saracen sword in a golden sheath, exquisitely engraved and ornamented with the fairest of gemstones. Long goatskin gloves bedecked his hands and arms. He was sitting drinking with his fellows and a few singing-girls when into his hall waddled Olaf the Stout, a thick-necked potbelly despite his young age, flat-footed and knock-kneed. The girls burst out giggling at this visitor, from whom dangled rings, brooches, pins, and many other baubles, besides numerous crumpled cloaks, some too long, others rather tight. The king slammed his tankard down on the table and asked what scullery boy this was.

The newcomer said: "I lead a band of Vikings in the fleet of King Thorkell Strutharaldsson the Tall, and my name is Olaf, son of Harald Grenske of Vestfold in Norway. My great-grandfather was Harald Tanglehair, who subdued all of Norway. I wish to speak to you, King, in private."

King Cnut sent the others out. He spread his mantle over his shoulders and bade the visitor sit at the table and drink. "Before you speak to us, Olaf," says Cnut, "will you perhaps lift up one or two of those hoods that you have pulled over your hair, one on top of the other?"

Olaf the Stout turns bright red and says that he was raised aboard ships, and that it is therefore due more to his ignorance of the ways of courtesy than disrespect that he lets his hoods hang down while speaking with a man of such high estate as King Cnut. And now, having adjusted his hoods, he turns to the matter at hand and says:

"We, the Vikings of Thorkell the Tall, have sailed here in one hundred and forty-two ships, and have made our pledge to King Æthelred to defend this land against you. Though we Vikings always feel it an honor to battle doughty warriors, such as those in the army gathered here by you, King, I can tell you, in short, that I am weary of winning countries for other kings. I am eager to yield the ships under my command to you, and to become your man, if, in return, you concede us something that we should consider an honor to receive from you."

King Cnut asks: "What is it you would have in exchange, comrade?"

"This I offer you," says Olaf. "As I am considered to have a smooth tongue, I shall use it to persuade the men in Thorkell's fleet, first discreetly, and then openly, of this my proposal: it is my desire that we abandon Æthelred and ally ourselves with you. I know there are many tried-and-true men in our band who would willingly become good friends of yours, if you were to grant them shires or towns for their bread-and-butter, although some would content themselves with silver or gold. We would prefer to win your favor with peace rather than war."

Cnut asks what Thorkell Strutharaldsson's position is in this matter, and whether he is willing to fight the Danish army in the hope of taking over Æthelred's power and kingdom. "Or do you present yourself to me, Olaf, as a traitor to both of your overlords, Thorkell and Æthelred?"

"Thorkell," says Olaf, "is quite intent upon battling you Danes. Should this happen, every single individual in England who believes his life worth fighting for will ally himself to us: countryfolk and townsfolk, young and old, women and men. I have personally witnessed that it is by no means child's play for a royal army, whether foreign or native, to do battle with the common folk in England when they choose to defend themselves. If it comes to such a battle, many a valiant warrior will be laid low by ignoble weapons."

"What reward do you ask, Olaf, for preventing Thorkell's fleet from opposing us?" asks King Cnut.

"I am offering to make Thorkell's entire fleet yours, and we shall pledge to defend you in England. I wager my life on its success. If this plan of ours works, everyone will be contented.

For my part, I demand a reward of fifty light ships, to allow me to sail to Norway and take possession of my inheritance, and there become king."

King Cnut springs from his seat and gives Olaf Haraldsson's ale tankard such a whack with his own that it skids off the table onto the stone floor and breaks. He grips his sword by the hilt and says:

"What a foul monstrosity, when unmanly, beggarly sons of bumpkins from Norway presume to be born to reign. I find it hard to see whether your childish stupidity springs from recklessness, or your recklessness from stupidity, in bringing such business to me. Do you honestly consider me, Cnut Sweynsson, to be so degenerate as to make a present of the kingdom of Norway to a vagabond boy who is no kin of mine? The kingdom that my father, by his prowess, won from King Olaf Tryggvason – who, in terror of my father, leapt from his ship? What a great child you are, Olaf, to imagine that you can turn your fear of me into profit, and in reward for your cowardice, come off with fifty ships and the realm of Norway to boot."

At this response, Olaf's face loses whatever color it has, and he replies: "I do not propose these things to provoke your hostility, King, but rather, I stand before you because I wish sincerely to become your honorable friend. Nor have I spoken any word that might be taken as treacherous to you. Sire, I ask that you grant me the favor of looking magnanimously upon this errand of mine to you. Our fortunes may be dissimilar, but I beseech you never to believe that I tremble before any man..." – yet as he says this, Olaf Haraldsson is quivering like a leaf in the wind – "...and let us cease this talk, if you so please, and do not blame me for it – and let us not carry it beyond these walls."

Olaf Haraldsson then bids King Cnut farewell, though the king's hand remains resting on his sword-hilt. When this visitor is gone, he calls to his fellows to return and drink, along with the singing-girls.

Olaf Haraldsson's tankard lies broken on the stone floor.

32

THE FORECASTLEMEN who had accompanied Olaf
Haraldsson to meet Cnut Sweynsson return to their beds, but
Olaf himself cannot sleep. He stands long by the bulwarks of his
ship, watching little waves ripple and break against a land breeze
at flood tide beneath the Lodestar. After lingering there for a
time, lost in thought, he notices men in a little ferryboat rowing toward his ship. One of them hails the watchman and asks
to speak to Olaf Haraldsson. As this newcomer greets Olaf, he
tosses back the hood from his head and raises his eyes to heaven
and his face to the moon. It is Bishop Grímkell. He says:

"A visitor sits in council with my foster-father Thorkell, and
the topic is you."

Olaf asks who the visitor is.

Bishop Grímkell replies: "An envoy of King Cnut Sweynsson."

Olaf asks what message this envoy is delivering to Thorkell.

"The envoy has come with the news," says the bishop, "that
you have resolved to conspire against and betray my foster-father Thorkell – your scheme being to appropriate enough ships

to sail back to Norway, and then seize the realm from Cnut and murder his jarls."

Olaf asks whether Thorkell has made known any plans of his own.

Grímkell says: "The last I heard, my foster-father King Thorkell had resolved that you – 'that little whelp,' as he said – should be hung no later than daybreak, though even sooner would be better."

At these tidings, Olaf Haraldsson sits speechless and still. Bishop Grímkell continues:

"It occurred to me," says he, "that it was you, Olaf, who spared me when you Vikings clipped the ears and noses off Christ's friends, and pelted the body of God's blessed friend Ælfheah with joints and horns."

As Bishop Grímkell stands there gazing toward heaven, per habit, with the moon shining on his face, Olaf the Stout grasps his hand and says:

"Tell your friend Christ, Grímkell, that now I entreat his aid alone. I will follow wherever he leads, and give myself entirely to his power, for we are in sore need."

Grímkell gazes skyward, whispering. "One day," says he, "I witnessed you inspecting your troops – among whom was an Icelander, deemed the most idiotic man in the fleet. He addressed you as King. I do not know what you yourself make of this matter, but I know that when Christ wishes to make prophecies, he chooses to speak through the mouths of fools rather than philosophers."

"How am I, a sea-tossed farmboy from Vestfold – who has, however, a quantity of silver, though no other ships apart from these two flimsy old tubs, crewed by a few ragged vagrants that have flocked to me in their despair, seventy men in all – how am I to wrest Norway from the hands of so mighty a king as Cnut?"

In a quiet voice, Bishop Grímkell says: "When King Christ wishes to display his omnipotence, he always avails himself of a man frailer and paltrier than others, such as when he chose David, a little boy, to strike down the giant Goliath. Christ will assuredly make you king over Norway if you swear him your allegiance."

Olaf asks what Christ will have him do now.

Grímkell replies, saying: "I am called the laughingstock of clerics and the most contemptible of bishops that anyone has ever known, possessing no benefice or bishopric apart from Thorkell the Tall's bed and table. I have no spiritual father and am the apostolic successor to none but a drunken fool from Armenia who anointed me with water and chrism behind horse rumps at a market in Rouen. Yet none can repudiate my having been made, by this divine and indelible ordination, the equal of the aldermen who rule Christendom and the clergy ranking closest to the Pope, through the blessing of Christ and gift of the Holy Spirit. As I am least of the brothers bearing the name

– 264 –

of bishop, Christ wishes, through prophecies and miracles, to make me the equal of those glorious Christian saints whose names will live as long as the world lasts. Now that we are both in desperate straits, Olaf, you must repent cutting off the noses and ears of holy men in England and pelting an old man with knucklebones – he who, in the eyes of Mary and Sunniva and Belinda and other beloved kinswomen of God, is regarded as one of the doughtiest of men since the beheading of John the Baptist, on which account he is now their invited guest in Heaven. This very hour, you must put to sea and sail to Norway to christen the rabble inhabiting that land – and I will act as your bishop, by the will of Christ, and thus shall we ransom ourselves from the eternal flames of Hell."

33

JARL HAAKON ERICSSON ruled Norway as a vassal of the Danish king, Cnut Sweynsson, to whom he was nephew. Books state that he was one of the handsomest men in the North. He was much the same age as Olaf Haraldsson, who was now sailing to Norway. Neither ambition nor tyranny had anything to do with Haakon's rise to power – rather, it was as if he were born for high office.

Norway is a desolate and sparsely populated land. Since time immemorial, petty kings had ruled small kingdoms scattered throughout it, and they still did so in name. Some of these kings were said to be of noble blood, while others had become vassals of the marauder from Estonia, Olaf Tryggvason, who had ravaged the land with fire for several summers and declared himself its monarch. Most of the kings had retained their titles and lands under the jarls that were appointed by the Danish kings to collect tribute from Norway after the Estonian reaver leapt into the sea. A pact made with these kinglets stipulated that they would retain their titles and estates only if they swore fealty to the Danish king. The petty kings were satisfied, and the commonfolk even more – for, as the old saying goes, "the farther away the king, the better off the people," when the king is unable to unleash his noxious wraiths upon them: tax-extortion and confiscation of property, levying and quartering of troops, manslaughter and lechery. Every last resident of the land praised his own great fortune when King Cnut the Dane, who laid claim to the kingdom of Norway, abandoned the North entirely and betook himself to the British Isles, to vex the inhabitants there with his tyranny.

Haakon Ericsson, having few ties to the Norsemen and ruling the land for an even more distant overlord, as well as lacking the pretentiousness of native noblemen, enjoyed the high regard of the populace. Under him, everyone was free to do as he pleased in most things, and freedom of this sort naturally channeled the people's conduct toward peaceability. Moreover, Haakon was lenient in his tax collection and paid only rare visits to the freemen – sparing them the burden of preparing him feasts – and never with a large retinue. Instead, he spent most of his time quietly in Viken, diverting himself with sports, the arts, or hunting, or chanting from hymnbooks with the clerics visiting on official business from the archiepiscopal see of Bremen – for in Viken, Christianity had long been fully and perfectly established. Haakon was so well-loved by the people of Norway that he had need for neither an army nor a naval fleet.

Jarl Haakon Ericsson of Norway was born to Christian parents and baptized as an infant, sparing him the distress suffered by some of those who accept the faith as adults, when they are overwhelmed by guilt for their former transgressions against the true God, and plague others so zealously with their pious turmoil that it would have been better if they had never repented. Nor was Haakon's popularity diminished in any way among the peasants when he let each man believe in whatever god he wished, or in none at all, if he so preferred. Ever since the passing of Olaf Tryggvason, the men of Norway had not had their eyes gouged or their tongues torn out, nor had they been mutilated in any other way for their faith or had their houses burned down for the sake of their gods. Haakon was no less a friend to the heathens than the Christians, but all his friends desired to be Christian for love of this young man. Many noblemen had greater expectation of prosperity from Christ than from other gods, and ordered churches built for him or made donations of land and property, while German clerics from the archbishopric of Bremen journeyed all the way north to Rogaland to sponsor converts and sing Masses, taking back with them young men from the farms who were eager to study the clerical arts in the South.

Olaf Haraldsson thus made his way home to a prosperous, peaceful land, where folk were no less Christian than most of the populace of Europe at the time, not counting the residents of episcopal sees, monasteries, imperial cities, or the courts of sovereigns.

Books narrate that Olaf the Stout landed in the central part of Norway. Upon landing, he immediately set out for Ringerike to visit his stepfather Sigurd Syr Halfdanarson, accompanied by Bishop Grímkell, and leaving behind a contingent of nearly seventy men to guard his two ships.

Sigurd Halfdanarson was a fine husbandman and extremely hard worker. He owned one of the largest herds of cattle in Norway and was the greatest cultivator of his lands, which included many vast, profitable estates in numerous districts, and every petty king in Oppland and Gudbrandsdalen was indebted to him in some way or other. Sigurd Syr not only collected rents on tenancies, he also outfitted trading ships, and his merchants brought him home silver and valuable objects and useful wares from foreign lands. He had become Olaf Haraldsson's stepfather by his marriage to Olaf's mother Åsta Gudbrandsdatter, when Olaf was a young lad.

Olaf the Stout's father, Harald Grenske, had been burnt alive as a consequence of wooing a woman. He was one of those Norse-speaking vagrants – men of uncertain pedigree – who flocked to Norway from distant lands with pretensions to its throne. All such men harped on the same claim: that they were descendants of Harald Tanglehair. A bully by this name had indeed surfaced in Norway six generations earlier, or a good hundred-and-fifty years ago. This thug had carried on murdering peasants and burning settlements in Norway for seventy consecutive years, and extorted wealth and property from most of the chieftains who did not flee westward across the sea or shift their households to remote skerries. He declared himself king following what was the prevailing custom in the North according to some scholars: namely, that the scoundrel who had the greatest stamina and best success in decimating the populace in a particular place should have that name. These agitators considered their agnate kinship to Tanglehair sufficient proof of their birthright to rule whatever little strip of Norway they could sequester, and they counted the entire country as their legitimate property as long as they could wrap their claws around it. Harald Grenske was one of these pretenders to the throne of Norway, though he diplayed little propensity for success in most respects. Olaf's mother, Åsta, married the gentleman Sigurd Syr Halfdanarson for his wealth, and it was considered extravagant of Sigurd when he granted the boy an inheritance and built him two small ships, calling them his tooth-fee.

Sigurd Halfdanarson never claimed his dues by force, but dealt with every matter in a wily, cunning way. He was considered peaceable and conciliatory, but not high-minded. His family had deep roots throughout the country, and he remained on good terms with leading farmers in Gudbrandsdalen and Oppland, to whom he was tied by kinship. He felt it no unfair advantage on their part if their tenants allowed the local assembly to bestow the title of king on them, according to ancient custom, or for them to bestow the title on themselves if others did not want to, least of all if they conscientiously paid their rents on lands that they leased from him.

Sigurd Syr had little inclination for novelties in religion and custom. He disliked Christianity, yet made no objection to his tenants or debtors practicing it. He worshipped the phallus of a stallion of his that he considered the best of all horses, the most divine, and had dedicated to the god Freyr. In honour of this horse's phallus he had raised a tall standing stone on a slope of his homefield. He erected a wooden fence around the stone, offered sacrifices spring and fall to the phallus, and drank its health at Yule banquets. It is said that when Bishop Grímkell beheld this stone, he was stricken with profound grief on Christ's behalf at such an abomination, and wept loudly.

When the twenty-year-old son of Sigurd Syr's wife, Åsta, returned to her after eight years abroad on Viking expeditions, she had their home cleaned thoroughly and hung with tapestries, juniper burned and hogs slaughtered, making ready to receive him in the most magnificent manner possible. Upon his arrival, she bade King Olaf Haraldsson welcome and kissed his hand and foot, before leading him to the high-seat and sitting at his right hand, directing Bishop Grímkell to his seat at her son's left. Squire Sigurd was taken somewhat aback when he was shown to an inferior seat in his own hall, and he laughed. After sitting at table for a time, mother and son declared their aim: that Olaf Haraldsson should be king of all Norway. At this, Squire Sigurd laughed even louder.

When Olaf saw that his stepfather took this as a joke, he laid his knife on his plate, his face pale, and said: "You would do better to restrain your mockery of the matter now raised, Squire Sigurd. It is my firm intent to become king of Norway, and to drum up the necessary forces to do so, even though they may seem meager to others at the moment."

Sigurd Syr stopped laughing. Instead, he asked how a young vagabond, barely out of puberty, lacking the support of kin, and with only two flimsy little ships, could come up with such an idea.

Olaf replied: "The wealth of my kin may have been dispersed, but I am of no shabby extraction – my cousin was King Olaf Tryggvason and my great-grandfather Harald Tanglehair, and they both subdued all of Norway. This inheritance is my birthright as much as it is any other of my kindred's. Though I have but few ships, and no troops apart from a handful of foreign ragamuffins, I have made a pact with and sworn an alliance to the king to whom the realm of Norway is but a leaf in a bird's beak – and that is Christ. For him, I have pledged to free the souls of men in Norway from everlasting fire, and he in return will grant me his spells and miracles and other marvels. As a token of this pact of ours, he has sent his son Bishop Grímkell, who was anointed and inspired by the Holy Spirit in Rouen to guide my hand in raising anew in this land the banner of Almighty God and of my kinsman Olaf Tryggvason."

Sigurd said: "Who the true sons of Harald Tanglehair are has never been ascertained. In fact, he begat children with maidservants and vagrant women from one end of Norway to the other for seventy years, since noblewomen had little desire to take such a louse-ridden man to their beds. Every single dimwit who has since commenced upon dastardly deeds in Norway calls himself Harald's direct or distant heir, and everyone always laughs, as I laughed just now, when these pretenders have nothing to back their claims of patrilineage. Yet it cannot be denied that some people who wish to solve their own problems and others' with fire and warfare may be descended from Harald Tanglehair, including Olaf Tryggvason and other landlopers such as your father, Harald Grenske, who was burned alive while wooing. However, as vague as the lineage is of those men who claim to be related to Harald Tanglehair, I assure you that the lineage of White Christ is even vaguer. You will therefore need to use plainer words in order for me to understand what support and arms you may expect from him."

Olaf rose to his feet and delivered the following speech:

"Christ has promised me such support," said he, "as we have never had from the gods to whom we sacrificed of old. He has taught us how pressing it is for all men to redeem their souls from fire and the serpent. Not a single king that makes war in Christ's name will ever end up as unfortunate as we Vikings were when we fought without the gift of the Holy Spirit and for no godly cause, and when wrinkled old townswomen doused us with piss. Christ will levy me the troops that we require for each battle, and the pope and the emperors in Rome and Constantinople will ally themselves with me, as will Robert Capet, along with the host of bishops and archbishops that Christ has anointed, and myriad saints and arch-saints, angels and archangels, and the rest of the residents of Heaven accustomed to supporting every king who marches to battle for Christ, reinforced by war wagons and Greek fire. And I assure you that every king who saves the souls of the rabble will be raised to everlasting glory in the Kingdom of Heaven, even though he himself may fall. Now the people of Norway have a choice: either to be redeemed from fire and the serpent, or to die."

Following her son's declaration, Queen Åsta Gudbrandsdatter rose from her seat – her neck and cheeks flushed. She stepped forward and said:

"I have always known you, Squire Sigurd, to be a peaceable man, yet I never thought that you were a poltroon. No man could ever level such a charge at King Harald Grenske, even when he returned penniless from his Viking expeditions and consigned himself to death by fire. In short, I would choose to be married to a beggarly man who risks his own life to acquire the title of king and glory, even if he were burned alive, rather than a swine monger who considers heroism and royal propensities laughing matters, loads his cellars with butter and lines the bottoms of his coffers with silver, and, in his impotence, makes offerings to Freyr's rod. Now the moment has come when I give you a choice, Sigurd: either aid my son with your wealth, your strong ties of kinship, and your good repute in his quest for the throne of Norway, or you shall never join me in my bed."

Squire Sigurd smiled, and said: "We must not let my churlish disposition prevent us, Mistress, from drinking welcome toasts to your son, as is befitting. I must be growing old, Olaf, for I find myself lacking the heart to contradict your mother, Queen Åsta, even more so now that she has gained such powerful backing. It appears quite clear to me that the god you named will stretch his hand far to provide you with the backing you need, though such a god seems rather dull to me in comparison with our friend King Freyr, who has a bigger penis than the other gods."

34

KILLING HAAKON, Cnut's jarl, seemed unpropitious to Olaf, yet he was more anxious about incurring the wrath of the Norwegian populace by slaying such a tolerant and peaceable ruler for no good reason, knowing too that such a deed would be condemned by Christian lords abroad, and by none more than the archiepiscopal see of Bremen, which then administered canon law in the North. He did, however, send spies out to keep track of the jarl's movements, and around the same time that Squire Sigurd Syr commenced secret negotiations with estate holders and other leading men in Gudbrandsdalen and Oppland to solicit their support for the new claimant to the throne, Olaf learned that Haakon had just left Sogn, sailing south to his winter residence with only one ship. Olaf and his men launched their two ships and sailed north, hoping to catch Jarl Haakon. When they learned that the jarl's ship had anchored for the night in a certain sound, they set an ambush for him, navigating between skerries in the darkness until the jarl's men were suddenly surprised to find two ships lying alongside their own, and fighting men leaping aboard.

That night, Olaf Haraldsson took Jarl Haakon captive. When the jarl asked what brigand had seized him, Olaf told him his name and his lineage, as well as his plan to take over the kingdom of Norway. He would give Haakon a choice, he said: leave Norway immediately, after swearing an oath that he would make no attempt to defend the land against him, or else be beheaded that very night. The jarl was inexperienced and rather feeble of character. He was hardly prone to great exploits, and would not battle against Olaf the Stout. The jarl swore the oath demanded by Olaf and was granted permission to leave. At dawn the next day, the jarl and his men put to sea.

As regards Cnut Sweynsson, he had taken from King Æthelred the one thing that was left him – his wife, Queen Emma. First, Thorkell the Tall had laid hold of all of King Æthelred's goods and chattels, and then Sweyn Bluetoothsson had claimed his land and kingdom. Now Cnut took Queen Emma as his own wife, after banishing King Æthelred to the forest, where he and several of his marshals and captains lived as outlaws, stealing peasants' chickens for their sustenance until the peasants drove them away. King Æthelred then fled to a remote skerry, where he lived out his days munching fox flesh and gnawing roots. When he gave up the ghost, Æthelred was king of seven birds of bone.

Upon landing in England, Jarl Haakon Ericsson goes straight to meet his kinsman King Cnut, and tells him the news:

a squat, knock-kneed, rotund peasant boy has come to Norway, wearing a blue cloak over a red one, his right shoe on his left foot and his left shoe on his right. He commands two old barges crewed by a handful of foreign vagrants, and claims that he intends to subdue the entire country. King Cnut laughs and says that they should wait until spring to send men to Norway to kill Olaf the Lout. Later, Cnut bestows the title Jarl of Northumberland on his kinsman Haakon, who now ceases to be part of our story.

Old accounts report that while Jarl Haakon's ship is still being readied to turn its prow seaward, a man in colorful clothing comes walking back to the aft deck and raps on the bulwark with the shaft of his spear, in the manner of a king's man requesting silence at court. Cupping one hand to his mouth like a horn, he calls out, asking whether King Olaf Haraldsson is near enough to hear his words. Olaf's crew wonder who this man might be, addressing their leader by the title of king, and they reply:

"The king is indeed here."

The finely-dressed man says:

"You are welcome to this land, King Olaf Haraldsson, to raise folk from ignominy and mediocrity and restore the kingdom of Norway. I have composed a lay for you, and will gladly recite it to you if you grant me leave to do so."

Olaf the Stout's face lights up at this salutation, but he says that he finds poetry hard to grasp and rather tedious. "Yet," says he, "what is the name of this man, who alone of all men in Norway chooses to greet me in a becoming manner?"

The finely-dressed man replies: "No Norseman am I, though I speak the Danish tongue. I am an Icelandic skald. It is my hope that the king most nobly born in Norway since Yngvi-Freyr will not turn a deaf ear to my praise."

"It is odd," says Olaf the Stout, "that you have never set eyes on me until this very day, although my reputation hardly precedes me. Only tonight I took captive Haakon and his crew, including you, yet you have found the time to compose a lay about me. What Icelander are you, then?"

"My name is Sigvatur, of Apavatn," says he, "the son of Þórður the Skald, who, for the longest time, served King Thorkell Strutharaldsson, your leader on Viking expeditions, and who now sits by a little lake on a heath, keeping an eye out for the strange fish that swim in it, and expects soon to die. He has relayed to me your bold exploits for me to work into verses, and in my lays your name shall be preserved throughout the course of the ages. Would you like to hear, King, what the cuckoos sang to me about you, or will you send the author of your glory away with your enemies?"

Olaf says that the jarl's ship is not to sail until he has spoken with this man, and he orders manropes drawn between that ship and his own. Skald Sigvatur now boards Olaf the Stout's ship. He has naught with him but his spear, inlaid with gold, and the clothing on his back, covered by a red pelisse lined with fur. On his arm he wears a fine gold band. He is a lively man, black eyed. Jarl Haakon Ericsson sits at the helm of his vessel, his fur cloak wrapped about him, and watches silently as the skald changes ships.

Olaf Haraldsson greets his visitor and asks: "Why do you abandon your master now, when fortune is divided so unequally among us rulers?"

"I do so," says Sigvatur, "because I have augured from birds that you will come to rule this land. We skalds are the voices of royal fortune and heralds of the heroes who conquer lands. I ask now for silence. I will make your former deeds shine with the same majestic luster destined for you by the Norns. And I hope to be able to join your retinue."

Olaf the Stout replies: "It will suffice if you join my retinue on the day that I deem it important for me to have the support of a skald, seeing as how you depart from this jarl of yours when you witness him hounded out of his realm – yet he is a greater ruler than I, and a better Christian, and one of the most stately men in the North, and of such high pedigree that he is granted his authority by Cnut. I have a suspicion that so noble an over-lord as Cnut will find for this jarl a greater and better abode than I will ever possess, though he now sits wrapped in his cloak, meek and pale."

In the evening they went ashore to feast at one of Sigurd Syr's farms, and there Olaf the Stout and his men heard the praise-poem that Sigvatur Þórðarson had composed about Olaf's fifteen greatest battles. First, the lay told of how Olaf, when twelve years old, had ravaged Gotland, occupied the island and made the Gotlanders his tributaries. Then various battles of his were described, fought in locations that no one has ever been able to pinpoint precisely. Here, praise was given to Olaf's victory in Kennemerland, a place that people say is part of Friesland. These verses told of how the high-minded farmers of that land rode to shore to welcome Olaf's ships and greet the seafarers with gifts, and how Olaf immediately assailed them, killed them all, and took possession of their gold and silver. Next, the lay extolled Olaf's victory at Canterbury, when, the English annals say, most men were mutilated, and the venerable man of God, Ælfheah, was pelted to death with knucklebones and horns. On Olaf's part in this achievement, Sigvatur sang: "Gentle helms-man, you took the broad burg of the Cantware by morning." The lay moved on to Olaf's great exploit of reddening Ringmere Heath with peasants' blood – it being customary in poetry not to mention peasants as anything but vermin of the sort that men kill in their tunics. Again, the lay lauded Olaf's sacking of London, leaving English carcasses floating down the River Thames. Finally, Sigvatur's poem celebrated the glorious battle fought when Olaf assaulted Hill-in-France – when Chartres went up in flames. These verses lauded Olaf for "razing low a high Hill."

The Icelander's eulogy of the gentle helmsman Olaf Haraldsson was, however, too much of a hotchpotch of complicated geography and obscure tales of voyages to remote regions for anyone to keep straight. Few in the company were old enough to have visited all the territories where Olaf had roamed, and even they recalled only a small number of the names of places they had actually harried. More specifically, these vagrants understood little of the Danish tongue in poetic form, scarcely any of them being from the North: some came from England and Ireland, Orkney, or Shetland, though most were foreigners. Yet they knew themselves to be valiant warriors and mighty champions, and thought their leader could hardly be overpraised – so to them the lay seemed quite fine. Olaf the Stout, for his part, accepted Sigvatur the Skald as a member of his retinue from that moment on.

35

THAT WINTER, Sigurd Syr spent a great deal of time on the road, his horses loaded with costly wares. It appeared that this farmer, who had passed his days ingloriously at home, was in possession of far greater wealth, both in money and valuables, than a Viking could gain through deeds of everlasting renown in distant lands.

Great deliberation and scheming now took place in Gudbrandsdalen and Oppland, as well as in Viken, the Fjord regions, and anywhere else that Sigurd Syr had friends, kinsmen, or stewards. First there were private conversations, then feasting and drinking, and then, as winter drew to a close, the peasants were summoned to assemblies. In some districts, the petty kings made public their willingness to renounce their titles, if their tenants consented, and to pledge their allegiance to that noble man who had come to Norway to unite the country in the manner of his deceased predecessors and rule it as sole monarch: Olaf the Stout. The populace made little objection, as it is difficult to keep kings on their thrones when they no longer wish to occupy them. Olaf personally attended many assemblies, and folk marveled at his lordliness – wearing, as he did, numerous colored cloaks, his fingers and arms weighted with gold rings, spindle-limbed and potbellied, averse to the whimsicality of youth. Some peasants welcomed his rule with applause, while others grumbled under their breath. Several lords sent their sons to him at the behest of Sigurd Syr, to swell and enhance the troop of men that he had brought with him from abroad. Olaf now rode throughout the districts with his company and took oaths from various leading men, with Bishop Grímkell constantly at his side, carrying a large cross and gazing heavenward. It seemed that wherever Sigurd Syr had been with his pack train that winter, Olaf was welcomed with open arms. Everywhere he went, Olaf announced his wish to baptize the populace, following the example of Emperor Charlemagne and Olaf Tryggvason, the sovereigns considered to have been the staunchest champions of Christianity among all the secular lords in the world. Olaf decreed that churches be donated more money and land than they ever had before, and declared Christ his half-share partner in land and movable property throughout Norway, while Grímkell took young men under his wing and taught them the *signum crucis* and how to sing the *Credo* and paternoster and the psalms, and then ordained them priests. Olaf went a step further than the emissaries from Bremen in his ordinances, stating that those who refused to accept the faith or to practice Christianity under his rule were to lose nothing less than their lives. He vied so hard with the archbishopric of Bremen for the favor of Christ that he baptized more people in Oppland in just a few days than the German suffragan bishops in Viken had managed to convert over the course of many generations, refuting those who said that an oaf and his excommunicate, vagabond cleric had come to Norway from westward over the sea. Olaf imitated the habit of many a Christian ruler, who, for their own amusement, would name twelve of their most trusted officers their apostles, after Christ's forecastlemen – moreoever, Olaf named his three highest ranking men after the kings of the East who brought gifts of gold, frankincense, and myrrh to honor the Lord.

History has shown time and again that when a king sells his kingdom, its people are rarely as easily sold – and so it went with Norway now. In many places throughout the country, the peasants stubbornly resisted the new order that always accompanies a regime change. Yet it turned out that the populace did not harbor sufficient hatred for this Olaf, who was a complete stranger to them, since no headway was made in gathering an army to oppose him, and even when meager bands of troops did come together in various places, they were quickly dispersed. The stronger the foothold gained by the claimant to the throne, the harder he pressed his advantage. Olaf quickly reverted to his old Viking tactics, searching out those he reckoned unfaithful to him, taking them by surprise and slaying them or burning them alive in their houses, and then confiscating their property, while having his friends prepare feasts for him and his men.

This book will not recount the stories of Olaf the Stout's burnings and murders in Norway, nor attempt to retell the *Saga of King Olaf the Saint* any more than is needed to elucidate how the fates of our two heroes from the Vestfirðir, whose tale we began to narrate quite some time ago, played out in the shadow of greater events in the world. Of Olaf, we shall relate here only what bears on the unfolding of our heroes' destinies.

In Norwegian law, king and slave were treated as equals in certain respects. By law, those who burned others to death were the worst class of criminals, and if a king did the burning, he was condemned and outlawed no less than a slave, was labeled an incendiary, and forfeited his life and whatever wealth he had in land and movables.

It is not known whether it was ignorance of the law or childish recklessness that caused Olaf the Stout to begin ravaging Norway with fire, the one crime that not even a king was permitted in that land. The brows of many furrowed when the king, whom Sigurd Syr had bribed men into accepting and others had formally taken as their master at assemblies, turned up in Romerike with three hundred men, burned the authorities in their homes, and took possession of their lands in the name of Christ.

As this news spread, a number of nobles met to discuss what steps to take now that such an arsonist had come to Norway. Assembled in this council were several who had held the title of king, among them one that had fled Romerike when Olaf torched it, as well as kings from Gudbrandsdalen, the king of Hedmarken, and the king of Hadeland. They met at the old assembly-place and manor in Hedmarken called Ringsaker, located on a grassy bank of the great lake that fills the valley there, called Hedsævi of old, but which Snorri the Wise has called Vatn. Most of the leading men in Østlandet had gathered for the assembly – those that had not accepted bribes from Sigurd Syr or sold their lands and titles. These were husbandmen who had never participated in Viking forays and knew little about war; their knowledge and skills were acquired only in peaceful locales. They were kings of the sort that knew how to forge iron, cast copper, and engrave silver, or else how to fashion houses to look as if they had built themselves. They could carve runes on sticks and dragons on columns, and praise in verse the virtues that gain a man respect at assemblies and a reputation that lives on after death. They were taciturn, but could recite every law valid in Norway. Over ale, they told tales of the mingling of gods and giants, and shared stories of what went on up north beyond the great gulf, where ogresses dwelt.

Assembled thus at Ringsaker, the petty kings settled on a plan, in response to the woeful state of affairs in the land, to levy an army against Olaf the Stout, and they appointed a rallying day. Each king was to contribute three hundred men to this army, each man with whatever weapons he possessed, and the others with anything that might serve for a weapon. Having made this decision, they called for drinks and turned to lighter subjects, passing the cup between them in a friendly drinking bout before going to sleep.

Turning back to Olaf Haraldsson: after setting Romerike ablaze, he convened an assembly and issued orders, while Grímkell began teaching vagrants the paternoster. As they occupied themselves at these tasks, Olaf received word from down south in Ringerike that the kings were conspiring against him, and would meet at Ringsaker in three nights. Olaf announced this news to his troops at once, bidding them make ready swiftly and ride to Ringsaker in Hedmarken to attack the kings.

After riding long and hard, and finally drawing near to the kings' assembly-place, some of the men in Olaf Haraldsson's band, those born and raised in Norway, began to harbor doubts, anxious about burning more people at present. Moreover, some in the company claimed kinship to the kings, and discontented murmuring arose among the ranks. Those closest to Olaf said it was not a criminal act to maim or burn heathens, while others denied that kings in Norway should be burned alive in their houses because Christ built the halls of Heaven, not Þórr.

When Olaf the Stout heard of the wrangling going on in his

army, he consulted with his captains, then convened an assembly in a clearing and addressed his men. It is said that he had greater skills in persuasion than most others in Norway, whether speaking to someone in private or before an audience at assemblies.

In his address, Olaf explained how all the great kings in Christendom had always proclaimed the true faith with fire and sword, and how Charlemagne, the most glorious of all emperors in the sight of God, had, in one morning, beheaded four-thousand eight-hundred Saxons, after first baptizing them all in the name of the Father, Son, and Holy Spirit, thereby redeeming their souls from fire and the serpent. He declared nothing to be better than torture and flame for persuading people to repent and reform and for bringing them, through vivid visions, to an understanding of the salvation that Christ granted men, particularly if the leading peasants were roasted alive, mutilated, or beheaded. As an example, he described how that very pillar of Christianity, Otto the German, the Holy Roman Emperor, had traveled south and blinded the anti-pope John, sliced off his nose, and plucked out his tongue, so that the true pope, Sylvester, might ascend to his throne and the majesty of Christ be exalted.

After declaiming to his men for some time on the necessity of fortifying Christendom, Olaf asked his friend Bishop Grímkell of Canterbury to step forward and have his say – the man who, by rightful ordination and anointing, had received the gift of the Holy Spirit to act as Christ's spokesman after only the pope himself. Olaf bade Grímkell express, in plain language, whether it was Christ's will that manslaughter or burnings be abandoned in this world or that the torture of heathen kings and the anti-pope be forbidden. "In what other manner," said he, "are the people to be saved?"

Grímkell raised his cross and stepped forward at his lord's behest, and there in a forest in Norway delivered a discourse that old books render in the following words:

"Verily, Christ is king of kings as he is of all men, but the hour has not yet come when all kings acknowledge Christ. For this reason, that peace does not yet reign which Scripture states will be so great that the dead shall awaken, and so enduring that men shall beat their swords into ploughshares. But as long as that peace remains unestablished, we have the words of all the eminent bishops and Church fathers and holy doctors, as well as the decrees of the Lord Pope. And Christ himself, who rules over Judgement Day and the world's end, says, when he preaches the sword, that it is neither prudent nor sensible to enact and unreservedly observe laws that prohibit the slaying of men or the destruction of settlements that deny the redemption of the soul."

Bishop Grímkell of Canterbury continued:

"I was present when Archbishop Ælfheah, my spiritual father, was pelted with bones and horns by heathen Norsemen, and dozens of my brothers from my school days were mutilated, as well as my maidenly sisters. Now the day draws nigh when heathen Norsemen shall, in their own homeland, be dealt the same measure, full to the brim and well shaken, that they dealt us in Canterbury. My spiritual son, King Olaf, has imposed this penance upon himself: to consign every man born of woman in Norway, king or slave, that denies the redemption of the soul, to torment and flame, and upon completion of his atonement, he will be proclaimed the most glorious king in the North."

Olaf the Stout's forces made the journey so speedily that the kings had no warning of their movements. Olaf's men concealed themselves in the woods and arrived at Ringsaker by night, and were blessed by Bishop Grímkell before commencing their work. The kings had no backing but pages and grooms, and they woke in the night to find that Olaf the Stout's army had surrounded the buildings.

The sun had risen and was shining on lake and forest when Olaf Haraldsson had the kings and other leading men lined up along the courtyard wall at Ringsaker. Most were wearing only their nightshirts or other scant clothing. The weather was calm, says Snorri. Olaf ordered the kings bound. Then he stepped up to the line and called on someone familiar with the prisoners to state the name and origin of each of them. Some of the king-lets had kin in Olaf's army, and these entreated him for the lives of their kinsmen. From several nobles he took oaths and handshakes as promises that they would leave the country and never return to Norway, yet he spared no man who claimed kinship with himself. A few men offered to kiss his foot, and these he dealt with according to his whim. One or two elders among them declared that they would never plead for mercy from a kinless boy, an incendiary and a thief, who was no more of a Norseman than Olaf Tryggvason, the Estonian. Olaf the Stout ordered that these men be led away immediately and hanged at once.

Then Olaf Haraldsson opened his bag and drew forth the tools that were dearer to him than most, which he had bought in the British Isles and kept handy ever afterward – namely, his instruments of torture. From the line, he selected those whom he intended to torment, while prescribing how the kings were to be restrained during the procedure. Before the torture began, Bishop Grímkell bade the men say the paternoster and sing the *psalterium beate Marie virginis*, that is, the Psalm of Our Lady. Olaf's men looked on, as did the manservants and housemaids of Ringsaker, some from the stable doors, others from doorsteps or windows, as this brash, portly fellow, fairhaired and beardless, faced the bound and barefoot kings of Norway, most of them hoary-headed, long-bearded, and disheveled from sleep. There, as is told in Icelandic books, Olaf Haraldsson blinded King Hrorek of Hedmarken, then pulled the tongue from the mouth of King Gudrod of Gudbrandsdalen and clipped it in two at the roots, before wrapping the eyes of the one and the tongue of the other carefully in his handkerchief, for a keepsake. The elders who had defied Olaf were led off to a granary. There, holding his cross, Bishop Grímkell sang the sacred psalm *Miserere*, gazing humbly toward heaven as ropes were tossed over the rafters and the old men strung up. In this manner, Norway was dedicated fully to Christ. Dwelling in those woods were black grouse and capercaillie: these birds shook the night-dew from their wings just as King Olaf Haraldsson was washing the blood from his hands.

The king commanded his men to set fire to the buildings that had housed his enemies in this place, and declared that a church was to be built there afterward.

When Ringsaker was resettled and a church constructed there, the farm was moved and rebuilt farther up the lakeside. Now only grass is found on the bank of the lake where the kings of Norway were led out, yet black grouse and capercaillie still chatter in the foliage. The sun's rays shone on the gently rippling lake as I passed by there one morning in late spring.

36

NOW THE STORY moves west to Ísafjarðardjúp.

As far as people knew, life was happier in Ögur than any-place else in the Vestfirðir, or even in the districts beyond. Ever since Chieftain Vermundur contributed land and other kinds of wealth in order to make his kinsman Þormóður a worthy match for Þórdís Kötludóttir, and their wedding was held and Þormóður settled down to farm, folk in the district forgot both his past faults and the fact that it had been only a very short time since he and his crony Þorgeir Hávarsson had spent their time freebooting in those parts. Vermundur had also paid full compensation for the sworn brothers' questionable exploits on Hornstrandir, in which Þormóður had played a part. Folk in Djúp still recall that during the years when Þormóður lived as a husbandman in Ögur, he seems not to have been disliked in the district – from the day that he settled down to farm, no one has any stories of him ever imposing on other farmers or making his presence felt in any way other than perfectly peaceably. He showed not the slightest interest in grabbing after distinction or power in the district, but remained quietly at home on his farm, interacting only rarely with others and taking as little trouble to make friends as enemies. As mentioned earlier, in his youth he had been more agile at games than most others there in the west, and a vivacious reveler at gatherings, but after he returned from his Viking forays at Hornstrandir, and he and his sworn brother had parted ways, he stopped participating in most of the games and attended not a single social gathering. People also have it on good authority that the entire time Þormóður Kolbrúnarskáld lived as a farmer, he associated with no other woman but his wife Þórdís. The capricious girl who opened her window one night out of curiosity, was in fact her husband's one true love – the kind of woman who embraces a man's heart with both life and limb. That is why it is said that in the west there has never been a love as good or better between husband and wife.

Djúp shone with light from Gimlé, the name that ancient lore gives to the southern hall of the sky. Þórdís Kötludóttir of Ögur reigned in this light – not, in sooth, a curious maiden who let an athlete in during the night against her own will, but rather, a distinguished matron in a bounteous district, reserved in speech, yet warm. She had eyes that sparkled heavenly blue though her gaze was steady, and her hair was more deeply ashen colored than in childhood, yet just as plenteous. Her skin was so drenched in sunshine that she shed a golden light all around her, as if the very luminance of the sky had taken on the appearance and shape of a woman. It is frequently attested in the old tales that such women changed shape in their sleep and flew through the sky in the dress of swans.

Þormóður Kolbrúnarskáld worshipped this golden image of womanhood above everything he owned, and after her, the two daughters that she bore him. These he called his Moon and his Star. It is said that he loved his wife and daughters so dearly that he spent days on end thinking of them and nothing else, and could never sufficiently praise the good fortune that sometimes can fall into a wretched man's lap during his lifetime – dead though he soon may be. On the other hand, no one recalls Þormóður as having a knack for farming, though almost any task he put his mind to came easily to him, and credible report has it that he abandoned his poetry and other lore entirely during his blissful days at Ögur.

One morning early, during haymaking, just after folk at Ögur have risen and are readying themselves for their daily chores, a sight catches their eyes through the main door. There, out by the homefield gate, is something new, and entirely unexpected: a man's head. The head is impaled on a stake and faces the farm. It is big and bulging and far from pleasant to behold; most resembling a seal's head turned inside out. The lips are eaten away, as is the tip of the nose. The jaws gape widely, the tongue sticks out between the teeth, the eyes are glazed and sunken, and the hair is filthy with old, crusted blood and gore. Few people have ever beheld so ogrish a head.

While the entire household is shuddering at this sight, a woman calls for Slave Kolbakur and tells him to make quick work of it, before the master and mistress rise, and take down this curse-pole that wicked men have raised against them. Kolbakur retorts that although he is a slave, the women ought to pay attention to their own work before his. "This head," says the slave, "is not intended for me, and I will not take it down."

Just then, the two girls come out of the house to fetch their toys. The slave says: "Go back inside, little maidenettes, and tell your mother that here by the main gate stands a head that she alone may get rid of, if she wishes."

Just before mid-morning, Þórdís Kötludóttir is standing in the courtyard, surrounded by her servants, her hair radiant with a golden luster. She immediately asks what head this is that has been raised there in the night. No one will answer her plainly or admit to recognizing the head. Slave Kolbakur speaks up:

"This head rode into your yard, Mistress," he says, "and you must decide whether or not I bury it before your husband wakes up. Your choice is this: will you have it buried without asking his leave, or wait until he wakes, when he will choose between your head and it?"

His mistress laughs and says that if this is a head of destiny, then it is not for her to do away with it. "And it is of little use for me to bury it, for some day, every man will encounter that same head. Go inside now, my little goldcrests," she says, "and wake your father from sleep and tell him that there is someone at his door who was bound to come sooner or later. I always knew that he would show up on a fine morning such as this, with the sun shining on Djúp and eiderducks leaving their nests."

The little girls run inside to their father's bed. The older of the two gives her father's foot a kiss as he lies there, while the younger pokes the tip of his nose with her forefinger, waking him. Þormóður sits up, grabs both girls, holds them in his arms, and asks them what is new.

"Father," says the younger girl, "there is a head outside, fixed on a stake. No one has ever seen a head so ugly!"

"What sort of head?" says he.

The elder girl replies: "I think, father, that it is the old Devil who has come, he who was hounded and tormented most by God, and bound tightly – and whom we call the Midgard Serpent. When that serpent gets loose, the world will end."

"This is weighty news," says Skald Þormóður, and he puts the girls down, throws on a cloak, and pulls shoes onto his feet. Then he goes out. When he comes to the door, he sees his wife standing in the yard, along with his entire household, all staring at the huge, hideous head. They are astounded by the head and wonder how it has gotten there. Farmer Þormóður goes straight to the stake, and after staring at the head for several moments, says:

"I recognize this head clearly, though I am not familiar with all of its journeys. This is the head of my sworn brother Þorgeir Hávarsson, come to pay us a visit."

At this announcement, he lifts the head from the stake and kisses it. The little girls burst into tears when they see their father kiss such a horrifying head. Þormóður Kolbrúnarskáld bids his household, old and young, to keep calm, and tells them that he will certainly give this head a worthy welcome. He asks his wife for a cloth of the finest weave to wrap round the head, and then lifts it in his hands and carries it carefully to a storehouse at the edge of the courtyard. He then bids the servants attend to their chores.

After finding a place for the head in his storehouse, wrapping it in the cloth, and speaking to it for a time, Þormóður sends some farmhands of his around the countryside to make inquiries into the movement of people or boats over the last few days – who has been out on the roads, whether any seafarers have come ashore. He learns that two tramps had been seen in the mountains, apparently having crossed over the heaths from the east – between them they were carrying a pole from which hung a bulky object. Those that saw it thought it might be part of a ram's carcass, which they had perhaps been given as alms. Folk had presumed them to be Butraldi Brúsason and his lackey Lúsoddi, who were forever roaming about the Vestfirðir.

As soon as Þormóður hears this news, he launches his boat and sails to Vatnsfjörður to have a word with Vermundur. At this point in the story, the chieftain is much in decline from old age, yet he recognizes his kinsman Þormóður and has him sit by his bedside and report the news. Þormóður tells him plainly about Þorgeir Hávarsson's head having been impaled on a stake before the door at Ögur, and asks whether Vermundur has heard what person may have been carrying this head around the Vestfirðir.

Old Vermundur replies that, dead or alive, the head that Þormóður speaks of bodes evil, and he is certainly not the one who lugged such a monstrosity around the Vestfirðir. Þormóður asks about Butraldi and Lúsoddi – where such miscreants are likely to be hiding out just now. Vermundur says that as far as he knows, the two of them have gone to Greenland. "Good-for-nothings from the Vestfirðir are better off there," he says.

Þormóður says that it sounds to him as if Vermundur has better knowledge than he does of the goings-on in the district. "I would ask," says he, "that you do not mock me or make sport of me in this matter. You know well that we were once good friends – I and that king's man whose head was just now mounted on a stake before the main door at Ögur."

Vermundur says: "I would have thought you might be more obliged to thank me for buying you the most excellent match for a wife in all the west."

Þormóður asks if Vermundur knows for certain whether the wretches he just named are Þorgeir Hávarsson's slayers.

Vermundur replies: "I do not know who cut off Þorgeir Hávarsson's head – and I do not care. Butraldi and his man may well have bought the head off of some rascals up north. Whatever the case, it seems fitting to me that this head has been paid its due. The king of Norway sent Þorgeir on a perilous mission to kill some farmers out here in the west who had beaten some of the king's merchants last year and appropriated their wares at the price it suited them to pay – and by my advice, they paid no more. We men of the Vestfirðir have no qualms about letting King Olaf know that he cannot wantonly send his bravoes to kill our liegemen, good farmers, before our very eyes, though I may be old and decrepit."

Concerning the events leading to Þorgeir Hávarsson's death, as well as the place where he lost his life, we shall never gain a clear answer from men of learning – the old books differ widely on these details. Yet on one point all the authorities agree, and not a book has been written nor a tale told that holds this in doubt: that Þorgeir Hávarsson was killed in his sleep, not cut down in battle, and what is more, that he lost his life not to the weapons of a hero or indeed of an honorable man who had earned distinction or a good name. All the books tell the same story: that he was killed by abject nobodies, and that wood from his weapons and shards of his shield were used for kindling. Some tales relate that in a harbor where ships lay waiting for a fair wind, some scullions left their cauldrons to go gathering sticks and twigs for their fires, and found the hero asleep in a booth at midday, with a driftwood log for a pillow. His neck lay exposed on the log, as it might on a chopping-block, with his chin facing upward. The scullions felt that the man was in an exceptional position for beheading. They crept up and hewed off his head, there as he slept, broke the shafts of his spear and ax, and clove his shield, as well as the block upon which they had sundered him, and used the wood to stoke their fires. That day, they had no need to gather any more brushwood or driftwood. Old books also relate how rogues from Greenland cut open Þorgeir's body and pulled out his heart, because they were curious to see how such a jewel was made – one that never quaked before life or death. The story goes that Þorgeir's heart was very small, and incredibly hard, and that after peering at it for some time, the scullions simmered it until it was tender, divided it among themselves and ate it, in order to increase their strength and valor. It is also thought that by the time King Olaf sent Þorgeir Hávarsson to Iceland to kill certain Icelanders in the west with whom Olaf had grievances, Þorgeir held a grudge against the king. He felt that, as one of the king's men, he was never given enough opportunities to face dangerous situations and undertake tests of courage worthy of his mettle. Folk thus believe that King Olaf sent Þorgeir to Iceland to kill Icelanders simply because there was a good chance it might turn out to be the last journey Þorgeir ever made. During King Olaf's reign, his envoys were much disliked in Iceland, and whether they came in peace or not, they constantly made it their business to try to persuade Icelandic chieftains to hand the land over to the king. Stories have also circulated on Hornstrandir, in the Jökulfirðir, and in Djúp that Butraldi Cow-sucker and Þorgeir's betrayer Lúsoddi, who were frequent hangers-on at fishing stations and harbors, gave the scullions brushwood for Þorgeir's head and carried it on a pole westward to Djúp, where they asked Chieftain Vermundur what he would give them for it. Some books say that Vermundur's response to this question was that it was not for him to accept this head, but that he would provide them with victuals and other assistance after they had found a place for it.

Farther south, in Borgarfjörður, Þorgeir Hávarsson's mother Þórelfur had died, while Þorgeir's kinsman Þorgils Arason was at Reykjahólar, increasing his fortune. Þormóður Kolbrúnarskáld now rode from the west to meet Þorgils and reported the latest news to him, that his kinsman Þorgeir Hávarsson had been beheaded somewhere up north – he who was born a greater hero than any other in the Vestfirðir, and was one of King Olaf Haraldsson's men. Miscreants had killed the warrior in his sleep, brought his head south, and mounted it on a stake before his door at Ögur.

"It is of no concern to me where the head of this manslayer was mounted," said Þorgils Arason, "and the difference between my kinsman and me is that I have profited most by killing no one. Nor will I, in my old age, start combing the countryside for people to kill, like lice, though some miserable rats might easily be rousted out of dark corners here and there and dispatched. I advise you to follow my example, good lad: go home to your farm and make yourself rich by giving men life."

When Þormóður arrives back in Ögur, he goes straight to his storehouse to greet the head of his sworn brother Þorgeir. As he lifts the costly cloth from the warrior's face, it looks even uglier than before, and fills the storehouse with its stench – carrion flies have laid their eggs in the head. Þormóður strews salt on it, hoping to defend this noble head as best he can from the persistent visits of vermin.

It is now so late in the summer that no more ships will be departing for the year, and Þormóður remains at home on his farm. In the fall he grows extremely reticent and averse to human interaction, paying little heed to what is going on around him, and sinking ever deeper into his own thoughts. When his wife sits at his knee, he strokes her hair. When his two little girls are playing, he stares at them as if from a remote distance, or as if beholding strange visions at the very limit of the sea, but he no longer calls to them to sit on his knees. He meanders aimlessly both outdoors and in and does no work, but mutters dark verses to himself, in low tones. Many a night, while others sleep, he rises quietly from his bed and goes to the storehouse, where he spends hours speaking to Þorgeir Hávarsson's head.

37

SLAVE KOLBAKUR had a superb cock that crowed numerous times every night. This bird kept many people at Ögur from sleeping, crowing as it did in the evening when folk went to their beds, and again at midnight, and then just before daybreak, when it would crow for quite a long time – and it would be wide awake again at midmorning. Many a night, after the skald had gone to his storehouse to strew salt on the hero's face, his wife lay awake in bed, unable to sleep a wink for the crowing of the slave's cock.

One morning before dawn, when Þormóður is out in the storehouse and the cock has just finished a long bout of crowing, Þórdís of Ögur finally has her fill of losing sleep due to this bird. She steps into her slippers, dons a mantle, and hurries out of the bedchamber. She goes straight to the loft where Kolbakur is sleeping, lights the slave's lamp, and wakes him.

He sits up and asks what is on his mistress's mind.

"I have come, Kolbakur," says she, "expressly to throttle that bird, whose nightly crowing vexes us to no end."

He says: "The bird you speak of shall commit no further outrage. I shall wring its neck with my own hands, if you wish."

Having made her intention known to the slave, and he having responded so well to it, she remains sitting there on the edge of his bed, weeping.

The slave asks what is causing her so much woe.

"My love for my husband Þormóður," says she, "is so profound that it gives me no peace, by night or by day. I am never so busy that if I hear his voice from a distance, I do not run and sit at his feet. You, Kolbakur, who have seen carved stone crosses in Ireland, higher than the hills – what remedy do you have to free me from this affliction, and him from his fetters?"

"So many years have passed," says Kolbakur, "since I asked for one night of union with you before Þormóður and his kin from Vatnsfjörður rode from Ögur to wed you, and you refused and rejected my entreaty, though your refusal, you said, was based less on your love for him than on the fact that you were betrothed to him by contract. You said that the hallmark of a good woman consisted less in loving her betrothed than in refusing to betray him."

"I have come to you now," says she, "not because I am bound to him solely by the laws of men, but rather, because I love him above all things, created and uncreated, that are to be found on Earth or below it."

"Speak, Mistress," says he. "I am your slave."

"We here at Ögur enjoy more good fortune and other bounties than most people in the Vestfirðir, as if the gods had come down to us one morning and cast their favor upon everything around us, on the air, the sea, and the earth. Here, milk and honey flow into the mouth of every living creature. It is little wonder that my daughters have the hue of stars, when their father towers high as the sky itself, above all other men, like a young stag slung with dew, supple and slim;* such a radiant ideal among his people that even when he went freebooting around Horn in his youth, most men spoke fairly of him, and women barely acknowledged the existence of any other man in the Vestfirðir. Tell me, Kolbakur – you being an Irishman – what malice might Josa mac De have in mind, to bestow such great happiness on a woman?"

Kolbakur replies: "Most would say, Mistress, that as good as your husband might be, in and of himself, he owes most to your gifts of love."

"Outrageous rubbish," said she. "Little did I suspect you to be so foolish, Kolbakur, as not to know what a dungeon and snake pit a woman's embrace is to a skald and hero. I am the bane of a hero's or skald's glory, the wispy fetter forged for the Wolf from cat's tread, fish's breath, and bird's spittle.* I am the wall standing between the skald and seductive sea voyages, between him and the clamor of battle and the favor of kings – and therewith: a reputation that never dies."

Kolbakur says: "Would it please you, Mistress, if I were to go out one morning after he has gone to sleep, and remove the head from his storehouse and bury it deep in the ground?"

"No," says she.

He asks her why not.

"For this reason," says she. "However deeply or secretly we dig, this ugly, useless head will remain closest to his heart, and there rule over other heads, not only my own and those of other women whom men desire most, but even over that of the evil woman who dwells in the darkness of the Abyss – this head will rise ever higher in his mind's eye the deeper we dig in the ground."

"What shall we do, then?" asks the slave.

"I am so overwhelmed by Þormóður's grief," says she, "that I will do everything in my power to release him from me."

At her reply, Kolbakur remains silent for a long time, until his cock wakes and begins crowing in its pen beneath the rafters. The pen has a small hatch on top, and after the bird has crowed for a little while, the slave says:

"If you please, Mistress, draw the bolt on this little hatch, and there you will find the bird you hate and wish to see dead. Apart from that, I have no other advice to give you."

When the mistress returns to her chamber at dawn, she finds her husband lying awake in bed. His wife looks pale and bleary-eyed to him, as if she has been crying, and he asks where she has been for so long during the night. She slips beneath the cover, cold and terribly drowsy, and answers him with a yawn:

"I took it upon myself," she says, "to silence the bird that was forever keeping us awake at night."

She lies down and falls asleep almost at once, but he lies awake a long time, without taking his eyes off her. Her fair hair is darker than of old, her milky bosom fuller. Is this the woman, superior to all others, who once woke him with the rustling of her wings in an unfamiliar fjord, came to his bedside with her swan-dress draped over her arm, tapped him, the skald, with her wand and bade him follow her? Who is this, who has curled up in his bed, shivering in the morning chill, and fallen asleep straightaway with an unexplained, half-dry tear in the corner of her eye?

That same day, Skald Þormóður goes up to the loft where the slave has his workspace and a sleeping-alcove beneath the sloping roof. The slave is very skilled at most crafts, and the loft is full of tools and items he has fashioned: plates and bowls, baskets and churns, ladles and drinking horns, and numerous other utensils. The slave is on his knees, joining the staves for a bucket. The staves are standing upright, and he is fitting the rings around them.

Þormóður silently examines several half-made items before sitting down on a block of wood. He has his ax – which he normally does not carry at home – hanging by its strap over his shoulder. He loosens the ax from its strap and stares at its edge for some time. The slave turns to look at him with his squint-eyes, whose aim is always difficult to pinpoint.

The farmer breaks his silence thus: "You have a bird that keeps my lady and me awake at night. Any man who raises such a creature is an enemy of ours. Take up your weapons, and we shall go out to the homefield and fight."

Kolbakur slaps the palms of his hands against the two sides of the loosely girded bucket, causing the staves to fall from the rings into a pile on the floor. Then he stands up.

Slave Kolbakur says: "Once, long ago, I was duped into setting an armed ambush for you, Master, and ever since, I have never regretted any deed as deeply. I was also taught in Ireland that only those with craven hearts put their trust in steel. Yet I tell you, Master, that my life has seldom been less precious to me than now, and I will not beg for it if you are intent upon killing me."

He brings forth a chopping block and places it at Þormóður Kolbrúnarskáld's feet, then lies down on the floor with the block beneath his neck, baring his throat, his chin pointing upward. "I have," he says, "heard it said that this is how Þorgeir Hávarsson was beheaded, and I am certain that I will be no better at it than he was."

Þormóður flings his ax aside and tells Kolbakur to stand up. He says that he has no mind to take his head. "I have," says he, "enough heads for now."

The slave rises slowly and silently from the chopping-block, before starting on righting the bucket staves again and fitting them against each other within the rings. Þormóður sits watching him work for some time, without saying a word. Finally he stands up.

"It may be," he says, "that you speak the truth: that slaves will inherit this land when we heroes and skalds have fallen into oblivion, and my children will learn your wisdom – that only cowards put faith in steel. I look forward to being dead when your Irish wisdom prevails in the world."

Saying this, Þormóður Kolbrúnarskáld turns and leaves the loft, and he and the slave do not cross paths again.

38

THAT WINTER passes without further incident, apart from Þormóður becoming ever more withdrawn concerning most things, with no one knowing why. He generally goes to bed before the others, and is sleeping by the time his lady joins him. Many a night, however, when it is quiet in the house and most of the household is asleep, the farmer dresses and goes out to the storehouse where he keeps the hideous head, and to which he alone has a key. He sits by the head through the night, sprinkling salt into its nose and mouth and saying things to it that others can only guess at. He never speaks of this head to anyone else, or of what he intends to do with it – whether he might bury it in a churchyard or heap stones over it in the wilderness – and no one volunteers to ask him.

Folk also notice that something seems to be sorely distressing the mistress at Ögur, yet no one is able to guess what it might be. In the mornings, pale and ill, she pours the milk from the troughs, and sits teary-eyed at her loom during the day. People wonder even more at the mistress's sadness as it becomes more apparent each day, as spring draws near, that she is with child.

One night late in winter, Þormóður Kolbrúnarskáld is out talking to the head of his sworn brother Þorgeir Hávarsson, and he happens to return to his bedchamber earlier than usual, only to find the bed empty and cold. He lies down but cannot sleep, and after he has lain there awake for quite some time, his wife comes in from outdoors, steps out of her shoes, casts off her mantle, and curls up beneath the cover. Both lie there awake for some time, on their own sides of the bed, without exchanging words. He hears the woman sobbing quietly, and speaks:

"Difficult paths, my lady?" he says.

She replies: "Only those onto which my love for you has driven me, and which have become more difficult than I can endure without losing my health and mind."

"Strange paths, my lady," says he, "yet stranger is your love for me, if it is true that you have been with child since Yule. The last time that I lay in your lap was the night before the head of my sworn brother Þorgeir appeared here by the homefield gate during haymaking. You would be near delivery now, if it was I who begot the burden you bear."

"Day and night since I saw you playing on the ice," says she, "and you came to us women and spoke to us, I have not lived a single moment without your image engraved in my mind. Every motion of yours has nourished me, and every minute when you were so distant that I was unable to hear the tread of your shoes was like black night to my heart. Yet the torment I suffered when you left me to go raiding with Þorgeir, and were confined in the prison of the evil woman who dwells in the Abyss, was far less painful than my sufferings over these past years, knowing you to be helplessly shackled in the fetters of my passion, bereft of your fate and your fame."

He says: "Brynhildur Buðladóttir has stated that it is wiser not to put one's trust in women, for they always break their vows, and no man shall ever be able to say truly whether a woman loves him wholeheartedly. All their oaths are vanity, hollow and pointless."

She says: "We women dare least, since it is we who risk most, to love you heroes and skalds wholeheartedly, for when we least expect it you no longer sit at our knees, having gone off to far countries to win thrones for kings and accomplish exploits whose praise will be sung as long as the world lasts – and leaving us betrayed."

Þormóður says: "It is a sign of my affection for you, my lady, that I turned aside from my path to glory and settled down to farming. Weighty ideals and words have been remote from me for some time, as well as exploits most worthy of verses. For I have loved you so dearly that I have striven not to involve myself in anything that might displease you. What is more, I felt that my regret would be unbearable if I were to forfeit, in any way, the blessings that you have given me, or to choose to pursue a different lot. You have also borne me daughters, which, I must admit, made me anxious at first, for I thought that if your love made me meek, theirs would make me weak. As it turned out, when they lay suckling at your breast and I watched their toes wiggle as they suckled, and later, when they smiled at me and reached out to me with their tiny hands and arms, dimples at every joint, it was as if, for a time, the power that conquers lands and laughs at its own death dozed in me – until I beheld the head of my sworn brother Þorgeir Hávarsson at my homefield gate."

After conversing for quite a long time at daybreak, and saying all they feel they have to say, Þormóður and his wife fall silent and go to sleep.

Now the day draws nigh for Þórdís Kötludóttir to bear her child, and when the time comes, she delivers a boy, beautiful and fair of form, fiery-haired and squint-eyed. Þormóður Kolbrúnarskáld comes to see the boy, and after looking him over for several long moments, greets him, bidding him welcome to rule lands, Iceland as well as Ireland, before reciting a verse on the greatest tidings in the world just then: that King Brian had fallen at Clontarf, yet had won the day. He laughs – and then leaves, without another word.

Women are appointed to tend to the boy.

Most sources say that that evening, Þormóður Kolbrúnarskáld went to bed like the rest of the household at Ögur. Yet after lying there for a time, until he felt that the others were asleep, their beds warm with the savor of restful dreams, he got up, slipped into his clothes, pulled on heavy shoes, tossed a thick cloak of homespun over his shoulders, then took his weapons and went out. Summer was drawing to a close and the night was dim, but the farmer knew all the stepping-stones over the farm's creek, crossed them, and headed for the mountains.

In the morning, when folk woke at Ögur, their master was not in his bed, nor could he be found anywhere on the farm. The day passed without him returning, and no one knew what had become of him. More days passed, but nothing was heard of Farmer Þormóður. When they went to inspect his storehouse across the yard, however, they found Þorgeir Hávarsson's skull on a shelf, polished with great art – it was the finest of treasures. Folk in Djúp were much amused by this head for a long time afterward, and a proper burial for it was constantly postponed. For three full generations, it remained part of the homestead at Ögur, but it was lost when all the buildings went up in flames toward the end of the days of the lawspeaker Markús Skeggjason.

39

GREENLAND, THEY say, boasted one of the most sparsely populated human communities in the world. Norsemen from Iceland inhabited that land for twelve generations until they all died out; the last survivor there, having breathed his last, fell flat on his face with no one else to bury him. This was nearly a century after the last ship traveled there.

When Þormóður Kolbrúnarskáld came to Greenland in search of the slayers of his sworn brother Þorgeir Hávarsson, a colony of Norsemen had existed there for a generation. The land's bounty then was much less depleted than later, and ships visited most years. The Norse colony was divided into what were called the Eastern and Western Settlements.

Sources state that when Þormóður reached the Eastern Settlement, he went to meet the greatest chieftain in the fjords there, a man called Þorgrímur Trölli – it being customary for newcomers to present themselves to the highest authority in the colony. The inhabitants there found it rather peculiar that a man of renown should have come from Iceland in the east, leaving behind his home and the bounty of Ísafjarðardjúp to step ashore at Brattahlíð like any other seaman, with no other belongings than the clothes on his back and his rather shoddy weapons, only in order to hunt down two paltry wretches who had drifted thither from Iceland a few months earlier – Butraldi Brúsason the Cow-sucker and his bosom pal Lúsoddi – but he declared that he would take no rest until he had killed those two scoundrels.

It is said that the Norsemen in Greenland were little given to fighting and killing, apart from when they undertook to slaughter the trolls that dwell near the boundaries of the world, and which they called skraelings. They felt that their own group was meager enough without killing each other, and they constantly feared being overwhelmed if the trolls decided to attack them in any large number.

Þorgrímur Trölli said that he was indeed the man best informed of people's comings and goings in Greenland – with the exception of the bishop in Garðar – nor was it to be denied that two men from Iceland had turned up there. They were not particularly distinguished, but Chieftain Vermundur of Vatnsfjörður had provided them passage. "What we do not understand," says he, "is that although these men appear quite unlikely to do us Greenlanders any excessive harm, they are hardly the type of champions or warriors that might justify a first-rate farmer to leave his homestead and happiness in Iceland to chase them all the way here."

Þormóður replied: "Truly, I would have preferred to wreak vengeance on doughty men and heroes, or any man who might have struck down my brother in battle, and it is more tragic than words can express that measly rotters should have beheaded the warrior in his sleep. If, however, each and every man responded so leniently to his obligation to pursue justice for his brother, and upstanding men averted their eyes from enormities or injustice, unless these were perpetrated by respected, tax-paying landholders or other pillars of the community or prominent leaders, then malefactors and cowards would indeed hold their heads high in the North, leaving skalds without matter for their verses, and crofters and others of little means or backing without protection and security. Then rulers would be more like senseless beasts than men."

Þormóður Kolbrúnarskáld mingled little with the colonists in Greenland, and as a result, he received few invitations to the feasts of noteworthy men. Nor did he waste much effort on the summer tasks that are obligatory in Greenland, when men rise earlier and retire later to their beds, eking out hay with a scant supply of iron. Some folk there cut the grass with their knives or tear it out with their bare hands, while others keep nightly vigil over their small strips of grain, spreading homespun over the ears to protect them from frost. Still others drive fish into inlets and catch them in their hands, or batter seals with cudgels.

When the work foremen asked Þormóður what tasks he would choose to do on Þorgrímur Trölli's farm, he said that he had come to perform great exploits, not to bother about food. For this reason, he was greatly disliked by many of the inhabitants of the Eastern Settlement. The foremen informed him that it was the law in Greenland that he who refuses to work shall not eat, and that Greenland's inhabitants were more used to providing themselves with sustenance than cultivating heroism or listening to doggerel. There was always a hint of animosity in people's voices when they spoke to the skald, and few were willing to give him shelter.

Through relentless inquiries about Butraldi and Lúsoddi, Þormóður discovered that the Greenlanders had soon grown tired of these two derelicts, and that they had been unable to settle down anywhere – indeed, they had been fonder of begging door to door than working for their living. In the spring, the leading men had had them removed to the Western Settlement, where life is tougher and beggars succumb faster than in the east. Once he had learnt all he could about his most pressing concern – revenging Þorgeir – Þormóður would change the subject and ask people if they knew where in Greenland might be found a woman greater than all others, who had been exiled here by Vermundur of Vatnsfjörður, along with a shaggy slave from Norway.

Þormóður has described how he lived with penury and sickness through his first winter in the Eastern Settlement in Greenland, and came to know the hardships that folk are forced to endure most winters in that land. Always, at the close of winter, there was a dearth of provisions, greatly reducing people's access to the necessities of life. The cold bit painfully, there was little fuel, milch cows went dry for lack of hay in March, and scores of sheep froze to death as they grazed on frozen ground. The cattle had to be lifted to their feet in the byres. Folk there had nothing to eat but old curds when they could not catch any fish, and their fishing gear was poor and meager. Moreover, the sea ice reached all the way to shore, and they lacked the necessary clothing and equipment for traversing it to fish or hunt. There was often such a shortage of meal for bread and porridge that folk picked and ate various seeds and grains on hills and heaths in order to replenish their strength. Their richest fare was old seal meat, but it is dreary stuff when eaten dry. These winter deprivations made most people lean and sick, and many dropped dead along with their livestock during particularly bad years. Yule feasts were not held in Greenland, but instead, fervent vows were made to the blessed Nicholas of Bari, the saint in whom the Greenlanders put most faith after Þórr was gone. The church at Garðar had been consecrated to Nicholas by order of the Lord Pope.

In Greenland, the ice hardly ever breaks sooner than expected, emptying from the fjords and allowing sea voyages to resume, yet eventually it does happen. At the coming of spring, Þormóður took passage with some men removing to the Western Settlement. Usually, it was a six-day journey by six-oared boat between the two settlements in Greenland. This time, however, the men encountered headwinds and were tossed about for much of the summer between the mainland and the islands, forcing them to sustain themselves by fishing and hunting, before reaching the Western Settlement when the haymaking was nearly finished. Here there were fewer folk, and life was even harder than in the east. Bare cliffs jutted out into the sea and long fjords cut into glaciers, leaving no soft ground for a blade of grass to grow. The colonists here were in far greater need of blessed Nicholas of Bari than in the Eastern Settlement, and churches had been built to him beneath the glaciers at the behest of the venerable Lord Pope. When Þormóður Kolbrúnarskáld inquired about Butraldi and his companion Lúsoddi, he was told that these vagrants had gone and joined the hunters who traveled to Northern Seat each spring to hunt walruses and whales – the tusks of these great fish being among the most valuable articles of trade known to the world, next to gold and ivory.

Northern Seat was the name given by the Greenlanders to the regions lying closest to Ginnungagap, the home of the frost giants, where there is nothing but ice and darkness. To those parts of Northern Seat nearest the Greenland colonies, it was a sea journey of five days short of a month. Men went there in spring and returned in the fall, while some remained up north over the winter, accumulating wealth, and some even longer – yet such expeditions were often fraught with hardship and peril. Many never returned from Northern Seat. Venturing thither was thought fit only for daredevils and the desperately poor. For those, however, who did manage to return from Northern Seat with the fruits of their venture, their advancement was practically assured.

Tales were told that due north of Northern Seat were to be found the abodes of the troll-races and sorcerers that the Greenland colonists called skraelings, after the way they wrapped themselves in scrappy, tattery skins and furs the likes of which Norsemen were ashamed to wear. The Norsemen refused to consider skraelings as human and declared them unfit to live, calling it a mockery of human beings for monsters to take on their form, with eyes and noses and other human features. Each summer, this foul rabble, as the Greenlanders called the skraelings, migrated overland to the east, where they would pitch their tents on islands and skerries and hunt whales and other great fish. Whenever the skraelings were sighted on land, the Norse chieftains sent out a call to arms and sallied out to kill them. The Norsemen soon learned that the skraelings' sorcery was so potent that they were never in mortal peril on sea or land. To them, every sort of weather was fair, and they were never more entertained than during the tempests that froze the life out of Norsemen or drowned them. These folk always had an abundance of food, in both good and bad years, and their bodies wobbled with fat. They feasted joyously while everything undertaken by the Norsemen – reputed to be wise, industrious husbandmen – went amiss, their colonies under constant threat of hunger and want, their crops failing and their livestock perishing, their children dying in the womb. When the sky darkened with piercing winds, heavy snowstorms, and harsh frosts, the troll-folk were settled snugly in their castles of ice, entertaining themselves by singing the *Hymn of the Moon Man* backwards and forwards, night and day, and not giving a hoot whether the storms went on for days or blew over. The Norsemen, on the other hand, found it particularly bizarre that this race had no weapons and no knowledge of the arts of manslaughter and murder, and let themselves be chopped up like brushwood and their dwellings be set on fire when their sorcery was powerless to save their lives.

When Þormóður heard the news that Þorgeir Hávarsson's slayers had eluded him once more, he realized that it would now be more difficult than ever to catch them. Knowing that he no longer had a chance to go north that summer, he changed his tune and finally began asking whether anyone had heard of a woman bigger and stronger than any other in the Western Settlement, yet more supple and pleasant in games of love, and who had traveled from the Vestfirðir to Greenland at the order of Chieftain Vermundur. The Greenlanders replied that they were unaware of a woman as distinguished as the one Þormóður described, but that there was an old woman from Iceland dwelling with a crooked, frowning fellow as her servant on a headland near the seal breeding grounds, where she rendered whale blubber into oil that was to be paid as an annual tribute to the bishop of Garðar. This woman had a stranger name than most, for she was called Sigurfljóð, and her servant she called Master Loðinn, yet more often, Slave Loðinn. These two could not be said to be overflowing with beauty and grace.

For days and weeks, Þormóður continues to wander around Ánavík in the Western Settlement, despondent and helpless. As before, better-off men give him a rather chilly reception, if any at all. Worse still, he has been sick for the longest time, from lack of care and eating execrable food. Very often he loses himself in thought, brooding on things hidden from others, and putting off going to the headland to visit the woman said to be living there. Every day he takes long walks by the sea, stopping to sit on rocks on the shore and watching the seals that bear their pups on the skerries, or trying to augur the future from seabirds' cries. Every day he notices smoke ascending from the rocks at the far end of the headland across the fjord. Every day he walks a bit farther up the fjord than on the previous one, before turning back. One morning he sets out early, and reaches the fjord's head near midday. There a crofter gives him goat's milk to drink, and he sits on the hayfield wall for a long time, pondering over which side of the fjord he should walk down. In the end, he decides to walk down the fjord's far shore, in the cold shadow of the glacier, and sets out toward the headland, more distractedly than determinedly. When he reaches the tip of the headland near evening, the sun is shining in his face. White smoke appears against the sky beneath the sun, and the wind carries the stench of whale oil to his nostrils. At that point, he resolves not to turn back.

A man is sitting among bare rocks by a stone hearth, with two kettles over the fire. In one he is rendering liver, and in the other, blubber, feeding the fire with seaweed and driftwood. This old fellow has not groomed his beard or hair for many years, but his eyes, keen as a hawk's, can be seen gleaming beneath his extremely shaggy brows. A large, finely-made knife, smeared with blood and blubber, lies on one of the hearthstones.

Þormóður Kolbrúnarskáld greets the man at the hearth, unfastens his own sword and lays it on the hearthstone nearest him, and then lies back on the rocks, winded from his walk. The man does not look up from his oil.

Þormóður asks: "What man does Kolbrún love above all others at this particular moment?"

The old fellow looks up, his eyes flashing beneath his shaggy brows. "You will find out soon enough," he says.

"When?" asks Þormóður.

"On the day," says the other, "when the weapon of the man she loves most, second to you, pierces your heart. What are you searching for in this foul hole, you fool?"

"Glory," says the newcomer.

"I never heard of anyone gaining glory in Greenland," says the man. "Whom do you plan to kill?"

"Butraldi," says Þormóður, "and the lad accompanying him."

The man laughs and says: "So you are going after the shrewdest champion and greatest well-pisser ever born in Iceland? I can assure you that he will come off better than all his enemies, as always. In Djúp and on Hornstrandir he got whatever bounty he demanded of people, and was wont to eat dairy food as he pleased. Most years, people and livestock drop dead from starvation in these parts. Butraldi and Lúsoddi soon realized it would not take long for the Norsemen at this fishing station to die out, and that there was little hope of betterment for idlers here. But up near the northernmost glaciers, a race of people enjoys a life of such plenty that they pop seal blubber into the mouths of newborn infants, and of dead men when they expose them to be consumed by birds. Butraldi and Lúsoddi have gone off with the men from Northern Seat to mingle with that race."

Nearby, under cover of an overhanging crag, stands a hut made of rocks slathered with seaweed, with doorposts of whale bone. After the old man and the visitor have been conversing for a while, the door of the hut opens, and a woman wearing a bearskin comes crawling out beneath the low lintel. This woman is not only large in stature, but also fuller of bosom and much plumper in the belly and loins than other women. Her eyebrows are black as coal, and her hair wolf-gray. She has a thick neck, powerful-looking teeth, and the largest eyes of any woman. Her skirt is tucked up beneath the bearskin, revealing stouter calves and sturdier knees than most others have, and the sight of her confirms everything the old tales tell of ogresses and sorceresses dwelling on the northernmost promontories, where sea-tossed sailors wash up when their ships wreck. No sooner is this woman out the door of her hut than she comes straight to the hearth and takes both the weapons, the old man's knife and the newcomer's sword, each lying on its own hearthstone, and fastens them to her belt beneath the bearskin.

Þormóður gets to his feet and greets the woman, and she asks him the news, and who he is, and how it happens that such a young, handsome man does not groom his beard in a more gentlemanly manner before presenting himself to a woman.

He tells the woman that his name is Vígfús,* and that he has not come to Greenland in order to have his beard trimmed or his hair styled. "I was born and bred in Iceland, in Djúp, where Butraldi Brúsason and his toady Lúsoddi killed my brother. I have spared nothing to pursue them after hearing that they fled hither. I intend to hunt them down and kill them here in Greenland."

At this announcement, the mistress of the hut roars so loudly with laughter that it echoes off the cliffs and wakes seals on the rocks. After laughing her fill, she turns to the other fellow, still crouching over the hearth, and says:

"Away with you now, Slave Loðinn, for I wish to speak privately with this visitor."

The slave walks off without a word. He is a broad-shouldered man, somewhat bowed, but otherwise looks every inch the warrior. Þormóður Kolbrúnarskáld walks over to the woman and kisses her.

Mistress Sigurfljóð addresses him: "Now, Þormóður," she says, "there is no need to beat around the bush. The woman that so long ago took into her bed the little lad who was supposed to sleep with the dogs is now part of the distant past. Yet I've always known you would come here in the end, even if nothing were left to welcome you on this headland but my cairn. How could you forget me for so long?"

He says: "Not a night have I gone to sleep or woken in the morning without your bird crowing on the roof."

"We women are always delighted," she says, "to hear you men prattle, best of all when we have grown plump and gray. Truly, you and I kindled well together at one time, though I was no great beauty."

"You are the woman," says he, "who has always prevented me from being able to love another. Were I pledged to the fairest Valkyrie, we could never delight in each other's love with your image standing between her and me."

"It remains to be seen," says she, "whether the woman you find here has the strawberry mark that might still elicit verses from a true skald."

"I have been called the greatest husbandman in Djúp," says he. "At my side stood the choicest of women, whose wealth and beauty made me the envy of most of the leading men in the west. Yet one midsummer, on a heath, when the sun of my life shone brightest on this skald, and the earth breathed its headiest perfume, I could no longer bear it. I ordered my servants to ferry me out to Snæfjallaströnd, and did not stop until I had reached the darkest and most rugged of all the fjords in the Jökulfirðir. There I sat on a grassy wall, listening to the stream as it gurgled past the ruins where your bower once stood. Year after year, at the height of midsummer, I sought out the cold fjord beneath the dark cliffs where I had writhed, sick in your arms, through those long winter nights."

"On the first day you came to me," says she, "I enjoined you and Þorgeir to go kill my lover – and indeed, no woman could do her husband a greater favor."

Þormóður says: "I am father to two little maids with the fairest eyes and softest hair in both Strandir and Djúp. Ever in my mind are their little toes as they lay suckling at their mother's breast."

The woman says: "Less toilsome days would I have had, Þormóður, after old Vermundur, my former friend, banished me to Greenland, if you and I had been granted a son. I must tell you that if I had loved myself more than you, I would never have allowed you to leave the Jökulfirðir for Djúp. Yet when I gave you to another woman, I had full possession of your love and the power that goes with it."

"That woman loved me no less than you. Whereas you called on me to kill your lover, she went by night to her slave's bed, enabling me to pull on my shoes and depart for the freedom that begets heroes and skalds."

40

TWO DIFFERENT accounts are commonly given of how long Þormóður remained in Greenland: one says that he was there for three winters, and the other, seven half-years. No decision regarding this will be made in these pages, though surely it is hardly fitting to measure in years, rather than hours, the time spent together by a man and woman after he has searched for what seems like ages before finally finding her. It may be, moreover, that to some learned men, seven half-years' cohabitation with a woman seems no longer than three winters does to others. Yet most books agree that by the time Þormóður Kolbrúnarskáld was finally rescued from Greenland, he was a grizzled old man, whether his stay there was long or short.

It is said that at the beginning of Þormóður's stay on the headland, some of his days were agreeable, despite his present life being so unlike his previous one, and despite the glorious deeds he had long yearned to accomplish being postponed. It is also said that Mistress Sigurfljóð left little undone to distract her guest from the stench of the liver-works there on the headland, amidst the kettles, hearths, and casks. After Þormóður's arrival, the mistress brought out her tapestries and textiles and hung them up to decorate the inside of her hut. She draped a curtain before the bed and led her guest to his high-seat on a weathered whale vertebra flanked on either side by carved and painted pillars. She had fires lit on the floor and water heated for baths. When the household made itself ready for bed, the mistress spoke harshly to Slave Loðinn, saying that his night quarters were to be outside with his oil buckets, or else in the sheds where they hung blubber or fish, and if this was not to his liking, he was free to stretch out by the stone cairns where sea-birds or shark-meat were cured. When winter arrived, it seemed quite proper to the guest that Slave Loðinn, who was little given to heroism or the poetic arts, should rise at nightfall from his seat near the doorpost and drag his sleeping bag out to a shed, to sleep amidst the dried fish and whale meat.

As time went by, however, Skald Þormóður fell ill from lack of dairy foods, an illness that afflicted most Norsemen in Greenland, and which was compounded by a grainless diet, lacking, as they did, even bread of unthreshed grain – and when they baked and ate food made with wild seed or lymegrass, they hurt their teeth. Long-lasting intestinal complaints were common, and led to anemia, emaciation, and palsy. It was a sign of Mistress Sigurfljóð's exceptional knowledge, as well as her fluency in speech-runes, that the longer Þormóður dwelt with her, the more eager he was to hear her wondrous discourses – for him, her runic lore in Greenland the Dark filled the place of the bounties he formerly enjoyed as a man blessed by kind fortune in bright Djúp.

As for Mistress Sigurfljóð, she was too heavily shrouded in mystery for anyone in Greenland to deem her a woman of rank, mainly due to her acting like a witch and wrapping herself in skins like a troll-woman. It was also rumored that she had been forced into exile from one land to another for persecuting her lovers, until she was finally marooned in an oil-making encampment on a headland in Greenland. Although she lacked most domestic comforts, however, including the clothing that the Norse women in that land weave from wool, it was no secret that she had spent the fruits of her and her slave's labor on valuable items of trade, and would one day find opportunity to travel back to the North to visit her old home and haunts.

Holy Scripture says that the man who is fettered to a place by his flesh, and who feels as if everything around him is orchards and roses, will one day go walking and notice that the orchard is naught but burning desert, offering neither water nor shade, only barren rocky wastes where there is not a single blade of grass for a bunting's beak. Whether such wisdom comes gradually, or is revealed to a person at a single moment one day, will not be debated in this little book.

Greenland's short summers appear to have grown shorter or even to have dwindled to nothing, and the farmer who once lived in Djúp, where good fortune grows with the flowers, hears his own voice ask amidst the cold crags of Ánavík, where no flower will ever grow: "Why am I here?"

One morning as he is lying in his and his mistress's bed, his eyelids part to reveal a monstrosity next to him, bigger and more bloated than any other creature that has ever taken on a woman's form, and in his drowsy state, he feels as if he has strayed into some hidden quagmire, whence no path leads back to the abodes of men, much less of kings, while his ships are burning behind him. His mind now roams from the brink of despair to distant places where kings heap glory on men, and when he rises from the bed, he finds himself saying:

"What might King Olaf be telling his skalds today?"

She wakes and asks: "What does it matter to you?"

"Might not the king be wondering," says he, "why I have not kept my vow? Þorgeir remains unavenged, preventing me from concluding my lay to warrior and king."

"Do you wish then that I were no longer dearer to you than anything else – including Þorgeir's revenge and praise of kings?" says she.

He replies: "These nights, I lie down to sleep with my heart full of grief, knowing that you are the woman who distracts me from my obligations – as the old saying goes: 'Voice of council or king.'"*

"What can idiotic kings and their worthless gifts do for you?" says she, "or the twaddle of peasants at assemblies?"

"We skalds must never let it slip from our minds for even one day," says he, "that heroes make kings, and kings rule lands."

"Do I not rule you, then, skald?" says she.

"Even if you do, my sworn brother is unavenged – and it is but a pitiful possession that you rule while such a binding task remains unfulfilled. I will never be able to stand before King Olaf Haraldsson with my head held upright until the deed is accomplished."

"How lamentable it would be to let that king cut you to pieces for hounds and ravens rather than dwell in the kingdom that is mine," says she.

He says: "How lamentable it would be to have forsaken both the woman in Iceland who had more of the sun's radiance than any others, and my little daughters, whom I called my Moon and my Star, only to lie here until my dying day in this desolate hovel, filthy with whale oil and postponing my end with fox flesh and dulse. A life void of exploits is foul indeed, yet fouler still is a death void of glory – and I shall spare nothing to find Þorgeir's killers and slay them, before going to meet a death befitting a skald in the service of a king, according to the fate spun for me."

"In Norway," she replies, "I have a greater and better kingdom than Olaf Haraldsson."

"What kingdom is that?" says he.

"A kingdom supported by an even greater number of nobler champions, eager to fight for me according to my will."

"I never knew," says he, "that you had your own warriors to defend you, apart from Slave Loðinn."

"Three twisted narwhal's tusks lie hidden in my bed," says she, "two of which I had intended to use to secure passage for Loðinn and me to Norway. The third was reserved to purchase us a dwelling place in the Fjord district, where I was born. In my dreams I have beheld a hall there in the heather. My slave, Loðinn, has in truth been the man bound to me longest in faithful love, so that the worse I treat him, the more certain I am of his dedication and forbearance – and when I treat him worst, then is he most devoted. In brief, I have never had a better man than him, nor will I ever. It is up to you now, Þormóður, to go and kill Slave Loðinn, and I will provide you with a weapon to do so. Then you and I will go home together to Norway, where you will see what pillars support my high-seat in the heather. You will then have the benefit of my magic to make you the most renowned hero in the North."

He says: "I do not wish for things acquired by magic, but only what I gain through my own energy and accomplishment. I would rather fight and die for a king who rules over kingdoms than conquer a place using magic or other craven abominations."

She says: "I assure you, I will defeat that king, and you shall gain only what I purchase for you. Know that I am no shield-maiden whom you can turn into your scullion – in truth, I am the woman who inhabits the Abyss. Through me, all your bright shieldmaidens shall be made widows, and the kings in whom you placed greatest faith shall fall. Though you were to journey to the world's end, there you would meet only me."

That day, the woman is somewhat melancholy. In the evening she tells Slave Loðinn that he may sleep in the hut with them.

Next morning, when Þormóður rises and goes out, he sees two weapons lying on hearthstones before the door: his own sword and Slave Loðinn's knife, which Mistress Sigurfljóð had once fastened beneath her bearskin. Without a word, Þormóður Kolbrúnarskáld takes his sword from the hearthstone and walks off.

41

NOW SOMETHING must be said of the race called the Inuits, who make their abodes at the heads of Greenland's northernmost fjords, as well as on headlands, skerries, and islands. In Greenland, the land rises from the sea only to be covered by high glaciers – all the way north to Scythia the Cold, some say – where there is no human life. It is also said that the name this race has given itself means the same as our word for "men." The Inuits are some of the most peaceable and prosperous people ever described in books. They have no herds, and use the land for neither hay nor other crops, but are such great hunters that their shots never go astray. They catch polar bears in stone traps, and drive reindeer either into pinfolds, where they fell them, or else into the sea, where they harpoon them from boats. These beasts they take mainly for their hides, as well as their tongues and loins. They hunt seabirds with darts, and drive fish onto shoals to spear them. Much of their time is spent on sleds, driving their dog-teams over the sea ice – when they encounter an opening in the ice, they lay putrid swim bladders and seal livers at its rim, and when a shark comes to investigate they stab it with salmon-spears. They fit themselves out in skins, which the Norsemen find a contemptible habit, worthy only of trolls, and wear undergarments made of bird skin. They use one-man boats, called kayaks, or "keiplar" in Norse, made with such ancient sorcery that no storm, skerry, or other dangerous obstacle can damage them. They have a second kind of boat, the umiak, made of skins and crewed by women in breeches, and none has ever been reported to have run aground or sunk. These things have given rise to the saying that the Inuit are ignorant of the art of drowning at sea. It is also said that although the weather is harsher in that land than anywhere else in the known world, the Inuits call all weather good, and are fully content with the weather as it is at any given moment. The cold in that land can be most piercing, yet no one freezes to death. Blizzards there blow long and hard, burying the earth in snow and ice and preventing any vegetation from growing, yet we have never heard tell of a single Inuit succumbing to the elements. Nor do the Inuits consider Earth to be one of the elements – yet they call fire their truest friend, second only to the gods in whom they put most faith, namely the man who rules the moon, and the one-handed woman whose realm is the sea, mother of the monsters of the deep.

Reliable sources say that although the Inuit are great hunters, fowlers, and fishermen, expert with spear and bow, the sight of human blood can bring them to tears. They scarcely understand the forces and instincts that drive other peoples to manslaughter, and have no knowledge of the tools of the trade used by murderous folk in other lands. The Inuit have thick black hair and rather large mouths. When some who had been hunting in the south brought tales of the manners of the Norsemen settled there, and when the Norsemen slew their first Inuit, these people were so utterly baffled by the newcomers' bizarre, depraved behavior that they named the Norsemen after this characteristic occupation of theirs, calling them "killermen" or "mankillers" to distinguish them from men – genuine men – the Inuit. Just as the Inuit are completely ignorant of warfare, so too are they ignorant of vengeance and other practices pertaining to justice.

The Inuit do not live separately, but in hunting bands. These hunting bands travel south to the same hunting and fishing grounds each spring, pitching their tents in temporary camps and seldom lingering long in any one place, before returning north at the close of summer.

The Norsemen made a point of attacking the Inuit wherever they found them, whether in groups of whose movements they had gotten news, or as isolated individuals. If they came across their huts or skin tents on an island or headland, they set these abodes aflame or destroyed them some other way and slaughtered every person they found. Due to the Norsemen's having fair skin, colorless hair, and bright eyes, the Inuits lengthened the names they had given them to white or wan killermen, or pale mankillers.

It so happened that after a group of Norsemen reduced one of the Inuit hunting camps to cold embers, killing anyone who had not hidden in clefts in the rocks, and wrecking their gear as best they could, they were hit by a fierce storm, so that their boat capsized off a headland – something that would never happen to the Inuit. As the Norsemen in Greenland were unable to swim, and thereby to save their lives, all on board perished except one man who had come from Iceland – the skald Þormóður Bessason. He happened to be a good swimmer, and managed to stay afloat until a wave washed him onto a bank of seaweed, where he had no other recourse but to shout for help. A short time later, the storm abated. The remainder of the hunting band that the Norsemen had raided now fled northward with some of their dogs to safer haunts, using boats of theirs the Norsemen had overlooked when they burned the camp. As the women rowed by the headland, they heard shouting from the bank of seaweed. There the Inuits found Skald Þormóður more dead than alive, freezing cold, drenched, and bedraggled, with his good leg now broken too. Since the Inuits have no sense of retribution, they rescued their enemy, Skald Þormóður, from death and set his broken leg, singing all the while. They gave him warm seal's blood to drink, and to eat, fermented seabird, still feathered, and had their dogs sleep curled up against him. A number of corpses had been washed onto the seaweed – Þormóður's fellows – so the Inuits put seal-blubber in their mouths and carried the bodies up onto the rocks. Although the kind-heartedness of these people outweighed their wisdom or learning, they were well aware of the danger they faced, having a pale mankiller in the midst of men, and despite his being sick and spent, they were fairly certain that as soon as he recovered, he would leap up and kill them. Every place that they stopped for the night, they had him lie down with the dogs, and those in charge of these animals watched over him. When night fell, however, the dogs barked noisily, and some bit fiercely – hardly pleasant company in those cheerless places. Þormóður realized that he had little choice but to go along with his hosts no matter how far astray they led him, rather than be left behind, alone, a helpless man more dead than alive in the middle of a wasteland. Summer was drawing to a close. The Inuits broke camp, loading all their belongings onto the women's boats, including newborn infants and dogs, while any man capable of doing so paddled his own kayak. Quite often, the men rolled their kayaks over as a gesture of affection for the women, keeping them keel-up for long spells in a display of gallantry.

Þormóður was astonished at the sluggish pace of these people on their long journey. They paid no heed to the hours, but just trundled along, like folk that sometimes appear in dreams: no one was in a hurry; nothing spurred them on. Þormóður's spirit grew numb watching people drift along without any urgency, as if playing children's games rather than attending to their needs. It was often near evening when they finally launched their boats and started out. They did, however, inch their way farther northward each day, putting ever more distance between themselves and the Norsemen. Yet their day's navigation often amounted to no more than paddling round the tip of a headland to the next fjord – that was far enough – where the women would paddle to land and unload their belongings, along with their children, dogs, and Þormóður Kolbrúnarskáld. They would then drag their boats ashore, pitch their tents, and prepare and eat their supper with great fuss, before lying down to sleep for the night. Or they would paddle up a fjord, close to shore, aiming for its head, but then land and settle down for the night after only a short distance. They always hugged the coastline, never venturing out into straits between headlands; and sailing was unknown to them. Upon reaching the head of a fjord after several days' paddling, they would start paddling down the shore on the other side. If there was a promise of good prey, they would remain encamped for several days. At times they would drag or carry all their boats and all their belongings over an isthmus behind a peak to the next fjord. Women would pitch the tents in the camps, using their paddles as tent poles, while some of the men would go hunting foxes and hares in the surrounding area, or else try to track down musk-oxen; others would keep watch for sea-dwelling creatures: seals, whales, walruses, and bears. They stored caches of food in various places, and always left behind whale meat and seal meat in their camps as provisions for when they returned, or for other hunting bands, but took tusks and hides with them, as well as a large amount of blubber. Whenever they crossed paths with other hunting bands, they celebrated merrily, staying together for several days, boiling seal-blubber, feasting, and singing "ay" and "ee."

The news that one group that had gone south and returned with Þormóður Kolbrúnarskáld among their belongings aroused a great deal of curiosity in the hunting bands. Most men had never set eyes on a pale mankiller. Some asked what creature it was, and why it was being kept with the dogs. The others explained that Skald Þormóður belonged to a race of colorless Inuit who acknowledge no virtue but murder, and that pale killermen had come to their fishing grounds in the south and slaughtered everyone they could get their hands on, among them several men exceptionally skilled at driving their dogs and women expert at rendering blubber. All now praised their great fortune that the Moon Man and Mother of Sea Creatures had spared them from acquaintance with these pallid folk, apart from what their wise men might have related to them in song.

Þormóður now lay by night with the dogs, here and there near the northern boundary of the world, where death dwells.

His life was quite dismal, and the killers of the warrior Þorgeir Hávarsson were as far away from his weapons as ever. Again and again, his heart ached with a single longing: to survive until the day, which now seemed so far away, when he could stand before the mighty king whom Þorgeir had served and who now ruled the kingdom of Norway so honorably. Even if the vengeance that would make him worthy of coming before the king eluded him, he still yearned to extol such a king in verses that men would recall throughout the ages. And although he might never wreak his revenge, the skald hoped that in the eyes of the king, his journeying so far and so long to hunt down the warrior's slayers might be sufficient redress for this failure.

He tried to shut his ears to the relentless barking of the dogs during the night by exalting King Olaf in his mind, lauding him for his champions, and envisioning in his mind's eye the moment when he, a skald, would arrive at the king's hall and enter and bow to his lord. As he pondered these things, time passed and his broken leg healed, yet it was crooked and hardly fit for walking on, while the other one had been lame ever since rocks rained down on him on the mountainside at Ögur.

After traveling northeastward for several weeks, the hunting band came to confined regions where glaciers descended to the sea between bare mountaintops. The weather worsened considerably and the group was often forced to wait for days, hindered by snowstorms, yet eventually they reached their home and dwellings: stone huts on promontories, some dome-shaped, others formed of whalebones with hides stretched over them. Awaiting them here were the stay-at-homes: old folk and children and a swarm of dogs. When they arrived, they hauled their boats ashore, greased them carefully and hung them on tall frames to keep the dogs from gnawing on them. Then they worked on patching up their dwellings and tents and sleds and other gear for the winter. It is the Inuits' custom in winter, when the weather allows, to drive their dogs in the moonlight over ice-covered fjords, far out to sea, to hunt seals – and here more than elsewhere, they feasted on seal and walrus. Some of them worked on covering the huts with seaweed, then with snow, while others hung their insides with hides and arranged cooking utensils and oil lamps in them, for there was no lack of fuel in blubber and oil. In that land the moon shines in winter, but not the sun, which is why the Inuits honor the Moon Man above all. Little by little, the light of the sun vanished, until finally, folk could see only the faint outline of their hands before their faces for an hour at midday. By that time, Þormóður Kolbrúnarskáld had earned the dogs' trust, and those that had been fiercest toward him at first no longer seemed likely to tear him apart. At the same time, his esteem rose among the men. They made him foremost among those creatures, just one rank below the dogs' respected keepers. They dressed him in good tunics and hose of sealskin and gave him hides to sleep on, and housed him in a shed reserved for pregnant bitches and sick old dogs that were so smart and faithful that no one had the heart to kill them. Snow shelters were built for healthy, vigorous dogs, or else they were left outside to be snowed over. The creatures were tied together with ropes of seaweed, these being the only ropes that they did not gnaw off. After snowstorms lasting several days, folk would have to dig their dogs out of the snow to feed them. The noble skald Þormóður, however, found his life tedious in the extreme, hearing nothing but the whine of the wind and the howling of the dogs and hardly ever seeing any daylight. He felt that he would have died and descended to Niflheimur had he not kept the glorious image of King Olaf Haraldsson, Þorgeir's lord and that of both the sworn brothers, steadily in his mind's eye, as well as his hope and dream of someday truly becoming one of the king's men.

42

THUS DOES Þormóður Kolbrúnarskáld spend his days in this place, plentifully fed with seal-blubber and blood and fermented seabird, which the Inuit eat with its feathers still on, and ptarmigan with its crop, but for quite some time he has little interaction with men – the Inuit being afraid that if he gets too close he will kill them, after the manner of his people. Despite the abundance of food, however, he is malnourished, and often ill. It so happens that one morning, in one of Greenland's frequent cold winds, he wakes in the dog enclosure to find a father and his daughter sitting near his bed. They begin singing "ay" and "ee" and drumming. They have come to see how he is getting on, and offer him warm seal's liver, which they consider a wonderful delicacy. Once this father and daughter have risked their lives singing for this mankiller and serving him these tidbits, and he has listened to their song and eaten the dainties, the attitude of the entire hunting band toward its guest changes significantly, and many that had paid him no more heed than a gust of wind cut slices of their food for him as a sign of goodwill, and even deign to look at him. In the evening he is brought to a hut shared by seven families – no less than thirty people dwell in it, night and day. There to greet him is the girl who had woken him that morning with delicacies and song. She welcomes him warmly and bids him sit and enjoy himself with the others. This girl is named Luka. They pass the evening with no small measure of singing and drumming. It appears as if the hunting band has forgotten the damage and injury done them previously by the pale man's people, and when folk retire to their beds, Þormóður is not sent out to sleep with the dogs, but instead invited to snuggle into a wondrous skin sleeping bag, sewn shut and adorned with variously colored skin beads. Next, the maid Luka comes and slips into the bag with him. In Greenland, pretty young girls often use urine for washing their hair and other ablutions, and rub themselves thoroughly with unguents that the Norsemen might liken to whale oil. For now, however, Þormóður Kolbrúnarskáld hardly moves a muscle.

The next evening, when the girl crawls into his sleeping bag again, he turns away without a word, and on the third evening, he spreads himself so wide that she has no room to slip in beside him. She goes and sits by the wall and cries, greatly astounding Þormóður. Other women come and try to comfort her, while the elders in charge of the drumming start singing "ay" and "ee" over and over, dramatically rocking forward and back, while some bow their heads to their knees as they sing. Their song's subject is how a pale mankiller refuses the company of a human woman in his bed – how a pompous guest disdains a hunting band abounding in blubber. Bitter sorrow has come to afflict good men: "Ai-a, are you not filled with shame, when the gills quiver on a stranded sea trout that swam hale of late in the eddies, beating its tail, a-i-a, a-i-a?" All of those who had gone to sleep now rise from their beds and join in this song, with bitter and piteous wails. Finally, several men step forward and offer to lend the pale man their unbetrothed daughters for his nighttime company, if he prefers them to this one, and still others are willing to lend him their wives if they will consent, while Luka can have whatever man she chooses. When Þormóður glances over the other women, feeling fairly certain that they will not smell any different than the maid Luka and that he who will not share his bed with a woman in a hunting band will be sent off to the dogs and wake flea-bitten, he realizes that his best option is to accept his public obligations, and says, in the end, that the maid Luka should indeed come sleep with him in the sleeping bag that she herself had softened with her own teeth and adorned with precious beads. He admits that a girl with such an outstanding sleeping bag must indeed hold a high place in the hunting party. These declarations of his are rejoiced at by everyone there, and one and all exuberantly praise the man who made the moon his hunting camp, while some extol the one-handed Mother of Sea Creatures. The girl returns from the wall where she has been weeping, at first a bit bashful, wiping off tears with the back of her hand, thankful that he refused the offer of other women, yet still racked by sobs. Þormóður is moved by this girl who values her own happiness to the point of tears, in contrast to the dry-eyed women from whom he had parted, the most eminent in the North, who had tossed his life-egg between them like a toy at Hornbjarg. He says that it makes little difference what people call fragrance – what to one race is fragrance, is to another stench. "This girl shall indeed be my wife."

And time passes.

Upon coming from the Norse settlements to this remote place, Þormóður Kolbrúnarskáld was astonished to discover such a great discrepancy: whereas in the settlements, men were sorely oppressed by crop failures, hunger, and distress, deadly illness, and loss of livestock, here, north of the very limits of human life, there was a glut of amenities: tools and equipment, dwellings and boats, clothing and shoes, bountiful food, and an endless supply of fuel for lamps and fires. The Norsemen in the south had had little to sing about, and their skalds were dull and inept, while here, all the songs were long, and everyone was a skald. When one person started singing a song, the entire hunting band joined in and did not stop until the next morning. In the Western Settlement, the Norsemen were in constant peril from the weather both at sea and on land, but here in the north, the cruel winters, with their never-ending blizzards and deadly frosts, flung no such javelins at people. The Inuits sat round their soapstone kettles, never more content than when their dwellings were completely snowed over, leaving not a trace of them on the snowfields beneath the helm of the moon, apart from when doughty men were forced now and then to dig their way up through the roofs to make holes for the smoke. Their lamps burned brightly night and day, and the dwellings of the Inuits were always so warm beneath the snowbanks that they all spent their days naked, apart from little strips of hide around their loins. Each of them had his own chores: some did the cooking and cleaning, some carved stone and made vessels, while others fashioned harpoons and other spears from bone, though they did not use sharp-edged iron tools to craft these things – instead, they scraped bone with harder bone. To fasten different pieces together, they had thongs instead of nails. Some softened skins for clothing with mallets and scrapers, or with their teeth, while women sewed bird skins into undergarments, using whale sinew for thread and hares' teeth for needles. Moreover, there were men who worked steadily at cold-hammering native iron – but no one in this place coveted renown in arms or glory as a lord of men. Þormóður mingled freely with these people, who were more peaceable and concordant than any other race – so much so that there was no conflict between them, and each and every one was a pillar of support for his neighbor, and nothing caused apprehension but a man who took no companion. They lived happily and prosperously in a land where Norsemen had experienced nothing but hardship and death, and had mastered every skill needed in that land to partake of and rejoice in the bounties of life. They had been granted all the good fortune that flows from blubber, which is far more trustworthy and benevolent than anything gold can give. This peculiar guest of theirs, however, actually thought little about all this, when he finally found himself living among people who had become, in their own country, true creators of their own good fortune. At times, when Þormóður wished to try his hand at a particular task, he found he had no knack for any of the tools or equipment used by these people in their crafts and other arts, despite his having been considered masterful in all such things back in the days when he dwelled in Djúp. He was as good at learning their language as a dog is at distinguishing the sounds of human speech. When these people gathered in a circle to sing their songs, with everyone joining in, he, the skald, shut his ears to their song as tightly as he could. The subjects of the songs of these people, who had never accomplished a deed of renown as far as anyone knew, he found quite trivial, and to him, it was simply idiotic that they had never once given a thought to the honor to be gained in declaring allegiance to a magnificent emperor or king or other lord who had covered himself in glory by means of victorious battles or grand conquests, or by maintaining a retinue of champions and skalds. It was bewildering to him how this Greenlandic rabble completely lacked any eminent men who were capable of taking advantage of those beneath them. He himself stated that when he was living among those people, his mind returned to the same thought, night and day – that it was an utter disgrace that freeborn heroes and skalds, as well as their kings, should lack the vigor necessary to wipe out such a stupid and loathsome race.

It is said that during his time in this abode, Þormóður Kolbrúnarskáld developed a taste for warm seal's liver. Yet folk began to grumble when Mistress Luka brought the pale man better and more plentiful morsels than what other men in the hunting band received from their wives, and also when she fed him, while others had to feed themselves. A wise man who was an acquaintance of the Moon Man was called upon to meet with Þormóður and Luka, and he informed them that no wife in a hunting band was to shower more affection on her husband than other women did on theirs. Nor did it please the group when the pale man grumbled ill-naturedly to himself while the rest of them sang, and folk wanted to know the reason for it. Þormóður replied that it was fair that he be granted more seal's liver than most men, since he was a liegeman of Olaf Haraldsson, the most praiseworthy king in the North, and it was for his sworn brother's sake that he served this king and constantly sang his praises, whatever others might sing. The Inuits understood little of what he said. They were completely ignorant of the customs and laws of other lands and had never heard of kings or warriors. "Does this Olaf," they asked, "drive dogs better than other men?"

That winter passes like others that are no shorter, until cracking sounds begin to rend the night, and those in the know announce the tidings, that the Mother of Sea Creatures is breathing a warm breath toward the land from the farthest seas where she has her abode. When the sun drives its bright celestial dogs south of the glacier, and the Moon Man, the guardian of midnight, returns to his bed, men wake their earthly dogs, brush snow off their sled-runners, and go to see what gifts the one-handed woman has left on the rim of the ice.

Þormóður remains at home, with his mind on grander exploits than killing seals or walruses. Time passes sluggishly, slowly, and in order to while away the hours he takes to seducing the women tending to their chores in his dwelling, their lawfully wedded husbands having journeyed out onto the ice. Once again, folk begin grumbling at this behavior of his. The women grow jealous of one other – many of them harboring a desire to sleep with this colorless mankiller – while the menfolk are swollen with grief at the thought of the women's disdain of the honorable behaviour expected of them. Eventually, Mistress Luka discovers her sister, the maiden Mamluka, beneath the mankiller's hide one evening. Upon finding Mamluka there, Luka attempts to chase away the maiden, but the lovestruck girl refuses to get up, so her sister sits herself down by the wall and starts wailing. Her mother goes to Luka and squats beside the girl and wails as well, with all her might, as do her cousins and other female relatives, filling the room with their cries, but the other girl refuses to get up from beneath Þormóður's hide.

Among the Norsemen, men who seduced other men's wives could be killed with impunity, but the Inuits have no idea of justice of this sort, as previously mentioned. Reliable sources say that although the Inuits never resort to revenge, they consider one crime far worse than any other evil deed – to the extent, in fact, of it being unatonable: when a man abandons his wife without grounds and leaves her in tears, and takes up with another woman before her very eyes. A heavier penalty and harsher forfeiture is imposed for this crime than any other that might conceivably be committed in a hunting band. This terrible punishment is carried out as follows: people take a snow bunting and blow into its nose – exhaling their repugnance of the deed. Then the bird is left where the criminal dwells, and the other men walk away. From that day on, the hunting band neither lays eyes on the criminal again nor acknowledges his presence among them. From then on, he is on his own – and he who is on his own there is dead.

Now the nights grow lighter – the time has come for the band to embark upon its summer hunting and fishing. One evening they notice that a bird has flown into the dwelling, beating its wings against the ceiling in the great distress of its avian heart. On the bird's arrival, the group falls silent. All at once they are overwhelmed with fear, and they scramble to their feet and rush out of the dwelling. Þormóður's in-laws leave one by one, his wife and sister-in-law and the entire clan, as well as the other women who have previously had relations with the guest, each of them taking whatever they have in their hands, until Þormóður and the bird are the only ones left. He sits there for a spell, listening to the bird beat its wings against the ceiling, and expecting the others to return – but this does not happen. Finally, Þormóður gets to his feet and opens the door for the bird, which flies off, following the path laid down for it by the Moon Man and the Mother of Sea Creatures. Þormóður goes outside and shouts that the bird has flown away, but no one pays him any heed. By then, the nights have grown light enough for work. There is a hustle and bustle on the hard-crusted snow around the winter camp, and to Þormóður, it looks as if everyone is preparing for departure that very night. But when he tries addressing anyone with the few words he has learned of their language, they all turn a deaf ear. When he touches someone to get his attention, the man walks off without a word. No one glances Þormóður's way, any more than if he were wearing a helm of invisibility. Then, like so many men who fail their lovers, he flees back to the comforts of his wife. He goes to Luka, who is busily occupied, and asks why she has not brought him something to eat, but his wife neither sees nor hears him, and when he nudges her, she acts startled, as if some unexpected, foul thing has fallen from the sky. She hastily brushes herself off, walks away, and hides behind a group of unrelated people. No one bids him start preparing himself to join the hunting expedition. After finishing gathering and bundling up their possessions, they drive their sleds and boats over the ice in the direction of the sea. As the yelping of the dogs and creaking of the sleds dwindle in Þormóður's ears, he realizes that he is dead. That night, he lies awake, racking his brain over what he can possibly do to regain his life. When he goes out the next morning, he is in for another shock: the old folks remaining behind in the winter camp neither see him nor pay him any notice, but pass by him like fleeting shades. As for those left behind to look after the dogs and household things in this abode over the summer, he is invisible to them as well. He has the suspicion that among the group, there are several other men who have been made outcasts for some reason, and are therefore as good as dead. The dogs that had greeted him earlier in the winter when he brought them food no longer give him as much as a sniff.

The next evening, when he crawls all alone beneath a shabby scrap of hide in the empty dwelling, having had nothing to eat but what he has picked out of the rubbish heaps, his mind drifts to the sorrowful fate of the skald who was one of the greatest heroes and lovers of women that ever lived in the North: not even dogs sniff at him; he is buried alive north of the world. As he lies there, pondering what chance he has of reawakening to life and exalting King Olaf, whose power and majesty he believes surpass those of any other king, he hears dogs barking and the swishing of sled-runners over the hard-frozen snow, and then the rustling of skins outside the dwelling door, as one always hears when Inuits walk by. Now the stone slab is lifted from the mouth of his tomb, and a person comes to where the skald lies dead, and in the next instant is sitting at his bedside, and has touched him, mouth on skin. He recognizes from her breaths that it is the maiden Mamluka, his crime. She takes a warm seal's liver from her bosom and hands it to him. He thinks that what the maiden says is this:

"We set off for the south, away from your corpse. Yet when night fell, and we had pitched our tents, and all had gone to sleep, I could not sleep, and the one thing I knew was that I had to return to you, despite your being dead. For I love you so much that I would prefer to be with you dead, rather than not at all."

There she tarries for a time with the skald in the dark of night, feeding him liver and wrapping him in a good hide –

before turning away. She does not hear what he says to her, makes no reply to any of the dead man's questions, but loves him as disconsolately as only a woman can do, and departs.

Reliable sources say that in this manner, the maiden Mamluk was the dead Þormóður Kolbrúnarskáld's wife for three nights, returning each night from her hunting band's camp after all had gone to sleep – but on the fourth night, she failed to return, nor did she ever return again.

43

NOW, FOR THE moment, we shall shift our narrative from the cold abodes of trolls back home to the North, and tell of events that occurred there during these years. In brief – King Olaf Haraldsson was toppled from his throne and driven from the country, exiled by his enemies. Many accounts are given in Icelandic books of the ruin of his kingdom, according to the testimony of heroes and skalds, but few of them will be detailed here. Yet there is no concealing what wise men have considered to have weighed most heavily in Olaf's downfall: namely the utter lack of benevolence and the huge resistance that Olaf encountered from the peasants of Norway, despite his having for a time made great strides in consolidating his rule among the good nobles of that land, whom he had bribed or won over in some other way. The peasants constantly sought for an opportunity to murder the king, along with the nobles whom Squire Sigurd Syr had induced to support him. The Norwegians never viewed King Olaf Haraldsson as more than an incendiary who could be killed with impunity according to the laws of the land, whether by a slave or a free man.

In his youth, Olaf the Stout had become accustomed to the Viking habit of salting down cows in distant lands, and now, after becoming king, he quickly took up his old habits, making plans to plunder his neighbors of their livestock, and then deploying his troops to pillage cattle, sheep, and goats, as well as stoats, in several of the Norwegian districts that paid tribute to Swedish kings with the consent of the kings of Denmark. These deeds gave rise to such ill will between Olaf and one Swedish king that it could never be fully assuaged afterward, not even when Olaf became the king's son-in-law. As the saying goes: "What you build, you live in." The Swedish kings that called themselves lords of the Uppsala domains, Olof Skötkonung and later his son Anund, who was christened Jakob by clerics, plotted constantly against Olaf Haraldsson. They considered these raids of his daft, and attempted to decoy him into fool's errands. Nothing made them hotter than when someone called him a king in their hearing.

The Swedish kings habitually provoked the Danish kings and the Norwegians into conflict with each other. The Danish kings called themselves the sovereigns of the North, despite not truly being so, except for the times when they were surrounded by weak and worthless kings at loggerheads with each other.

Olaf, King of the Swedes, was stunned and flabbergasted when he received news of an impudent, reckless move on the part of his namesake the Stout – a move no less impudent than his current enterprise of killing the Swedish king's men and plundering goods and chattels in the Swedish tributaries in Norway.

The Swedish king Olaf had numerous children. Some were fathered in secret, or with his mistresses, while others he had by his queen. The king had presented his daughters with an magnificent manor in Götaland, rich in meadows, woods, and lakes. Each spring he sent his daughters to dwell there in the company of those henchmen of his who seemed better suited than others to taking care of women.

Around that time, it so happened that noblemen in Norway, friends of the Swedes entrusted with looking after the king's daughters in summer, contrived to have Olaf Haraldsson make a covert journey to Götaland to hunt in the extensive, game-packed woods there, and Olaf asked to spend the night at the king's daughters' manor. He was announced as a count of the Holy Roman Empire, there on a pleasure trip, and was welcomed with a most excellent banquet. The Swedish king's two daughters were then in their prime. One was named Ingegerd, a radiant, tall-statured woman, who had a swan-dress and could fly, and when she wanted, she flew off to determine men's fates. She was the king's lawfully begotten daughter, and the best match in the North. Ingegerd had an illegitimate half-sister, dark in complexion, named Astrid, who could be as chatty as anyone when she wished, but also extremely ill-tempered and rancorous. She was a shrewd woman and a good drinker, but it was thought unlikely that she could be married off to a foreign potentate. Some sources say that she was dwarfish.

The sisters agreed that this young king had certainly made his mark among nobles esteemed for deeds of renown, having subdued Norway of his own volition and in valiant style, killing five kings in one morning. They declared him fit for the company of the truly illustrious, despite his being called a cow-salter in Uppsala. That evening, they drank to the king's health with great courtesy.

When Olaf the Stout woke the next morning, he asked for the hand of Ingegerd, the king's daughter, in marriage. She received his proposal politely and took it up with her guardians, and they promised to bring the matter before her father, King Olaf, in Uppsala. Olaf the Stout sorely regretted having to take his leave of the ladies, particularly Princess Ingegerd. They accompanied him to the gate and bade him farewell on a hill overlooking the sun-splashed lakes of the kingdom of Sweden, its golden pastures and dark forests. This pale lad, with his sullen, evasive gaze, lacked all mirth and was bereft of playfulness, having experienced little of what normally constitutes youth. On land he had a waddling, wobbly gait. He was stout above and slender below, with a pale layer of down on his cheeks and the hands of a surgeon. Yet at that hour, this lad appeared in the eyes of the king's two daughters as nothing less than the hero of a lay. Ingegerd approached him and vowed to do her best to convince her father to accept his proposal, and bestowed him a parting kiss. Olaf then turned to Princess Astrid, who had less to say than usual. To her, he said the following:

"What keepsake will you, Astrid, give this wayfarer who is about to return from the golden peace of Sweden to the land of his enemies?"

She unfastened a gold pin from her neckline and handed it to him. He thanked her for the gift, and in return, fastened her mantle with an inferior pin of little worth. She then responded with these words, whose meaning has long been disputed:

"The woman who mocks you most shall harbor you, but she who pines for you daily shall show you the door. She who deceives you shall possess your life, but she who loves you shall destroy it."

At that, King Olaf returned to Norway.

The king of the Swedes took this news far worse than the report that the king of Norway was slaughtering both his men and livestock.

As much as the Swedish kings have always been far mightier and greater rulers than the kings of Norway, there are fewer tales concerning them, since Icelandic books focused more on raising the Norwegian kings above their usual pettiness. It was the belief of Swedish kings that the kinless marauders or foreign renegades who were constantly turning up in Norway and claiming kinship to Harald Fairhair were poor matches for the daughters of the kings of Uppsala, who could trace their descent with certainty thirty generations back to Yngvi-Freyr, without a single woman in the line. The Swedes felt obliged to put the kings of Norway in their place, especially if they began stirring up trouble in districts neighboring their own, and it had not been very long since the Swedish king Olaf allied himself with the Danish king Sweyn to kill Olaf Tryggvason. It was very much in Sweden's interest for the kingdom of Norway to remain poor and disunited and be ruled by petty kings, each feathering his own little nest. Thus was Olaf, King of the Swedes, stricken speechless when he learned that his daughter Ingegerd and his portly namesake were consorting.

The Swedes held lands and kingdoms in the Baltic regions, and Swedish merchants traversed the whole of Russia, all the way to Constantinople. The Swedish kings had kinsmen among rulers in the east, men who controlled vast realms but were prohibited by the emperor in Constantinople from holding a loftier title than knyaz – that is, prince. Around that time, Yaroslav, son of Knyaz Vladimir the Saint, was undertaking to subdue Russia. Opposing him were his brothers, three or four of them, and Yaroslav had sworn an oath to spare nothing nor lay down his weapons until he had defeated them all. Since Knyaz Yaroslav found himself hard pressed in battle against his brothers, with rather little backing from the native lords, he sent envoys to Uppsala to request support from the Swedish king based on bonds of kinship, promising in return greater privileges for the Swedish merchants in Kiev than they had previously enjoyed, and taxable land for their livelihoods when they spent the frigid winters in the east. The Swedish king Olaf declared that Yaroslav should have as many troops from him as he needed, and ordered his vassals to levy troops on the coasts and islands east and west of the Baltic – everywhere that he ruled. But Olaf added a confidential stipulation: that when Yaroslav was victorious over his brothers, he was to wed Ingegerd, Olaf's daughter, and grant her a half-share in his lands and kingdom, and the Swedish king's agents were to accompany her and act as her stewards and advisors there in the east. Thus, the next news that Olaf the Stout heard of his betrothed, Ingegerd, after their meeting in Götaland, which we have just described, was that the girl had left Sweden and been wed out east in Russia to Knyaz Yaroslav the Wise, son of Vladimir the Saint.

Just when Olaf the Stout feels most cruelly betrayed by Ingegerd, whom he loves beyond all other women, and deceived by her kin in all other respects, it so happens that Ingegerd's illegitimate sister, Astrid, declares her love for him. The single most important factor in sealing the peace treaty between the kings of Sweden and Norway is the support and authorization of noblemen from both lands for this match – and finally the Swedish king yields to the persuasions of his nobles and weds

Olaf the Stout to Astrid, his illegitimate daughter. Yet relationships between fathers and sons-in-law can be chilly, and there is as little trust between the two kings as before, despite the treaty's bringing an end to mutual slaughter and plunder.

At that time, regents of Cnut Sweynsson ruled in Denmark, while he himself occupied the throne of England. Foremost among Cnut's regents was his brother-in-law and bosom friend, Jarl Ulf Sprakaleggsson. Those were bountiful years in Denmark, both on land and at sea, and the commoners' welfare improved, as always happens when lords of the land remain distant, taking their wars with them. As might be imagined, the noblemen in Uppsala took a dim view of the wealth accumulating in Denmark through peace, and the Swedish peasants began grumbling discontentedly at the harsh treatment they felt they were getting from their tax collectors in peacetime – besides being mobilized to make war on unfamiliar peoples in the eastern part of the world, while the Danes, on the contrary, enjoyed wealth and plenitude. A dangerously unwholesome friendship sprang up between the Swedish and Danish peasants whose lands bordered each other, and some of the Swedes' leaders declared their willingness to accept the laws of Denmark rather than remain the subjects of the Swedish king.

Just as Denmark's wealth grew in the absence of kings, however, so did the populace of Norway suffer ever-increasing hardship under the rule of King Olaf Haraldsson the Stout. Every penny in the land went toward keeping his army primed and ready against the Norwegian peasants, as well as toward the furtherance of Christianity and the construction of warships.

After some time, Norway found itself devoid of grain, and many men in that land whose livelihood had previously depended on two goats, now had only one. Others – far more numerous – who had previously gotten by with one goat, now found themselves with none, and were forced to remove to the woods with their broods and gnaw on bark or dig for roots. At this point, Olaf the Stout sent word to his father-in-law, the king in Uppsala, petitioning him for grain and meat, or bright silver to trade with foreign merchants for food. His peasants, he complained, had nothing left with which to feed his army – many had been reduced to beggary and were dependent mainly on Christ's goodwill for their sustenance. They were now paupers of the Church, which had taken control of much of the best land and property in Norway.

The Swedes, for their part, rarely had enough grain or meat for themselves, but they did have good mines that supplied plentiful ore. They were better at forging iron than most peoples in the North and always had arms to spare, even when they had nothing to eat. The king in Uppsala sent word back to his son-in-law the Stout that he had neither grain nor meat to hand over to the Norwegians. "But," he said, "the land lying here next to us has more than enough grain and livestock. It is called Denmark.

You pirates must have taken a giant step backwards if you now sit and watch hungrily while other men stuff their own bellies on your doorstep. No one has ever heard of the Norwegians having to beg their bread from Swedes, and we are certainly not about to change that – but I will supply you what you need in weapons and ships in order to drive the wolf from your door."

Historians reckon that the beginning of the end of King Olaf the Stout's reign in Norway was his going to war against the Danes, into which he was duped by his father-in-law, the king of the Swedes.

Olaf assembles all the ships that he can get his hands on, mans them with peasants who have lost their livelihoods in Norway, gives them whale meat to eat, and sails on a fair wind south to Denmark. Awaiting him there are several ships under the command of Swedish noblemen, sent by the king in Uppsala to reinforce him. No sooner does Olaf the Stout reach Denmark than he falls back into his old Viking habit of pillaging the countryside, slaughtering the sheep and cattle and salting them down. He duly proclaims that his is an army of defenders, come to deliver Denmark from tyranny. The Danes, having been caught entirely off-guard, suffer immense losses of people and livestock before their lords manage to call men to arms throughout the country and engage Olaf's forces. They send word to King Cnut in England, informing him that an army has come from Norway to free Denmark, and entreating their overlord to respond quickly. Cnut does not tarry, and musters a huge army in no time – all English soldiers. He has aremarkable number of ships, too, huge ones, and so well equipped that a fairer fleet has never set sail against the North. All the ships are painted above the waterline, and many have gilded heads at their prows, and sails striped with blue, red, and green. When their arrival in Øresund is reported, the Swedish king's ships prepare immediately to sail for home, while Olaf the Stout's fleet flees in terror toward the Baltic, where many a vessel, being poorly rigged, is lost in storms. Of the ships that seek harbor in Sweden, the Swedes seize those of any worth as payment for old debts, and pillage others. Those that remain unscathed in the harbors, and which no thief or villain has a mind to plunder or dismantle, are trapped there and prevented from returning to Norway by the fact that Cnut's entire fleet is lying in wait in Øresund. Winter draws on, and Olaf the Stout's troops remain cooped up in their ships with few provisions of their own, and none provided by the Swedes. In the end, the Norwegian peasants decide that their best hope is to abandon their ships and attempt to journey home on foot, traversing the breadth of Sweden in winter, and the king is persuaded to consent to the expedition. At first, King Olaf has horses to ride, but his troops eat them, compelling the king to march like everyone else, though he has men carry him over gullies and rocky terrain, due to his ungainliness and clumsiness on dry land. The Norwegian troops are often forced to resort to looting, for the Swedes still refuse to assist them, beating them instead like dogs every chance they get, and even enslaving some. It is a long time before this forced march fades from the memories of the peasants who manage to make it home barefoot to Norway.

Olaf is left with very few men. He is unable to gather new forces to defend his kingdom against the peasants, and has lost his fleet. The peasants harass him so relentlessly that by summer he has no other choice, due to the riots and uprisings throughout the land, than to take to his heels once more and flee with his household by the shortest route out of Norway, eastward over the mountains.

Now that Olaf Haraldsson the Stout has been ousted from his throne, things go as they so often do for deposed kings: most people lose their love for them – particularly those who once put their faith in them – and so it was with Queen Astrid. Her life seems to her to have taken a cruel turn – clambering over mountains out of Norway, over scree and sharp-edged rocks, her husband banished and disgraced and their young son crying, with no companions apart from a few ribalds whose service Olaf has purchased with silver. Gone too is every other close, trusted friend of King Olaf – the farthest from him now being those who had formerly sung his praises with flowery words and courtly affections, such as his marshal, Skald Sigvatur of Apavatn. Gone too is the Englishman, Bishop Grímkell of Canterbury, whose life the king had saved on the banks of the Thames, and whom he had made his court bishop, father-confessor, and most intimate friend, in defiance of the episcopal see of Bremen and the Lord Pope himself. All are gone.

Writers of old have hinted that King Olaf was so loathed by the populace that he was reduced to plundering and robbing to feed himself, his queen, and their son as he made his way out of Norway.

When Olaf Haraldsson and his ragtag household come down out of the forest lying between Norway and Varmland, envoys of his father-in-law, the king of the Swedes, are there waiting for them, to take his wife Astrid and their son and return with them to Uppsala.

The king asks: "What will you do with me, the son-in-law of the king of Uppsala?"

The envoys reply: "You can look after yourself, fool!"

There at the edge of the forest, King Olaf parts from his queen. Yet he will not give up their son, for he fears that the kinsmen of the boy's mother will do him harm, so before the queen leaves the mountain, he persuades her to allow him to take the boy with him. Queen Astrid then rides to her kinfolk in Uppsala.

After begging from door to door in Varmland with his son for a time, King Olaf makes his way to the coast and takes passage for himself and the boy on a merchantman sailing eastward that fall, back to Russia.

44

AT AROUND THE same time, a ship returned from Greenland to Nidaros after a two-year journey. Such a homecoming was always considered great news in Norway, for not all ships returned from voyages to Greenland. Though tusks from whales and walruses might be had there, and these being people's only source of ivory in the north, merchants were reluctant to visit those parts for fear of sea ice and prolonged storms, which churned up breakers more powerful than anyone had encountered on other seas. When the ship anchored, and its crew members spoke to the first person they met on one of Norway's rocky reefs, they were told of the changes that had taken place there: King Olaf Haraldsson had been toppled and driven to the East by his enemies, and most of his friends had turned against him.

This news grieved and distressed the crewmen – to think that they had set sail with the king's wares two years ago and returned to the same land, yet it was now the land of the king's enemies. To them, Norway seemed to hang like a necklace that has lost its gemstone – what good was it, though Norway's meadows blossomed and its forests abounded in leaves, if its people no longer united round its trunk? As so often happens, however, the crew had lost sight of the comforting fact that one man is always replaced by another, and a king by a king – but more importantly, a penny by a penny.

Word now spread that King Cnut Sweynsson of England had anchored his fleet in Viken, intending to take over custodianship of the Norwegian king's realm – following the old custom that the kings ruling Denmark should also possess Norway, regardless of whomever else might temporarily raise his banner there. Envoys were dispatched by Cnut to every part of Norway to persuade the nobles to swear oaths of loyalty to him – in return, he offered his vassals more power and loftier titles than ever before, and privileges and honor far beyond what Sigurd Syr had sold them when he traveled round the country with his train of packhorses. The noblemen were promised greater fiefs for their livelihoods and more lenient taxation than before, as well as the full backing of the English army. Convinced that the English fleet was far more capable than King Olaf's starving servants of thwarting the insolent peasant rabble, the leading men in Norway soon abandoned any reservations they had about submitting to Cnut.

That evening, curious townsfolk gathered at an inn in Nidaros to hear the sailors' tales of Greenland and to discover what valuables they had brought back with them. Among the ship's crew was a man of rather dubious appearance. His cheeks were sunken and haggard, and he was scarred and marred, tattered and tousled, wearing threadbare shoes and clutching a raggedy skin about him. The townsfolk asked who this ragamuffin might be – whether he was a Lapp or a Finn, and why such men did not stay put in Greenland. The crewmen replied that he was an Icelander, and that he had seen places farther to the north than any others – places where it was horrendously cold, and nearly as infinitely dark as the long night of the grave. Trolls had left him on a skerry not far from the Western Settlement in Greenland, and there he had sat beneath a distress flag for six days and nights before the ship's crew found him. His extremities were nearly frozen, but the crewmen saved his life. Unknown trolls had encountered the man on the coast at Northern Seat and brought him south to that skerry.

Norwegians have always found it highly laughable how Icelanders trace their ancestry to kings, and now the townspeople of Nidaros ask this newcomer: "What kings did you have for forefathers, Suet-lander?"*

The ragamuffin replies: "King Olaf Haraldsson's warriors were my closest kin, and he who had the noblest heart was closest of all."

They, in turn, reply: "King Olaf the Stout's army was made up of none but cowards and moochers, and here in Trøndelag you are better off never speaking the names of firebugs and thieves. It is clear from your arrogance that you are a true Icelander, though worse for wear."

The ragamuffin retorts: "We Icelanders are the only men in the North who can neither be forced into submission nor bought."

They laugh, saying that it is astonishing to witness a dust devil in calm weather. "How does chopping up suet on the remotest skerry in the world inflate folk so?"

The ragamuffin says: "It cannot be denied that when Harald Tanglehair set Norway aflame, we betook ourselves west and made ourselves Icelanders. This we did because we had no desire to associate with men who allow themselves to do battle and murder for money. We took no possessions from Norway apart from the lore of skalds, warrior ideals, and tales of ancient kings. To Iceland, we brought Mímir's head, and Boðn, the vessel of the mead of poetry, yet here you remain, dull-witted, bereft of skalds, and speaking a corrupt language, with no glory of your own making. Norway will never have any glory, apart from what Icelanders bestow on it."

The others retort that it is high time to have done with the glory bestowed on Norway by Icelanders. Icelanders had never portrayed Norwegians in poetry or sagas as anything but bullies and crooks, mustered by their rulers to ride roughshod over the populace and trample it underfoot. Icelanders consider none to be men apart from those who kill people en masse. The townsfolk say that that lout with the title of king, Harald Tanglehair, from whom the Icelanders had fled, was not a whit worse than any others the Icelandic skalds had praised to the sky, such as Olaf the Stout.

A distinguished man steps forth from the host's table in an inner nook of the inn. He is finely attired, elegantly groomed, black-eyed, and wearing a sword and arm ring. As he draws nearer, the patrons who have been making fun of the Icelander over their mead fall silent.

The courtly man speaks up: "Good sirs," he says, "it is my understanding that this man you are teasing is a countryman of mine, and I ask you to regard his sore and battered feet and consider what a difficult road he has traveled. Look, too, at how weathered and furrowed his face is. This man has certainly traveled far longer and harder roads than you. I would hazard that he has experienced a thing or two more than some of you who lie about here among the skerries of Norway, men of little spirit and narrow outlooks. What man are you, Icelander?"

The ragged old man whom the townsfolk have been mocking rises from the table, clad in a hairshirt beneath hide tatters, his feet swathed in rags and his toes stricken with sores that reveal white bone, and limping on both legs. Several of his fingers have been lost to frostbite, while the others, still whole, are twisted into his palms. His ears are missing as well, and the tip of his nose is blunted. Most of his teeth have come out, his pate is white and bare, and his beard hoary. He has neither weapons nor shield, nor a single possession of any monetary value. Now he rises from his seat before the stately lord, his countryman, who has defended him out of kindness, and states his name and lineage.

"My name," says he, "is Þormóður, and I am the son of Bessi, from the Vestfirðir. Some called me Kolbrúnarskáld at Djúp and in the Jökulfirðir, when I was younger."

At this disclosure, the nobleman goes to this countryman of his and embraces and kisses him and bids him hearty welcome. "My name is Sigvatur," he says, "and I am the son of Þórður. My father and I have often extolled the glory of kings, though such a thing passes now, as before, for a fleeting honor. What fate did the Norns spin for you, Þormóður, whose verses every child in Iceland knows? You look to me rather ill-treated by the sisters."

"I was the richest farmer in the west," says the skald, and he smiles. "And I was wed to the noblest woman in Djúp, a Valkyrie in beauty and grace, and by her had two little daughters with the nimblest toes and sweetest laughter in the Vestfirðir. They used to wake me in the morning, one by kissing my feet and the other by pressing her forefinger on the tip of my nose."

The royal skald bids the serving-maid bring him and his fellow skald ale, and a salted pork joint, as well. "Tell us freely, Skald Þormóður, of what has been on the lips of many: your journeys beyond Iceland's shore."

The courtier has the sores on the newcomer's feet cleansed and bandaged. Þormóður starts in on his story, looking down at his feet:

"It was known to all in Iceland that I swore an oath of brotherhood with the warrior whose like had never before been born in the North. I loved him above all others and he me, though we were not granted the good fortune to remain together long. It was in our pact that nothing but the death of both of us should sever our brotherhood."

"I have heard tell of the warrior Þorgeir Hávarsson, but the more I have heard, the less I have understood what sort of man he was," says Skald Sigvatur.

Þormóður says: "The sort of man in whose chest laughed a heart that was no bigger than a rowan berry, yet as hard as an acorn."

Sigvatur replies: "Such a warrior must truly have had much to commend him. What further proof do you have of his merit apart from his small heart, Þormóður?"

"That the king," says Þormóður, "to whom that heart was pledged is the greatest in the North and all the world. This is in fact why he has become my king as well."

Sigvatur then says: "I think I have some knowledge of the king to whom you refer. I was his marshal and faithful friend for no less than ten years, and we conversed on many a topic. Yet I do not recall ever having heard the king mention the small heart you describe. Nor does it appear that that heart alone was sufficient to bring victory, either to its owner or to the other to whom its support was pledged: King Olaf. Both have been laid rather low, and some think the sun has not shone brightly on Norway's mountainsides for some time now."

Þormóður replies: "Þorgeir has in fact fallen in the king's service, and still lies unavenged, though little has been spared to redress that. Yet for Þorgeir's sake, I have composed a lay in honor of King Olaf Haraldsson that will be sung as long as the North is inhabited."

With a smile, Skald Sigvatur says: "We skalds have no idea which lays will remain longest in memory. I, too, composed verses honoring King Olaf."

Þormóður says: "I abandoned my farm in Djúp, where the ram trundles in its wool and a single fish is worth as much as a bull. I handed over my swan-winged Valkyrie to a slave. To my two nimble-toes, who gazed at me more trustingly than anyone else ever did, I left Þorgeir Hávarsson's skull."

"It is a bad bargain to compose lays for lords, Skald," replies Sigvatur, "while letting others pull the biggest and choicest fish from the sea. I would never have become a skald if I could have had such excellent fish. I became a skald following my forefathers, because we had nothing to live on. I was sent, an impoverished child, for fosterage at Apavatn, where odd little trout swim with inverted fins and carry poetry in their heads – and he who sinks his teeth into those heads is never the same again."

"I went," says Þormóður, "to Greenland according to my oath to Þorgeir to pursue his slayers, who were, in fact, so contemptible that they were hardly worth killing. One was a well-pisser, and the other was a lice-ridden tramp."

Sigvatur asks why Þormóður was unable to kill these sons of the Evil One.

Þormóður says that the little snakes always slipped from his grasp. "When I sought them on Hornstrandir, they had gone to Melrakkaslétta, and when I came there, I was told that they had gone to Greenland. When, after weeks of being tossed on the waves, I finally made it to the Eastern Settlement, they were reported to be in the Western Settlement. In the Western Settlement I met my old concubine, who had cast a love spell on me, and this woman offered me refuge and rest for a time – insofar as those things can be had in Greenland. But Þorgeir Hávarsson's slayers had escaped to Northern Seat, where they mingled with trolls. When at last I escaped that cruel woman, after being constantly confounded by her sorcery in the darkest of places, I determined to make my way north to the farthest reaches containing any seeds of human life, to see whether I might be fortunate enough to carry out my revenge, and I joined the company of men who gather narwhal tusks and slaughter trolls. Yet after the trolls that we had gone to slaughter saved my life, and cured my broken leg and frostbite, and elevated me to the rank of their dogs, I felt as if those two churls, Well-Pisser and Louse-Crop, were nothing but the offspring of my delirium – once I had come north of Northern Seat, I forgot the purpose of my journey. It seems rather likely to me that Þorgeir's slayers now occupy a place below Niflheimur, in the ninth and worst world. However," says Þormóður in conclusion, "it is my hope that King Olaf will, when I finally manage to stand before him, take into account the long road that I have traveled, enduring great tribulation and prolonged times astray, despite my plans having come to nothing. Not all men would have been willing to undertake such a journey for the sake of a bond."

Sigvatur is much impressed by this story of Þormóður's, and asks numerous questions about the habitations of trolls in Greenland. Þormóður tells him of those great wonders: of the creatures that dwell there in human form, but do not hold man-slaughter to be the highest of accomplishments, or know what it means to accomplish deeds of renown. Nor does that race submit to a king or lord or bishop, and it has neither lawmakers nor tax-paying landholders, nor anyone of rank apart from the man who has made the moon his abode, and the one-handed woman who dwells in the depths of the sea. Lastly, Þormóður recites to Sigvatur and the others gathered in the inn the great lay that he composed with a fiery heart for King Olaf Haraldsson while he languished in those regions where Allfather dwelt with frost giants before he created earth, sea, and air.

Sigvatur listens attentively to the lay, as do the others drinking in the inn. After Þormóður recites the final lines, they continue to sit silently, reflecting on the praise bestowed on King Olaf Haraldsson. At last Skald Sigvatur Þórðarson has his say:

"This is indeed a fine lay," he says, "and far better than those that I composed for that king, yet it has one drawback. A good lay is of little worth if it is composed too late. Praise bestowed on a king other than the one that now rules the land is worse than silence, however well-worded it may be. A lay for a fallen king is no lay. A lay for a victorious king, who now rules the land – that alone is a lay. Olaf Haraldsson is farther from you, Skald, here in his own royal residence, than when you tarried with trolls in Greenland and had the least hope of meeting him face to face."

Þormóður says: "Þorgeir and I often spoke of how a valiant heart remains the same in victory or defeat. And it is my belief that the king who is lord of Þorgeir Hávarsson's heart, alive or dead, will truly possess more power in the end than other kings against their enemies, and that his banner will wave throughout the ages, though he falls. For not even on the bow of Bifröst, whose end touches the sky, nor in Djúp, where I had my domain and my bliss, nor in Greenland, as far north as Northern Seat, where fish have more precious tusks than anywhere else, nor even north of Northern Seat itself, where trolls rule, is there any power or glory – except in the breast that holds a gallant heart."

Sigvatur says: "I know, Þormóður, that you have put yourself in greater peril than others due to your prodigious fortitude, which would never allow you to shirk from journeying to the ends of the Earth to fulfill an obligation. Yet of all the perils that a fearless heart can stumble into, I wish to warn you, from true experience, of one that is worse than being tossed about off Greenland's shores and cast up in Northern Seat, and that is, to bind yourself to a sovereign, no matter how noble he might be. He who pledges his faith to a sovereign is truly worse than dead. For a sovereign is the first to be strung up on the gallows. Where do we, his friends, then stand, when our refuge is hung? Secondly, a sovereign is always prepared to yield his throne and lands to his enemy, and his entire army as well, particularly his vanguard of champions, and to conspire with his superior and vanquisher to murder his closest friends and confidants – those who have been most faithful to him. A sovereign is the only man in any land who is free to join the ranks of his enemies at any moment it is to his own advantage, and each and every person that puts faith in his sovereign also puts himself in danger of being murdered by him before all others – and especially before his enemies. It is said of Þorgeir Hávarsson, who was a greater braveheart than most of King Olaf's champions and far more faithful to him than any other man, that when the hero displeased the king, the king sent him on a perilous mission to Iceland, to kill Icelanders – a mission that came to its expected conclusion. It is wise to bow to a king as long as the peasants put up with him on the throne. When the throne starts to wobble beneath him, however, it is advisable that a skald address his lays to the king whom the peasants are more inclined to endure. If a foreign army invades one's land and overmatches the king's own forces, it is wiser to trade one's loyalty to it for gold, in the manner of noble lords, than to sing the praises of the king who is abandoned or doomed."

Þormóður says: "When in Iceland I heard tell of Sigvatur Þórðarson, I never imagined that he, when his luck waned, would be first to betray his troth to his king – who, through the valor of his champions, conquered Norway. In the old lore that I learned from my father, a far different kind of gallantry is extolled."

"Friend," says Sigvatur Þórðarson, "splitting hairs is unbeseeming for skalds. What matters more is that the peasants here in Norway have toppled King Olaf, and that a foreign lord has arrived with fourteen hundred ships, and, according to old custom, has purchased the allegiance of every good man in Norway with any authority. You are now standing in the English king's realm – not in King Olaf Haraldsson's. That is a fact. If a skald or hero in Norway does not understand this fact, then it will cost him no less than his luck and his life. And then, every man may think what he pleases of gallantry."

Þormóður says: "Things look quite hopeless for me, then, wanderer that I am, having abandoned my wealth and love, children and farm, field and pasture, in order to win justice for my brother – and paying, over and above all these, with my hands and feet, nose and ears, hair and teeth, all in the hope of earning the friendship of the noble king whom Þorgeir chose for us. You are one of this king's right-hand men, wearing his costly arm-ring and the scarlet cloak he draped around your shoulders, yet here you are feeding me hearsay that the king wished to destroy the heart to which I had pledged my faith, and which was so fearless that in times of prosperity as well as suffering, the memory of it was ever my lifeline – particularly when my own heart quaked in the face of death. I would have been better off losing my life in the arms of a wicked mistress, or among trolls, than to have to listen, weaponless and defenseless, to such malicious slander."

"Even the wise may be mistaken, comrade," says Skald Sigvatur, "as you are when you accuse me of slandering King Olaf Haraldsson. I assure you that I have never had a better friend. I call him a paragon among kings in his generosity to his friends and his guilelessness in most of his deeds. Yet it is no secret that King Olaf was a man of little wit, and in the same measure, of little education, having been brought up aboard ships and trained in the work of marauders since childhood. He never learned how to walk properly on his own two legs on dry land, and instead waddled about, ever on his sea legs. Christian counts and bishops who lead armies in the south bribed him and his fellows to burn and slaughter for them in France, after first baptizing them, for Christ demands that the champions who serve his kings profess the true faith. Such was King Olaf's learning that he knew only two solutions to any predicament: one being baptism and the other murder. Due to his childish ignorance, he constantly had to have others at hand to tell him when to baptize and when to strike. Yet I believe that King Olaf would have done right if he had been able, even to any small degree, to distinguish between good and evil. And because of his utter childishness, I felt more pity for Olaf Haraldsson than most men, and loved him better."

45

BOOKS RELATE that following King Cnut Sweynsson's departure from Denmark to take over the throne of England, he sent Harthacnut, his son by Queen Emma, back east to Denmark to be brought up by his brother-in-law and bosom friend, Jarl Ulf Sprakaleggsson, whom he had appointed his regent there, to defend his kingdom while he was away ruling distant lands.

Eventually the Danes, weary of Cnut Sweynsson's prolonged absence, claimed Denmark for their own, letting it be known that they were no slaves of kings. The Danish noblemen were more than uneasy with the idea of the land having no king to rule it, as well as no army that a king could use to strike fear into the heart of the populace, in the manner of good rulers. Therefore, Ulf Sprakaleggsson, in consultation with the nobles, ordered that land and privileges be granted to the peasants and lightened many of their obligations and debts to their lords, demanding, in exchange, that they accept as their king his foster-son Harthacnut, an ignorant child. Upon conclusion of the bargain, Jarl

Ulf took all power and authority in the Danish realm for himself, without asking leave of his friend Cnut Sweynsson.

Now we shall briefly relate the events that occurred in Denmark at the same time that the English army frightened Olaf Haraldsson out of Øresund, along with the Swedish ships that the king in Uppsala had sent as allies, or rather, as decoys to lure the Norwegians into their predicament. Once the cow-salters from Norway were chased off and peace was restored to the land, Cnut went to see those whom he had assigned to keep watch over his kingdom in Denmark. He left his ships and rode to Roskilde, which was under the regency of his brother-in-law Ulf Sprakaleggsson and Ulf's foster-son Harthacnut. Emissaries of the see of Bremen had founded a monastery in that town, and it boasted a cathedral as well, which stood for many years, and was dedicated to the Holy Trinity and named the Church of Our Holy Lord.

Jarl Ulf Sprakaleggsson prepared a great banquet to welcome his suzerain, Cnut Sweynsson, and Cnut's captains. A splendid company of Danes gathered there to regale Cnut, who now named himself Cnut the Mighty or the Great, in commemoration of the victory that he had won against the English king Æthelred and Queen Emma. Jarl Ulf was then the wealthiest man in Denmark, and his banquet in honor of Cnut reflected this – but we shall not recount here what fare was offered to the guests.

Norse books recount that Ulf Sprakaleggsson was a hot-tempered man, but an excellent administrator of his kingdom and a superior leader in every respect. That evening, the two friends, King Cnut and Jarl Ulf, play a game of chess. During the match, the king becomes distracted and makes a wrong move – what Snorri calls a "finger-breaker" – but then wants to take his piece back and make another move instead. When he attempts to do so, Jarl Ulf is none too pleased. He tips over the chessboard, stands up, and walks off. Shortly afterward, everyone goes to bed.

There are two different accounts concerning what subsequently occurred between the brothers-in-law. In this book, we prefer to follow what was put down in writing in English annals the same years that these events took place, and we do so first because Cnut was king of England at the time, and thus we feel it right and necessary to give ear to his own clerics and advocates, who would not have wished to denigrate him in any way, and in the second place, because some of the Icelandic accounts of these events seem more dubious, having grown muddled in the memories of historians, storytellers, and knowledgeable women in a foreign land for seven full generations before being written down.

The accounts state that Cnut had, for a bodyguard and valet, a youth from Norway named Ivar. It was the custom among rulers never to surround themselves, for any reason whatsoever, with natives of the lands they ruled, believing that their lives were at risk in such hands due to the ill will that might be borne by the populace toward its ruler. Cnut Sweynsson thus allowed neither Danes nor Englishmen in his bedchamber, knowing, as he did, where his enemies were to be found.

On the evening of the chess match, after the king has gone to his chamber, he bids his valet get up and go and kill Jarl Ulf Sprakaleggsson. The young man dresses himself in haste and leaves, but returns a little later to report that the jarl has gone with his bishops to chant compline. Cnut has Ivar extinguish the lamp, and they go to sleep. After vigils, however, King Cnut rises from his bed and wakes his servant, telling him to put on his shoes and go and kill Jarl Ulf Sprakaleggsson. Ivar goes out into the night and is away for a long time, but finally returns to tell the king that Jarl Ulf has gone to town to visit his mistress – in whose vestibule are two lions with fire burning in their eyes and jaws, and in whose forecourt eighteen vicious bitches guard the lions. They lie down once more to sleep, the king and the Norwegian Ivar, but toward dawn, King Cnut wakes again and calls to his valet, saying that the time is drawing near for jarls to be returning from their mistresses, and that the Norwegian is to go and lie in wait for the jarl and kill him. The valet rubs the sleep from his eyes and goes out. In town, the cocks are crowing. Quite a long time passes before the Norwegian Ivar returns once more to the king's bedchamber, with bad news: Jarl

Ulf had driven home to his wife, King Cnut's sister, and they had bolted their bedchamber door from within, while four chambermaids slept, with great modesty, in the anteroom – an iron-clad knight keeping watch over each maiden. Just then, the first bell chimes matins in Our Holy Lord's Church. King Cnut says that of all peoples, the Norwegians deserve the least blessings, and to be beaten more than any other men. They sleep now for the remainder of the night.

The king rises early the next morning and goes to attend Mass in Our Holy Lord's Church. At the same time, his brother-in-law Jarl Ulf arrives at the church. They greet each other, proceed to the chancel, and sit down side by side before the altar to heed the service. King Cnut responds over and over to the chanting with bitter sighs and warm tears. At the Canon of the Mass, it is a sign of great courtesy for good men to fall to their knees and cover their faces as Christ descends to take up his abode in the bread, which clerics call transubstantiation. When the Mass reaches this point, King Cnut the Mighty kneels next to his bosom friend and lays one hand lovingly on his breast to find his heart, at the same time reciting several holy words from the Psalter in Ulf's ear. As he speaks, his other hand drives his dirk between the jarl's ribs and through his heart, killing Jarl Ulf Sprakaleggsson instantly.

It is a mark of how great a man King Cnut was in the estimation of the bishops and archbishops, and of the Lord Pope, yet particularly in the eyes of White Christ himself, that no one with the title of sovereign in Denmark has ever been more or better renowned before or since, though one were to search far and wide. For he is the third king in all of Christendom to have been granted the designation Magnus, which in our tongue is "the Great." Jarl Ulf was carried quietly out the chancel door while the bishops concluded the Mass. Maidens of Christ then wiped the blood off the stone floor, and clerics purified the Church of Our Holy Lord with a blessing – and it was all as if nothing had occurred.

That same day, Cnut the Great has his son Harthacnut brought to him, and there on the town square, in the sight of the peasants, he deals the boy a fitting chastisement with a switch. Then he takes him on his knee and kisses him, and says that the boy shall sit next to his father on his throne. Norse books record that when these things had been done, the entire populace of Denmark rallied to King Cnut and submitted to him out of love. The king then appointed other regents to govern Denmark, men who play no part in this story.

Now we shall return to the tale of Þormóður Kolbrú-narskáld, who has made it to Norway after being battered and afflicted by storm, starvation, cold, and other hardships in Greenland. When the Icelanders in Nidaros witness the woe-ful state of this skald and countryman of theirs, they fetch an aged peasant woman, an expert healer, to treat the man, and he remains bedridden on a farm for the rest of the summer. The flesh grows back over the abscesses on his hands and feet, and his internal afflictions subside – those that he had contracted from the bizarre fare he lived on while dwelling in the troll-world. When he is finally able to return to his feet, he is, of course, quite unsteady, since both of his legs are lame, and neither his hair nor his teeth grow back, nor the fingers or toes that frostbite had taken. His youthful beauty can never be reborn, and the clothes that he wears, though gifts of mercy from goodhearted folk, are very shabby. In the fall he is left there penniless, after the other Icelanders have sailed away on their ships. Gone, too, from Nidaros is the nobleman Sigvatur, the king's skald.

When Þormóður ventures to converse with the Norwegians or to entertain them with good lays or tales, they give him but poor reception. It was an age in Norway when folk prized southerly fashions, and they preferred hearing stories of the miracles of holy men and godly women and the sacred chants of monks and priests to fixing in their memories the tales of the men of Hrafnista, King Hálfur's champions, the Völsungar, or other excellent men of yore. The Norwegians feel quite strongly that they can do without any long, complicated poems croaked out ad infinitum by a beggarman from Iceland. When the skald goes to meet the high-born men and wealthy shipowners in Nidaros and offers his services as their minstrel, these magnates choose instead to hire southern dwarves to perform magic tricks for them. When he offers to recite them the *Greenlandic Lay of King Olaf and his Champions*, they all declare that Olaf is the one king they would choose least to hear praised.

Not one man of distinction in Norway could be found who did not consider it an advantage or an honor to serve the king of England. When Cnut landed in Norway with an English army aboard fourteen hundred and forty ships, their sails striped blue and red, most of the Norwegian elite enthusiastically praised his fleet. They told Þormóður that no savvy, silver-tongued skald composed praise-poems for royal absconders, and that any man who did not follow a king who commanded an invincible army was tying his luck to a foxtail, even if noble men were in the habit of scratching the ears of fugitive kings during the brief time they hung onto their thrones. Þormóður's only option now was to go from door to door and earn his living in such labor as tends to extend one's days rather than one's fame, for instance, mucking out peasants' pigsties and leading their goats to and from pasture. Wherever Þormóður Kolbrúnarskáld dragged himself throughout the villages of Norway, folk inferred from the poor fellow's tattered clothing and carriage, which was typical of those scarred by sickness and decrepitude, that he was a mere derelict. Boors and vagabonds laughed at him and called him mad, and young lads shouted insults at him. Having been a skald and sportsman in Reykjahólar and Vatnsfjörður and the darling of women in the Vestfirðir, a Viking on Hornstrandir and a prosperous husbandman in Djúp, he found it strange to pass his frostbite-damaged hand over his bald, earless head or damaged nose, or to pull a white wisp from his beard.

It was paramount in Þormóður Kolbrúnarskáld's lore that all powers and authorities with jurisdiction over any matter in Heaven or on Earth should be noble and praiseworthy – in particular, the men who rule empires, as the gods rule over the world and the celestial bodies. He was thus assailed by great perplexity upon finding himself mucking dung and swineherding as a result of his loyalty to Þorgeir Hávarsson's king. He began to question whether he had learned his lore correctly, and whether he should continue to extol eminences who had been laid lowest: one butchered on a chopping-block in the north, the other driven alive into exile. Ever more often, the skald's mind wandered to the power and authority of Cnut Sweynsson, who had landed in Norway under countless sails, as previously told, and won a greater empire than any other king in the North, according to report. Eventually, the skald persuaded himself to rework his lay for King Olaf in praise of King Cnut Sweynsson, and to eulogize the overwhelming victories that King Cnut had won in England against King Æthelred and in Denmark against Jarl Ulf, as well as when he subdued Norway simply by spreading word of his coming under striped sails.

King Cnut now sent his treasurers by ship, loaded with English money, to hold private talks with noble Norwegians, he himself having settled in with a great force on Zealand, at Trelleborg. Reliable sources state that an Icelandic merchant conveyed Þormóður Kolbrúnarskáld to Denmark aboard his ship, declaring that such an excellent skald had little opportunity for glory among crofters in Norway, and that the refuge and home of such a man was solely with kings who rule over numerous empires at once.

Trelleborg was designed by foreign architects using Roman arithmetic, under the direction of Cnut's father, King Sweyn Bluetoothsson. It was there that Cnut and his father gathered mercenaries that they managed to recruit both inland and on the isles, billeting them and training them for use on campaigns in other lands – it was at Trelleborg that Sweyn had mustered the forces he took to England to harry King Æthelred. At this particular time, Cnut's English army, which he had sent to terrify Olaf Haraldsson the year before, was stationed at Trelleborg. Within the fortress's ramparts stood thirty tall wooden houses, and in a nearby estuary of the Great Belt dawdled numerous ships, painted beautifully above the water-line.

When Þormóður Kolbrúnarskáld appears at the rampart gate, the guards announce that for beggars to approach king's castles is an offense punishable by death, especially those that limp so badly that they are useless for war. "And," they say, "it is beyond belief that a beggarman should seek audience with a king such as Cnut, the greatest champion since the passing of

Charlemagne and equal in rank and dignity to emperors, high kings, and the Lord Pope himself. Where are the clothing and weapons that you would wear to present yourself to such a king?"

"I am an Icelandic skald," says the visitor, "and I have given my clothing and weapons, as well as my toes and fingers and nose and ears, and my teeth, which used to sneer at stately men, and my hair, which was the delight of women, to gain the renown necessary to address statesmen who rule the world with might and wisdom. I handed over my farm to slaves, as well as my wife, who can fly like a swan, and the same for my daughters, who had the nimblest toes in the west of Iceland. I pray you deliver this message to the king, good fellows: that I have journeyed through colder and darker lands than most men, and over surging seas, and lived with trolls north of all human habitations, and I have kept safe, in the fair wind of the moon-bride,* a lay in alliterative verse, longer and better than any that even the Lord Pope himself has managed to deliver to his master, King Christ, whom the trolls claim has his kettle on the moon."

The guard retorts:

"King Cnut will not suffer to have leprous tramps in his sight tonight, when he is receiving Skald Sigvatur Þórðarson, formerly King Olaf's marshal. He has stopped here on his way to Rome, and we have just ushered him into the king's hall, wearing a sable mantle and gold-broidered shoes. He is assuredly a far greater skald than you, though we in the king's guard find monkeys, dwarves, and pipers far more entertaining than any of you Icelanders."

This book will not describe the feast that Cnut Sweynsson held at Trelleborg on Zealand after he had reconquered Denmark and its associated territories and was making ready to leave the country. Learned men, however, say that one of the guests was Skald Sigvatur Þórðarson of Apavatn in Grímsnes, arrayed in precious velvet and an engraved sword, with numerous gold rings on his fingers and costly arm-rings of the sort that can only be had from emperors or suffragan bishops. It is presumed that at this feast, Sigvatur recited the lay whose refrain declares that none towered higher under Heaven itself than King Cnut: "Cnut reaches to Heaven." This lay tells of how Cnut received word from the east that things were going awry in his realms in the North – those enemies of his that he feared least, such as Olaf the Stout and his followers in Norway, had been ousted by the populace, whereas in Denmark, those he distrusted most, his brothers-in-law and bosom friends, had taken power. The lay does not tell how Cnut scared King Olaf away from Denmark, but instead focuses its praise on Cnut's mustering of an English army to defend Denmark from Danish peasants: in control now of those lands, says the poem, was something the king considered far worse than the rule of either his friends or his enemies – namely, the impudence of the peasants, who aspire to take possession of the lands they inhabit and rule them themselves. In his lay, Sigvatur names such conduct "Danish robbery." The lay suggests that it was not due to paltriness, but rather, unwillingness, that Cnut chose not to launch military campaigns against his enemy Olaf Haraldsson or his friend Jarl Ulf Sprakaleggsson and Ulf's son Harthacnut, who had snatched Cnut's kingdom in Denmark from him. It is only when Cnut is informed that the peasants there are poised to take matters into their own hands – rule by peasants, he feels, is something infinitely worse than the might of his friends and enemies combined – that he sets out with fourteen hundred and forty English ships, to show these upstarts in Norway and Denmark that he towers highest under Heaven of all kings on Earth, and is nearest to God, and is such a dear friend of Christ and his mother that he is free, without any word of rebuke from the Lord Pope himself, to murder his friend before the high altar at Mass, during the *transsubstantione panis*. The lay repeats the same refrain after recounting the king's mighty exploits – so glorious a king is Cnut that he alone can be seen beneath the arch of Heaven: "Cnut reaches to Heaven."

Following the feast, King Cnut leaves the North and returns to rule England. Skald Sigvatur Þórðarson, for his part, has enough cash in his saddlebags when he reaches the mainland to buy himself horses and ride south over the Alps to Rome that fall.

46

OLAF HARALDSSON left Sweden along with his son Magnus, and sailed in the fall with merchants all the way to Kiev, to the realm of the Grand Knyaz Yaroslav the Wise and his Grand Knyaginya, Ingegerd of Sweden. There he hoped to find support and refuge.

The town is located on the southern bank of the Dnieper River, where it is broadest, resembling a great lake. Buttercups as big as loaves of bread grow in the meadows there. Sometime in the past, bellicose Swedish merchants had pushed their way into power and subjugated the folk that inhabited the region's wide plains or woods. Grand Knyaz Vladimir the Saint, the father of Yaroslav the Wise, had been baptized a Christian in Constantinople, and decreed that all of his tributaries were to be Christian. Of old, the leading men and great lords of that land were called boyars and bogatyri. Vladimir waged a long and vicious war against these people, with the support of foreign kings, both the Byzantine emperor and his Swedish kinsmen. Many places were conquered and Christianized during that war, while those of Vladimir's men who fell in battle were proclaimed holy martyrs by the patriarchs – death on the battlefield was their salvation, their exemption from Purgatory. Their skulls were the greatest of treasures, and the source of numerous wonders and miracles.

Standing on the banks of the river was a splendid royal castle, surrounded by an orchard and high towers. The towers were manned constantly by watchmen, on the lookout for the approach of Cumans or other enemy armies from across the plain or down the river – these lands having never submitted entirely to their sovereign. Located within the town walls was a monastery that grew into one of the greatest in that part of the world, as it was in possession of several items of profound interest to most Christians: first among them, a finger of the blessed protomartyr Stephen. Learned men argued that this finger was one of the best safeguards against shortages of butter, and was extremely effective against grasshoppers, besides being a powerful counter to the usury of Jews. Also preserved in this monastery, whole and intact, was the earthly body of the blessed Knyaz Vladimir, Yaroslav's father. This body, replete with fragrance and glory, stirred consciences deeply and gave rise to many a miracle throughout the region and beyond. This monastery, moreover, possessed more skulls of those that had given their lives in the service of Holy Wisdom than any other monastery thereabouts, and these skulls begot an abundance of miracles for the welfare of the people. Many bought candles and lit them before these skulls, for the salvation of their own souls and those of their kin.

At the behest of the praiseworthy Lord Patriarch, who, in the East, holds the same position as the Pope in the West, Yaroslav the Wise undertook to erect the Cathedral of Holy Wisdom, which has stood there in some form ever since and has always been counted as one of the major cathedrals in that part of the world. For its construction, enormous finances were required. People were exhorted to make monetary donations, any sum they could do without, in memory of saints and martyrs, for the sake of their own souls and the souls of their kin, and many an individual's reputation was enhanced if he donated generously to Holy Wisdom and lit candles before the skulls.

It is said that when Olaf Haraldsson arrived in Kiev in the fall with his son Magnus, and sought out Yaroslav, the knyaz scarcely deigned to acknowledge this banished king of Norway who had come to his country as a fugitive, devoid of the glory of royal birth and of power. Worse still, his shoes were ragged, and his kirtle was filthy with grease stains. His son wore no shoes at all. Yaroslav also found it strange that the man who was formerly his rival should now seek his friendship, and said that he would rather be a better friend to such an excellent king as Cnut the Great than feed and shelter those who were traitors to him. What is more, he said, he had not gone to such great pains to kill his four brothers in battle simply to give away land in Kiev to foreign fugitives. Yet he would, he said at last, condescend to allow Olaf to accompany the Swedish merchants, after they had dragged their ships ashore for the winter, to the districts where they traditionally gathered tribute for their livelihoods while wintering in Kiev.

Folk say that in the eyes of a woman, no suitor is so contemptible that, even if she has spurned him disgracefully or betrayed his trust, she will not, ever afterward, have more affection for him than for any other man. The older she grows, the more eager she will be to aid him as best she can, regardless of his predicament. In like manner, Knyaginya Ingegerd decided to ensure that Olaf Haraldsson was well looked after in Kiev and granted whatever position in their court he himself chose, and she provided him with raiment befitting a nobleman. Her sister's son Magnus, she said, would be brought up with the knyaz's children.

In those days, the Norse tongue was not commonly spoken in Kiev, except among the Swedish guard serving there, whose duty it was to fight the commoners and keep them subjected to the Grand Knyaz. Clerics and notables there spoke Greek, which they called the world's most important language. In that town, only beggars and lepers spoke the vulgar tongue. There were few in Yaroslav's court who deigned to speak with Olaf Haraldsson, he being held in such low esteem. Olaf's lack of friends caused him no small amount of grief and sorrow. No one there paid any heed to him, apart from the woman who had disgraced him most with her falsehood and deceit, and who now granted him alms out of pity. Olaf grew disgruntled at how no one seemed to want to listen to him whenever he ventured to speak, especially when they knew that he was more eloquent than most in his own tongue, able to deliver elegant, authoritative speeches to large crowds, and to recount glorious exploits from his Viking days and other adventures.

Now it happened, as we find so often in the old tales, that the king, feeling foresaken, turned his mind ever more frequently to that lord who is praised by his friends as most trustworthy and most patient in listening to those who find themselves in dire straits – namely Christ, King of Heaven, who shall sit in judgement over mankind on the Last Day. Olaf began frequenting houses of worship in order to speak to the saints and apostles, those most favored by Christ, as well as to holy maidens and commanders of the angelic hosts. He put himself in the hands of these holy beings, hearkening tearfully to the prolonged chanting of monks, which, in the Greek tradition, is often most melancholy and plaintive. However, those who governed the Christian church in that part of the world were not great friends of the Holy See in Rome. In Greek they were called metropolitans, and were governed by archimandrites and patriarchs. They had all been excommunicated by the Lord Pope, as he had been by them. Yet Olaf Haraldsson could not distinguish their

Christianity from that of his old friend Bishop Grímkell of Canterbury. In most respects, the Greek and Latin rites seemed the same to him.

Olaf, having gotten a grasp of the monks' language, spent long periods conversing with them and listening as they told their wondrous and compelling tales full of miracles, revelations, and the remarkable visions of the saints – all the while picking lice from their beards with great dexterity. By the bounty of Holy Wisdom, King Olaf now came to understand how tender an embrace Christ offered to those who had squandered their kingdoms: how patient he was in lifting them to their feet if they submitted to him, honoring every man's supplications, whether he were emperor of his land or an exile. He spoke often with the monks about his wretched state, landless and penniless as he was, dependent upon the charity of strangers and detested almost everywhere. Yaroslav would have none of his service, nor would he grant him land for his livelihood, either to govern or to plunder, as he had been accustomed to doing since childhood. Despite the coldness shown to him by Yaroslav and his court, the more Olaf's heart was moved by the truths of these miraculous tales, the more he felt visited by Christ the Emperor's grace.

It is said that Knyaginya Ingegerd insisted that Olaf Haraldsson, her first suitor, be granted a place in Kiev where he would enjoy more respect than he was given by her spouse, Yaroslav. By her intercession, Olaf was invited to dwell in the monastery and mingle with the men who consecrated themselves to God through their holy way of living. Yet it was God's law that no childbearing creature, other than the queen of the land, should be allowed to cross the inner threshold of a monastery.

Ingegerd Olafsdotter was a tall woman, fair-complexioned and haughty, like those other women of the race of swans, of whom but few are seen in the North, and none elsewhere. She paid repeated visits to her brother-in-law Olaf in the monastery to discuss the news from the North, where her thoughts were constantly fixed. She spoke candidly to Olaf, telling him apologetically that her kin had held the Uppsala domains for thirty generations in the male line and put little trust in men of dubious lineage who rose independently in Norway and claimed the title of king – there were too many examples of how quickly such kings were slain in Norway when someone stronger undertook to attack them. Nonetheless, she did not feel that her sister Astrid, born of a serving maid, had made a match any worse than her own. She said that it was certainly a kingly feat to dispatch one's own brothers from the world, as her husband Yaroslav the Wise had done, but as knyaginya, she found it far less honorable for Yaroslav to have four wives in addition to herself, as well as seven concubines. She added that it was better to rise under one's own power in a kingdom temporarily divided and to fall prematurely in battle, than to rule Kiev in name – without being allowed the title of king by the Byzantine Emperor, only that of knyaz. "And those black-browed, meddling slatterns of Constantinople, naked to the navel, mocked me, calling me a shieldmaiden of the race of trolls, suckled by a she-bear!"

Around that time, monks were zealously gathering all the skulls of holy men and martyrs they could get their hands on from the company of the elect killed by the boyars and bogatyri in the fight against King Vladimir the Holy, when he set out to force the people of that land to take baptism. The monks' plan was to entice the people of Russia, as well as Bulgaria the Great and other kingdoms, into making pilgrimages to Kiev to venerate these holy and blessed saints, whose skulls, by the mercy of God, bore such beneficial fruit. Any person who wished to bring these skulls a monetary offering for the sake of Holy Wisdom, was promised in return forgiveness of sins and mitigation of their pains in Purgatory. They could also expect their sores and boils to heal, their calves to fatten well, and excellent yields of turnips, as well as respite from crawling creatures and the Cumans, that vicious race that eats human flesh. Likewise, whenever paupers came across a comely man's or woman's head on their path, they could bring it to the monastery, and receive from the monks cabbage gruel with a scrap of meat in it as a reward.

When this king from the North enters the monastery, destitute and weary, the monks ask how he means to employ himself between holy offices, since Satan, the Evil One, the rival of Christ as he is called, is particularly fond of assailing the idle, and with great cunning. King Olaf replies that he is in fact known to have expertise in many crafts, for instance in fashioning shrines or carving bone. "Yet when I was a Viking, I was best known for my surgeon's hands," says he – and true enough, he kept in his bag, which never left him, a set of small knives, supple pliers, and awls. With these tools, he said, he had earned a good reputation after joining the army to defend England, then France, and finally Norway, by gouging out eyes or tearing out rebels' tongues, or torturing captives and hostages. Upon beholding these tools, the monks assign Olaf the task of removing the flesh from the bone on the heads of the martyrs and other holy men, digging out their eyes, pulling out their tongues, extracting the soft tissue from their palates and jaws, and then polishing their skulls. These venerable, fruitful skulls of saints, the sources of numerous outstanding miracles, were preserved in the Cathedral of Holy Wisdom in Kiev down to the days of Bishop Sigurgeir, and were seen by us, who, in our great poverty, have put together this little book.

47

LEARNED MEN have often noted how King Cnut Sweynsson granted his vassals in Norway more power and privileges
than they had ever had before, making them feel much better
equipped to control those districts that were a constant bone
of contention between them and the Swedes – and how these
vassals behaved like others who enjoy the protection of a mighty
king, believing that his kingdom will last forever, and acting as if
they have free reign under his aegis. Anund, king of the Swedes,
began to feel that it was becoming too crowded on his doorstep. The Norwegians appeared to be growing too bold, now
that they had an English king ruling them – one mightier and
in command of more troops and ships than any king of Norway
had ever had.

King Anund Olafsson of Sweden, however, having wed
Cnut's sister, deemed it fitting to proceed cautiously in his
dealings with the Norwegians – neither straightforwardness
nor force would do any good. He pondered how he might get
the better of the Norwegians in some way, or how much Cnut
would give to retain control of Norway, or recover it, if it should
be torn from his hands. He admitted that he had made an error

in judgement the year before by providing Olaf the Stout too little support when the peasants closed in on him, especially since most of the peasant leaders had now sworn their obedience to Cnut. He considered it better to have a petty man for his neighbor in Norway than a sovereign in England.

Now, as more and more of King Anund's stewards complained to him about the Norwegian encroachments, Anund finally lost patience and convened a secret council with the lords whose advice he normally respected. Little of their plans was revealed to the populace. In the fall, however, King Anund sent men east to Russia with silver, with the aim of meeting Olaf Haraldsson the Stout and offering to buy him the horses and gear he would need in order to leave Russia that winter. A fleet would be awaiting him on the eastern shore of the Baltic, to sail with him to his wife Astrid. That fall marked a year since King Olaf had come to Kiev.

On the day the Swedish envoys presented this offer to Grand Knyaz Yaroslav, Knyaginya Ingegerd paid her customary visit to the monastery to speak with her brother-in-law, King Olaf. He was at his assigned task, using pliers to pluck the soft tissue from a saint's jawbone. A scent of incense filled the monastery, serving both to invigorate people's hearts and to mask foul odors. The knyaginya took her seat opposite Olaf the Stout and watched for a while as the king dug dexterously at the saint's jawbone. Then the knyaginya, who was somewhat downcast, said:

"Visitors from out west in Sweden have come to our palace," said she, "with the following message: you are to return home with them to my sister Astrid. First, though, you are to reconquer Norway, and for your campaign, my brother Anund in Uppsala will supply you with all the vagrants, beggars, and thieves that are to be found in the kingdom of Sweden, both east and west of the Baltic. Famine threatens my brother's kingdom, making it easy in most areas to hire troops for war, whether in Estonia, Osel, and Gotland or in Sweden itself. These men are promised outstanding spoils in Norway."

Olaf Haraldsson immediately stopped working and set aside the saint's skull, with the pliers between its jaws. He said:

"As far as I can see, if what you say is true, these things will be of no small consequence – though your tone as you tell me is not particularly encouraging."

She replied: "How necessary do you feel it is to regain the hand of my sister Astrid?"

"If we are called upon to re-establish the kingdom of Norway," said he, "it is the will of Christ and not men, though, for the time being, I had thought to fill a different role for the examiner of monks. May I remind you, Ingegerd, that although I was but a man of little worth in your eyes when I ruled Norway, and you disgraced me by taking up instead with that inveterate adulterer, the Nidhogg of his family tree – despite your being promised to me by your own consent – that man will never bear the title of king. Why should you show more interest in me now, when I rule over no one, apart from these rotten heads?"

She said: "You wish to punish me now for your own grudge against me, when you, a mere sailor, proposed to me, hardly more than a child, and a vain one at that – and I was led by my own childishness into a union with a man who had more might and renown. Now I have learned that the more mighty a king is, the less his wife has of his love. I would rather be the friend of a man who, for the monks, polishes the skulls of beggar-kin, or that murderers sell to bishops for a sup of cabbage gruel, than be wedded to a king who rules the land of his enemies. You and I share the same language and complexion, things that make compatriots of two persons in exile. My sister Astrid has our Norwegian jarls for chess and private conversation as she fancies, though she has always been easy to please, with a figure like a dairymaid working her churn and shaping butter pats, and grinning like a serving wench. If you go, I will be left here alone, with the earth beneath me scorched to its roots."

King Olaf then said: "What Christ wills, we must venture, and kingdoms are not purchased cheaply – but as far as women are concerned, we take things as they come. For a woman, there is more honor in being the friend of a king who hews heads off living men than one who polishes those of dead men, and Christ must certainly have great deeds in store for me if the news that you have brought me is true."

Knyaginya Ingegerd replied: "It may indeed turn out," says she, "that you come to possess the one kingdom that Christ grants you, but Norway, never – and that you will enter the one bed that Christ selects for you, but that of Astrid, your spare horse, never. From now on, our destinies are entirely our own."

At these words, the knyaginya burst into tears; she rose and left the room without any other word of farewell, shutting the door behind her. Olaf Haraldsson the Stout wiped flesh and blood from his pliers and awl and small knives, and praised Christ the Lord.

As for Anund, King of the Swedes, he assembled a fleet of ships from the lands that he ruled east of the Baltic, intending it for the use of Olaf Haraldsson the Stout when he reached the coast. That winter, Olaf headed westward with a fine retinue, harnessing draught-horses to sleighs and driving over the ice, accompanied by guards to protect the silver they carried. The Swedish jarls in charge of the expedition had given their pledge to their lord, the Swedish king, to address Olaf as king when speaking to him.

When the company arrived at the coast, they found the fleet ready to sail, and the Swedes announced that King Olaf was to command it. Not everyone in the fleet was what might be called irreproachable: outlaws had been levied, and large numbers of slaves, whom powerful men could not be bothered to feed during famine, as well as all manner of riff-raff and knaves whose kind are hunted down in the woods like wolves. For their fare, these men were given hard stockfish one day and porridge the next. There was not a single Christian within the fleet, and hardly a man who spoke the Norse tongue. King Olaf was regaled by the Swedish king's stewards on the mainland and isles with proper feasts and worthy gifts. His life had certainly changed since he had traveled east, not so long ago, as a passenger on a merchant vessel, leading his barefoot son by the hand and ignored by all.

At that time, Christianity had gained only a small foothold east of the Baltic, and the Swedish stewards doggedly resisted gathering taxes for pope or patriarch. There were, however, some old merchants who had agreed to be prime-signed when they were abroad, and some built chapels to Saint Basil of Cappadocia after retiring from their trading ventures. Good Swedes were loyal to Þórr, while the commons, who did not speak Norse, put most faith in the god named Jumala, who holds a fine staff in his hand. Yet nothing further shall be told here of his excellence.

As mentioned previously, King Olaf had become such a great friend of Christ after being expelled from his kingdom that it vexed him when he could not hear Holy Mass and chanting in Greek or Latin, or the sounds of bells ringing. Above all, he drew satisfaction from pondering the subtleties of Christ, who had entrusted his page with a heathen army to spread the true faith in Norway. Yet as glad as Olaf was of this fighting force, the lords in the east were no less gratified, in this time of famine, that the king of the Swedes should have thieves and paupers and other wicked rabble rounded up on the mainland and isles and shipped off to be slaughtered west of the Baltic.

Gotlandic books tell of how King Olaf Haraldsson, during the course of this expedition, sailed his ships to that island and received a better welcome than when he had landed there during the Viking raids of his youth and been given a drubbing by the islanders, which, naturally, inspired nothing less than a special praise-poem later, lauding Olaf's victory over the Gotlanders. In Gotland, folk were not yet Christian. King Olaf commanded every member of his fleet to donate a penny from his pay for a church on that island, and in return, the islanders gave Olaf twelve rams and promised to build a church and appoint a priest to it at the appropriate time. There, Olaf gathered more paupers and thieves, conscripting them with the same promise as in the east: that as soon as the army reached Norway, they would have all that the land produced at their disposal and be free to divide the spoils among themselves, according to Viking custom.

Olaf Haraldsson sailed into Lake Mälaren with the force he brought from the East, and was met at the estuary by the king of the Swedes, who was affable and relaxed and had much to tell: first and foremost, that Cnut had abandoned the North entirely, while churls were making an impertinent show in Norway, claiming the land was theirs to rule. Yet there was a positive side to this: since Cnut had purchased the loyalty of the peasants' leaders, they had hardly anyone at their head, and thus had little hope of victory against a hardened army. The Swedish king had also made inquiries concerning Olaf's kinsfolk and friends in Norway who might be expected to support him, and secretly sent men to meet them. These, he learned, were entirely prepared to back Olaf if he came with an army capable of defending the land against the peasants. When the kings agreed that Olaf's force was still too small to redeem Norway, he received his brother-in-law's permission to levy as many troops as would follow him from throughout Sweden, and the king promised to help him with this levy. Sweden was then suffering a great famine – beggars roamed the country in bands or took to the woods or outlying islets. The kings dispatched envoys to conscript these people and send them to defend Norway, with the promise that this army could sieze all the treasure there that they could lay their hands on, and take the crofts of the Norwegian peasants for their own. Unsurprisingly, many men believed the Swedish rulers were offering them a most promising expedition. This force comprised more highwaymen, bark-eaters, and brigands than any before it. The rank and file were fed gruel, those above them lutefisk, and the captains meat. At first, the men were not given weapons, so that they would not kill each other – there was a great deal of quarreling among the ranks of this army, which was a mishmash of every sort of derelict and outlaw, none understanding the other's tongue. The captains limited themselves to showing them the chests full of weapons to be used against the Norwegians. The men were poorly clad, and wrapped their feet in birch-bark until spring arrived with warmer air. Olaf found no Christian men among the forces that had been levied in Sweden to reinforce him. In fact, another generation was to pass before Sweden became Christian, apart from the kings in Uppsala who took up the faith in name only in order to establish relations with kings farther south and with foreign barons, as well as to be known as friends of the Lord Pope. In Uppsala stood a temple to Freyr, larger and more sumptuous than any church in the North at that time – and all learned men agree that the Uppsala kings did everything in their power to prevent Sweden from adopting the Christian faith. They wanted their land to preserve the peace and quiet that it had enjoyed since antiquity, and made only those concessions to rabble-rousers and foreigners that were strictly necessary for peace.

After arriving in Sweden at the invitation of his wife's kin, and in perfect friendship, King Olaf felt that things had taken a strange turn. He was put in charge of all the bandits of the kingdom, its tired and hungry crofters, louse-ridden tramps, foreigners, and plenty of other heathens, but was denied the service of priests. When he complained of this predicament to the king, he was told that the bishops had it on good authority that in Kiev, King Olaf had consorted with heresiarchs and reprobates who obeyed the Patriarch in Constantinople. That form of Christianity was subject to the Lord Pope's lesser excommunication, while the Lord Pope was subject to the Patriarch's greater excommunication. No cleric from Bremen would have dared risk his salvation to sing Mass for King Olaf without having the formal permission of the Lord Pope to do so. It should be noted, as well, that though he was given a friendlier reception by his queen's kin than before, Olaf was not accorded the same by the queen herself – she did not ride to the ships to visit him. At the arrival of Midwinter Night, as the heathen Yule was called by the Swedes, the king in Uppsala sent large bull carcasses down to the coast, where Olaf Haraldsson's tents were pitched, and with them barrels of mead – though Olaf was as far as ever from the lap of his lady, Queen Astrid. Olaf was expected to celebrate the Yule feast with his troops on the shore, and not in the royal castle in Uppsala, and the Swedish king's men paid little heed when he attempted to protest. Being most dissatisfied with this arrangement, Olaf mounted and set out for the castle, taking several of his men with him. He hoped to meet with his queen Astrid before others could interfere, and when he arrived at the castle, he was told that she was in the mead-hall. Word was sent to her that a visitor had arrived and wished to speak to her, and she was informed of his manner and appearance. Queen Astrid ordered that the visitor be shown to a room distant from the hall, and went there to meet him. When she saw that it was Olaf, her husband, she was clearly quite astonished, but greeted him courteously and asked for news of the east, and what business he had here.

King Olaf replied: "I would never have thought you would feel the need to ask your spouse and lord for news, or enquire on what business he had come, while you pass the evening in a mead-hall after your husband has returned home to you – he who was driven away from you, betrayed and in great distress."

Queen Astrid said: "It should have been clear to you long ago, Olaf, that we daughters of the king in Uppsala prize tangible realities above promises. It is little to my or my sister's taste to be wed to kings that have been driven from their realms. I have the choice of many a good man with whom to quaff mead in the evenings, some of them high-born, and governing territories in Sweden as good as all of Norway, even if it were yours. We wed ourselves to kings for the lands that they rule – not for love or the fame augured you by birds. Since my kinswoman Ingegerd refused to marry you because you stood on only one foot in Norway, why should I be true to you when you stand on none, a knock-kneed, potbellied sailor? I demand just one thing of you: that you reconquer Norway before I set eyes on you again."

48

WE MUST NOT wholly neglect to recount the travels of Bishop Grímkell the Englishman from the moment that he was left kingless in Norway with Cnut as his enemy, and the see of Bremen refusing to have anything to do with him.

As long as Olaf held Norway, no Christian overlord had a say in whom he made his court bishop, and Olaf, like other kings of Norway after him, was little inclined to comply with orders from Bremen in any matter.

After the Norwegians expelled Olaf from the land, and Cnut had purchased full authority in Norway with English coins and ample promises, and all of the great lords in Norway had become the best of friends with the English, each with his own particular bribe and promise of profit, the friends of Olaf, who, for some reason, had not had the opportunity to betray him – among them Bishop Grímkell – found themselves much beleaguered. Cnut's bishops now confiscated the field that Grímkell had ploughed and sown – with the Bremen clerics taking their share – and all men of God in the North become his vilifiers and foes as quickly as they had become sworn enemies of King Olaf Haraldsson. Most good men wanted Grímkell to be excommunicated, while others preferred to go after him and kill him. With his life in peril from these men of God, Grímkell kept himself hidden in Norway for the time being. Yet when he heard that the king of the Swedes had resolved to bring Olaf back to Norway, he reflected on his situation, before deciding to take passage on a merchant vessel to France, where he joined a group of pilgrims. By Yule, they had crossed the Alps, and at Easter they arrived in Rome.

Bishop Grímkell was clad as a pauper, staff in hand. The accounts say that he carried in his scrip no treasure apart from an old, fermented cheese – one of those sorts produced in the North that stink most of all things known in Christendom and cause thieves, pilferers, and cutthroats to avoid any pilgrim who carries such an abomination.

In that age, Rome's golden crown shone more radiantly than ever before in the distant regions of the world. The apostolic and Catholic faith had spread not only eastward to Poland, but as far into the lands of the North as Iceland, and then west to Greenland. Those who were most remote considered Rome to be nearest Heaven, and dubbed it the White Queen of the world, resplendent with maidenly lilies, as it says in the pilgrims' song: "O Roma nobilis orbis et domina albis et virginum liliis candida."

At the same time as the beauty of Rome shone brightest at the margin of the world, it suffered the bitterest tribulations within its own walls, as recounted by sagacious historians. It had not been long since twelve popes in two decades were laid low by their rivals, poisoned or murdered in some other clandestine way, while others were first beheaded and then hanged by their feet, not counting those who were blinded, had their noses chopped off or their tongues torn out, or ended their lives in dungeons or snakepits, or were paraded backwards on asses in the city streets and torn limb from limb as they rode. When the pilgrims arrived from the north, the Lord Pope happened to be hanging by his feet on a gibbet, his head impaled on a stake alongside, on Monte Malo outside the city walls, where the pilgrims traditionally fell to their knees in prayer in view of the Holy City. By that time, Rome had been under the control of gangs of robbers, foreign and native by turns, for many generations: there were the counts of Campania, Tusculum, and Sabina, all calling themselves consuls and senators of Rome, and there were counts palatine and, after them, Guelfs and Ghibellines, Orsini and Colonna, and numerous other villains. These gangs had done much to the ruination of this city, making quarries out of the ancient temples and arches and monuments and forts and walls, and piling up the stones into breastworks to defend themselves against each other. Lime-burners ground ancient marble and mixed it with lime to make mortar. The temple of Jupiter was used as a stable, and every statue and sculpture in Rome had long since been smashed. Most of the city was nothing but weed-covered ruins and pasture, and whenever there was a lull in the conflict or a brief period of quiet, the livestock – goats, pigs, sheep, and cattle – grazed on the surrounding hills. At such times, too, peasants from Campania could be seen toiling here and there, having been given leave to bear stones away on their own backs and those of their asses, to build cowsheds from ancient temples and palaces. Despite the city of Rome boasting more churches than any other, historians relate that at that time, none of them, apart from the apostolic basilica, possessed a silver chalice until one hundred and seventy years later, when Pope Innocent, the third by that name, gave each and every cathedral in the city a monetary gift to be used to purchase a valuable chalice. By then, all of Rome's scholars were dead and its schools had fallen into ruin, and not a person was to be found in the city who could play the organ. For the Romans, the finest model for imitation was St. Peter, who had mastered no skill apart from catching fish, yet still held the keys to Heaven's gate.

At that time, Rome was so plagued by disease that in some years only a few, and sometimes none, of the pilgrims who journeyed to the Holy City from distant lands managed to return to their homelands. The city festered with more foulness, rottenness, leprousness, corpse-stench, and starveling-stink than any other place in the world. Learned men, however, are of the opinion that the foul odor from the cheese that Bishop Grímkell brought with him from the North did little to bring relief to the Romans' nostrils, but rather, the opposite.

In those days, an all but impossible fish to catch for a penniless man was an audience with his Apostolic Lordship. None but those with bags full of coins – open ones, at that – had the slightest chance of obtaining a letter from the Pope or his Curia. It soon became apparent, too, that the cardinals sitting in council with the Lord Pope had more pressing obligations than to pave the way for a wandering bishop from the North. The Pope's doortenders gave this bishop's request for an audience with the apostle Peter a flat "No!" for an answer – the bishop being of such low esteem that he had not even hired a company of soldiers to protect him against highwaymen and criminals, not to mention the fact that he smelled no better than the city's rubbish heaps, where the lifeless bodies of plague-stricken people were dumped.

It is said that Grímkell's presence made most people stare: he was tall and gracefully built, with the kind of visage that one often sees in depictions of God's holy men and saints. He had flowing black hair and a noble, melancholy pallor, while his eyes gleamed like the black gemstone *carbunculus*, which skalds call a wonder of the world. He still directed his gaze rapturously toward Heaven, as he had done in his youth when standing by the blessed Archbishop Ælfheah's side.

After making many fruitless trips to the Apostolic Palace, to be met only with bluster from the guards, Grímkell returns to the palace door one day and opens his scrip, releasing its stench. From it he pulls a bright silver penny that he hands to the door-tender, while announcing that his name is Grimcetillus, court bishop to King Olaf Haraldsson of Norway, and that he seeks an audience with the Pope. Then he walks away.

Several days later, while Grímkell is sitting in his lodging, chanting and weeping with deep, heartfelt compunction, as was his wont, a messenger from the Lord Pope's palace turns up and announces that Bishop Grímkell is granted the opportunity, that very day, to appear before the vicar of Christ and successor of Peter – Pope John, the nineteenth of that name – in the Apostolic Lord's Palace of the Lateran, and to make his petition there.

Pope John the Nineteenth, whose worldly name had been Romanus, was a Roman layman from a line of Tusculan counts. Besides being head of the Church, he was also the highest secular authority in Rome, consul and senator. He had never been ordained a priest, nor been to school to learn to read or to sing in Latin, and could converse only in the peasant dialect called *lingua volgare*, the vernacular. John had gotten hold of the Holy See by means of bribes, with the support of Conrad, the king of Germany. Conrad had pledged to keep other robbers away from John's throne, and John, in return, to crown Conrad Holy Roman Emperor.

Bishop Grímkell of Canterbury was led through a succession of chambers in the Apostolic Palace to the Apostolic Lord's *salutatorium*, having come to try his luck on this old, smoothly worn stone floor beneath a Roman vault grown with cobwebs full of enormous spiders. He found Pope John sitting on his throne, bedecked in a red cope embroidered with gold and flanked by the venerable cardinals he habitually kept at hand. Sitting motionless in one corner was a German monk, the only man in the papal palace who knew how to use a pen, and who had been appointed by the Emperor Conrad to advise Pope John and manage his affairs, and more especially to oversee the Apostolic Camera, that is, the papal treasury. He bore the title of *camerarius*.

These authorities of the Lord sat on tall-legged chairs fashioned in the ancient Roman style, with high backs and narrow seats. Along the walls stood stone vessels and wooden shrines, besides goblets and drinking bowls from Constantinople. Next to one wall there was also a *lectulus* – a small canopied bed draped with a Saracen cloth of gold weave. Behind the throne stood a copper crucifix, a gift from Ireland after iniquitous men had destroyed all the images and statues in Rome. On this cross, legends of the saints were beautifully embossed, and in the center the Lord was depicted in his imperial vestments, his hands raised in blessing. His head was in Paradise, where angels stood on each of his shoulders, while his feet were on Earth, where they were flanked by a godly pair: the apostle John and the Sancta Virgo, the two who loved the Lord best and grieved most at his departure from the world.

Now, at one and the same moment, Grímkell's saintly visage appears to those in the Curia, and their nostrils are assailed by a horrendous stench. Grímkell falls to his knees before the Pope and reverently kisses his foot. The Lord Pope bids his guest have his say, and Bishop Grímkell addresses the Most Holy Father and the Curia in these words:

"I, Grimcetillus, most wretched of clerics in God's Christendom," says he, "would first ask of my Apostolic Lord that he recall when evildoers pelted clerics and priests to death on the banks of the Thames. That day, I pleaded with the saintly old Ælfheah, whom I served in my youth, as bones and horns battered his feeble body: 'Will not my master allow me to step forward and receive the blows intended for him?' – and that is the beginning of my story. After that, for fifteen years I toiled in the service of the Lord at the fringes of the world, namely in *Norvegia*, as court bishop to King Olaf Haraldsson, who formerly ruled that country. None versed in chant had ever gone to those parts before we ventured there to preach Christianity to the rabble that shares the lairs of wolves and dragons. My king is now exiled, and I wish to beseech my Most High Lord Pope that those poor servants of the Lord who once put most faith in God be not driven into the wilderness to dig roots and gnaw bark. I also beg that other men of God be not allowed to endanger the lives of their brethren who have, year after year, battled wild beasts and dragons *pro Christo*. I beseech my Apostolic Lord to bear in mind that King Olaf and I baptized more people in Norway in two summers than the bishops of Norway under the episcopal see of Bremen did in a hundred and fifty years. We built three hundred churches, and King Olaf gave Christ land and abundant riches in Norway, together with his heart, his soul, and his body. My first prayer and *supplicatio* is for safe-conduct, and following that, I beg the Lord Pope to grant me a letter conferring on me the same rank and authority as the bishops of Bremen in Norway, in the places where I have preached the gospel."

During this address, His Apostolic Lordship gives a great yawn, scratches himself, spits, and snorts, before saying in his dialect:

"My goodness, this man stinks. What is this churl harping on?"

The Pope and his cardinals now confer for a time, and the Lord Pope does not seem very well disposed. Eventually, the cardinal who is the Pope's closest confidant, says that Christ certainly did not consider the fact that the churches in Norway were granted logging and hunting rights much of a windfall. Great offerings could hardly be expected from the monsters and dragons of the Norwegian woods, against which this man had battled for fifteen years. "The Pope finds it rather bizarre," says this cardinal, "to hear of Norway being ruled by a king other than our friend Cnut, king of the English, who inherited Norway from his father. As far as we know, no other king has been named in connection with that realm. Our Apostolic Lord declares that he will never betray his friend Cnut, who holds sway over Norway, nor lend an ounce of support to any disreputable pretender to Cnut's throne. Never shall Pope John let it be forgotten that when he crowned his friend, Conrad the German, Holy Roman Emperor, Cnut was the only king of any distinction willing to do us the honor of journeying to Rome in our support. Once he was in our presence, we bestowed a plentitude of benefices on Cnut for his bishops, and he in return pledged us ample tribute from throughout his realm, which he has in fact always paid punctually. We would never do Cnut an ill turn – such as might jeopardize our collection of Peter's Pence from England."

Grímkell then says that King Olaf Haraldsson is expected to return from the east that summer, leading an invincible army to conquer Norway. The land's defenses will be scarce, he adds, since Cnut has left to govern England. "Where," says Grímkell, "shall the bishops of Bremen and Cnut's men find refuge when King Olaf comes to avenge his woes? Would it not be beneficial for one who both bears letters from the Pope and is a faithful friend of Olaf to step in and attempt to allay the king's wrath when he sets about stringing up his foes?"

The cardinals discuss the situation for some time, inquiring of each other what sort of man this Olaf is, who presumes to usurp the throne of King Cnut Sweynsson, and whose court bishop this pilgrim claims to be. None of the Curia have ever heard of King Olaf Haraldsson, and they are at a loss as to how to respond. Finally, the German monk speaks up – he who has a better knowledge of papal business than any other cleric in the Lord Pope's household. He says:

"This Olaf belonged to a band of Scandinavian pirates that foreign kings hired to fight for them. He was among those enlisted by the Duke of Normandy to burn Chartres Cathedral. Then he brought fire and destruction to Norway for a long time, but fled to a tributary of the Emperor in Constantinople and the Patriarch, our enemy, to consort with heretics. For his conduct, he is excommunicated by the laws of God. Moreover," says the German monk, still addressing the Pope in the vernacular, "this little fellow Grimcetillus, who has just come rather close to blaspheming Christ, received his miter and crosier from Armenian schismatics behind horse rumps in Rouen."

When His Apostolic Lordship hears this, he pounds on the arms of his throne, declaring that any viper in clerical garb, ordained by schismatics, is to be boiled in the same cauldron as forgers. "And," says the Pope, "that stuff in this imbecile's bag – is it the flesh of the venomous beasts and dragons he has been slaughtering for fifteen years in Norway?"

The cardinal translates the Apostolic Lord's words for Bishop Grímkell, as follows:

"Our Apostolic Lord has heard," says he, "that Gregorian schismatics from Armenia ordained you too near to horses' rumps in France, O Grimcetille, and any cleric ordained by a wandering bishop is excommunicate. What do you have to say to free yourself from this predicament, my son?"

A wise English cleric has written that neither logic nor rhetoric nor a just cause are of any use when speaking to a deputy of Christ, let alone to Christ himself. For Christ is not only the intellection of all creation, but also the beginning and end of all logic and rhetoric, and what Christ requires of men is not their wisdom and mastery of dialectic. In the eyes of Christ, it is the value of our gift, measured in struck silver or some other sort of earthly wealth, that matters – and naught else. It would seem that Bishop Grímkell had acquired this wisdom somewhere – for, after being reprimanded by the cardinals for some time and prescribed sackcloth and ashes as penance, this pilgrim speaks up once more, saying:

"If," he says, "dust and ashes may again be so bold as to address their Lord, in the same way that Patriarch Abraham was permitted to do so, it must first be pointed out that no one knows where the esteemed Lord Peter the Apostle – at whose feet I shall soon grovel in the dirt – went to school, or where that blessed fisherman received his tonsure. It is hardly any secret to the world that when the supreme defender of Christianity was elected and elevated to the Apostolic See, the Holy Spirit had gone for a walk." Bishop Grímkell now falls flat on the stone floor at the feet of the Lord Pope, supplicating with tears and sighs, until he rises to his knees with these words: "Here we see evidence of the holy doctrine and teaching which says that the Lord is extolled highest and his omnipotence most exalted in those points of grace least comprehensible to human understanding. He who lacks tonsure and schooling has become most noble in word and deed of all the popes since the passing of Gregorius Magnus. Therefore, I beg my Apostolic Lord and venerable gentlemen in the Curia to bear in mind that this wretched acolyte, who received his ring and crosier in the midst of horses, with no holy relics at hand apart from Cabbage-Christ and Onion, still was able to convert King Olaf Haraldsson to the holy faith, and thereafter all of Norway."

At these words, Bishop Grímkell lifts his cheese from his scrip, lays it on the floor at the Pope's feet, and swiftly sticks a knife into it. A flood of gold and silver pieces pours from the cheese, like a swarm of maggots. The coins are both fair and bright.

"Here have I brought you," says Grímkell, "the belated first-fruits of my bishopric in Norway – gold and silver from myself and King Olaf Haraldsson."

At the sight of these tokens, His Apostolic Lordship's tongue is tied, as are those of his cardinals. The Pope steps from his throne and lies down on the floor to examine the coins, followed by the cardinals. Emperor Conrad's monk, however – he who knows how to use a pen and manages the Apostolic Camera – says that at present, there is no question whatsoever of them making a vagabond or itinerant cleric an equal to the spiritual leaders of Norway – the bishops of Bremen, or those of Cnut Sweynsson, King of the English, who, in the eyes of God and all Christendom, is the rightful possessor of Norway. "On the other hand," he says, "it is right that Grimkell be granted a letter declaring that the archiepiscopal see of Bremen and other lawful successors of the apostles are not to do him any harm, and he is neither to be excommunicated nor sentenced to death by them – rather, they are to recognize and tolerate their poor brother, who is replete with good will, until it be revealed whom Christ wishes to hold the throne in Norway.

"But on the day," says this monk, "when King Olaf Haraldsson attains the throne and the kingdom of Norway by the will of God, or is exalted by means of remarkable confession and penance, or above all by a special death that may be reckoned martyrdom, so that the heavenly angels rejoice and the clerics and the commons see that the Lord has chosen Olaf to bear him witness with various exceptionally clear signs – on that very day, Brother Grimcetillus shall be elevated to the rank and dignity that beseems him."

49

IN NORWAY, the bird cherry blossoms last of all trees. Whereas birch, linden, and other trees bud before the spring nights regain their full light, the blooms of the bird cherry do not open until summer wanes. Olaf Haraldsson now spent an inordinate amount of time making preparations for his expedition from Sweden, reinforcing the troops and fortifying their leadership, stilling quarrels among his men, and stocking up on various necessities. He sent word to his friends and kin in Norway that they were to gather forces in secret and join him after his march westward over the mountains from Jämtland that summer. Their watchword was to be that they should be fully prepared by the time the bird cherries blossomed.

Although these messages were to be delivered secretly to King Olaf's men in Norway, the old adage, that many a man has an enemy among friends, seemed to be proved true again: news of the king's intrigues spread no less among his foes. On hearing these rumors, the peasants grew restless. They were convinced that if Olaf regained a foothold in their land, his rule in Norway would soon be enforced in the same old way:

he would start burning and murdering, torturing, seizing property, and committing other such injustices. They denounced Olaf Haraldsson as a criminal, forfeit of his life according to the laws upheld at most Norwegian assemblies throughout the land's history. Now, as before, the peasants vowed to end this king's days as soon as they had the opportunity to do so.

As regards Þormóður Kolbrúnarskáld, the story goes that he returned from down south in Denmark and traveled from district to district seeking out leaders who had won honor and fame, and inquiring as to where champions might be found who, with intrepid hearts, had distinguished themselves in battle. He wished to compose quatrains about some, rhapsodies about others, and lays for those that deserved them. Yet it was the dawn of a new time in the North, when leaders relied less on valor and heroism than on the favor of kings and bishops. They considered it more advisable to become the vassals of sovereigns, or to buy their way out of the clutches of the monster Christians call "sin" than to earn the praise of skalds – thus, limping vagrants were not called upon to extol sovereigns. The skald often pondered whether his sworn brother Þorgeir Hávarsson had not been the last true warrior in the North, apart from King Olaf Haraldsson, who had been driven from his kingdom by crofters.

Now this wayfarer gets wind of the news that King Olaf Haraldsson is expected from the east that summer, to lift Norway out of its ignominy. At this revelation, life returns to

Þormóður's limbs, which had been frozen in Greenland. There seemed to be hope that the North would be freed from the fetters in which it had been festering for some time, now that the sworn brothers' king was to lead an invincible army into Norway to reclaim his heritage. The skald envisions the king at the head of his retinue, rising in the east with the radiant crown of his glory, consecrated to the gods. Now Þormóður speeds, though lame, through wood and meadow, from district to district, heading north to Trøndelag, for it is there, he hears, that the king will be descending from the mountains at the blossoming of the bird cherry. When he comes to the long, deep valleys of Norway, where the paths follow rivers and lakes over great distances, drawing ever nearer to the mountains that form the country's natural boundaries, it looks to Þormóður as if there are more folk out on the roads than ever before. Most of the travelers are poor people, carrying their belongings on their backs, laborers and crofters. Some lead packhorses, most often traveling two by two, and never in groups larger than five, always with a short distance between them. They hardly ever acknowledge each other or exchange more than a few words when they happen to meet. Yet there are even more men roaming off the highroads, leading their horses or carrying their loads through forests and over heaths. All these men appear to be running their own errands, rather than those of any authority. When Þormóður addresses them, they reply curtly. One says that he is moving house with all his possessions, another is going to trade his labor for butter and flour. There are, in addition, many saltmakers out and about, and salmon fishermen, as well as herring fishermen and others on their way home from the fishing stations.

One day, after coming down from a mountain, a saltmaker turns to Þormóður Kolbrúnarskáld and says:

"What beggarman are you who so often crosses our paths of late, and where are you heading?"

He says: "I am an Icelandic skald, seeking your king."

The saltmaker replies: "Strange that Icelanders should now wish to have arsonists lording it over them, after having fled from Harald Tanglehair's rule here in Norway."

Þormóður replies: "Stranger that Norwegians do not want rulers that win them glory through stoutness of heart."

The saltmaker replies: "We have had plenty of kings in Norway, but the only ones that proved of any use to us were those that we sacrificed for good harvests and peace."

Þormóður says: "From my father and other good men in Iceland I learned most of the lays that have been composed in the Norse tongue, and none of them ever told of any man winning glory for this land apart from its kings and their champions, after slaughtering their enemies and setting their lands and property aflame. These are the men most extolled in Icelandic poetry, though few of them were born for long life – not salmon fishermen and saltmakers."

A crofter says: "The mill that my grandfather built on his homefield, Jarl Haakon Sigurdarson demolished. My father built another mill, and King Olaf Tryggvason knocked it down. I myself built a little mill when I was young. King Olaf Haraldsson burned it when he harried us in Romsdal."

A backwoodsman says: "I kept three cows in a clearing and the king's men salted them all down, calling it their tax."

Among this group is a stately, ruddy-faced old man, who says: "I had toiled hard to dig a well, deep and clear, when King Olaf Haraldsson turned up with fifteen of his commanders, bearing the sign of the cross. The three highest in rank, he called his Wise Men from the East. The other twelve, he called his Apostles, after the great squires who paid homage to Christ. All of these men, both the commanders of his army and the king himself, came and pissed in my well."

A herring fisherman says: "Great misfortune has befallen us Norwegians ever since we stopped sacrificing our rulers and started eating whale meat."

Þormóður grips one of the peasant's clubs, laughs, and says: "What do you think you wretches can do with your staves against the king's men's storm of steel?"

The peasant replies: "In war, those get the worst of it who put faith in steel."

From exchanges such as this, Þormóður came to realize that other company would serve him better in his quest to meet the king, but when he arrived in Trøndelag, no matter where he turned, he encountered people quite unlikely to share his path.

Groups of them emerged from every gully and rift, from behind trees and boulders, or edged their way along overgrown forest paths, shieling paths and cattle tracks, all seemingly with one and the same destination. For the most part, they looked alike, with unkempt beards and their hair tucked into the necks of their tunics. There were also young men with downy cheeks and chins, poorly shod, sunburned, and loudmouthed. Sticking out of their saddlepacks were clubs, spades, and forks, as well as the occasional spear. At nightfall, they all lay down to sleep wherever they found themselves. Some donned hair sacks, while others lay on the bare ground. They were all Christians, and the next morning clerics rode among the sleepers, holding their crosses aloft and ringing bells for the men to rise and heed the sacred song. They exhorted the men, bidding them never, as long as Christ lived, to forget the murders, burnings, and pillaging committed by the malefactor who was now headed for Norway with a foreign force to make war on them anew. They declared the native army assembled here greater than had ever been seen in this poor country, and bade the Norwegian peasants stand fast and rely on their numbers to drive out that band of foreign brigands. Snorri relates the words of the bishop who addressed the peasants of Norway on behalf of Christ: "The time has come," said the bishop, "to slaughter this rabble for the eagle and the wolf. Unless you prefer to drag the carcasses under mound and cairn, let each man lie where you cut him down."*

50

IN NORD-TRØNDELAG lies Verdal, at the border between
the kingdom of Norway and Jämtland in Sweden. It is there
that the highroads meet, and there that the waters flow, where
mountains and ridges overlook a broad valley dotted with forests, fields, and rivers. Ewes and lambs graze among the thick-
ets, while cows lie chewing the cud at the base of ancient cairns.
In the middle of the valley stands a farm, backed by a copse of
aspen and maple, birch and linden, and bird cherry as well. The
dandelions growing there are the same as in Iceland. This farm is
called Stiklestad. Learned men say that it is often a valley, where
the landscape slopes down to a place of rest like the benches in
the Hippodrome of Constantinople, that is the stage for events
that determine the destinies of kings – and it is here, in just such
a valley, that King Olaf Haraldsson fell, the day after this book
ends. When we who composed this narrative came to Verdal one
day a thousand years later, and beheld the blue heaths to the
east – whence the king led his final march into Norway, bereft
of clerics, forsaken by skalds, abandoned by friends and lovers,

but backed by a foreign, heathen army – the stones were then silent in Stiklestad, of course, and nothing remained of King Olaf's saga but a soughing in the leaves.

Now to tell of the eve of King Olaf's fall, when the peasant army has assembled at Stiklestad, beneath the holy cross, and the king's forces are on their way down from the mountains. An Icelandic skald has also made his way to Verdal, seeking the king he has chosen as his own. No book says what gift of divination allowed this skald to envision that this king, whom the peasants of Norway now meant to crush, would someday become the only king in the North surpassing Cnut the Great in glory and praise – and his praise flourishes no less in Heaven than on Earth. To him have bowed not only earthly dukes and emperors, bishops and popes, but also saints, martyrs, and virgins, as well as all the heavenly powers, archangels, thrones, dominions, and cherubim. Yet King Olaf has never been cherished by anyone as much as by Icelandic skalds – for in fact no book has ever been written in the world about kings, or about Christ himself, that can hold a candle to the account that Snorri the Wise composed, called the *Saga of Olaf the Saint*.

Skald Þormóður Bessason hobbles about Verdal, wondering what door in the camp of his king's enemies he shall knock upon to beg for the supper he needs to prepare him for what is forthcoming. The men have pitched their tents on the bank of the river and lit fires, and physicians have gathered there around their kettles to simmer grasses and herbs. A man crosses Þormóður's path. He has a gray beard and is wearing a worn tunic with a long hood pulled over his head, looking like most other peasants gathered there. Yet when he speaks, his voice sounds familiar to Þormóður's ears.

"Nearby is a woman," says the man in the tunic, "who has gotten wind of your coming, Þormóður, and she wishes to meet with you."

Þormóður asks where this woman might be. The man in the tunic tells Þormóður to follow him. Squatting by a hearth near the river is a woman wearing a skin kirtle, simmering herbs in a kettle. Her face is ogrish and her eyes bigger than most women's. She stands and welcomes Þormóður eagerly, but when she tries to greet him with a kiss, he turns away, saying that he has no idea who she is. "Who are you," he asks, "and why are you here?"

She says: "I am Kolbrún, your lover, who has your life-egg in her keeping. I have come from Greenland to kill my rival, Olaf Haraldsson, the king chosen by you and your sworn brother. I am preparing healing potions for those who carry out this deed."

He says: "You shall be cursed for it."

"It remains to be seen who will be cursed when it is done," says the woman. "But I will promise," says she, "to spare your king, as long as you rework his lay in my praise."

"What will you reward me for that lay?" says he.

She replies: "I have a thatched cottage in the heather and two young she-goats," she said, handing her guest a cup of goat's milk.

He says: "I once had a manor in Djúp, more bounteous and brighter than any other place in the world: the sea full of flounder, flocks on the slopes, mouse-gray cows of the stock of mermen, their udders full to bursting, waddling to the milking-shed at sundown. There I loved a swan whose like has never been seen among queens. In my hayfield in Djúp, I bade farewell to two girls, ever so small. I handed it all over to a foreign slave for the sake of the glory that is superior to every other possession, and the praise that the skald is elected to offer to a mighty king and his champions, so that he may live among gods and men throughout the ages. Now, after I have squandered everything out of devotion to the heart that alone of all hearts in the world knew no fear, and to the king who ruled that heart, and have finally come within reach of my king, you offer me a hovel in the heather and two kids!"

"Never," says the woman, "will the king you seek come to possess the kingdom in Norway that is mine."

To these words he makes no answer, but thanks the woman for the fare she has given him, and then hobbles off toward the mountains in search of his and his sworn brother's king, whom he, with his skaldic foresight, knows will become the most renowned and glorious king, honoured with more praise than any other Norse king throughout the ages.

Twilight was at hand. After it grew dark, the mistress summoned her slave, Loðinn, who was sitting a short distance away among a group of peasants busy fashioning clubs from roots or whittling sticks into arrows. She said:

"We arrived too late to prevent the coming of that vagabond who betrays us – that skald of Olaf the Stout, so devoted to folly. What would you suggest we do with him?"

"I am unaccustomed," said Slave Loðinn, "to being asked for advice on how you should deal with your vagrants."

She admitted that was true. "I have long been a stingy mistress to you – and even less a woman," said she. "That man who just now walked away from me is to blame."

"I am your slave, Mistress," said he.

"If that be true, it is time to finish it," said she, taking something from beneath her belt and handing it to him. "Here is my knife. Go now and do not come to my tent until you can show me Þormóður Kolbrúnarskáld's dying blood on its edge. At that hour, it will be revealed whether you are a man or a slave."

51

ÞORMÓÐUR Kolbrúnarskáld now leaves the rebel encampment for the mountains to find the king. Having reconnoitered Olaf Haraldsson's army, the peasants knew that he was near. That day, the horses' bundles had been untied, the chests opened, and the weapons dealt to the king's troops. King Olaf had not trusted his men to keep the peace among themselves, should they have gotten hold of weapons before the time came for the armies to clash. Shoes were also handed out to those whose feet had suffered in the mountains, and tunics to those who had marched to Norway shirtless. Now that they had reached Norway, the men's thoughts and hopes focused more and more on their shares in the booty of food and clothing and valuables promised them by the king.

Þormóður has not gone very far before he meets one of the king's outposts. These men speak in the dialect then common in the East, and now, upon encountering someone who can speak the Norse tongue, they ask Þormóður his name and business. He tells the truth – that he is an Icelandic skald, come to meet King Olaf Haraldsson and deliver him a lay. One of the men says:

"We have been ordered to treat any man who does not trip over his words when speaking the language of this land of Norway like any other usurper and traitor to his king."

The sentry who speaks the Norse tongue replies, saying:

"No order was given about how to treat an Icelandic skald who asks leave to rattle off rhymes to the king. What do you think, comrades?"

A third sentry says: "I think it is a good idea for us to try out the spears they gave us tonight on this tramp."

More king's men, all heavily armed, gather round to have a look at this skald. Some come and poke at him to determine whether he is concealing a knife or other dangerous implement, but soon find that he has nothing on him apart from his staff. Several officers step up and question the newcomer concerning the Norwegians' war capabilities: what their numbers are and what weapons they bear. Þormóður answers frankly that it is the most un-warlike army that he has ever seen, lacking in most of the things that help bring victory in battle. None in that army has weapons of the sort praised in poetry, whereas clubs and root-bludgeons are prominent, as well as churn-staves and beams. "It is sheer recklessness," says he, "for porous wood grown from the soil to challenge royal steel to battle."

Eventually, several of the sentries are ordered to show Þormóður to the king's tent, which is located at the foot of a heather-grown hill topped by an ancient stone cairn standing out against the sky. Serried ranks of guards surround the king's camp. The king's men's horses graze in gullies and hollows, while baggage and saddlery are piled on level ground. The majority of the troops have nothing to distinguish them apart from the weapons they had been issued that day, scarcely marking them off from the beggars who roam from house to house during bad years. Nowhere near are any knights on fiery, golden-bridled stallions, wielding famous old swords, or any of those champions who chomp the edges of their shields, roaring and making all sorts of other grand and manly shows to terrify folk, or yet those great and noble vassals who are bathed in the grace and goodwill of a mighty king.

The men now crowd round Þormóður to hear his business, most of them making fun of this poor wretch who has come straight from the enemy army the night before battle, completely unguarded, to request an audience with the king himself. They inform him that the king has more pressing issues at the moment than listening to the bosh of beggars from Iceland – he would be better off telling them how fat the pigs in Norway are, and whether the cattle are well-fed. "We have had enough of the Swedes' barley gruel," they say. Some have heard as well of the wealth of women to choose from in Norway – which meant that they could look forward to softer beds the following night than they had lain in for some time. They were far more for bawdy talk and lewd ribbing than for bringing such a miserable tramp before their king. "Why are you lame in both legs?" they ask.

"Because," says he, "that is the only cure for being lame in only one leg."

As they stand there gabbing with this beggarman, an officer passes by with a small escort. He addresses the men, asking if they have everything they need. Most say yes, though some are reluctant to answer. The officer says: "By tomorrow evening, you will have even more." This man is not stately in appearance. He is, in fact, corpulent, and waddles more than walks, with chubby cheeks and a sparse red beard. He is wearing a blue cloak of fine cloth, very creased, clotted with horse hair and mud, a tall, Russian fur hat, and high, dirty boots. A sword hangs from his belt, the tip of its scabbard poking out from beneath the hem of his cloak. Old books state that even though King Olaf had not learned the art of swordplay, which made him resemble Ása-Þórr, he still always wore a sword, in the manner of lords and noblemen. The king has not had his hair or beard trimmed or groomed in a long time, and his face is grimy with dust and streaked with sweat.

When Þormóður realizes that this is King Olaf Haraldsson, he steps forward and addresses him, speaking loudly and clearly:

"I am the skald Þormóður Bessason from Iceland, your

champion Þorgeir Hávarsson's sworn brother. Pray listen, my lord, while I sing you a lay."

The king asks what beggar this is, daring to open his mouth in his presence. "Trolls take you Icelandic skalds!" says he. "Few have done me worse than they. I have had more than enough of these Icelanders' boasting. Where is that man tonight," says the king, "who always boasted so highly of his loyalty and devotion to me when I needed them most – Sigvatur Þórðarson of Apavatn?"

"Of your friend Sigvatur, my king, I can inform you that he has gone to Rome to pass the time, out of pessimism about the outcome of the battle awaiting you. But I have traveled treacherous paths to stand before you."

The king casts him a glance and asks curtly: "What paths have you traveled, then?"

Þormóður says: "In order to stand before you, sire, I have given these things of myself: I abandoned my farm in Iceland and left behind the treasures of mine that I could not, for love of them, take my eyes off at any hour of day or night, and placed them all in the hands of a foreign slave, in hope of the glory that skalds reap from such a noble lord as you are reputed to be, endowed with the might to rule the world. That being done, I went westward to Greenland, and then far north of the world of men for three-and-a-half years, intending to avenge Þorgeir Hávarsson, the greatest warrior you had in your kingdom."

"I cannot comprehend what this man is prattling about," says the king. "The impertinence of you Icelandic starvelings toward your lords is an unparalleled abomination. What warrior does he claim to have been best in our kingdom?"

Þormóður replies: "Your glorious champion, Þorgeir Hávarsson. No man has ever been born in the North with such an unwavering heart."

"This wretch must be mad," says the king. "We certainly do not recall having ever heard that name – though some Icelandic imbecile by that name may have stumbled his way into our band back in our Viking days."

These things being said, the king departs to attend to more pressing concerns.

After stopping here and there to inspect his forces, and speaking some encouraging words to most of the men he encounters, the king has horns blown in the night to muster his army to assembly. He summons his interpreters, announcing that he wishes to address all the men before they sleep. Those who are not already asleep gather together at the forest's edge to hear the king speak. These are the words of Olaf Haraldsson:

"Good fellows," says he. "It is known to you all that the land to which we have marched is named Norway, and some of you have doubtless heard tales of that land, though very few of you have ever set eyes on it. Now we are going to set it ablaze with fire.

"That land, Norway, lying just beyond the border, was my, Olaf Haraldsson's, inheritance, by virtue of my noble birth. When miscreants managed to usurp the kingdom, some of them petty extortionists who titled themselves kings, others foreign thugs such as Cnut Sweynsson, who designated himself supreme monarch, I wrested the country from their hands, partly by prowess and gallantry, partly by trickery and guile. My supporter in all things was the Emperor Christ, the son of the Virgin, who rules over the Kingdom of Heaven. I know that you have little knowledge of him, but when opportunity allows, I will make it plain to you that he has a far finer weapon than the god Jumala, who carries naught but his simple staff, completely lacking a crossbeam. Though none of Christ's features are as comely as those of Jumala, what he has above and beyond Jumala is that he was not begotten by a man in his mother's womb, as Jumala was begotten by Kumala, but was born of an immaculate maiden by the intervention of the dove that learned men name Holy Wisdom. Moreover, to the Swedish men in our army who are friends of Þórr, I wish to make it known that White Christ, who was my benefactor in Norway, is so mighty an emperor that when his stake, which learned men call a cross, was measured against Þórr's hammer in Saxony in the days of Charlemagne, men with sharp eyes and measured tongues testified that Christ's was nine times higher than Þórr's and twelve times heavier. Monks taught me these things from Latin books. After I brought the

Norwegians this most outstanding stake and bought them peace and happiness, their livestock yielded little milk, whereupon I led an army to Denmark to salt down cows, and I had houses of God built all the way north to Rogaland, so that chanting and bell-ringing and the paternoster might be heard throughout all the land, while giants and ogres fled for their lives. Who then should rise from the hair of the earth but churls and fishermen, pitting themselves with insolent rage against their lord, and at the behest of our enemies?

"My good men, now the rulers in Sweden, my wife's kin, have granted me, in you, a doughty and valiant army for the reclamation of this land, and we have brought fifty horseloads of steel, whereas the Norwegians have only their clubs. I now designate you the defenders of the kingdom of Norway, and the time has come for us to burn the Norwegian peasants' dwellings to charcoal. It is my command that you spare no creature that draws breath in Norway, and show no man mercy until I have once again gained complete control of the land. Wherever you see a churl with his brood in field or meadow, on the highroad, or in his punt, cut off his head. If you see a cow, slaughter it. Set each and every house ablaze, and send barns up in flames. Millhouses – topple them; bridges – break them. Wells – piss in them. You are the liberators and defenders of Norway, and whatever you come across, rightly or wrongly, dead or alive, milk and meat or money, is to be your spoils of war – all except for gold, which the king alone claims. Let nothing withstand you until you have laid Norway at my feet.

"Good men, let us go now and set Norway awash with flames. And when we have burned, scorched, and decimated the land, I will name my right-hand men and grant estates and titles to those who make the greatest achievements in the work that we shall commence in the red light of dawn. Some of you shall then be titled jarl or hersir, others count or baron, some alderman or lord, and some, finally, knyaz or bogatyri. You shall have equal share with me in the revenue and bounty of the land in Norway, besides other wealth, and we shall all sit at one and the same table when we feast. Yet first I would ask of you, though you are heathens, not to take it amiss if I maintain something of my loyalty to the emperor who tumbled the Romans and other evildoers into Hell at the hour when he was hanged on the gallows. In return, I will allow you to keep your idols. Those who put their faith in Jumala's staff shall serve him, and Þórr's men shall exalt his hammer as they wish. The same goes for each and every man, whatever stump or stone he believes in. Yet I beseech you not to hold Christ in lower regard than Jumala, for it is of vital importance that this army earns the rightful blessing of the Lord Pope in Rome and the venerable Father Patriarch in Constantinople, as well as the good graces of the emperors, kings, and dukes who rule in the South, yet particularly the mercy of Christ himself, who has made all of these authorities his foot pages.

"After we have subdued Norway and put to death the rabble that has risen there against its king, we shall rebuild the country, erecting forts and castles with tall towers, and build ships and conduct Viking raids throughout the world. We shall sow fields more spacious than have ever been seen in Norway, and tend fatter herds, and for our labor we shall purchase slaves who will submit to us body and soul until we free them and declare their children equal to our own. We shall lay stone roads over the length and breadth of Norway and drive wagons like King Óðinn. We shall raise towns and cities with splendid houses and monasteries, horse markets, butchers' stalls, and extraordinary brothels, and buy Saracen fabrics and ornate swords, pepper from India, gold and ivory from Africa, and silk from the Orient. We shall erect a cathedral of Holy Wisdom in Nidaros, as glorious as the Hagia Sophia in Constantinople, and on its altars display golden shrines holding the skulls of saints, bigger and better than elsewhere in Christendom."

52

IN THIS BOOK, we shall not gather everything else that has been told of the sworn brothers Þorgeir Hávarsson and Þormóður Bessason, who were among the greatest and most renowned heroes in the Vestfirðir. Our account of their king, Olaf the Stout, is likewise drawing to its close. Other scholars, more sagacious than we, have done the task of extolling the glory of Skald Þormóður and King Olaf from the moment when they both fell lifeless at Stiklestad, the morning after the conclusion of this our narrative. The tale of King Olaf's glorious sainthood began when his devoted friend, Bishop Grímkell the Englishman, returned from Rome, and, going over the heads of the bishops of Bremen and the Christians of Norway, disinterred the king's corpse, which the peasants had dragged off and buried beneath a pile of stones, and declared its sanctity in the name of the Lord Pope. With an abundance of melodious requiems, the Church, for its part, celebrated the papal decree declaring this man to be the true King of Norway throughout the ages, in the light of this world as in Heaven, *in nomine Jesu Christi domini nostri.*

At the same time, news spread that Bishop Grímkell had been reconciled with the archiepiscopal see of Bremen through the intercession of the Pope, and made suffragan bishop over God's Christians in Norway. Now it went as it so often does, that those who bestow posthumous glory on kings also rewrite the stories of their lives, and thereby create saints for generations present and future.

The death of Þormóður Kolbrúnarskáld at Stiklestad has been exalted by Icelandic historians in immortal books, ensuring that the skald's renown survives as long as that of the king whom he sought and found.

On this the final night of our narrative, when the army has gone to rest, and the men have laid themselves down beneath their shields throughout the forest, having plucked moss and leaves to cover their feet and keep them warm, the king finds himself unable to sleep. It is commonly held that the speech he made that evening heartened him less than his followers. Many a foreigner in the army has fallen asleep hoping that he will, with the help of Christ, Þórr, and Jumala, and the steel that cowards esteem higher than the gods, subjugate all of Norway and kill all the Norwegians apart from those who wish to become their docile slaves. Not all, however, who await these great events can sleep. Here and there a man can be seen sitting upright in the grass, scratching himself and yawning, while others lie around him dozing, or nibbling on morsels from their satchels to while away the night before death.

That night, the king has no one with him but a Russian foot page who cannot speak the Norse tongue. Up until now, the king has trusted only this boy. Yet after the king has lain down, thinking that the boy is still awake, his mind turns to all the tales of kings being murdered in their sleep by their foot pages the night before significant events. Unable to fall asleep, the king crawls out of his sleeping bag and leaves his tent.

A waning moon hangs over the cairn behind the king's tent, and the cairn's topmost stones stand out against the sky. It appears to the king as if three men are sitting atop the cairn, brandishing their weapons: cross, hammer, and staff. The king stares at these men as he stands before his tent flap in the night, and says:

"I expect these must be the brothers Jumal, Christ, and Þórr, sitting there with their weapons."

A sentry steps forward, marches over to the king, and asks:

"Did you say something, sire?"

"Nothing of any importance," says the king. "I thought, however, that it might be amusing to augur the future from birds tonight, though I in fact had none when I conquered Norway the first time, with only two creaking tubs and a scurvy crew. Summer is beginning to wane, and I lie cold at night, with no companion whom I trust. Was it as I thought? Was there not an Icelandic skald limping about here earlier this evening, requesting an audience with us? Where might he be now?"

The sentry says that if no one has killed the man for amusement, he cannot be far away.

The king turns away from the sentry and takes a few steps up the slope behind his tent. The moon is now very close to touching the cairn's topmost stones. The king lies face down on the ground, heavy-hearted. Finally, he raises his eyes to the cairn and addresses it:

"Cairn-dwellers," says he, "whatever your names be! Take the hand of this inglorious arsonist, bereft of the backing of champions and the service of clerics, devoid of women's love and skalds' praise, a man friendless and alone. Your names are worthless to me, but your comfort is everything."

After groveling in the grass beneath the cairn for a short time, he notices a man sitting several steps away in the shadow of a rock, watching him, having overheard his anguished plea. They stare at each other for several moments. Then the man says:

"None but foxes dwell in that heap of stones."

The king asks: "Who are you?"

The man replies: "I am the Icelandic skald."

"Welcome, skald," says the king. "Did I hear correctly earlier this evening, that you composed a lay for me?"

"You did indeed, sire," says this man. "I have composed a very precious lay for the greatest hero in the North, and for you, his king. This lay I paid for with my bliss and sun, and my daughters, Moon and Star, and with my own beauty and health, hands, legs, and feet, hair and teeth, and lastly with my lover herself, who dwells in the Abyss and has my life-egg in her keeping."

"Ease your king's mind awhile now, skald," says Olaf Haraldsson, "and deliver me your *Lay of Heroes* by this cairn tonight."

After some hesitation, the skald replies: "I can no longer recall that lay," says he, and he stands up slowly and hobbles away, leaning on his cudgel, and disappears behind the cairn.

By then the moon has gone down, and night shrouds valley and hill at Stiklestad, as well as the bird cherry, late to blossom.

ENDNOTES

PAGE 11: Tense shifts between the past and present are common in the Old Icelandic sagas. Shifts to present tense often occur at particularly dramatic moments, as if to quicken the pace of the narrative according to the action, although this is not a hard-and-fast rule. Throughout *Wayward Heroes*, Laxness imitates this style, and it has been partially preserved in this translation.

PAGE 16: "Brynhildur" refers to Brynhildur Buðladóttir, a renowned shield-maiden and Valkyrie who appears in many Old Norse and Germanic works. She was imprisoned by the god Óðinn within a ring of flames on Mount Hindarfjall. "Swans" spinning men's fates refers to the Valkyries and their role determining the fates of warriors in a well-known Eddic poem.

PAGE 18: Easterling (Icelandic: *Austmaður*) was a term used in medieval Iceland and the Orkneys for persons from Norway or the Scandinavian continent in general.

PAGE 18: The Icelandic word *loðinn* means "hairy" or "shaggy."

PAGE 37: The windows in old dwellings in Iceland were usually round openings in the ceiling, fitted with frames stretched with transparent membranes (sheep or calves' bladders, or fish skin).

PAGE 37: Mardöll is one of the names of the Norse goddess Freyja, who was associated with love, beauty, fertility, war, and death.

PAGE 40: Kolbakur is quoting verse 70 from the Old Norse *Hávamál* (*Sayings of the High One*), a collection of gnomic verses from the Viking age, preserved as part of the Poetic Edda.

PAGE 41: *Hávamál*, verse 71.

PAGE 45: White Christ (Icelandic: *Hvítakristr*) was, in saga-age Iceland, a common name for Jesus Christ, derived perhaps from the white robes that Christians wore for baptism.

PAGE 78: A reference to an Icelandic legend about a farmer who receives cows in reward from a merman whom he accidentally fishes up from the sea one day; from one of these cows, a greet breed descended – all grey, and called "sea-cows."

PAGE 83: Irish for Jesus.

PAGE 92: *Lús* in Icelandic means "louse."

PAGE 94: The stars of Orion's belt.

PAGE 109: Hlórriði is one of the names of the Norse god Þórr, who drove a chariot pulled by two goats, Tanngrisnir and Tanngnjóstr.

PAGE 116: The constellation Pleiades. In Iceland, time during winters was reckoned by its position above the horizon (here "midmorning" means 6 AM).

PAGE 123: *Hávamál*, verse 71.

PAGE 134: The Holy Roman Empire.

PAGE 140: Stones that were imbued with the magical power to help alleviate the pains of labor.

PAGE 180: Prior to besieging Canterbury in 1011, the Viking fleet docked in Greenwich, on the Thames, and returned there with the captives from Canterbury.

PAGE 182: A "tooth-fee" (Icelandic: *tannfé*) is a gift given to a child when he cuts his first tooth. The practice continues in Iceland today.

PAGE 198: A type of provisional baptism involving being marked with the cross.

PAGE 203: Olaf Tryggvason steadfastly (and often violently) promoted Christianity in Norway and elsewhere in Scandinavia (including Iceland).

PAGE 204: Munvegar (literally, "paths of joy"), is associated with the realm of the Norn Urðr in the Viking Egill Skallagrímsson's poetic lament for his dead son, *Sonatorrek*.

PAGE 206: *Hávamál*, verse 1.

PAGE 222: In Old Norse society, a *níðingr* – truce-breaker, traitor, coward – was the most contemptible form of villain.

PAGE 308: In stanza 38 of the Old Icelandic Eddic poem *Völsungakviða in forna (Helgakviða Hundingsbana II (The Second Lay of Helgi Hundingsbane))*, the hero is described as a stag slung with dew.

PAGE 308: "The Wolf" refers to the monstrous wolf Fenrir of Old Norse mythology, destined to devour the god Óðinn after breaking free from his chain forged by dwarves from these three elements (as well as a woman's beard, a mountain's roots, and a bear's sinews), which are impossible to break.

PAGE 330: In Icelandic, "eager for killing."

PAGE 336: *Hávamál*, verse 114.

PAGE 378: A derisive Norse nickname for Icelanders, who commonly used suet and tallow from their herds of sheep.

PAGE 400: A kenning for the mind.

PAGE 443: From the *Saga of Olaf the Saint*.